THE

BARGAIN

A Port Elizabeth Regency Tale: Episode I
-IV

Vanessa Riley

Books by Vanessa Riley

Madeline's Protector

Swept Away, A Regency Fairy Tale

The Bargain, A Port Elizabeth Tale, Episodes I-IV

Unveiling Love, Episodes I-IV

Unmasked Heart, A Regency Challenge of the Soul Series

Sign up at VanessaRiley.com for contests, early releases, and more.

ISBN-13: 978-1-943885-18-3

COMING TO LONDON HAS GIVEN PRECIOUS JEWELL A TASTE OF FREEDOM...

Dear Beautiful Reader,

The Bargain is a serialized story or soap opera told in episodes. Each episode averages from three to eight chapters, about 15,000 to 30,000 words. Each episode resolves one issue. Emotional cliffhangers may be offered, but the plot, the action of the episode, will be complete in resolving the main issue.

My promise to you is that the action will be compelling, and I will tell you in the forward the length of the episode. This episode, Episode I, is three chapters long, 15,000 words. Enjoy these Regency Tales set in South Africa.

Vanessa Riley

Coming to London has given Precious Jewell a taste of freedom, and she will do anything, bear anything, to keep it. Defying her master is at the top of her mind, and she won't let his unnerving charm sway her. Yet, will her restored courage lead her to forsake a debt owed to the grave and a child who is as dear to her as her own flesh?

Gareth Conroy, the third Baron Welling, can neither abandon his upcoming duty to lead the fledgling colony of Port Elizabeth, South Africa nor find the strength to be a good father to his heir. Every look at the boy reminds him of the loss of his wife. Guilt over her death plagues his sleep, particularly when he returns to London. Perhaps the spirit and fine eyes of her lady's maid, Precious Jewell, might offer the beleaguered baron a new reason to dream.

In this episode:
The vastness of the cresting ocean isn't enough to drown Precious Jewell's high spirits or her dreams of doing for herself, but a false move and an old nightmare have placed her in more jeopardy, Lord Welling's bedchamber.

Captaining his schooner to Port Elizabeth was his only refuge, until his ship was invaded by land lovers, his son and his challenging caregiver. Perhaps, Miss Jewell's vivacity and audacity are just what he needs to quell rebellion amongst his crew and his heart.

The Bargain is the first Port Elizabeth Regency Tale.

ILLUSTRATIONS

Illustrations

A portion of the Portrait of Catherine Worlée, Princesse de Talleyrand-Périgord (1762-1834) inspired the portrait of Eliza Marsdale set on the cover. The work of art, Portrait of Catherine Worlée, is in the public domain and can be found at Wikicommons.

The cover is an inspired work of Sanura Jayashan commissioned for this book.

Dedication

I dedicate this book to my copy editor supreme, my mother, Louise, my loving hubby, Frank, and my daughter, Ellen. Their patience and support have meant the world to me.

I also dedicate this labor of love to critique partners extraordinaire: June, Mildred, Lori, Connie, Gail.

I give special thanks to Piper, the lady who held my hand and led me to discover Precious Jewell's fire.

Love to my mentor, Laurie Alice, for answering all my endless questions.

And I am grateful for my team of encouragers: Sandra, Michela, Kim, and Rhonda.

CAST OF PRIMARY CHARACTERS

Baron Welling (the second Lord Welling): the late uncle of Gareth Conroy.

Precious Jewell: a slave brought from South Carolina in 1815 as the personal maid of the late Eliza Marsdale Conroy.

Eliza Marsdale of Charleston, South Carolina, married Gareth Conroy. The marriage was arranged by the (2nd) Baron Welling and Eliza's father, a wealthy cotton plantation owner.

Gareth Conroy: the third Baron Welling, succeeded to the title upon the death of his uncle. He has been commissioned to lead the colony of Port Elizabeth, South Africa.

Jonas Conroy: the son born to Eliza Marsdale. She died shortly after childbirth.

Mr. Palmers: the butler for Gareth Conroy. He runs the staff at Firelynn Hall.

Old Jack: a groom employed by a neighbor to Firelynn.

Mr. Narvel: Gareth Conroy's typical first mate.

Mrs. Clara Narvel: wife of Mr. Narvel.

Mr. Grossling: A member of the War Department.

Ralston: Gareth Conroy's first mate on this voyage to Port Elizabeth.

Prologue: London, February 4, 1816

Her mistress's groans pierced the air, breaking Precious Jewell's heart again. The birth had gone all wrong. Eliza wasn't going to make it.

Precious coddled the newborn in her arms, smoothing linen about his tiny body. He looked mighty content for all the ruckus his early comin' caused.

Lowering her gaze to the sweat-dampened bed sheets, the spatters of crimson swaddling the blanket by Eliza's stomach, only questions remained. Why Eliza? Why now?

The doctor shifted from his post at the door. "There's nothing more to be done."

His starched tie fell asunder. He looked very different from the know-it-all who'd arrived hours earlier. If the man had only listened and taken the babe sooner, Eliza wouldn't be so weak now.

"I'll get the vicar." The cowardly man left the bedchamber.

The butler stalked away from the bed, and passed

Precious as if she wasn't there. He rounded to the window. Palmers's old stone face looked broken. "How will we tell His Lordship?"

Useless menfolk. Thinkin' of other men, not Eliza.

They should be encouraging her mistress, not counting the seconds for the reaper to appear. "She ain't gone yet. Maybe you should send prayers to that Sunday God of yours."

Palmers returned to the canopied bed. "Watch your tongue, Jewell. There's no need for your opinions."

"Stop you two." The weak cry slipped from Eliza. "Let my final moments be of peace."

Tears pressed on Precious's eyes. Oh, how flushed her poor friend looked. "Let me give you something to drink, Miss Eliza. You might get strength from water. Don't you want some…?"

Eliza's head slowly shook. Her pinkie shifted and waggled. It was her way when she wanted to appear demure, but still show disapproval. "Not now. Something more important."

Precious moved to the head of the massive bed frame. "Open your eyes and see your son. You gotta fight for him. Your husband needs you too."

The lady's pinkie started to shiver like it would fall off. "He's made his choices." The kitten-like voice bore a sharpness, a biting pain. "Let him burn for going off to his uncle. Tell him that."

Palmers spun and clutched his dark mantle. "He's to be the baron tonight. He had to be at his uncle's last breath. Duty claimed him, ma'am. You will be the next Lady Welling."

At this, Eliza's eyes opened. Red-rimmed pupils flashed before settling on her son. "For a few minutes, I have a title. Write my father of it. He's paid for it."

"Hush now, Miss Eliza. You should save your strength. In a few days, we'll be getting you styled for another cluster of parties. You'll be the new Lady Wellin'. I mean Welling."

Gasping, as if her lungs leaked, Eliza closed her eyes. "What's that worth? No more promises on things...can't touch." She clenched her teeth together as her body vibrated, her fingers latching onto the mound of bedclothes.

Precious turned. The babe shouldn't witness his mother's passing.

"It's fine, friend." Eliza's voice became softer. "Let me see him one more time."

Wiping a tear on her emerald sleeve, Precious rotated the babe to a secure position within the crook of her arm, and slipped back to the mattress. "He's beautiful. Your son's beautiful."

Eliza's hand moved as if to touch the boy, but then dropped to the bed. "Promise me, Precious. Love him for me. You must do this."

"I'll do what I can for him. Now hush with this fever talk."

"I free you, Precious. Let everyone know that I freed you. And you will mother this child for me."

Was this one of Eliza's jokes? She needed to be careful. That Sunday God might be watching. "Do you want to try to hold him? Maybe the warmth of his little body would keep warmth in yours--"

"I'm serious. You're free if you will love my son."

The solemn vicar and the doctor stepped into the room. The clergyman started reading from his Bible.

Eliza screamed, then took a breath. "Precious Jewell is

a free woman. No more my slave. She will care for my son, Jonas."

Palmers stepped backward and moved to the window. "His father should name him, and as his heir to the barony, perhaps he should be Gareth, the lord's namesake.

"It shall be Jonas." With a shaking limb, Eliza lifted a weak hand and brushed the foolscap on the baby's crown. "Promise me. I've done some bad things. Giving you freedom is a good thing. Promise, P."

Even as Precious nodded, Eliza's hand fell with a slap onto the bed sheets.

Her eyes closed, never again to see the morning.

The baby squirmed, then started to cry.

Tears leaked from Precious's eyes too, for Eliza would never hear Precious yell, "Yes!"

Chapter One: Danger in The Streets

The rain soaked through Precious's blouse down to her corset, icing her skin. The harshness of the cold water couldn't chill the fright pushing in her lungs, unable to break free. And though Lord Welling didn't mean no harm, his grip on her waist intensified the fear trapped in her flesh. Would the nightmares ever go away?

Her slippers slapped at the sidewalk. She slowed her steps. Lord Welling wasn't a brute. Eliza would've said something. Maybe.

No, he was just a thief who stole her hopes. Her heart slowed as she stopped running. Nobody chased her yet.

Bending over to catch a breath, her mobcap flew with the wretched wind. Everything in her head ached, down to her eye sockets. It was cruel to hope and to have kept freedom pent up in her skull. She should've asked before now and not believed for two years she was free.

Turning her face to the dark night sky, she let the pounding rain drench her cheeks. The sloppy drops spit at her, but something needed to remove the tracks of salt.

Maybe the God Eliza swore was real would do that one thing now; use His rain to cleanse her of hope and despair.

Yet, how could there be a God, and a good one? He let Eliza die. He let a whole world of people be set in chains. "Not fair. When will it be fair?"

The sound of horses' hooves pounded behind her. Her heart slammed against her chest. Lord Welling had sent men to retrieve his property. What punishment would he give his runaway slave?

But where else would she go? The coins sewn into her apron were still at Firelynn, wrapped about the baron's hand. Precious had nothing.

Empty, she turned to surrender, but the carriage passed her by. A sigh of relief escaped her mouth. She was safe for another few minutes, but the dark streets of London weren't good for black or white, servant or free.

Out of options, she listened to the pain in her temples and plodded back to Firelynn. If she humbled herself, Lord Welling might make her punishment light. He'd already given her the worst blow. What damage could a caning on the backside do now?

Still not free.

Her heart wept on the inside. Her chest shuddered. All the plans, the dreams, gone with his words. No, Lord Welling couldn't do more harm.

She brushed at her chin then reached to her soggy flopping hair. Her thick curls spun tighter about her thumb, drawing up and unraveling from the weight of the rain. Goodness, she must look like a wet mop with her soggy braids slapping at her jaw. What a sad lump she was.

Hunching her shoulders, she walked a little faster. Such a cold she could catch being waterlogged. A shadow moved between houses. She bit at her lip to keep from uttering a shriek. Chiding herself, she pressed forward. Counting at least as many birthdays as Eliza, all eighteen or twenty of them, Precious was too big to be seeing ghosts.

Yet, the thing moved again. The beast or man came out of the dark, his twisted jowls highlighted by a flash of thunder made her arms pimple.

Tugging at the tucker bibbing her neck, she tried to ignore it and hurry past.

"Blackamoor." The voice sounded loud and cutting. A man followed. His boots knocked a steady gait behind her. "Come here, you."

What was she thinking or not thinking, wandering the streets of London at night?

Swoop. He jumped in front of her, blocking her way. His eyes held flames. The devil was in him, she was sure of it. "Why not stay and play with Old Jack?"

She shook her head and backed up. "I must be heading to my master at Firelynn."

"Black-a-moor, I'll be your master tonight."

Spinning, she dashed to his right. Crunching down, she sprinted and sped as if she were back in the woods in old Charleston chasing rabbit.

Blam, blam blam. His heels knocked against the cobblestones lining the ground. He reached and clawed at her sleeve. "Wench, I called you!"

There was evil in his voice. It didn't sound human. How could anybody bent on destruction sound otherwise? This attack would be her fault. She'd asked danger to kiss her, to tear at her clothes and make her vulnerable.

She balled her fist about her collar and ran faster. Her skirts were heavy with water, but there was a light ahead. Maybe a groom or stable boy could be alerted in the mews. Yet would anybody care a whit about a runaway?

The sky moaned but the rain settled into a drizzle. A light fog swallowed the earth, but the beast kept chasin'. From the cut of the buildings, Firelynn was only three blocks now. Surely, the library door was still open.

"Black Harriot. Give us a taste of your finery!"

She wasn't a prostitute. Her ears and her heart burned. Hadn't she vowed that no one would make her feel that low again?

The man's shadow overtook hers. The stench of gin and sweat caught her as he got a firm grasp of her shoulder.

She struggled and swung with her arms, but her slippers tangled in her wet skirts. She tumbled. Smack, she landed so hard onto the cobbles her stomach deflated like a ripped sack of corn, dribbling pops of air from her lips and nose. Her cheek met a loose stone and stung. Flat upon the soggy ground, she was helpless and ashamed.

"Blackamoor, Jack will be good to you if you give me a show." The beast grabbed her by her braids and hauled her up, but she managed to scoop up a rock from the ground. "You'd make a nice one to bed tonight. More than Old Jack could hope for."

He twisted her hair and jerked her to him. This couldn't be the first woman he'd treated like a whore, but it would be one he'd never forget. Balling her hand about the stone, she punched him in his breeches. As he

8

stumbled backward, she slung the cobble at his head.

The thud of the hit deafened. The rock surely crunched his jaw, breaking bone. "Augh! You hellcat. You'll pay for that."

In the moonlight, the shine of his blade blinded. He meant to kill her. Her heart pounded as she hefted her skirts and tried again to outrun him. If only she hadn't fled from Lord Welling.

An arm grabbed about her middle. Fingers gripped her throat. A last breath whizzed from her lips. She fought the blackness and clenched to absorb the sting of the knife. *Lord, let death be quick.* There had to be freedom in that.

"Release her!" The deep voice penetrated her nightmare. She blinked and caught sight of a sharp metal point coming full bore at her.

Somehow, the pressure along her windpipe disappeared. She fell onto the street. Freed, she took a full breath and peered up.

Lord Welling stood there, wonderful and strong, with a gleaming rapier. The long, thin sword pressed at her attacker's Adam's apple. "Why should I let you live?"

"She broke my…She hit me with a rock. I'm entitled to something for the damages!"

A guttural noise flung from Welling's lips. He pounded forward. His dark cape fluttered, shrouding half his body. He looked more the villain than a hero, but part of her needed a villain, someone to steal away all the evil that had ever touched her.

From the howling squeal of the man who'd tried to humble her, her master's change of stance must've inflicted pain. Good. Had he made his rapier draw blood for her or for the sake of his property?

"Sir, don't force me to pay her debt. You won't like how I settle scores."

Lord Welling glanced in her direction. Even in the low light of the moon, she could see fury burning in his eyes. His attention swiveled back to the fiend. "There's a bruise to her cheek. Maybe I should take an ear for payment. That would do nicely and give my hounds a treat to eat."

"I ain't done nothin'. Tell him, witch!"

Precious didn't say a word, just pulled her arms about her knees.

"Tell him, please." The beast's voice cracked.

Good. Maybe he knew her terror. Oh, very good.

"She's your blackamoor, Welling. I ain't touched her. Keep her locked up 'fore something bad happens to her. And you shouldn't be so greedy. Give up your English Black since you'll be king of a whole city of them in Africa." The man backed off, turning toward the alley. "Well, I'll keep tabs on your piece while you're away. Next time, love."

Next time? Everyone knew the baron was leaving. Her stomach sickened and a silent tear dripped down her sore cheek. No papers, and now a fool wanted vengeance. Maybe it would be best to be sent back to Charleston. Those men weren't any better than these, and there she wouldn't fill her head with dreams.

Welling's boots appeared when her tears cleared. "Come along, Miss Jewell."

The tall man bent with arm extended, stooping low to help her from the street. "Sure you're not hurt?" His sweet blue eyes seemed large and full of concern, a little too much for just checking on his property.

Avoiding his hand, she nodded and slowly stood. At

full height, dizziness claimed her, but she couldn't let the baron know. She'd already caused enough problems.

"Very well, mouse. Back to Firelynn."

After a block or two of walking, she lifted her gaze to the baron. Her conscience couldn't take more silence. "Thank you."

One of his missing dimples popped as he slid his rapier under the crook of his arm. "I would have gotten here sooner, but it took a moment to find my cloak. And even more so to sober up." He laughed a hearty bellow. "Choose another night to frighten me out of my wits."

Something needed to fill up the stillness of the night, but all she could think of was Old Jack. He'd be back and without the protection of her master, he'd get what he wanted. With trembling fingers, she clutched at her blouse.

Her soggy slippers slapped at the stone steps as he guided her back the way she had escaped. "I didn't mean to make trouble."

He closed the patio door and pointed to a chair by his sideboard. "Warm yourself by the fire."

She nodded and sank by the hearth. The heat felt good, taking away the cold eating at her fingertips.

"Running in the middle of the night is a foolish thing, Jewell. I didn't know my words would affect you so."

"Anyone ever take your freedom with a word?" She covered her mouth and bowed her dizzy head. "I should remember myself."

A strong chuckle left him, so much so that she lifted her head to view him.

Shaking off his cape, she saw that the arm hidden in all the flowing velvet still bore her apron. Hurt, he came after her. Did property mean that much to him?

"Jewell, do you need a doctor?"

"No, sir."

He picked up a shiny tray holding his brandy bottle and two glasses. "Do me a favor and pour us each one."

Her reflection on the metal showed a wild urchin; braids everywhere, red marks indented along her throat, a bruised cheek. Her shaking fingers poured a half glass for him, but none for her. "You don't need more. You're so much better not under its influence."

A lazy smile and his other missing dimple bloomed as he picked up the drink and took a sip. "I'll keep that in mind. You remember that if that blackguard had succeeded in...you would have little redress."

"Yes, I'm property. No one goes to jail for damages to property."

"No, people do swing from the gallows for theft. A black or mulatto has little relief from the law. It might not be allowed for you to testify. So when I am gone, be very careful. You and I have made an enemy."

Fingers tangling in the righting of her loosed braids, she wanted to be out of her master's sight, but one thing stood in the way. Punishment. With a swallow, she stared at him. "May I have my due for runnin'?"

His face pinched as if he didn't know what she talked about. He shook his head. "Don't know if you're prepared for more wrath. Go to your room. I'll think of it tomorrow."

She backed out of his study, nodding, half-curtsying. This kindness felt odd. Why did he treat her so well with all the trouble she'd caused? Foolish English.

Not owning any others, he must not know the customs for doling out punishment. Or maybe he knew she'd pay soon enough at Old Jack's hands.

Chapter Two: London, February 4, 1819

Lightning crashed about the great windows of Firelynn Hall, but that didn't frighten Precious Jewell none. No, it was the tinkling of broken glass coming from downstairs that set the hair on the back of her neck in a tizzy.

She stilled her vibrating fingers against the stark white apron of her dark-emerald maiding outfit. The feel of the cloth was so starched and formal. So different from the plain hand-me-downs she'd gotten in Charleston, wearing them filled her middle with something, not quite pride, not joy either. Something. She reckoned three years in London offered better treatment.

Angered mumbles floated up to the echoing hall sending more trembles to her spine. The master fumed again, but time was running out. She couldn't put off her request any more. A drunken set down or slap couldn't be any worse than what she'd suffered. That was England's benefit. She hadn't been lashed for slapping a fresh footman or coal boy.

Yet.

Pushing herself forward, Precious forced her feet to work and crept until she made it to the edge of the stairs. Her body froze with toes dangling over the thick tread. She had every right to approach the master like the other servants.

Nodding like a twit, she tried to hold that sentiment in her tummy, clenching it tight within her middle. But the grand mirror exposed a small brown face with quivering lips. Lyin' to yourself in your head was as bad as lyin' out loud.

And she weren't …wasn't a servant, not without papers.

Thunder moaned and set the house to shaking. A wail sounded, shattering the little bit of courage she possessed. Little Jonas must be taken with fright. He must need her.

Her slippers turned a little too easy and Precious pattered back to the nursery. It was better to see about the baby than tend to herself. Well, that wasn't a lie. It just felt heavy like one. Excuses had a way of piling up on your back until you fell over. Right now, Precious would tumble with the slightest wind.

She pushed open the wide paneled door. Sure enough, Jonas stood in the middle of his bed covers. He cried, but this time the noise was muted. She'd heard him cry for hours like a banshee. He must know his Pa was in a bad way. She came closer, her voice set to a whisper. "Jonas, darlin'. Brave boy, you must settle."

The whites of the two-year-old's eyes loomed large. Tears pooled too, but the little man didn't let them go. He must know silence was better.

Heart aching, she picked him up from his crib.

"Birthday boy, all will be well."

Thunder groaned and light blazed through the thick glass panes. For a moment she fingered her apron to see if the Lord above had smote her for fibbing. Surely, a good God knew you couldn't tell a babe the truth that his father was demented with grief. "Jonas, sweetheart, go back to sleep; shut those blue eyes. You have your pappy's crystal blues, but all of Eliza's blonde locks. And she's looking upon you smiling and singing. But she sure would get me for letting you fidget."

When his mouth puckered, letting out a low spitting sob, Precious held him closer. Having him shouting would add more upset to the household. No, this little angel needed to be spared his father's wrath. Lord knows, Jonas hadn't seen enough of his pa, and viewing the man drunk or yelling wouldn't be good.

The cherub in her arms snuggled against the pleats of the low neckline, exposing her blouse. Paper or no papers, this time of caring for Jonas would end. Soon a proper governess for the boy would be sought, someone who could teach him all the ways of the English. Someone who was not a slave.

Precious jumped as Jonas touched her neck. He'd reached and gripped one of her fat braids slipping from her mobcap. The blackness looked like rope against his rosy palm. "Momma, make better."

Her pulse slowed as she sucked in a deeper breath. "I'm not your momma, Jonas. Call me Mammie Precious. Maybe your Pa will get you a new one someday."

An ache rippled inside. No one could ever replace Eliza, and definitely not these hoity-toity English misses. Precious had seen them, spying on the master, bribing a footman for his whereabouts when Eliza was barely cold in the ground.

The child yawned and burrowed into the crook of her arm. He wasn't paying her no mind. But, it wasn't best to pretend she'd get to be in his life once his pappy left for South Africa. Mr. Palmers would see to that. She shook her head, trying to rid it of a hundred horrible thoughts of her dealin's with the prideful butler and focused on the boy. "Your mother, Eliza Marsdale, was the kindest of souls, so good –"

Slam.

Crash.

The noise was very loud. Even Jonas's sleepy eyes popped open again.

Somehow she eased him back into the crib and tucked the blanket about him tight, all whilst her hands shook. "Now back to sleep, you. No more fussing. If your pa sends me away, know I love you."

The lad nodded and before his blue eyes could draw her back, Precious hastened to the door. Lifting her moss-colored skirts, she scampered down the treads heading for the master's study.

Mr. Palmers came out of the room. His stern face held a deep frown planted between old saggy jowls. He looked sad. As if he had just noticed her, he leveled his shoulders and snapped to attention. "What are you doing up, Jewell? Is the child well?"

"Yes, sir, but I must speak with Mr. Wellin'."

He looked past her, as was his custom when dealing with servants he felt beneath him. "It's Lord Welling. You've been here almost four years, and you still get it wrong. What will you be teaching his heir?"

She scrunched up her apron to give her fingers

something to do other than fumble. "You won't have that problem for much longer. I'm sure you'll find someone approp...perfect upon the lord's leaving next week. In fact, I'll bring it to Lord Well-ing's notice now."

As she stepped forward, Palmers blocked her path. "No. His lordship is in no mood to be disturbed. Return to your room. That's an order. You know what that is?"

She knew what orders were. They were ingrained in her brain, and the consequences of disobedience had cut scars upon her back. Precious nodded and forced her body to turn. Gall wet her tongue. So close. Too close to be chased away by a hoity-toity butler.

Palmers plodded past her and headed to the west wing. As she made it to the stairs leading to the basement, she watched his stiff form covered in the black livery uniform disappear into the dark passage.

Twisting stairs leading to her small chamber below sat in front of her. Forty-five steps and she'd be inside her closet-sized quarters, one shared with a scullery maid. In Charleston, the slave quarters were big but shared by four or five. Maybe the small cellar room was what the lowest of servants of the house could have. Once the master left, how much longer would Mr. Palmers let her stay in it? He didn't think she deserved anything but a hay bale, to be stabled like an animal.

If he tossed her out, would she become a Blackamoor at a brothel or worse, sold again and returned to South Carolina or Jamaica? Her fingers latched onto the waxed rail for strength. The smooth wood felt good beneath her thumb, cooling the fever of thoughts running rampant.

A memory of Eliza pushing her, encouraging her to slide down the big one at her pa's manor in Charleston fluttered in her mind's eye. Precious had held her breath,

17

put her bottom on the banister and slipped the length of it. For a few seconds, it felt like flying. It was reckless and heady and would've earned Precious a beating if Mr. Marsdale had caught her, but sailing free was worth it. Wasn't freedom worth every risk?

Thunder erupted. The storm pelted the roof in a steady punching manner. Her breath came in spurts as she remembered a backhand to the jaw and the stings of a whip all endured while protecting herself. The freedom to refuse sweaty advances was worth the beating, so complete freedom had to be, too.

Precious unglued her hand, pivoted, and headed for the study. Pausing, she counted the dents in the fretwork trim surrounding the threshold. At ten, she leveled her shoulders and knocked on Lord Welling's study door.

Nothing. No grunt. No deep voice, full of command answered.

But no turning back either.

She pried open the heavy double doors and slunk inside. The heat of the room stung her cheeks. The stench of liquor and cigar smoke hung in the air adding a sheen to the measly candlelight in the corner.

A few more steps and she spied her master.

Lord Welling slumped at the fireplace. His tall formed hunched over the white wood mantle as the huge portrait of Eliza hung over him. The fastidious man had his shirttails exposed beneath a rumpled waistcoat. A cranberry coat lay dumped on the floor. His head, crowned with thick brown hair, sat tucked in one arm. A clear goblet hung from the other.

How drunk was he? Could she reason with him cast to the winds? The first day she saw him, his lean face held a hardy laugh. His wit, Mr. Marsdale said, could dice up a hard turnip. Maybe liquor slowed his brainbox down enough to agree to anything.

"Aw, Eliza's Precious Jewell. My Precious Jewell."

His voice with the stiff accent would be perfect for sermon making. The authority in the deep tones prickled her skin, made her feel as if she'd been caught being naughty. She nodded. "Yes, sir."

He downed the amber contents of his drink then pounded the mantle. "Isn't—" A hiccup left his pursed lips. "Isn't your job to see that the child sleeps, madam? Aren't you missing a moment to mother him?"

Was he taunting her? Why? It was her responsibility to see about the child. His harsh tone almost sounded jealous. That couldn't be right. Alcohol was an evil thing.

"What does the mouse want?"

She should just say it. *Give me papers to keep me free, off slave ships and out of brothels.* Then no man could have the right to touch her. Looking into the baron's red-rimmed eyes, the words stuck in her craw. Courage dropping away, she turned. "Good night."

"So the mouse is running away? Fine. Leave me, too."

She weren't a rat, nothing that low. She fiddled with the pocket of her apron then rotated to face him. "You drink too much drink. There's no reasoning with a bottle."

Like a foaming wave at the ocean, laughter poured out of him. "Tell me something that's not so obvious." He straightened and waved her forward. "You should drink with me too. You know what tonight is?"

Of course she did. Everyone in Firelynn Hall knew. Precious just stared at him.

He grunted hard and eyed her too. "It's the day I let your Miss Eliza die."

Thunder crashed outside, and his hand closed tight about the glass, breaking it. Red poured from his palm. "Augh. Bloody thing."

Precious dashed to his side and drew his hand up in her apron. "Foolhardy man."

He winced and snatched his hand away. "I chose to go to my uncle, to do his bidding. Who knew they'd both die that night?"

She felt for him, remembering the arguments Eliza had had with the master about who he loved more. Sympathy ate at her gut, but it disappeared when Precious spied her pristine apron darkening with growing red spots. "You fool. You're bleeding to death."

Charging him, she seized his palm, and plucked out two shards of glass. The fire spit at her as she tossed them to the hearth. "You think dying will bring her back? Nothin' will do that."

His deep blue eyes beaded as he yanked his arm back. "That hurts, woman. Leave me. Let me drink to my lady gone."

Droplets trickled onto his waistcoat as he gazed at Eliza's portrait. The eyes formed of paint seemed focused on him, probably disgusted at his drinking.

The proud man would bleed to death. And, with the smears on her apron, she'd be blamed. Precious came in here for freedom, not a heap more trouble. She grabbed his hand again and bound it tightly, wrapping it around and around in her poor apron. "You got a boy. Eliza's son needs you."

Lord Welling stopped fidgeting and let her tie a knot. His bloodshot eyes widened and seemed to settle on her face. "Well, as I leave to go defend my uncle's work, it will be you who cares for him."

"He's a good boy, but he'll need his pa to make him a good man."

"How can I show him that? I scarcely remember what that is."

A final knot secured the makeshift bandage. The cuts of the glass had gone deep. "Start by not going to Africa. It's a bad place." She bit her lip, but the words burned too much to be silent. "My grammy talked of how it changed when y'all came."

"Y'all?" His stiff accent, sort of questioning, sort of condescending, grated on her ear. He wiggled his fingers within the wrapping of her ruined apron. "You mean the slave traders, those y'all? The house of Welling never participated in such transactions."

No, they just inherited slaves by marriage. The baron's hands weren't clean. They were wet in the stains of it, like now with his own spilt blood. She swallowed the irksome thoughts and focused on Jonas. That would be a reason for the man to stay. "Your son needs you here. There's nothin' worse than not seeing your pa. Even just a notion or whisper of him in passing, day to day is better than never."

His face scrunched and then tilted up toward Eliza's picture. "She hated it here. Thought the weather too foul. I should've listened and made her last years more pleasant."

That didn't make sense, but that's how guilt worked. She eyed his very lean cheeks through the lace of her floppy mobcap. His laugh dimples were missing. He was tall, too tall. "She was very pleased to be a baron's wife."

"Pleased? Was she pleased waiting for my return from tending to my uncle's affairs? Was she happy waiting for the accoucheur to deliver the babe alone? Was she pleased she never got her title, dying before my uncle? Only a few hours separated them from Heaven's gate. Well, at least she made it in."

Men were dumb about birthin'. "That baby didn't wait. Some women weaken in the process. It takes all they have to give life. The Lord just—" She snapped her mouth shut as a belly full of laughs rolled out of his lips.

"Stop, Jewell." He wobbled over to his sideboard and pried at the glass top of bottled spirits. The makeshift bandage must've prevented him from getting a good grip and popping it open.

She plodded across the thick carpet, coming again within a few feet of him. "You can't need more."

"I surely don't want less." His eyes widened and he drew himself up as if her boldness had suddenly penetrated his drunken brain. "I didn't ask you to be my keeper."

"But you're mine."

A lazy smirk appeared, making his eyes a darker shade of blue.

Such a turbulent river stirred within him, and sometimes it pulled her undertow, but Precious didn't like swimming or drowning. With a shake of her head, she looked away to the floor. "That's what I came to discuss before you are off to who knows where."

He set down the bottle and rubbed at his neck, shoving his loose hair to the side. He wore it longer than most. It gave him more of a pirate look like in the stories Eliza read. "I was wondering when the mouse would say her piece."

With a tug, he whipped off his rumpled cravat. "You've been skulking about ever since I returned to Firelynn Hall. Something tells me you have an ask. Say it."

He'd noticed her. Had he seen the many times she let her courage slide away? Not again. She planted a hand on her hip. "I need my papers, sir."

His eyes blinked, his forehead riddling with lines. "What papers?"

"My freedom." Her voice sounded horrible, hollow and low. A quick cough and a short breath allowed her to strengthen her tone and appear strong. "I need papers to show, to get my next employment."

"You need no other possibilities. You work for me." He pulled his massive arms together, almost missing the elbows he now cupped. "Why should you work elsewhere?"

"The missus. She gave me my freedom that horrid night. Mr. Palmers was there. He heard it."

The baron took a step backward, planting his foot close to the sideboard, almost falling. "You sly thing. You use the anniversary of her death to coerce me."

"I speak truth." She picked up his brandy container and shook it. "The only things you listen to are these spirits."

He reached for it. As if swimming in a mud hole, he stumbled forward with arms flying.

She put her hand on his chest to steady him.

He seized her arms, drawing her to his side. One massive arm pinned her against him. The buttons of his onyx waistcoat smashed into her cheek.

His breath, soaked in liquor, blended with the hint of vanilla of his skin, along with the scent of ash and soot from the roaring fire. "Mouse, give it back."

His words heated the crown of her head and his arms tightened about her. Shocked and shaking, she twisted and pushed to get free, but there was no budging from the baron's death grip. "Let me go."

"Shhh. You're talking too much." With his free hand, he slid his fingers down the length of her back. She could feel his pinkie tracing the eyelets of her corset. Squirming, she tried to shift to keep him from picking at the ribbons of her undergarment. Being fully clothed didn't stop her panic. She rocked and pressed against his iron-like embrace to be free. Never, ever did it settle into her head that Lord Welling was like the rest; a man who took what he wanted.

Brain swimming in a sea of choice brandy, Gareth Conroy, Lord Welling, held the thief in place. How dare the wench take his bottle and taunt him with it? He searched a little more, here and there, until his fingers claimed the dimpled glass from her fidgeting hands. "There, now I've found it."

He released his grip and the mouse scampered away. Must be the effects of the drink, but did the girl look scared? She couldn't have thought to keep it all herself. He sloshed the bottle. Amber honey flooded to one side then the other. There was enough to share.

Bosom heaving, she moved out his reach and trembled by the fire. "I need my papers." Her voice almost sounded as if she were choking.

With a grunt, he pivoted and put his full concentration on liberating the stopper. Another second or two of quick jabs popped the top. He flung it with a thud to scamper across the waxed sideboard. His vision split it into two, so he let it be and poured a glass. "The morning papers have upset me of the riots, but they are nothing to be frightened of. We are safe here."

Before he could fix his lips to the wiggling goblet of needed joy, the mouse came closer again. Her roasted-almond complexion bore hints of red along her cheeks. And, upon further inspection, he realized her curves held a sizeable endowment, not at all the scrawny thing that accompanied his wife from the Carolinas. "Miss Eliza gave me my freedom. Would you ignore her dyin' request, too?"

He swallowed a gulp of fire, but his nerves felt doused with kerosene. His temper, which had deflated in his game of find the bottle, now raged anew. The maid's word *too* held accusation. And it made the cold stuff in his veins burn. "Be careful, madam. I'm indulging this interruption to my privacy, but even amusements have their limits."

The censure in his voice did the trick. The pert Jewell lowered her chin as she clasped a wavering hand.

It must be the brandy, for something in him suddenly saddened at the loss of her fire. He lifted the glass again to his lips but stopped. Perhaps if he kept from further soaking his brain, he could figure out why the mouse ran in here. Was she dashing for a clock? He put down the liquor. "You were very dear to my wife. I'd find you in each other's confidence. I watch you sometimes with Jonas. Same love."

Jewell's countenance lifted. Her full lips parted and a resilient voice sounded. "Was always the way with us, since I could remember. That's why she freed me. You must make it right."

Now the mouse gave orders? The blend of audacity and humble pie tweaked his humor and his pride. "Lady Welling didn't have the power to free you. Let me acquaint you to English law. Once a woman marries, all her money, possessions, even her rights become her husband's. So how could my wife give what she didn't have?"

Thunder boomed, and the girl's chestnut eyes widened so much that flecks of emerald and gold showed, just like Eliza's. He reached for the girl to catch a part of his late wife, but Jewell ran.

She passed through the patio doors, the one leading to the smallish garden and then to alley. From the popped opening, the wind hissed and spit into his study.

The fool girl left him for the rain and the evils of dark London streets. He wobbled to the glass panes and leaned against it, staring at the sea of blackness, but couldn't find her. The buckets of water dumping from above hid her. Yes, God was good at taking things away from Gareth.

A jolt went through him as he turned and witnessed his Eliza's painting bearing down on him, judging him for things out of his control.

Gut burning, he put his sore palm to his head and tried to block the disappointment his love had had in him and his own noisy conscience.

The cackle of taunting thunder forced him to swivel back to the window. How could he let Jewell go and take the last traces of Eliza, too?

Chapter Three: A Painful Peace

Nothin' worse than preparing for a caning and having to wait for it, waking every morning with dread in her belly, all day walking on tiptoes. Yet, no punishment came for Precious. Three days passed and no whip or stick befell her backside. It was as if she hadn't run, hadn't needed rescuing by the master. Had he been so drunk he'd forgotten?

That couldn't be it. He was lucid, with eyes that sparked. Well, they possessed a brave fire before he started drinking the brandy again.

She shook her head and put her mind to Little Jonas. Her skinned knee stung as she knelt four paces in front of the boy, but the thick carpet of the nursery offered some cushion. Smiling, she held her hands out to him. "Come on, little man. Take another step."

The boy giggled and tottered, then stopped when he wobbled and almost toppled to the floor.

"Try again, little man."

He puckered his lips. "Uh uh."

Patting the thick brown carpet, she tried to entice him, but those rosy cheeks weren't havin' it.

"No, Mama."

"You want me to wait? Waitin's no good." Waitin' was bad. Had she gotten the courage to confront Lord Welling sooner, she could take back a year of dreams. Thinkin' you're free, only to be put back in a box; that was no good.

Jonas started to laugh. "Mama funny."

"Sweet child, I'm not. Mammy, some say in Charleston. I—

Before she could finish, the door to nursery creaked open. Precious barely lifted her gaze, expecting Mr. Palmers or a lower floor maid, but the sight of her master made her jump. "Yes, sir."

"Mama, eh?" His eyes held a smile as he stepped closer to his son.

Cringing, she felt an extra lash would be added to her for this. Wiping her brow, she spoke with muffled voice. "I always correct him, Lord Welling. I meant no disrespect."

He waved at her as if to stop the explanations. "He's walking now? Time keeps moving."

"How much you'll miss when you venture off to Africa." The words flew out of her mouth before her good sense started her brain to working.

Folding his arms, his shoulders tugged at his dark blue coat. "The plan was for his mother to be here with him as I went about my duty. With her gone, I don't have other options. My inheritance..." He looked away, half-pivoting, so all Precious could see was his ramrod-straight back and a freshly bandaged hand pulled to his buff breeches.

Little Jonas moved and waddled forward, lunging at his father's boots. The child was all giggles, clutching the master's leg, falling upon the highly polished Wellingtons.

The baron bent as if to hug the boy, but his arms stayed fixed.

Maybe a little encouragement would set things right between Jonas and the baron. "Pick 'im up, sir. A child needs to know his father's love."

Lord Welling lifted his head; a dimple peeked like he'd swallowed a laugh. "I thought you said the whisper of it was fine."

Gall swam in the back of her throat, but she knew it was better not to say her thoughts on his tweaking. Moving forward, she lifted the child and swung him around. Maybe the jokes would keep Jonas from knowing his pa's rejection.

But the boy stuck his arms over her shoulder toward the stupid man. Poor baby wanted to know his pa's heart.

"Papa." The child's sweet voice sounded strong and sharp, enough so it cut at hers. "Hug."

"Stop, Miss Jewell." Lord Welling came behind her and patted his boy's head.

She pivoted to face him and rotated Jonas so that they could both see the sight of the baron shifting his stance.

Was it fear? No. Something kept him from loving this little boy. What?

Since she'd already earned punishment, pushing the man a bit more couldn't make things worse. Precious snuggled Jonas then shook her head at the baron. "He won't break, sir."

Wide blue eyes seemed to penetrate her skull. The man looked well, sans the alcohol. He raked an index finger through his dark brown hair. "I was never very good with children. I was my father's only."

Encouraged by the small smile hovering on his lips, she pattered forward and stuck Jonas against his waistcoat. The boy latched onto the large bone button at the top of the silk beneath his bright white cravat. "Take 'im, sir."

Hesitation ripped across his face, firming up a mouth now pressed into a line.

This close, the woodsy scent of him tickled her nose as surely as if he'd stroked it with a feather, but she forced her expression to be as blank as his.

He couldn't know the silliness of her thoughts or that she'd already begun rethinking her boldness.

His hand whipped backward. For a second, she tensed as if the baron would slap her, but then his palm clapped about Jonas's middle. The grasp was awkward, but it didn't seem like the boy would fall. In fact, he grabbed fists full of his pa's waistcoat like he'd seized reins.

Backing away, she headed to the door. "I'll let you two alone."

"Jewell, no." His voice sounded rushed, as did the pounding of his boots along the floor. "A young child needs a woman's care."

He deposited Jonas into her hands, popped to the threshold, twisted the doorknob, and then stopped. "I've some thinking to do about Port Elizabeth. Maybe Jonas will visit. You will have to attend him there, too."

Before she could ask his meaning, Lord Welling pried the door open and shot through to the other side.

Had she heard him clearly? In case he returned, she plastered on a fake smile and spun the boy to the window. Did the master want Jonas and Precious to visit his mysterious city in Africa? When and for how long?

30

Staring out at the sea of townhomes, she wondered if this Port Elizabeth looked like London, thick and overcrowded. Maybe it had rolling hills and wide spaces like Charleston. What were the people like? Maybe they were kinder and she would be away from all the things that put fear in her bosom.

Through the glass, she watched Lord Welling don his top hat and climb into a carriage. He surely didn't fret another moment about this invitation.

Africa? Didn't her people come from there? Weren't her people scooped up from a village and sold like meat at the docks? That's what her ma had said had happened to hers. Cold sweat moistened her palms. Precious would have to be extra careful and not run too far from the baron's protection. She could get caught by a slaver and end up in worse straits. The thought of someone like Old Jack owning her made her toes feel numb again, just like in the rain.

She shrugged. The baron's offer couldn't be a serious one. It was just something to say to hide his awkwardness with Jonas. Her heart fumed again. It was meanness to taunt the part of her that still dreamed of living and doing on her own.

Jonas kicked and made an impatient pucker with his lips so she set him down on the thick carpet. He took a few steps then toppled over, laughing.

Precious smiled and tried to focus on his joy, not the sense of hope and dread warring in her lungs. Coming to England from America had given her new privileges and a taste of freedom. What would a visit to Africa bring?

Chapter Four: A Bargain

After a day at his solicitor's, a reward of beefsteak smothered in onions should've brought a sense of accomplishment to Welling's gut. It didn't. The food went down, as did the crusty bread of the hasty pudding, but he didn't feel satisfied. No, every bit dropped into the pit of his stomach like a rock sinking in a pond.

Watching Miss Jewell, with Eliza's eyes, playing with his son, showing love to his boy bothered him more than it should. By leaving Jonas for Port Elizabeth, was he again choosing his uncle over his late wife?

And what of the fussy maid? Until Eliza's death, he'd always thought of Jewell as her baggage, her slave. Yes, that was a nice and tidy way to keep what he'd seen happening to the blacks in West Africa, the slave ships, the breaking of men and women, out of his mind. Those trips with his uncle were supposed to enlighten. What light can be seen in such brutality? Port Elizabeth was down in the southern tip of Africa, so it would be different. Under his control, it had to be.

He poked at his plate. His hands weren't so clean anymore, but letting the last traces of Eliza go was out of the question. How would he…Jonas get on? Pushing a sliver of meat across the blue Wedgewood dish, he stared at the carmine red walls. How long he'd sat there wasn't apparent until he blinked and saw that the candles along the dining room mantle had diminished to a couple of inches. Wiping his mouth, he wrenched out of his chair.

Perhaps, a drink would do. He never allowed himself to indulge in alcohol as a way to end his day, but on the anniversary of Eliza's death, he gave himself leave to swim in fine brandy. Right now, he felt the same edge, the same rawness in his soul. One glass of brandy would help. It had to.

With his palm still raw from the last time he indulged, he plowed through the door. The muted sound of an argument stopped him.

Whipping to the left, he saw Palmers hovering over Miss Jewell. In the darkness of the hall, he heard the butler's sharp tone. It sounded accusatory. What had the minx done?

Palmers gripped her by the shoulders. "Your apron was found in the master's bedchamber. It's bloody. You have a bruise on your black face. What has occurred, Jewell? Did you attack Lord Welling? Have you forgotten your place?"

The girl straightened her carriage, though her arms vibrated. "No, I haven't. How could I forget? You remind me daily."

Something primal stirred inside at seeing Jewell shudder, but he was proud her wits were sharp. Though he felt like throttling the old man for putting angry hands on a woman, Welling marched to him at a steady pace.

"Let her go, Palmers. She's done nothing untoward. I had an accident and the young lady bandaged me up with her apron."

Like his fingers had touched fire. Palmers released her. "Sir, I suspected—"

"Not that I would harm a woman, but it never crossed your mind that *I* might be the villain?"

"Sir, it's not in your blood to be savage."

Miss Jewell took her apron from the man. Her head shook from side to side and her almond eyes held daggers. "But it's in mine. Right, Mr. Palmers?"

The old servant straightened, his nose twitching as if smelled a skunk. "Watch your tongue. I am your superior."

Welling hated the haughty tone of the butler, so like the gentry when he'd introduced Eliza, his American heiress bride. Gall and spittle filled his throat. Jewell and Eliza deserved better. "You are in charge, Palmers, but superiority is a matter of opinion."

Folding up the stained apron into a neat square, the spitfire stared off into the distance, but her voice sounded deep like she gargled with marbles. "The old bird likes threatening me. Mr. Palmers, don't you have silver to count, a room to check to see that I've cleaned?"

Sarcasm and pride, two things he didn't believe a slave would possess. What other things was she capable of? Remembering his position, he waved her off. "None of that, Miss Jewell. Wait for me in my study."

She lifted her chin and swept down the hall. Grace filled her agile limbs. She didn't shrink like a servant or slave, for that matter. Must be the American part of her aiding her boldness.

Chiding himself for watching her a little too long, he

whipped his head back to Palmers and counted the seconds until he heard his study's door slam. "Why do you think so little of the girl?"

Palmers straightened his onyx livery, his wrinkled palm latching to the jacket. "The bruises to her. She's a slave, a savage."

"Seems to me, since you were the one manhandling a woman, there's savagery in your blood." He hardened his countenance and stared at the old bird. "Don't touch her or any other female like that again."

The butler nodded, but his mouth twisted as if he sucked lemons. "I hadn't thought she'd fallen under your special protection. You always seemed so honorable...set in your grief."

Such wretched thinking. The man leapt from Jewell as an attacker to a doxy. Anger burned inside, making Welling almost ball his fists. Beating a pompous, ancient windbag wouldn't do. "For you, either the girl is treacherous or I brutalize my bedfellows. Palmers, your mind is more limited than I thought. Go to your chambers, old man, and treat Miss Jewell better. She's a good worker and very doting to my son. Consider this your only warning."

"Yes, sir. While you're here, you'll see I keep your orders." The man dipped and plodded down the hall and out of sight.

Standing in the quiet of Firelynn, Welling let the implied threat soak into his brainbox. What did Miss Jewell experience during the months of his absence? And even if he sent for his son and her upon occasion to visit Port Elizabeth, what would the years without his protection do to her?

With a shake of his head, he stepped into the study

rebuking himself for these cares, until he saw the maid standing in the shadow of Eliza's portrait. The likeness of Jewell's eyes to the one of the portrait was unmistakable, except for the shadows of anger crowding the girl's pupils. No, that intensity matched the Eliza of his dreams.

Jewell folded her hands behind her back. "What do you want of me?"

Closing the door, he thought of what to say. What did he want? Definitely something Jewell and time could never make happen.

He moved closer, taking in the maid's caramel skin, her straight posture, the sense of pride swirling about her surprising curves. "So you've made an enemy of Palmers. With Old Jack, that makes two."

Still fingering her ruined apron like it was prized silk, she lifted her chin. "And you, for denyin' my freedom. That would make three."

"I'm no enemy, Jewell. I'd think that the night of the storm would make you recognize this."

"So you don't hit me. Or leach after me. Or call me 'dirt' to my face. You still begrudge me my freedom. Maybe if you were in town more, you'd have me fetch a pet monkey and chase after you like the other pageboys."

"I don't have a pet monkey. And you are no pageboy."

He looked above her head, away from the girl's darkening cheeks to Eliza's wistful smile painted in oils, very unlike the frowns haunting him at night. "If you were free, Miss Jewell, what would you do?"

"I could seek employment. Maybe a family that needed an able worker. One that wouldn't be so threatened by a dark face. Yes, that would be good."

"You think Palmers is threatened by you? Old Jack

didn't seem that fearful when you hit him with a rock. No, he seemed riled."

"What else would you call it? They won't let me be. They look for evil in everything I do." She tugged at her tucker, pulling it closer to her throat. "Or they find new ways to humble me. A new family, a new place, would do better."

Jewell hated his household that much. So like Eliza. He turned his back to her and moved to the sideboard, splaying his fingers about the brandy bottle, but resisted the urge to taste and drown his conscience. "Jonas would miss you."

"Soon he'd be taken from me. It's better to do it now. I'll just be a faded memory."

He pivoted, his heart pounding with anger. "Memories don't fade. They find the means to return. Your leaving would be hurtful to my son. Even a bacon-brained idiot can see the strength of his attachment." He ran a hand through his hair, and softened his tone. "I won't have him hurt, not when I can prevent it."

She swiped at her eye and nodded. "Then good night, sir. Don't tell Palmers I'm no longer free. Then, he'll really be evil, very cruel with his gloating."

As she moved past him, he caught her arm. She flinched then stopped. "Yes, sir?"

He'd seen her tense like this before but thought it was his brandy-infused breath. She'd suffered something, but that mystery couldn't be solved now. He'd come to a decision, one she needed to hear. "I'm not done." Letting go of her, he pointed to the sofa. "Have a seat."

Her beautiful eyes grew large. She backed up to the flowery tufted cushions, but did not sit.

He moved his hand to encourage her to sit, lowering

his fingers as if he were leading musicians.

She jutted out her chin and then sank to the edge as if the puffy thing would bite her. "Yes, sir."

"I'm going to take Jonas to South Africa with me. You're right about him needing to be more entwined in his father's life."

A smile formed on her full lips. "That's very good."

"But, he can only come if you travel with him too."

Her mystical eyes squinted before she looked down at the floor. "I'll try to prepare him for the voyage. I know journeyin' by boat can be terrible."

She didn't understand and he needed her to. He stooped beside her. "No, Miss Jewell. You will come with us and live in Port Elizabeth. How do you feel about that?"

She picked at her apron. Her voice sounded low and humbled. "What does an owner's request mean to a possession? What is it you wish to hear?"

Perhaps it was selfish, but he'd hoped she would sound happy about this, maybe even display a little gratitude. Those few times Eliza was happy, her irises lit like a candle and her eyes danced.

No sparkle filled the maid's. They might've even held tears.

Jewell stood and curtsied. "Goodnight, Lord Welling."

Giving her freedom wasn't something he was prepared to do, and it made the paperwork in his jacket feel small, inconsequential. Yet, he wasn't forsaking his influence over the willful girl. "Wait, we are not done."

She released the doorknob and spun back to him. Her arms folded about her, and she heaved out a sigh. "I'm ready for my punishment."

"What?"

"For escaping." The girl came closer. Her fingers clutched the edge of her emerald bodice. "There's no cane in here, but the poker'll do." She gulped and shut her eyes. She turned her backside to him. "Wrap your jacket about it. That'll leave no marks."

Studying the curves of her pushed punishment far from his mind. No, a drunken vision of holding fire against his chest near the mantel stirred. He raked at his temples. "Jewell, no. Please face me."

She whirled around with fists levied. "Then what do you want?"

He pulled from his jacket the paperwork he'd gotten from his solicitor and draped it over her wrists. "Can you read, Miss Jewell?"

The girl glared at him, neither nodding nor shaking her head, but the almond eyes held flames. They bemused his soul.

Nothing meant more in that moment than seeing a glimpse of Eliza alive in Jewell. Memories of a fast courtship and an inferno of arguments and loving swept through him, fixing his boots to the floor, pinning his gaze. He blinked and remembered he was in Firelynn with his wife's maid, not Eliza.

He covered the ache with a cough. "These were to give you some papers to satisfy you here, in London, but I think these are exactly what you need to begin a new adventure."

Precious held her breath. The man offered her papers to dismiss her. Tossed out with no position to go to. How would she get on?

"Look at the papers, Jewell."

Her arms trembled beneath her thick cuffs and by

39

sheer will she chased the vibrations away. She'd show him and Old Jack and Mr. Palmers. Precious Jewell would make her own way, or die in the tryin'.

His brows furrowed. "Jewell, sit and read the paper. That's an order."

Not sure of what to make of anything, she half-pivoted and again eased onto the edge of the thick cushions. Servants weren't to sit in these places for entertaining, and never someone like her.

He took the pages and waved them before her face. "Read it aloud."

The scrawl appeared foreign, but there were words that she could make out. Servant, Five Years. "I don't understand."

He paced back and forth as if he searched for something to explain these papers. Maybe he couldn't make sense of them either.

Wrenching his neck, he stopped and planted a few feet from her. "These documents, if you place your mark next to mine, will make you an indentured servant. Immediately, you will no longer be a slave. After five years of faithful service, you will be free."

His words stung her ears. What did he mean? And why five years? "How is this free?"

Folding his arms behind his back, he stopped. Tall and warrior-like, he seemed to struggle. Maybe this fanciful notion of being free was too much for him, too. He cleared his throat. "This is the means to honor Eliza's wishes with permanent legal freedom. You'll have earned a tidy sum during your service, so that you have the means to settle where you like, and I will have assured consistency for Jonas."

The emotion running through her veins, making her

icy fingertips go fully numb wasn't gratitude. He didn't trust her. She clutched the papers to her bosom. "I suppose that I should be happy."

"You are all Jonas and I have left of his mother. My work to build a colony in Port Elizabeth will be grueling. I need to know that he is loved and kept safe, daily."

Why was the man so thick? She balled up her ruined apron, clutching the coins sewn inside. "I could serve as a free woman."

A smirk settled again on his face, but his eyes held no joke. "Free, you could leave us, and what would that do to him? I am not good with children. And there's nothing like a little inducement to bring out the best."

That didn't make any sense. She held her shocked self as if she were freezing. "I'd be a good worker, free. You know I do good work."

"Miss Jewell, you attempted to run the last time we were in this room. I won't have the leisure of retrieving you in Africa. No. I need to ensure your loyalty. You wanted papers, didn't you? This is my bargain."

She jumped to her feet and pressed toward the door. Opening it, she wanted to be out his sight as she tried to decipher the words on the page. "If that is all, sir."

He plodded ahead of her and elbowed the door closed. His mighty shoulders blocked her path. "I need an answer now. You leave this room without a signature then you will be a slave, my slave always. And when I am gone, Palmers will control your fate. It will be difficult to get new employ without these."

Taunting her, he waved the papers. "Or maybe Old Jack will help. He seemed very interested in your position. Be sensible. Take my bargain."

The man had all the power, but didn't he have it

whether she signed the documents or not?

"Why these?" Tears of frustration welled, but she swallowed them and crunched up the papers in her hand. "Why not just take me to Port Elizabeth, the horrid place where your people put mine in chains and began my way as a *savage*?"

"I'm not responsible for slavery, but I intend to clear up the conditions put in place by the English, Dutch, French - all the civilized societies - that took from Africa. So I'll start my penance for my people by ending my tenure as a slaver."

"This is just a change in title. You control my fate here *and* there. Nothin' substitutes for havin' my own say."

His chuckles were low and easy, but his stare sliced through her. "It's never that easy. And who truly has their own say, as you put it? No, we hope for the best in our circumstances."

"So, signing these papers will make you feel better?"

"I just want a servant, one dedicated to the happiness of my heir. I don't want you jumping when I enter a room. And, though your form is pleasing, I'd rather not have it turned to me expecting a lashing."

Her cheeks, even the bruised one, felt hot but his gaze did not break. "Jewell, I am leading the colonists to make peace with the Blacks and the small communities surrounding Port Elizabeth. I can't do that with doubts about Jonas's care and his safety."

Sliding the papers from her, he walked over to his desk and whipped out a bottle of ink, a sharp quill, and a blotter. Unfurling the parchment, he smoothed it onto the mahogany surface of his writing desk. "Come on, Miss Jewell. This is right."

How could it be, when he'd taken her excuses away? He'd thought about this, plotted it out in a matter of a few days. She took the quill from his hand, sliding the soft feather over her knuckles. "This will set me free in five years? I have your word on it?"

He nodded and pushed the papers closer to her. "Yes, five years and your service will be done. Then you will be free and have earned enough money to think of marrying or returning to England, or even settling in Port Elizabeth. Who knows? Some fellow there may catch your eye. You may not want to leave."

It wasn't that easy. Being pushed to sign things she could barely read, sucking in promises of some distant five years, hurt her heart. She put the quill down and stared at the smirk on his face. "So you've planned my future. You're acting more like an American master every day. Did you pick the buck I'm to breed with, too?"

With wide eyes, he tapped his lips then turned from her and went and stood near Eliza's picture. "My baroness wanted you freed. I'm giving you a mechanism that does so, but puts her son's happiness first. In five years, he'll be breeched, out of pinafores and in trousers. His need for a substitute mother will have diminished."

Mother to Jonas? What was the man thinking? She shook her head.

A sigh steamed out of the baron. "I'd like to think Eliza left this world in peace, knowing you'd protect her babe. She knew I would be too busy for the job. We owe this to Eliza."

Poor Eliza Marsdale. She'd loved every minute of carrying the boy in her womb. The notion of the babe gave her such pleasure. Didn't they both cry at the wiggle of Eliza's tummy at his quickening? She was good, always doting and lenient with Precious. A mumble of *yes* left her lips, but that wasn't good enough. She cleared her throat. "I do owe her, sir. Not you. Free me, and I will serve Jonas and you."

"I haven't in me to trust like that. You could change your mind and leave me."

His large blue eyes captured her and held her in place. She couldn't breathe or cede to his notions. Finally, she looked down to the polished mahogany flooring and pushed her slipper back and forth. "Miss Eliza trusted me, confided in me, thought me good enough to be freed. If you were me, wouldn't you want to be free too?"

"Jonas has chosen you, Jewell. I've heard him call you Mama on more than one occasion. Shall you allow your stubborn spirit to deny Eliza's joy?"

He'd spied on her and Jonas before today? When? And was she so wrapped up in loving the boy she hadn't noticed? The baron's tone didn't sound cocky, as it had before. No, it bore hints of sadness, maybe even defeat. She lifted her head and caught a glimpse of him, staring and stiffening his jaw. He wasn't use to pleading, but why did he need this?

Her chest constricted, and she felt for the quill. "You win."

Pushing fear and doubt to the back of her mind, she put her mark on the documents, where he had pointed. "What now?"

His hand, warm and strong, closed about hers. The odd mixture of his woodsy scent and fresh linen filled her nostrils. "This is for the best," he said. Taking the quill, he put his elegant signature above hers on both papers then offered her one page. "Keep this. The other goes to my solicitor. Now, off to bed. In the morn, pack and get Jonas ready. We leave at week's end."

She clutched the parchment and wrapped it in her apron. "Yes, master."

"It's Welling. Gareth Conroy, the third Lord Welling."

She backed away. "Yes, master." On the other side of the door, she took a whole breath. She was sort of free, but what did that mean in this Port Elizabeth place?

She started moving her slippers against the treads and down to her room when a tiny cry sounded. Jonas?

Pivoting, she decided to check on him and climbed the stairs to the second level. When she passed the hall mirror, she stopped and peered at her frozen cheeks, her poked out lips. Though her face still held a dark bruise, it did nothing to draw attention from the numbness straining her face. She had papers, but only as part of a bad bargain. What would become of her? Would she ever know freedom?

Pulling off her mobcap, she let her shiny braids fall near her chin and rubbed at her temples. Determination set in her jaw and filled her lungs with heat. It didn't matter what Lord Welling or whatever he called himself today said, or even what this paper held. She was free as soon as her foot stepped on the shores of Port Elizabeth. She'd show him. She'd show them all.

The End of This Episode. Tune in For Episode II. Learn more at VanessaRiley.com

Episode II
* * *

Episode II of The Bargain
Length: 8 Chapters (25,000 words)
Summary: Precious Jewell's Misadventures at Sea
Heading to Port Elizabeth

The vastness of the cresting ocean isn't enough to drown Precious Jewell's high spirits or her dreams of doing for herself, but a false move and an old nightmare have placed her in more jeopardy, Lord Welling's bedchamber.

Captaining his schooner to Port Elizabeth was his only refuge, until his ship was invaded by land lovers, his son and his challenging caregiver. Perhaps, Miss Jewell's vivacity and audacity are just what he needs to quell rebellion amongst his crew and his heart.

Chapter One: London, March 1, 1819

Sun poured through the bared windows of Firelynn.
Precious Jewell stood tall, fingering her apron, and tried
to absorb the difference. The gloomy shadows that
normally filled the nooks and tight dusting spots between
the heavy dresser and the burgundy papered walls of
Eliza's bedchamber had disappeared.

Precious took her cloth and oil polish and wiped down
the mahogany furniture again. It didn't make sense,
cleaning in a room that would be closed up. The baron
said he was taking her and Jonas to Port Elizabeth, but
mean old Palmers acted as if nothing had changed. Was
he right? Was this a whim that would pass?

Maybe Lord Welling would sober up and forget. Well,
he wasn't drunk when he gave her her papers. His
shocking blue eyes winced when she first refused to sign
them. No, the man had plans to take his indentured
servant and his son to Port Elizabeth, regardless of
Palmer's stubbornness.

One more pass with the rag and the surface gleamed.

For a few seconds, she imagined primping Eliza for a ball, pinning her gold locks up into a braided chignon. She was happy in this grand bedroom. A wave of sadness sank into Precious. Except for Jonas, she wouldn't feel her friend in Port Elizabeth. Would Precious forget the memories that gave her a small measure of joy, like Eliza teasing about her penmanship as she taught Precious letters, or even the one time she let Precious sashay around in one of her old party gowns?

Before her eyes got misty, the door to the bedchamber opened.

Palmers and two maids plodded inside. "Done in here, Jewell?"

"Yes, sir."

He looked at her over the high bump on his nose. "Good. You can help box up the late mistress's gowns. Seems Lord Welling wants them all given to charity."

Giving Eliza's things away! Precious nodded, but her heart split in two. Surely, it was good for him to put away the past. That had to lead to healing. Then maybe the anniversary of her death wouldn't drive the baron to despair. But to toss away her things? Precious felt some kinda way about that.

"Don't just stand there, girl." Palmers's crusty voice interrupted her woolgathering. "I said help."

When she scurried closer, they went into the connecting room where Eliza's dresses were stored. The door creaked open like unlocking a sealed tomb.

Stuffy. The stale air assaulted her, as did the smell of old lavender. Eliza's lavender. Oh, how Eliza loved the stuff.

Palmers lit a candle on each wall exposing the shelves

of tissue-papered dresses, all shades and colors.

Pushing past her sadness, and the heavy memory of Eliza twirling in the long mirror at the end of the room, Precious went to a close shelf and fingered the emerald taffeta. It was the gown Eliza had let her try on.

Thumbing the puffy sleeves, the soft cloth-wrapped buttons, she picked up the gown. The temptation to press it against her chest and angle in front of the mirror nearly made her palms tremble.

Suddenly the scent of Eliza, the memories, became overwhelming. She couldn't do it. "Mr. Palmers, I'm not well. I need some air."

He squinted over his nose again, but his thin lips pinched to a circle. "You're not one to shrink from work, are you? Nevertheless, I've no want of you getting sick in here. Go on. But be back to work in five minutes."

She dipped her chin and fled the room. Down the stairs to the main level, she wanted to whip through the kitchen and out into the mews, but she could hear Lord Welling's voice. He was down that way.

Not ready to see him in this near weepy state, she turned and headed for the library. Through there she could access the garden, and fresh air.

Her slippers pattered across the floor even as she tried to tiptoe. Once inside, the typically dark room had all its curtains parted. The sunlight blinded. It ripped apart the gloom of the study too. Then she almost screamed when she noticed Eliza's portrait sitting on the floor, removed from its place of honor.

Emotion lumping in her throat, she ran forward and touched the frame. "We're really leaving here. How can I do this without you?"

The door behind her swung open. Precious touched

her face, making sure that no evidence of weakness remained. She turned to ask Palmers how he wanted the grand painting wrapped, but it wasn't the butler.

Lord Welling closed the door with his foot. His stare didn't leave her or the painting.

His silence made her uneasy, and being in this room with him jumbled up her insides. In his study, he'd been kind to her after saving her from the brute, Old Jack, but this was also the place he took away all the choices that would have made her fully free.

With folded arms, he came closer. In the bright light, he looked younger, like the weight of the world had lifted from his broad shoulders. But his searching eyes, coupled with his closed lips, made her knees knock. Yes, he was her employer and could order her around like Palmers. But Palmers never made her this on edge. Never did she fear the power the butler possessed, not like this.

Slowing her knocking kneecaps, she put a hand to her hip. "A workman must've took it down, but left it here to gather dust. Do you know what you want to do?"

"Yes."

If it weren't a picture of Eliza, Precious would tell the baron what to do with it, and with his nerve-wracking self. "Would you like to tell me? I don't want to see damage to this picture."

He moved closer to the sofa. High black boots crossed underneath his thick legs as he tucked up his blue-black blazer and perched on the back of the high furnishing. "The workman will finish with it. It's coming with us to Port Elizabeth."

All of his other trips, he never disturbed a thing. He was here and then he wasn't. Eliza got used to it, and just kept her social calendar full to pass the time. Even with her gone, his routine never changed. Then it hit her, like a punch to the gut. "We...You're not coming back anytime soon."

"With Jonas coming with me, their are no obligations here to have me come to and fro."

She thought they'd journey for a few months, maybe a year, since he'd pushed her into five years of servitude, but to be away from Firelynn for years? She put a hand to her mouth. "You're never coming back?"

"Never is a long time, Miss Jewell."

"So is five years of servitude."

His dimple showed and for a moment, his countenance eased. His mouth almost formed a smile. "I don't think you'll miss London. Port Elizabeth, with its forests and close water, it might be like your Charleston."

"Oh, let it be nothing like that." She dipped her head and twisted her fingers within her starched apron.

"Jewell, you will like Port Elizabeth. It's new. Everyone is building. The weight of old things isn't so heavy with so much new to make you feel alive."

Except for Jonas growing, time stood still in Firelynn. Palmers was still mean. The dust continued to gather. And Eliza was everywhere, making her loss still fresh. Precious turned to her mistress's portrait. "Will you hang her in your residence, in a place of honor? Will it feel like she is there too?"

He strode close and clasped her hands, stilling her fidgeting and the very breath in her lungs. "You ever lost someone other than Eliza?"

She couldn't look up into Lord Welling's eyes. She simply focused on not moving. "Yes, my Grandmama. My ma, she was sold a year or two after I was born, so all I ever had was Grandmama."

"What happened to her?"

"Too much work when she'd become frail. She picked in the cotton all that day, made dinner for field hands, then never woke from her sleep." The memory of the woman's wisdom wrapped tightly about Precious's heart, like the stories she told about the fire, or hearing her sing during thunderstorms in their cottage.

"Isn't she with you, Jewell, in every step you take? She wouldn't want you to stay stuck in the past, stuck in some cottage in Charleston, where everywhere you turn you see your shortcomings. Everyday, all you feel is loss."

She nodded. There were other reasons than Grandmama's death that made her anxious to leave America, but he didn't have to know those particulars. "It was good to come away to London."

"I don't think Eliza wants that either. So, if I need to stay away from Firelynn to be free of the memories…her pouts, her cheery laughter, her disappointments," He blinked his eyes hard, then opened them wide, "then I choose Port Elizabeth. It's a new beginning. Maybe it's your new beginning too.

Fingers turning to ice, she broke free of his loose grasp. "You need to be free of this. Then you won't be so drunk. Jonas needs a father more each day."

He plodded over to his bottles of liquor and topped off a half-filled glass. As if saluting her, he lifted it to his lips. He didn't down it as she'd seen him do in the past. It was almost as if this effort was for show. "Well, I don't drink at sea. You'll have to deal with me with all my faculties working. "

The door opened and Palmers marched inside. "Miss Jewell, the packing of the dresses needs to be done."

"Yes, sir, Mr. Palmers."

The baron put down his drink. "Oh, yes, and do allow each of the maids to have one of the late Lady Welling's gowns. Make it a gift from their late mistress."

Frowning so hard his cheeks looked like they would explode, Palmers made a tsk sound with his teeth. "They are too fine for the help, sir."

A laugh, short and harsh, fled her employer's mouth. "And charity will have better use? I hadn't seen too many peers in the hospital lines. I'm sure the maids can make something out of the fabric. Jewell, that includes you. Which one of those fine creations would you choose?"

Without hesitation, her mouth flung open. "The emerald taffeta."

His gaze swept over her. She looked away before settling on staring at the jute rug on the floor. It wasn't indecent, his look, but more of what you see a man give at the bakery when fresh baked bread scents the air.

"Yes, the gown Eliza wore to her second London reception, the house of Lady and Lord Jerrings. Yes, Jonas Hunt, the new Lord Jerrings, was quite taken with her." A grunt left him, as if he'd remembered a bad joke. "Take it with you to Port Elizabeth and make something new from it."

Hating to agree with the scowl on the butler's face, she lifted her chin to meet Lord Welling's waiting glance. "I couldn't."

He folded his arms, picking at his brass buttons. "Then you won't. Palmers, have it and more broadcloth and muslin ordered to set sail with. There are no mercantiles in Port Elizabeth. Miss Jewell and the other women going with us will want material for a change of dress."

Palmers' gaze met hers, as if they both tried to

understand the baron's meaning. Then his man finally agreed, almost choking on the words. "Yes, sir."

"Good. Get to packing, Miss Jewell." The baron pounded past her and shoved his nearly full glass into Palmers' mitts. Halting, he half-pivoted. His gaze settled in Precious's direction and the painting near her side. "Be careful to follow my orders, Palmers. I'd hate for my plans to be ruined or delayed."

The door to the study closed behind Lord Welling, but his commanding presence remained. Even stiff Palmers looked shaken.

Precious pivoted to Eliza's portrait and touched the gilded frame again. This trip to Port Elizabeth would be new and different. But what were Lord Welling's plans? And why did it feel as if his latest directives had to do with Precious as much as the swirls of pigment?

Chapter Two: Boarding the Margeaux

One, two, three, four. Precious Jewell counted the tall poles anchored to top of the massive boat roped into the dock. Those beams seemed so high they punched through the overcast sky.

Pinching her fingers, she measured the swaying crossbeam attached to a middle post. An unfurled snowy white sheet wrapped about it, all spanning several inches betwixt her thumb and index. The distance must be miles wide.

Scared and excited, her throat dried even as her toes wiggled in her short boots. Swallowing, she lifted her chin to keep it from gaping. This boat had to be three times bigger than the one Lord Welling sent to Charleston to bring his bride and her slave maid to London. That one seemed so grand. The day her foot left South Carolina soil was the first day she could breathe. No more evil. Well, none that caused lasting damage.

Jonas snored. The soft noise tickled her neck. The

gingham cloth sling she'd made to carry him kept his little body close to hers while allowing her hands to be free. She shifted her satchel to her other arm. Skivvies, a fresh dress, a nightgown and robe, a few of Jonas's toys, and her indentured servant papers, all her worldly goods sat inside, and she wasn't trusting it to anyone.

The wind shifted. A ray of solemn light beamed down, warming her tight fingers. Everyone except for Jonas, all the workers and tradesmen and sailing men pounding to and fro, disappeared.

Staring and tracing the rope lines, her heart raced. Something new and magical would happen and this boat would lead the way. This beast of cedar and oak had to be larger than Firelynn Hall. Lord Welling probably needed one so big to carry her and all her hopes to this new land.

With a sigh and the forward shuffling of her feet, the world returned. Men, lots of them, stepped all around her. She clutched her bag a little tighter, but most didn't pay her any mind. They had work to do, carrying and loading crates onto the docked boats.

The hull of Lord Welling's boat were stamped with the letters, M-A-R-G-E-A-U-X, and bobbed up and down with the waves. The bottom of the boat, below the water's edge, must be just as big as the upper. A lot can be ferried in something like that. A lot of crates, trunks...enslaved peoples.

A gull shrieked overhead. It echoed in Precious's ear, sounding like captives crying out.

She shivered. Thoughts of Grandmama pressed her heart. The old woman shed tears, recalling how she bore the weight of the iron chains, the scorn of the white men beating them and yelling in a language she did not know.

The tales of being loaded into the dank abyss, the dark bottoms of a vessel such as this were rooted in the dear woman's nightmares.

Grandmama's brother died on the voyage. His body tossed overboard like garbage. How many others been killed, their freedom stolen on a big boat, one such as this?

Nausea flooded Precious. Her limbs shook with shame. How could her hopes be high when suffering and stealing still happened?

On the smaller boat with Eliza, all she could think of was herself and the chance to be away from her oppressors in Charleston. It hadn't gripped her like now, to think of her shattered family or the stolen futures of her forebears.

Heavy in spirit, she wiped at her eyes. That was yesterday, and what could one formerly enslaved girl do to change it? Nothin'.

Yesterday. She chanted it to her spirit, over and over, trying to recapture her joy.

Looking at cobbles in the dirt, she bumped into a woman embracing a man about his waist. Her dark walking gown blended into his short cape. Precious backed up, hating that she'd disturbed their moment. "Sorry."

The woman ignored her and snuggled closer to her man.

Precious scooted by, but couldn't help staring. Was it a homecoming or a send-off?

The couple walked away, hand in hand. Perhaps they had love. That emotion was a strange thing. Eliza and Lord Welling claimed to have it. Her mistress seemed happy, coming to London. What southern girl wouldn't be? Her fiancé seemed reasonable, handsome, and even-tempered. For an arranged marriage, that had to be good. But they quarreled often over his family obligations, until Eliza was gone.

With this past week of cleaning, she'd been wiped away from Firelynn. Her legacy, little Jonas, was all that was left of their union.

The boy snuggled next to Precious's bosom. She covered his face from the whipping wind. She thought about his mother more and more these days. Poor Eliza, Precious's long-time protector, would she be happy to see how this boy had grown? Would her heart leap as Precious's did when the baron began spending more time with him?

If Eliza had lived, they wouldn't be traveling to Port Elizabeth. She liked the parties of London too well. Entertaining, that was Eliza's fun. Oh, how she would have reveled in throwing a first ball as Lady Welling. Her friend died, hours before she could even use the title.

Precious's woolgathering sent her barreling into a thick man who bore saggy cloth bags.

Tall, and black as pitch, he doffed his hat to her. "Miss, you need to be careful." His head lowered, his gaze seemed to stop near Jonas's mop. "Your mistress about?"

Precious lifted her chin, a bit of pride buzzing like a lightning bug in her nervous stomach. "His mother is not, but my employer is somewhere." She stared him in the eye, something she rarely did with men, but she wanted him to know she wasn't enslaved.

"An American's tongue." He tossed the bags on his back. "Betcha you like it here better since you got rights. A slave's got rights here. I got mine." He adjusted his bundles and went on his way.

What was he talking about? She tugged her snowy mobcap over her ear. Whether the man believed her or not, she didn't care. Her freedom was true. She nodded, patted her bag with her papers, and kept trudging to the loading area of the M-A-R-G-E-A-U-X.

Mr. Palmers, the nasty butler, ambled down the wide plank leading from the ship's deck. The grim lines of his face stayed in a permanent frown. In fact, since Lord Welling announced his plans to take her and Jonas with him, the butler never smiled. He stopped next to her. "Don't disgrace His Lordship on this trip. You may have fooled him into thinking you're more than a backwoods savage, but we know the truth."

A thousand responses, all more hateful than the last, sprang to her mind, but she buttoned her lips. She'd save her good breath on someone more worthy.

"No retort? No drivel about nonsense?" He shook his head and tugged on his grey mantle. Such a puffed-up, mean-spirited bird. "Maybe you've learned some manners and respect after all."

Tongue burning with an apt phrase she'd picked up in London, she couldn't hold it inside any longer. "You bacon-brained fop, it hasn't been your doing. Go on now. Go play lord and master to the empty house."

As if he knew she and the butler would squabble, Lord Welling appeared, standing a few feet away with brows rising and tight lips.

She stilled her fidgeting fingers. There was no hiding her disgust of the butler, and, in another, hour she wouldn't have to. Palmers wasn't sailing. If all went well in Port Elizabeth, it could be a year or more before she'd see the troll again.

The crowd keeping the baron from them parted. He marched near, with a pretty young woman on his arm.

Who was she, and why was giggling?

"Miss Jewell, Palmers," he said, patting the lady's fingers, "this is Clara Narvel. She's joining us on this trip."

The fancy woman in a peach-colored cape and bisque bonnet must be a rich woman. "I am so excited, Lord Welling."

Precious didn't like the feeling stirring inside. A breathless, quiet anger, like somebody stole something, filled her middle. She looked down at Jonas and hoped her face didn't show the contempt brewing.

She rubbed her temples, and came very close to swatting her foolish self. Lord Welling hadn't done anything wrong. He wasn't betraying Eliza. He'd been widowed for two years. The handsome man surely couldn't expect to live as a monk forever.

Still, unease simmered as he swiveled this stranger with her cape billowing toward his boat.

"'Tis a good season for traveling," his voice sounded happy and strong. "You will like the Margeaux."

The buxom red-haired lady nodded and giggled again. "Captain Conroy, I mean, Lord Welling, I am so excited to be going with you."

She'd called him by one of his other names. The lady must know him well. This wasn't good.

The young lady's buttercup-yellow glove blended into his dark-blue tailcoat. The fluff of his town cravat was gone, replaced with a simple one that allowed the natural square of his jaw and long neck to be seen. He looked well without all the fuss, but Precious didn't like his black moon-shaped hat. Still, it was much nicer than the stuffy top hats that cluttered London.

Yet, she couldn't quite get over his bringing a woman who wasn't a servant or his wife on the same boat as Jonas. Precious swallowed, the answer stinging her throat. What better way for the boy to get used to a new stepmother?

Palmers gripped the ash-grey mantle shrouding his stinking bones, and craned his neck as if surveying the busy dock. "I didn't know more women would accompany you."

Well, well, the old bird was worth something after all, doing the dirty work of inquiring about all his lordship's guests. She caught Lord Welling's gaze and waited for his response.

The reticent dimple on the baron's cheek popped. "She's the wife of my lieutenant, the man I left in charge in the colony. This is her first trip to Port Elizabeth, too. Jewell, she'll be your traveling companion."

Once he said the Mrs. part, Precious felt her lips curling up. She would gladly share a cabin with the lady now.

Mrs. Narvel smiled bigger, showing a few white teeth. "Oh, and I can help with the little boy. My husband and I will need the practice, God willing." The lady patted the front of her cape, exposing a rounding stomach. "Soon."

A woman in love with her husband and with a baby. How very nice. Precious inhaled a little easier. "Jonas is not too much trouble if he gets his nap."

Palmers made a tsk sound with his teeth. "A pregnant woman? Is it safe? There are dangers to childbirth. More so at sea."

The woman looked up. A sense of serenity shrouded

63

her like a blanket. "All will be well. I'm but four months of figuring it out, plenty of time to travel and be with my husband to see the birth of his babe."

Head lowering, as if something had dropped weights on his shoulder, Lord Welling kicked at the cobbles. "It's my duty to get you to Narvel. A man can't miss such an event if it can be helped."

The old bird pushed close to the baron. "It's not too late to allow your son and his nanny to stay. I'm sure you can concentrate on your duties better without them getting into trouble."

Chin rising, Lord Welling stared in Precious's direction. Something flickered in his eyes, before he toggled his hat. "No, Palmers. I'd be more worried about the trouble they'd face without me. Go keep Firelynn in order. Come along, Miss Jewell, Mrs. Narvel. Let me show you to your cabin. Good day, old man."

Lord Welling, clasping Mrs. Narvel's hand, led her up the gangplank.

Waving Palmers good riddance, Precious stroked Jonas in his comfy bundle and followed after the baron. Her short heels clicked on the wood plank leading to the deck of the boat. Stopping midway, she glanced at the frothy water below. It looked cold and sort of brown. Would it be the same in Port Elizabeth? No, it had to be clear and blue to be everything she imagined. Yes, it had to be new, nothing like London and Charleston.

She started moving again, but stopped at the board's edge. A jump of a few feet to the deck lay ahead. By herself, she'd jump like a rabbit, but not with Jonas. Nothing came before his safety.

Turning, Lord Welling lifted his arms to her. "Hand me the boy and then I'll help you."

She unhooked him from the cloth sling and handed him into his father's large hands.

Jonas had awakened. His large eyes must have caught site of the baron, for he started cooing baby talk and ended with, "Papa."

The baron's serious face softened for a moment. "Mrs. Narvel, hold this precious cargo, while I help another. Right, Miss Precious Jewell?"

Without giving her any warning, his hands seized her waist. He swung her wide, the surprise of it knocking the air from Precious. She clutched tightly to her bag to keep it from ending up in the water.

Chuckling, he set her down. "Welcome aboard the Margeaux."

Panting, she squinted at him, giving him an evil eye. Lucky for her she had a tight hold on her satchel or she'd have dropped it. If Precious could get away with it, she'd box his ears. But first, she'd have to wait for the world to stop moving. "Marg-geaux, that's the boat's name?"

"Yes." He lifted his hands and pointed side to side. "She was my uncle's pride and joy. I come from a long line of sailing men. Nothing is better than being at sea. It's one of the few freedoms I know."

Precious couldn't respond, too disbelieving that a man born to a title could dare to think he wasn't free. Her fingers coiled tighter around her satchel holding the documents, which ended her enslavement. No. No freeborn man could ever understand.

He stuffed a hand in his jacket, and with the other he swiped at his chin. "You're in my territory, ladies. Now the rules begin. You must stay in your cabin at all times, unless I come and escort you. Being at sea can be a dangerous time. I need to know where you are every minute."

The sun decided to tunnel through the clouds and smite her. She blinked and surveyed the big beams she'd spied from shore. Massive, bigger than the girth of several men, they stood all around with ropes binding them together and to the deck. Her mind's eye became aware of the big male crewmembers staring at them, ten in all. "Why? How can you get lost on a boat?"

Lord Welling folded his arms, his tanned face looking very serious, but mirth stayed in his crystal blues. "Oh, it's very easy, Jewell. There are dark passages on the Margeaux, corners made for mischief. And the manners of my crew will evaporate as the trip gets long. So do as I ask this one time?"

He took his son back from Mrs. Narvel and put his big hat on him. "I didn't hear a yes, Miss Jewell."

Jonas grinned and kept raising and lowering the hat's brim, like a game of hide and seek.

She straightened the collar of Jonas's pinafore. "Of course, I'll follow my employer's orders."

"I guess that serves as a yes." With a shrug, he led them to a hole in the deck. "This way to your cabin."

Down a ladder he went, with Jonas held tightly in the crook of his forearm.

Mrs. Narvel went next and the baron helped her get to the last rung. "Your turn, Miss Jewell."

She could still feel the strength of his grip from his help on the plank. How long would the sensation of his hands about her middle, pressing into the boning of her corset, linger? No, she didn't want any more of that. Avoiding him, Precious quickly shot down the ladder. It was like a tree. And she'd been quite good at climbing trees and shoeing rabbits in Charleston's woods, before

Mr. Marsdale made her a house servant.

Lord Welling's hands touched her waist and the tingles started again. "You've got this little man?"

Once Jonas was in her arms, she backed away from the baron. "Yes."

Light spilling from the opening highlighted more boards and a corridor.

With his long fingers clasped behind her back, the baron led them to a door. It wasn't fancy but had trim and a brass plate. "There are two cabins on the ship; mine and one for my first mate. He's graciously given up…"

He opened the door, and they found a man lying inside. Pounding forward like he'd discovered an enemy, Lord Welling stepped close and scooped the man up by his shirt. "Who are you?"

The stranger popped free. The whites of his eyes shined brightly. "The name is Grossling, Lieutenant Grossling. I'm your first mate on this trip."

The name didn't seem to set Lord Welling at ease. No, it seemed to grate more, making his fingers tighten. "Ralston is my first mate this trip. Who sent you?"

"The war department, Captain. They've gotten letters talking about violent attacks by the Xhosa. We need to know how unstable the situation is and how well the colony will manage under your leadership."

"I see." The baron's face darkened. He didn't seem to agree. He took a couple of steps backward and leaned against the wall, folding his hands over his ebony waistcoat. "Well, this cabin has been reserved for the women. You'll need to bunk below with the crew."

The frown on Mr. Grossling widened. "What about giving them yours? I said I am an official with the war department."

"The captain's cabin is for the captain, not a paper pusher. And I don't share without good reason. A last-minute male addition is not a good reason. You should be lucky there is space at all. We are loaded to the gills, taking supplies to Port Elizabeth."

The man guffawed, but picked up his boots and his bags. "This is going in my report."

"Make sure to capitalize the words, chivalry and last-minute." Lord Welling pointed toward the exit. "There is only one man in charge on this vessel, Grossling. Leave."

Once the unpleasant man passed, the baron closed the door. Agitation lingered in his tense posture, casting shadows in his blue eyes.

Precious had seen the look before when she'd almost refused to sign on as an indentured servant.

He rubbed at his neck. "Ladies, I really need you to follow my warning. That fellow will be a bother."

Mrs. Narvel unpinned her bonnet and took off her cape. A big belly puffed up her flowery gown. "Yes, Lord Welling."

Making eyes at the little fellow, he stepped near Precious and Jonas. "I didn't hear you agree this time. Miss Jewell, you won't court trouble?"

She raked her fingers through Jonas's blond mop. "Only if trouble comes for me."

He plodded to the door, a shrug swallowing his shoulders. "Just stay below until I come get you and none will."

With that he was gone, the door rattling in its frame.

Precious put Jonas on the floor and fished in her sack for his blocks. Unwrapping them from a handkerchief, the boy started banging and stacking.

Mrs. Narvel sat on the edge of the bed. "Well, this is going to be a long trip. We should get better acquainted."

She nodded, but glanced at the lady's tummy. "You're about four months?"

The woman smiled and patted her belly. "Almost five, but don't tell Lord Welling. It will make him more anxious. My husband will be so surprised."

"Why? It's his right." Precious covered her mouth, but it was too late, the awful thing had sprung from her lips.

"Of course." Mrs. Narvel angled and leaned down, fishing off her cream boots. "His leave in London was so short. I didn't know until he was gone. How long have you worked for the baron?"

What could Precious say? Four years, two years, a few weeks since she had papers. A knock at the door gave a much-needed reprieve, a moment to think of an answer that didn't evoke sympathy or make her less than. "Let me get that."

Opening the door, she allowed two men to ferry in a trunk. They set it in the corner, taking up a good chunk of the small room. Once the men left, she turned to Mrs. Narvel. "I'd been with his late wife for a long time, but only in his household the last four years." She started digging in her bag to avoid more talk. She'd save the chatter for the voyage.

The air was warm in the small room, but hints of cedar offered the scent of newness. A little bit of hope stirred again. But what if this land of Port Elizabeth was just like London, or worse? What if she walked around free, but others who looked liked like her were enslaved. Her heart sank and all the hope died. *Oh, let it not be so.*

Trying to think of something else, Precious smoothed

the rumpled sheets on the bed. What about this fellow, Grossling? "That man the baron kicked out of here, do you think he could be a problem for Lord Welling?"

"No, he's too smart for Grossling to make hay, but we better mind the captain's warnings."

"I suppose." But how much trouble could two women cause on a boat this big? And what consequences would befall Lord Welling?

Gareth climbed the ladder to the deck. His palms felt slick with sweat, making the task a little harder than it should be. Back on deck, he wiped his palms on his breeches and surveyed his dominion. Men prepped lines, readying to launch. Others worked the gasket straps to unfurl the mainsail. One hand had begun to swab the deck boards to erase the footprints of the laborers loading the crates. The chimneystack of the brick oven below gleamed. The cook would soon be baking fresh bread and biscuits. His mouth watered, thinking of the delights. The Margeaux was in tip-top shape. This would be an uneventful voyage to Port Elizabeth.

He took a whiff of the fresh salty air, listened to the cacophony of gulls yelping overhead, and trudged to the rail. He lived more or less a solid life. Since the passing of his youth, he'd counted the costs of every action, like the digits on his hand. To date, he'd only claim to have made three mistakes, losing his first pay billet in a game of marked cards, not measuring the distance he needed to jump away from an exploding cannon, and choosing to attend his uncle's last moments on the earth rather than being at his wife's. Could bringing Miss Jewell and Jonas be the fourth?

Rubbing at his skull, he chuckled to himself, like a

drunk trying to deny the need for a bottle. The headstrong girl was too caught up in admiring his schooner to notice the hungry looks of his crew. Her emerald bodice fit snugly on her grown-up limbs, showing off all manner of curves. He chided himself, too, for she'd gotten his attention.

Swinging her around with his hands about her small waist was a mistake. Teasing the lively miss needed to be avoided at all costs, no matter how enchanting she was, or how much it amused him to see the crinkle on her brow deepen when he confused her.

Just like Eliza.

There was no doubt in his mind the two were related. By God's grace, he stumbled upon a piece of his wife. This time he'd do right. He'd keep Jewell safe, just like he should've done with Eliza. That might pay the debt he owed, to right that third mistake.

"Captain."

He pivoted to see Ralston, a tall, stocky man with a girth as bountiful as the jokes that often came from his mouth.

His first mate put his hands behind his back. "Captain, we are ready to make sail and be underway, but are all the women…are they stayin'?"

The man's thick Irish brogue butchered the King's English almost as badly as Jewell did upon occasion, but somehow Ralston's didn't sound as cute.

Fingers crossing behind his back for luck, he nodded. "Yes. They are. I assure you they will not be any trouble."

Ralston fingered a button on his short coat. "Aye. The two females making the trip. Is the redhead a mail-order bride for a colonist?"

"No, she's my lieutenant's wife."

His man frowned then swiped at his mouth. "Well, what about the other one? She's black, but not as black as some we've seen in Port Elizabeth. I'm thinkin' she'll get prettier with a little rum or a little time at sea." Horrid schoolboy-like giggles came out of the grown lecher. "Yes, I'm thinkin' she'll do."

Something primal rose up in Gareth at the thought of Ralston harassing Jewell. A growl inside almost ushered out, but he smoothed his fisting hand along his coat. "Let Miss Jewell be. She's under my protection."

The bubbly laughter poured harder out of Ralston's mouth, making his jet-black mustache twitch. Even his stomach jiggled with the horrible noise. "I'm not thinking of harming her. No, I had much more pleasurable thoughts of how to spend the time with the pretty blackamoor."

Pounding forward, he got into his first mate's face and talked really slow so the lout wouldn't mistake a syllable. "Ralston, leave her alone. Don't force my hand."

The man stepped back; his laugh had diminished but still sounded. "Oh, why didn't you say the chit was yours? Good for you, Captain. But if you tire of that little piece, give me first go."

He yanked the man by his ratty coat. "Ralston, so help me, you touch her and I'll…"

The laughter finally stopped from the fellow. He swallowed hard, his Adam's apple vibrating. Then Ralston wrenched free. "Don't get so mad. And don't blame me for looking for an opportunity. When they aren't waiting on you, you know what those Blacks are good for. Why else would they breed 'em like cattle in the Americas?"

He leapt backward, out of hitting range. "Well,

Captain. Take your time with that one. Learn the ways to control her and I bet that knowledge will be of use in Port Elizabeth. It'll give you an advantage over the warring tribes. Why make war when there are more pleasant things to be done?"

Stunned at the man's logic, Gareth mumbled a command, though it could have been a curse. He cleared his throat and started again. "Ralston, go check the main sail. We push off in the hour. Belay this foolish talk. That's an order."

His first mate saluted and trudged away.

Gareth pivoted back to the ocean, his ocean, and tried to put his mind upon a cresting wave, upon the gentle white foam, not the ugliness of Ralston's words. How would things in Port Elizabeth improve if all the colonists held this attitude?

The Xhosa, the powerful warrior group that inhabited the inlands of South Africa, sent a representative to the last council meeting. The man claimed that all the whites felt like this. And fool that Gareth was he said the tribe's experience was with the Dutch and the Spanish, not the English. English were different; English laws spoke to equality since the Somerset decision.

But how truly different were the Port Elizabeth colonists?

And how different was Gareth?

He'd ignored parts of that decision to keep Jewell under his influence. He wanted her close. For her own good, he couldn't risk her staying in London without his protection. And, like Eliza, she was too willful to be reasoned with, not without a bargain.

His conscience had been wearing on him since he presented her with the option of staying with Palmers or coming to Port Elizabeth as an indentured servant. Yes, England did afford slaves the right to choose not to leave her shores, but life in England was cruel to outsiders, those of different skin. The thought of the willful miss being tricked into prostitution or living in abject poverty wasn't something he could allow. That would never honor Eliza.

Maybe he should've trusted Jewell, but telling people what to do was in Gareth's blood. Growing up as a peer-in-waiting, with privilege and being set apart, a whole sphere apart from everyone, was all he'd known. Even when his funds were low, his assured elevation and family ties proved enough for the Marsdale family to consent to his betrothal to Eliza.

Perhaps his need to control things made him no different than his base first mate. Hadn't Gareth been fine with Eliza owning another person? To enslave, didn't that come with assumption of superiority, or worse, a belief that the enslaved was less than, not equal?

He reached for his hat to swat at his disturbed brow but found it missing. It was with Jonas. The happy little tot giggled with it, showing Gareth the same affection he offered Miss Jewell. The boy's smiles held Jonas's full love, with nothing held back. Though he too would follow in Gareth's footsteps and claim the barony, the child hadn't yet learned to look down upon anyone, any race, or any color.

Could he become like Jonas? Could Gareth unlearn these sentiments to help a colony of multiple races survive?

Or was this notion of equality a passing one, something made easier because of Jewell's connection to Eliza?

Chapter Three: Restless at Sea

Water lapped against the hull, pounding against the outer walls of the cabin. The whispers and coughs of the men below had finally ceased, but it still felt as if they were listening or commenting on her or Mrs. Narvel. It was too much for Precious. Her spirits swung too high. She couldn't sleep. Her soul stirred, and she couldn't be caged anymore in the small room. Every time the door opened from the cabin boy or another sailor fetching them food, she could see the changing shadows of light coming from the deck. The world moved topside, and she wanted to see it.

Being a guest was crazy and beautiful. It had to last. She looked up from the pallet to where the young officer's wife slept. Mrs. Narvel wanted to trade each night, like equals, but Precious let the pregnant woman have the bed. It was the right thing to do. Having the freedom to make the choice meant more than a soft mattress.

Precious lay back and set her restless head on her

quilt. A year ago, a few weeks ago, she'd have no choice in her duties or where to sleep. The last time she traveled over the ocean, Eliza lay in bed snuggled up in blankets, with hopes and dreams of a marriage to come. And Precious felt lucky to flop on a similar wooden pallet on the floor. Eliza treated her well, but she wasn't sleeping on the ground for anyone.

Choices. Yes, choices were a good thing.

Another wave crashed, but the rhythm soon blended with little Jonas's puffy breaths. He slept alongside her, his tiny little mouth puffing air. He'd adjusted well to the boat. Or maybe it was the joy of having his father about for more than a few days.

The hurricane lamp grew bright, casting an orange glow about the stark room.

"Precious, are you up again?"

The sleepy, high-pitched voice grated, but the woman, Mrs. Narvel, seemed to be a nice one.

But what did Precious know of things? She'd just spent two years thinking she was free. Oh, Lord Welling must've had a good laugh on that one. Well, at least he was laughing again. Two years of no joy was wrong, even for an infuriating man.

Sitting up fully, Precious set each foot on the floor, her bare feet thudding against the smooth worn boards. "Sorry to be shifting. Sleep doesn't have much use for me tonight."

Mrs. Narvel's apple-shaped head bobbed up, her red curls plastered to the sides of her butter-colored cheeks. "What are you going to do with another sleepless night? I haven't seen you slumber much."

The woman had been watching her? Precious bounced up and leaned against the wall. She took a finger and traced a crevice between the boards. "Guess I'll just do what I did the night before. I'll manage."

The hurricane lamp on the small table showed the lady's lips pinching. "You can trust me, Precious. I know some may give you trouble, but that's not in me. I know Lord Welling has faith in you, so you must be a good person. He doesn't trust just anyone."

Lord Welling trusted her? So much so that he couldn't let her be fully free, so much that he wouldn't let her go up top without his permission. Precious swallowed a bit of gall. Mrs. Narvel didn't need to know the particulars of the arrangement with her employer.

The lady picked up her book from the small table by the bed and waved it. "When I'm anxious, I take a hold of my Bible. I settle down with a Psalm. It's well with my soul. Here, read a little."

She'd like to trust those wide hazel eyes, but only Eliza's were ever good to her. And Eliza's word was bond. What good was that book with the golden leaves? With all the bad in the world, it couldn't be a good book at all. "I think I need some air."

The woman bounded up, tugging at Precious' grey robe, clasping her hand. "No, girl. You don't know how the men get up there. We haven't been to port in four weeks. A pretty thing like you could be in danger."

Raising a brow, Precious searched her companion's face for guile but found none. "I don't understand."

"These aren't regulars, soldiers bound to duty, but a crew of misfits put together by money. The Crown's hired mercenaries to try to keep the peace in South Africa." She tugged harder on Precious's fingers, as if keeping them would keep all of Precious safe. "We'll dock in another couple of days. Then you can stroll out, while they're onshore. Why do you think Lord Welling hasn't come for us?'"

Somewhere in the back of her mind, fear reached out and clapped her mouth, keeping her from uttering anything, just like it had before. Precious closed her eyes and shook her head, pushing away the bad memories of a small shed in the woods of the plantation. Almost panting, she pressed toward the door. "I have to have some air. I'll go mad if I don't."

Her words sounded almost strangled, but another second in this confined place would pull her into the past, and this time she might not escape. Siphoning a breath, she unlatched the door. "I won't be long, Mrs. Narvel."

"It's Clara, and do be careful. I'll take care of the little one till you get back."

Jonas always slept long, like he was afraid of missing tomorrow's allotment. "Thank you. He'll be no trouble for you. And you won't miss me."

Closing the door, Precious filled her lungs again. The cedar of the wood and the salt in the air already felt good, cleansing. Easing her way, with just moonlight as her guide, she found the ladder that led to the deck. Her eyes adjusted well to the night. They always had, more so now when she needed to see evil coming her way.

For a few seconds, she put her hand on the rung. It didn't bite. It didn't latch hold of her, or scream for someone to catch her. She took another quick breath. Everything would be all right.

Cinching up her muslin robe, she raised her head to the purpled bits of sky above. The peace of it called to her. If she stayed in the shadows, all would be well. Slowly, she took hold of the springy wood again and eased her way up. This part of the deck was empty. Maybe all the men Mrs. Narvel warned of were tucked into their hammocks, too. Feeling more confident, Precious pushed to the railing.

The water gleamed, reflecting distant stars. Hints of scarlet peaked within ribbons of ebony. The sky was beautiful. A new shiver, one of excitement, traveled up her arms.

But beyond, a good forty feet was a wall of ebony. Nothing could be seen beyond it. She reached out a hand and tried to measure it between her thumb and index finger, but how could she size infinity?

"Miss Jewell?"

The heavy voice sent a different vibration through her. She startled and clutched the rail.

"Miss Jewell, do you remember my orders? Woman, what am I going to do with you?"

Another emotion filled her, a mix of vexation and a desire to defend herself from being caught doing something naughty. She spun around.

Lord Welling stood a few paces away, shaking his head at her. His white shirt was open, exposing a few tuffs of black hair. His simple dark breeches blended into the night, silhouetting his thick form. There was a power about him now that she hadn't seen in London. Maybe it was hidden under the fancy ties and jackets.

Closing the distance between them, he folded his arms. "I thought I told you not to come out of your cabin. Did I not make it clear? Did I need to specify timeframes?"

He stood too close. Even in the onyx night, the stars and the lantern light in his hand made his eyes wide, deep blue, and menacing.

Willing her knees to still, she had to keep reminding herself that a servant didn't get whipped like an enslaved person, and, for all Lord Welling's bluster, he'd never tried to take a branch to her. She lifted her chin. "It's stuffy down there. I didn't think it'd hurt nothing. You're selfish for keeping it from me."

Dimple popping, he pounded his skull. "Mouse, scurry back to your quarters before you're caught by a very large rat."

His eyes were clear, untainted by alcohol. Why did that worry her? Could she handle him, sharp, with all his mind working?

Well, she'd try. She could stand up for her opinions just like Palmers or any other worker did. With a hand on her hip, she sharpened her tone. "Rats don't go after mice. If you'd ever spent time in fields, you'd know that."

"Hungry rats will devour anything." His head went sidelong as his gaze raked over her. "Barefoot, you'd make an easy meal. A charming one, but an easy one."

She refused to let her hand move to the belt of her robe. Something about letting him know his warnings trembled her bones didn't seem right. Instead, she pivoted back toward the ocean. "I'm not done getting air. I'll be a deck-side luncheon."

Chuckling, he plodded closer. "Jewell, you're no coward. I'll give you that."

She hid a sigh of relief in a deep taste of salted air. "The breeze feels so good. And the night sky, I miss a night's sky."

"Well, let's hope the red goes away before dawn. Like a red morn that ever yet betokened, Wreck to the seaman, tempest to the field, Sorrow to the shepherds, woe unto the birds, Gusts and foul flaws to herdsmen and to herds."

She swiveled and looked at his face; clean-shaven, speaking of mystical things, with his hair full out lifting in the wind. He was handsome if you like the sort, but he was full of nonsense, speaking nonsense.

A wave crashed against the hull, making her almost reach for him to steady herself. Forcing her hand to her side, she straightened her shoulders. Even if it got rocky, she'd stand her ground a little longer, just to prove her point.

"I can tell by the cross look on your face that you are not partial to Shakespeare. Then try this one. Red sky at night, sailor's delight. Red sky in the morn, sailor be warned."

The wind picked up her mobcap and set it sailing. He lunged and caught it, tucking it in his waistband. "You've had enough wind, Jewell. Let me escort you back below." He lifted his palm to her.

With braids dropping, curling to her neck, she stared at him, not wanting to move, not wanting to go back to the cabin. A small portion of her mind wanted him to speak more nonsense, to calm the edge in her spirit. "I haven't seen you drinking. We can smell rum from our room."

"No, ma'am, not out here in the open ocean." He trudged to the thick wood rail and clasped it in his big hands. "No, God has control out here, and I need to be able to hear Him. Can't do that cast to the winds."

Now he spewed a different set of nonsense. Precious didn't think the baron was religious. She squinted at him and looked out at the wall of blackness surrounding the ship. "I don't understand."

"Oh, Jewell, I learned the hard way long ago about

being too cocky, too full of my own power out here on the seas. That's wrong. God can strike at any moment, and you can lose everything if you're not paying attention."

There was sadness, a grieving music, to his tone, and it made her sad, pulling at her heart. She shook her head to clear it, and just stood near him, breathing in and out, looking at waves.

"You've had enough, my dear. I have to finish my rounds." He pivoted and took three long steps away. "Jewell, let me take you to your cabin."

"Why do you call me 'Jewell'?"

He lowered his well-muscled arm. "It's what we British do. Addressing by a surname is a sign of respect for one's heritage."

The boat rocked. The waves hitting below shoved the boat like one of Jonas's blocks. It made her reach backward and clutch the rail.

He extended his arm again. "Time for play is done, Jewell. You need to go below. The next few hours of ocean are going to be bumpy."

"I don't have a surname. Precious Jewell is my only name."

His clear eyes sharpened, and he stepped even closer. His palm went to her chin, gently, lifting and angling it in the moonlight. "Jewell's not a family name? Then who is your father?"

Stiffening, she stepped away from him. Now the railing pressed into her back, preventing escape. "I think I am ready to go below, but I can get there myself. Can I have my cap?"

"Mouse, I thought you had courage. You're going to let me continually frighten you." His chuckles, his patronizing laughter, burnt her ears. "I suppose that what's to be expected from a mouse."

The ocean pushed her forward, flinging her into him. He caught her and held her close. She could feel his heart thudding through her muslin nightgown. She pressed on his chest, but he didn't let go.

"Precious Jewell," huskiness set in his voice, "it's getting rough out here."

Tucking a braid from her eye, he released her. His breathing seemed labored, like he struggled for air. "Come along, Miss Precious." He rubbed at his brow, then clasped her arm and dragged her a bit. "You are going back to your cabin now. Work harder at listening. One of my crew might have found you out here, dressed in just muslin."

She couldn't take him forcing her to move any more than she could hearing him laughing at her, always sounding as if his thoughts were faster than hers. Anger pumping in her veins, she spun free of his arm.

But the ship shuttered.

Her feet went one way, her body the other. In an instant, she was dangling over the rail.

Chapter Four: Man Overboard

Gareth heard her cry. His heart plugged up his throat. The poor girl was out of his reach. "Hold on, Precious."

Running, he caught her fingers but the sweat on hands made her smooth skin slick. Grasping at her robe, he tried to pull her to him, but the crazed women fought him, punching at his arms.

"Don't touch me! You can't touch me!"

She was panicked and would fall. He'd have to manhandle her to bring back to safety. "I'm not trying to see your skivvy; I'm trying to save your life."

Her feet slipped against the hull as she tried to climb back. "Don't touch me again!"

Her pretty eyes were so wide they looked like they'd pop. She wasn't all there, couldn't grasp the danger.

He lowered his voice. "Woman, you have to trust me. Let me pull you into my arms."

Her countenance was blank. She probably couldn't hear a word he said, but if he didn't act soon, she would fall into the bottomless ocean. "Woman, I coming for you now."

When his hands sought her shoulders, he felt her wriggle free. The crazy girl fell into the ocean. "Blasted woman. Precious!"

She bobbed in the waves as they towed her away.

Running to the back of the boat, he scooped up a large bundle of rope and secured it to a belaying pin. Tying it about his waist, he climbed upon the bulwark, with boots planting on the smooth cap-rail. "Man overboard! Man overboard!"

He spied Precious struggling in the waves, head bobbing in and out of the water. The sound of men's boots pounded behind him. "For Port Elizabeth!" The chant flew from the top of his lungs as he leapt into the purple darkness.

He swam leeward, offset slightly to the right of the foolish girl. At least a minute of hard kicking and pushing against the waves set him to within a yard of her. "Precious, clasp my hand; this time like you want it."

She didn't answer. Her motion had slowed. The cold water probably drained her life away.

The iciness of it awoke any part of him that might've thought this was a dream gone wrong. "I'm not losing you, Precious."

Paddling harder, he closed the distance between them, aiming for the waterlogged mass of grey muslin. Where was her head? "Dear Lord, don't take my mouse, too."

As if she heard him, she popped up and caught a mouthful of air, arms flailing.

Good, Precious still had fight in her.

Now he wasn't taking any chances. He'd already lost too much by guessing people's strength. "Precious, it's me, Welling. Can you hear me?"

"Yes." The voice sounded small and tired and the urge to wrap her up in his strength ripped through him.

Battling against the ocean he revered, he got closer. "Do as I say."

His mouse didn't answer. Her head had sunk below the waves. The moving water pushed her away. He'd have one chance before the rope would snap him back to the boat.

He dove behind her and latched a hold of her back. She looked slight, but the fear in her could grab hold of him and drag them both to their deaths. He tightened his grip, his hands clasped under her bosom. "I've got you, Precious. Let me save you."

Her head nodded, and he felt her body relax and curve into his.

"You got him, Captain?"

"Yes!" Gareth responded, and kept Precious locked against his chest.

The rope about him tightened, cutting into the scar running the course of him, but he'd endure the sting of the old wound now that he had his mouse. The crew towed in their lifeline, bringing them back to the boat.

"Thank you, Lord." Precious didn't leave him. He hadn't guessed wrong about how to save her.

The stubborn woman stayed very still and quiet within his embrace. She hadn't fainted, but she probably wouldn't fully revive until he lifted her back on board.

Yet the questions in his brain wouldn't quiet. "Why, Precious? Why wouldn't you let me help you?"

Her teeth chattered. "I'm letting you help me now."

Did she want to jump? Was this a suicide? No, that couldn't be it, but there was something that chained her in fear. Only the pull of death had overcome it.

Almost near the hull, he lowered his voice to a whisper. "Woman, at least you waited for me to be sober this time before you frightened me out of my wits. I'll be good and drunk if you're going to keep this up on shore."

"Sorry."

His heartbeat slowed as his men raised them out of the water. Holding her tightly, he breathed into her drenched hair that had swelled to her ears, exposing a long beautiful neck. His lips brushed the salty skin at the nape. "I know. I'm glad I got to you, too."

Precious couldn't get warm. Unlike London's rain, the ocean was like a thawing winter puddle. Shaking uncontrollably, water dripping from her nightgown, she burrowed into the warm, masculine arms draped about her. Her left arm felt as if it had fallen off. It burned in its socket.

Lord Welling held her tightly as he climbed over the rail and jumped with a thud onto the deck. "See, I got you. You're safe."

His whisper kissed her ear, and she shook even more.

Lord Welling set Precious down by his boots. "You're a little cold, but you'll be alright."

Quivering as much from the cold trapped in her gown as from the touch of the man who'd now rescued her twice, she didn't know what to say. She surely would've died this time, not just on the inside.

No more breathing in and out.

No more caring for Jonas.

No more anything.

The light of torches added a halo about her tall rescuer as he talked with his crew.

Her eyes pinned him and all she could do was wonder

about the baron. Why did he risk his life? Was caring for the man's son enough to warrant such? Forget once being his property, did she have value to him now as a servant?

She moved her shoulder. It stung as if it had been cut with a knife. She bit her lip, holding in the pain. Tears came to her eyes but it wasn't the sting of the salt or her arm, it was the gnawing in her gut. A small hint of doubt built up on the inside, and she felt worse and worse. She wasn't worth saving. Why didn't he know that?

Lord Welling stripped the rope from around his chest. "Thanks, men. Here." He handed them the thick braided jute that had pulled them from the ocean as he pushed on wet fabric clinging near his heart. "Roll it back tight."

Her vision clouded as she coughed up salty seawater. Blinking, her eyes cleared in time to catch the heat of hungry glances from the four men standing around, tugging on slack rope, probably trying to appear busy.

She tried to cross her arms to keep them from ogling her wet bosom, but her right shoulder wouldn't move. How could she cover herself from the numbing cold and these men, their curiosity and lust?

She pushed at her brow. Her aches, her wet clothes, this was all her fault. One moment she was arguing with Lord Welling. The next, she fought evil in the dark. She couldn't see light any more until she fell in the cold water. Why couldn't the awful memories of that dark shed drown without taking her too?

Lord Welling's voice interrupted her building guilt. "Get the girl a blanket. I didn't pluck her out of the ocean for her to die of exposure."

A young lad nodded and started running, but the

bumbling man they'd found in the cabin stepped in front of the baron. "Captain, you yelled 'man overboard'. You could have been killed, over *her*?" A stubby finger pointed her direction. The snarl in his voice repeated his venom. "Over her!"

She swallowed, and waited to hear Lord Welling's reply to confirm the emptiness of her soul. He must hate her so for causing problems. She hadn't listened to him, so didn't she deserve what befell her?

The baron caught the man's hand and lowered it. "Lieutenant Grossling, what I yelled was correct. I was overboard. My men saved me. I saved her."

The lieutenant guffawed and shook his fists. "You are twisting things up. This is insupportable."

Lord Welling didn't move and, if his stiff stance was any indication, he didn't seem to want to budge. He kept separating Precious from the grousing bird. "You've been hand-picked by the War Department to accompany me. You're an observer. Stick to observing. We're still heading to Port Elizabeth without delay."

Mr. Grossling rent his robe, even pulled at his hair. "This is reckless. Simply reckless."

Lord Welling squeezed at his wet sleeve. He was just as waterlogged as she, but the chill didn't bother him. His hair hung down, matted to his lean cheeks, as if he'd been caught in a simple storm, not dunked in the ocean. "I lead this ship and this mission. I'll do what I think is best."

Mr. Grossling shook his head, his sharp nose whipping up and down. He was too puffed up to be satisfied with the baron's answer. He whipped his head around Lord Welling and stared at Precious. It wasn't lust in his face; no, it was a look she saw often. He had a bug in his britches over the fact that this man risked all to save a black and a woman.

Well, she had a bug, too. Why had Lord Welling done it? Jonas would have no parents left if Lord Welling had drowned trying to save her stupid self. And whatever this Port Elizabeth was, it would've lost a brave leader.

For a moment, she closed her eyes and felt anew the sensation of the cold numbing water dragging her down, and the baron's strong arms pulling her to safety, pulling her to the warmth of his embrace.

Short, hard steps tapped closer. "She's not even one of your crew member's wives. She's a black."

There, the grunt had said it. At least he'd named his hate and not pranced around it.

She was black, a mere servant, and Lord Welling valued her. She stared up at the baron. With all her heart, her shivering limbs, and with toes that were so cold they might fall off, she wanted to thank him. When he turned, she mouthed the words through chattering teeth.

Lord Welling's lips pursed, but a smirk soon came. "No, Grossling; she's more caramel. There's a difference betwixt caramel and black. My young heir will be able to teach you the colors, too, in a few years."

The gloss of Lieutenant Grossling's boot caught moonlight and some of the shine from the wavering torches of the crew. All heads were nodding, but with whom did the crew agree?

A clap and a few harsh chuckles came out of the War Department man, someone who seemed to be shaping up into Lord Welling's enemy. "Baron, you know what I mean. You don't jeopardize our mission for the likes of her."

The awful man stooped near her, his voice rising, like that would help convey his meaning. "Woman! Can you stay out of trouble for the rest our trip? This captain and crew have more important things to do than fish a servant out of the ocean."

Pushing wet hair from his brow, Lord Welling glanced in Precious's direction then back to the lieutenant. For a moment, it looked as if fire claimed the baron's eyes. "I think Miss Jewell is done playing in the water, but her safety is my concern, as is the safety of everyone who is under my command."

The man swiveled, folding his arms. His eyes cut in a sly manner. "Is she your…"

Lord Welling's muscled legs bent. His arms folded. He seemed poised to attack. "What, the nanny to the boy traveling with me? Yes, she is."

The fool backed up. "All for a dark nanny. You're going to a place of thousands of them, more blacks than you can count. Blast, you can get a Spanish or Dutch courtesan if you want. That is, if any are alive after the Xhosa have their way. Remember, Welling, you have a job to do. Peace won't come to Port Elizabeth if you drown yourself before we get there. Don't give in to carnal misalliances."

"I know what I have to do," the baron's tone sounded stiff, steeped in fury, "and I have just decided that it starts by valuing every life, not just the white ones."

The man guffawed as he tugged on his robe. "You're foolish, Welling. Nothing has changed from the war."

Slapping water from his sleeve at the boisterous man, the baron leaned back against the mast pole. "And why should it? My record was impeccable, but I never said my manners were. Now, Junior, go back to your hammock, before I forget to value your life."

The thin man scrunched up his face and marched along the deck to the opening. "This will be in my report. Maybe it is a bad idea to let you lead Port Elizabeth. You're not as steady as your uncle."

"But I am a lot more alive than he is at the moment. Port Elizabeth is a Welling calling. Good night, little man."

If his stomping was any indication, the troll would cause problems.

Precious tried to raise her arm to stop the baron from getting in trouble over her, but it radiated with pain. Her formerly numb arm screamed. Falling into the ocean hurt so bad.

A young lad came running with a blanket and handed it to her. So cold she could barely take it from him, she nodded and mouthed, "Thank you". Using her left hand, she worked the wool about her and her sore shoulder.

The baron looked down at her. His eyes scrunched up with concern. "Miss Jewell, what's matter with your arm. Is it working?"

Why was he so observant? He had other worries than her foolishness.

Before she could respond, Ralston started laughing. The raucousness was loud and spiteful sounding. He stroked his ebony mustache that covered most of his fat lips. "A fine fish you caught there, Captain. Before she spun herself in the cloth, quite a curvy little thing. But I suppose she's now your prize, aye, Lord Wellin'?"

The baron straightened, almost blocking the man from viewing her, but nothing could block a lustful eye. Mrs. Narvel's warning came to her. Precious pulled her naked toes under the blanket as best she could.

"Ralston, she's in my employ, just like you. So, unless you are ready to care for my charge's needs, let her be. Come on, Miss..."

The plucky man tugged on the baron's shirttail. "See, fellows? Since Captain Gareth Conroy has become titled the new Lord Welling, he's turned soft."

The baron pried his shirt free. "The liquor is talking, Ralston. Go below and sleep off the rum."

The man stepped so close to Lord Welling that they could've share the same breath. "Admit it; you just don't have it in you to pleasure a woman since your wife died."

The brute pedaled backward and shouted to the growing group of crewmen who'd come up on the deck. The number was up to eight. "Have you seen him wenchin'? I guess he's become too refined for this. Still mooning over a dead woman, or was it the war injuries that took your manhood away?"

The baron's hands had dropped to his sides, almost hiding his fisted palms. "Good joke." Though his words sounded light, the tension in his stance increased. A powder keg would explode soon.

Precious had seen the bucks go at it at Charleston picnics when the liquor had been flowing, but the baron was sober. Maybe he should pound Mr. Ralston for taunting him over Eliza. Why couldn't an honorable man be left alone?

Huffing, Lord Welling waved his arms at the crew. "The excitement is over, fellows. Go back to bed. We've got a busy day tomorrow."

Ralston made a circle, prancing with his finger in the air, inciting each of the crewmen to laughter. He again stopped at the baron's side. "Don't worry, Captain, we'll collect your due from the blackamoor. You just go on to your cabin, stare at the wife's picture, or read your Bible for priestly inspiration. We'll show her a good time."

A belly-rolling laugh belted out of Lord Welling. He ducked down and gripped his sides. "Ralston, you sure have me pegged."

More laughs came out of the baron, and even the formerly silent two or three men gave in to chuckles and hooting.

Precious's heart sunk. For a couple seconds, she let herself believe that Lord Welling valued her. He was no different; not when it came to pressure from his crew.

Yet, it couldn't be that simple, for why would he rescue her, keep rescuing her?

Lord Welling's laughter came harder until he had bent and grasped his sides. Then, as if the world slowed to a crawl, he rammed headfirst into Ralston's stomach.

The stout man gasped for air as the baron's fist pummeled his jaw.

Clutching his face, Mr. Ralston fell back, only to be tossed forward by a few crewmen. "Captain, what the h —"

The baron hit him again, bloodying an eye. "Just showing my jokes. Isn't that funny, taking a beating from a man filled with honor?"

"Captain's title or not, I'll not let you do that to me." Arms waving, Ralston charged at him.

Lord Welling ducked low, flipped the man onto his back, and tossed him over the rail. The sound of the splash silenced the remaining chuckles.

Getting the rope the men had coiled; he leaned over the side and tossed one end into the ocean. "Ralston, you still alive down there? If so, tie a loop about you."

The baron pulsed his hands, as if to shake off the

sting of battle. "You," he pointed to a tall, skinny man. "Let him thrash about for a bit, then pull him back on board. That is, if he learned something. Anyone else need a lesson?"

Silence and head shaking answered him.

Breathing hard, like steam filled his chest, he swiveled toward each of the men standing around with mouths gaping. "Anyone else think I'm too refined because I'm not a whoremonger?"

Again, silence and stunned faces prevailed.

Marching back to Precious, he gave her his arm and helped her to stand. His eyes seemed wild, whirling with thoughts. He put a hand to her cheek. "I do think Ralston was right. I have earned a reward from you, Jewell." He picked her up and tossed her over his shoulder. "She's the Captain's woman now; off limits to you all. You hear me?"

Almost in unison, every fellow with low or screeching voices responded the same. "Yes, Captain."

Blood rushing to her head, those words were the last words she could make out before the noise of his boots pounding along the deck covered everything.

Chapter Five: The Captain's Woman

Precious flailed against Lord Welling's shoulder as he climbed down the ladder to where the cabins sat. The jarring of the motion on her shoulder was enough to make her temples burst, but that was nothing compared to his anger. What was he going to do...to her?

His boots planted on the flooring, but he swayed a bit as the boat moved. "You shall be a delight, my dear." His words were loud, almost as if he intended others to hear.

He paused, as if he considered dumping her in the cabin she shared with Jonas and Mrs. Narvel, but that surely was wistful thinking. The taunting and the trouble she'd caused had pushed him too far.

Passing by her door, she wished she had just stayed inside and heeded her shipmate's warning. Then she'd still claim some dignity and maybe a small portion of the baron's respect.

Slam! Lord Welling kicked open the door to his cabin.

The room bore little light, just the small glow of a hurricane lamp. A bed made for two sat in the center. He strode inside and dumped her onto the firm mattress. Groaning, he marched away and bolted the door.

He laid his head against the paneled and trimmed wood. His fists flattened on the smooth part near the brass plate. With his shoulders sagging, he didn't seem so angry now. No, he looked more defeated. "Couldn't stay below, could you? It's hard enough traveling with women, but a hardheaded one is too much."

She looked to the footboard and counted the carved leaves notched on the frame. What was she to say to his back?

Sorry.

I didn't mean to fall.

I didn't want folks questioning your leadership.

Instead, she pushed herself to sit. Sucking in at the sting of her arm, she dropped the blanket and pried off her wet robe.

He turned. His angry face began to twist. His nose wrinkled, as if he smelled something horrible. "What are you doing?"

Her heart started pounding, but she worked the first button on her nightgown. She wasn't going to be a victim this time. No tears. She forbade them from coming. She'd allow him his due and get it over with. "At least you won't kill me, or threaten me when you take all I have."

His eyes scrunched up. He plodded to the light, rolling the knob to make the room blindingly bright. "Well, if you intend to give me a show, I might as well see everything."

She swiped at her eyes. "No jokes. Just come here and be done with it."

He inhaled a long breath. Then a chuckle crept out of

the grim lines of his mouth. "I think you need a little more practice at looking enticing, or at least interested."

With a shake of his head, he undid the ties to his shirt and pulled the wet thing free, exposing the hardened planes of his chest. The wet cotton plopped onto floor with a slap.

The light made his skin looked tanned, with tufts of dark hair in the valley below his throat.

A gasp left her, not just from the sheer strength hidden by his London clothes, but the horrid scar zigzagging below is heart, extending beyond the waistband of his breeches.

He plodded near and clasped the headboard, his eyes surely studying, measuring her. "Call me crazed, a man of sense and expectation, but a frightened woman doesn't make me feel romantic."

Trying to not look at him or wonder about the scar, she folded her naked feet up under her. "You're crazy. Men will do what they do."

He stretched and tugged the blanket back around her. The smell of him, woodsy and salty, reached her nose. At least he wouldn't reek when he got around to touching her. "You look chilly. I've been dunked in the ocean more times than I care to remember. I'm used to the cold."

How long would he let her agonize, thinking of being forced, of being told it was her fault, and then hopin' no babies birthed of the evil would come? Counting, sipping slow breaths, she again tugged the blanket down to her waist.

He sat in a chair, tapping the small table to his left. "Well, I should close up this Bible. Wouldn't want passages of caring for the weak or doing unto others slipping out and ruining this seduction." The leather book closed with a thud. He must've been truthful about his worship at sea.

Cocking his head back to lean on the heavily carved spindles of the chair, he lifted his boot to her. "Pull."

Stretching her unhurt arm, she clutched the nearly dry hide and yanked it free. The jarring sent up a vibration, making her bones ache. "You do the next one. I can't."

His face lifted and a small smile peeked. "Well, how could you with a hurt shoulder? You should truly learn to just tell me the problem."

She tested her arm, trying to move it. The sting made fresh tears come to her eyes. "Then how could you wish to ravish me in this condition?"

He propped up his head in hands and stared at her. "True, I prefer bedmates who are not writhing from the pain of an injury."

"Then, I can leave?" Hopping off the bed, she scooped up her robe.

He swung his leg wide, blocking her. "It's not that simple. The captain's mistress can't leave after five minutes."

"Mistress?" Her heart shriveled. He did intend to punish her.

"Yes, my lover. You're the captain's woman, Precious Jewell. No man on this ship will dare touch you if you are mine."

She wasn't worried about the other men right now, just this one with the intense spark in his eyes. "I'm no lover. Not when forced."

He sighed long and hard, but what could be frustrating him? He was about to take the rest of her pride.

"No one is forcing any thing, Jewell. I'm the last man you should worry about."

His gaze felt hot and thick, as if he measured the thickness of her nightgown or if he could see down through to her stays. She bundled the robe closer to her bosom. "Then let me leave or make good on your threats. I don't want to wait in fear of you."

His brow cocked. "So, mouse, you are giving me permission? How very interesting."

That didn't quite come out like she wanted, but something in her gut wanted an end to his game. "You think this is easy for me? Just get it over with. The waiting to be humiliated is the worst."

He rubbed at the light scruff on his chin. "You and my darling Eliza are very similar. She wanted things on her terms, but sometimes life doesn't play along."

She balled the fist of her working arm and shook it at him. "Just start already."

"Start what? Molesting you? You work for me. Blast it. I enslaved you but a month ago. A woman needs a choice. You can't choose under bondage or fear. You must always choose."

His deep voice grew lower, slowing, making each of his syllables punch her in the gut. "I know. I have suspected since the night of the storm that some blackguard didn't let you choose before. That's why you jump when I touch you. You freeze if my arms are about you. That's not what I or any decent man wants."

Backing up, the footboard poked her leg and stopped her retreat. There was no escape from his accusation. It was true, but she couldn't talk about that time with him or anyone.

Yet, the tremble in her body wouldn't quit. Oh, how

low Lord Welling must think of her. That was it. He didn't want another man's garbage. That horrible fiend who'd taken her trust, who'd erased every easy smile since, was still with her, still cutting up her insides. She rubbed her neck. Her voice filled with anguish over a nightmare that refused to go away. "Please let me go to my cabin. Jonas may have awakened with the ruckus. I won't come out for the rest of the trip."

"I can't let you out that door. How do I put this for your stubborn ears? If you don't look thoroughly ravished, the dogs will be on you again. I can't beat everyone up defending you."

There was no guile in his voice. He wanted to protect her. That silly notion made her want to cry aloud. Instead, she swiped at her nose and glanced back at him, hoping to look like stone.

His arms folded. His mouth huffed. "I've dumped the ringleader in the ocean. Won't be much of a crew if I have to throw them all in."

"You should. They all need a lashing for hurting women." She covered her mouth, hating that her fingers shook. Though she wanted to lie down and sleep off the pain, she stood up straight. "I can't be here, with you looking at me. I see enough pity in the mirror some days."

"Stay until morning. You'll be branded my woman, and left alone by the crew. Then, if you have the foolhardy notion to get some air, you can do it without fear of attack or anything that will have you swinging from the bulwark. Don't be fearful of my help."

The pain addled her thinking, but it sure did sound as if it was important to him for her to stay. She rubbed her arm. The pain radiated, more so since she had tried to let it hang normally. "Give me another reason, one that has meaning for you."

His gaze remained steady, unflinching. "I've said enough."

She shook her head, glancing at him, daring him to state his real purpose, but he refused to move. "I'll stay in my cabin until we dock at Port Elizabeth. I'll manage in my room."

"Your spirit is too high to be caged, but self-interest may help you make the right decision. Here's a new bargain for you. I'll take a year off your servitude if you stay put. It's worth it to me to not have another confrontation with my crew."

Was he so anxious over her safety that he'd ply her with an earlier release from their agreement? Lord Welling didn't seem fearful of his crew. And he'd tossed that big fellow as if he were paper. Perhaps, that fancy-looking man who questioned the baron before was at the root of this. Maybe more was at risk than Precious could surmise.

"Do we have a deal?"

His smile was too broad. Lord Welling's offer was cruel. Would he always search for another lever to push, another screw to turn to control her?

Thinking hurt now. Why couldn't she lie down in peace in her cabin? She sidestepped him, but he caught her elbow on the hurting side, sending her to her knees.

He sprung from the chair and whipped her up into his arms. Her warm cheek smashed against his cold collarbone, but she didn't care. It felt good to not lift her head.

"I didn't mean to injure you, Precious."

"Not you," she gasped and tried to blot out the searing

pain as she'd done before, but couldn't. Tears streamed out. "My arm hurts so bad."

He carried her to the bed and set her betwixt him and the headboard. With his long fingers, he tugged at one button of her nightgown. Then another. "I need to see the shoulder."

She couldn't breathe, couldn't stop him. She wiggled a little to keep him from seeing the scars upon her back. "No."

"Yes." He undid a final one and opened the gown. He pushed it down, exposing just her arm and more of her neck.

With a careful caress, he pushed at her stays and freed her shoulder. "This is bad, Precious."

Her arm looked inflamed, twice its normal size. Too scared, too injured to move, she let his fingers trail her arm. He pressed the high bone on top of the sore flesh with his thumb, and a noise like a wailing tomcat fled her lips.

His eyes narrowed and grim lines swallowed his mouth. "It's not broken, but you popped your shoulder out of the socket, either from hanging onto the hull or by hitting the water hard. I have to push it back in. Do you trust me, Precious?"

She glanced up at him between waves of throbbing aches. The curve of the muscles of his forearms, his solid chest with the horrible scar that looked as if something had tried to cut him in two, all made her feel safe. He knew suffering and perhaps could understand hers. Maybe that was why he was so kind to her. But it still didn't add up, the concern versus the battle for control.

"Precious, you still there?"

"Yes. Fix it. I've no choice, do I?"

His fingers stilled from the slight massage of her shoulder. "You have a choice. Do you trust me?"

As much as she wanted to pretend she didn't, she couldn't lie about how she felt. "Yes. I do."

"Good mouse." He put one arm behind her neck and stretched his palm to cushion her shoulder. With his other hand, he clasped the front of the joint. "This is going to hurt like nothing you ever felt."

"Doubt it. I know a lot of ache."

His chin nodded, and his gaze latched onto hers. Concern, and something else, some unreadable warmth, colored his intense stare. "Get ready to screech."

"Don't let me scream. They'll think you're hurting me. You're not like them."

His lips tensed. "You don't know what I'm capable of."

She lifted her good hand to his chest; her fingers couldn't help but fall on the deep scar. "I don't want to sound weak to them or you."

"I won't let them hear. You ready for me to make this shoulder right?""

She nodded and counted, "One, two, three, four, ready."

With a mighty shove, he snapped the joint back into place. The pop sounded like a china cup slamming against a rock. It deafened, but not enough to mask her howling.

Not that she could, not that she wanted him to stop, but, with his firm lips, he covered hers and caught all the remaining high notes of her scream.

The world grew black and inky, and his mouth stayed on hers, claiming her until she saw nothing at all.

Chapter Six: A Better Man

Gareth put his scope in his pocket and laid his hands at noon and three on the wheel. The setting sun had framed the right side of the ship, making the water have a blood orange color. If red stayed in the water and away from the morning, they just might make it to Port Elizabeth without a horrid storm delaying them. Well, no more woman-made incidents. His brain filled with thoughts of Jonas's stubborn nanny. Hopefully, there would be no Precious Jewell-made storms.

Three days ago, the girl fell into the ocean. Now she lay sick in his cabin with him and Mrs. Narvel taking turns caring for her. It was probably a good thing Precious was so bull-headed. Her fever had spiked pretty high before it broke, but she fought with all she had and then some. The girl warred hard against the ocean, and against him with the punch she'd delivered on the bow. That kind of fire comes from withstanding something horrid. What happened in the girl's past? Would it always drive her to be reckless, running away in the middle of the night or dropping into an ocean?

Eliza never said anything of Precious's story, just that she couldn't do without her.

The wind blew hard, kicking his thin cravat into his chin. She'd lashed out wildly, slapping at him at the height of her sleep. It made sleeping next to her difficult, but far more interesting than being alone.

What was he to do with Precious Jewell?

Ralston marched up side him. "Captain, I can take over the watch for you."

He folded his arms and stared at the Judas who almost made his men turn against him. "Not too busy stoking rebellion to do your duties?"

A sheepish, almost boyish grin peeked from underneath his mustache. He wrenched at his neck. "I'd like to blame things on the liquor, but that ain't it. I shoulda known you were still all man. Blast the rumors."

The false rumors that a cannon blast had taken all his strength had persisted since the war. Marrying Eliza and having an heir had squelched most of it, but now they appeared again. He turned and looked out at the vast ocean. Maybe focusing on the cold water would ease the volcano of anger ready to blow in his system. "Ralston, next time I'm not going to give you any rope, unless it's about your neck."

The fool clapped Gareth's shoulder. "Dunkin' me in the drink and taking that nanny woman, there is no more doubt about you now. I've done you a favor."

He pivoted and squinted at Ralston. "I don't think I need those types of favors."

"But the hellcat, she must make it worth it. I saw how you looked at her when you brought her on board, and then saving her. You know you wanted her, even if she works for you, even if she's a black."

Preposterous; he hadn't brought the girl along to find a way to seduce her. Right? She was a piece of Eliza, dear to Jonas. Yet, the drunk had noticed something, enough to guess that Gareth had become partial to Precious.

There was no more denying it. The playful cat and mouse banter with her was something he enjoyed until she flung herself into the ocean. And the feel of her curling into him, the surprising softness of her scarlet lips, it stirred something inside.

He rubbed at his skull and pushed away his own inner doubts of his motives. Ralston needed to be a better man. He would be next in command if anything befell Gareth. It would take both his first mate and his friend Mr. Narvel to command Port Elizabeth.

As twisted as Ralston's values were, there was good in him. Gareth had seen it when he helped to rebuild a cottage for a widowed colonist. No man had worked as hard as Ralston to get that roof back over the poor old lady's head after the Xhosa raiders burnt it to the ground.

But how could he get through to his first mate? Perhaps with the truth. "Wenching doesn't make a man a man. At what point does all the sin just make him corrupt?"

A belly laugh poured out of the fool. "None that I could ever see."

"You need to start spending time with the colony's vicar." Gareth started to pivot, but stayed in place. "Ralston, I don't know how you are going to do it, but I need you to shape up. We are in charge of how this new world of Port Elizabeth grows. We are to make it good, or it will die on the vine. Wenching won't work for that.

Women need protection, someone to count on. All the colonists need us to be fair, worthy to put their trust in."

The laughter had drained away from Ralston's face. The man gazed down and fidgeted with his hands. Maybe there was hope for him. Looking back from how Gareth had let Eliza down to how he'd been of use to Precious, maybe there was hope for him as well.

"Sorry, Captain."

He extended a hand to him. "Behind Narvel, you're the fellow I depend upon. It can't be if you have no morals. What if something happened to me or Narvel? I want the leadership of Port Elizabeth to fall to a man of conviction, not a war department bureaucrat."

Head lifting, with a glint in his eyes, Ralston stood erect. "You see that in me?"

"Yes, when you're not boozing or starting mutinies. Take the wheel. No drinking up here."

Smiling, Ralston stuck a hard handshake then took hold of the column. "You can count on me, Captain. But maybe you should head off to your prize. She hasn't left your room for days."

Nodding, Gareth headed for his cabin. Perhaps Precious was awake and felt well enough to answer some questions. At some point he'd need to figure out what had happened to her. That kind of fear couldn't be kept inside. It could come out again and endanger her or others.

"Have fun, Captain."

Gareth couldn't help rolling his eyes as he stalked down to the deck. He definitely couldn't give in to his attraction to Precious Jewell, who very well could be his sister by marriage; no matter how alive she made the dead parts of him feel.

* * *

Precious tried to open her heavy lids, but they must be sewn closed. Was she dead? Heart racing, she tried again, but couldn't. She must be dead or nearly dead.

Another moment of trying and she gave up and just let her fingers absorb the smoothness of the fine sheets. She must've fallen asleep in Eliza's bed again. Eliza would forgive her once she saw how tired and how hurt Precious was.

Well, as long as Mr. Marsdale didn't catch her, she'd be fine.

As long his nephew never caught her again, she'd recover.

He hurt her real bad last time.

Someone tucked bed sheets about her. She tried to stop shaking, but was too weak. She wanted to scream for Eliza, but her mouth felt dry, like bales of cotton.

A few blinks and she cracked her eyes open.

Mrs. Narvel's face became clear. She leaned over and mopped Precious's brow. "Your fever is almost gone. Oh, thank the Lord."

That was the woman on the boat. Precious and Jonas were on a boat. Where is Jonas? She shook and cried out through her stiff lips, but no one heard her. Her face felt wet. Why couldn't she get to Jonas?

"Will Mammie be fine?"

The sweet voice. It was Jonas. He must be well. *Oh come to me, Jonas!*

Her pulse slowed. She pictured him in his pinafore, playing with his favorite blocks, maybe looking at her with a shy smile.

"Yes, Miss Precious will be fine. Sometimes you need lots of sleep for the body to get better."

Click. Clack. The sound of a wood block hitting another one echoed. "I better with naps."

"Yes, sweet boy. Maybe Miss Precious might wake up today. It's been three since she became ill."

Days? As in more than one? The thought that she'd been laid up sapped the little bit of energy she'd started to muster.

And this woman with her pretty goldenrod dress had been waiting on Precious.

"Jonas, I need you to pick up your blocks and wrap them in the scarf. Lord Welling will be here soon.

Fluttering tired eyes, Precious caught a blur of a footboard. Leaves cut into the wood. Lord Welling's wood. Oh, now she'd been sleeping in Lord Welling's bed.

His words of her being the captain's woman burst in her head and made it hurt more. She didn't know if she was or wasn't. Everything had become a blur except the water.

The power of not being able to hold on to nothing, of not being able to catch a full breath, taunted her in mixed-up visions. But the frigid water that had grabbed hold of her and yanked her down was real. She surely would have drowned if not for Lord Welling.

A sense of gratitude, overwhelming tummy-twisting thankfulness flooded over her, until she tried to move her arm. Her body felt beaten, lashed at. Was it sickness or had he been repaid?

The only thing she knew for certain was that he'd kissed her. What happened after, she knew not. Another kind of empty filled her. Her chest rattled with a hollow cough.

The door to the cabin opened and Lord Welling stuck

his head inside. "Is all well in here, Mrs. Narvel. Has she woken up?"

"No. But the fever is much lower. By tomorrow she should be up for sure." Her voice got all squeaky. "She moaned some strange things."

The baron plodded near, his boots knocking against the floorboards. He bent and picked up Jonas. "Like what?"

"Bits and pieces, about being your slave and the captain's woman. Some other odd things, but is any of it true?"

"Miss Jewell is an indentured servant, but she was enslaved by my late wife's family."

The lady's voice became screechy. "Why didn't you just free her? It's England. Slaves have rights."

"But only in England. Now she has legal status wherever she goes, including Port Elizabeth."

"You could've kept her in England. She'd be free."

"Madam, it's never that simple."

Precious tried to open her mouth, wanting so for the lady to explain, but nothing came out. He left off something vital in his first offer back in London. What else would he ignore in order to have his own way?

Mrs. Narvel took Jonas in her arms. "Is it because she's your special friend?"

A harsh groan sounded, no doubt from *captain controlling*. "Woman, you are nosy. She works for me. She cares for, goodness, loves Jonas. She is in my protection, just as you are."

"I'm sorry, Captain. I like Miss Jewell."

"Go put this boy to bed. And, you, too, Mrs. Narvel. I can't have two women sickly on this voyage. I'll keep watch over Miss Jewell."

The look on the woman's face, dimpling forehead, flattening lips, mirrored Precious's turmoil. "Yes, Captain. But you could take our cabin. Jonas and I can sleep on the pallet."

"No. This is the captain's cabin."

Precious tried with all her might to sit up, to prove she could manage herself, maybe even go with the lady and Jonas back to their room, but even the slightest move made her shoulder radiate pain. A wince snuck free.

Mrs. Narvel took Jonas and stood. Her face still looked broken. "But she may awaken any moment now. We, I could…"

"I'll watch over her like I have the past two nights. I'm the closest thing to a doctor to care for the stubborn girl. Go on, Mrs. Narvel. You may take over again for me in the morning."

"Yes, sir." With Jonas waving, the lady left.

The door closed with a thud.

Lord Welling moved from the footboard and dumped his dark blue jacket into the chair. "Well, Precious Jewell, what shall we do to pass the time? Game of cards?"

He leaned down and put a palm to each cheek. "Much cooler. You got ocean water in your lungs, but you're going to be all right."

He balanced against the footboard and pried off his boots.

She felt the weight of the bed shift as he lay down beside her. He was fully clothed and inches from her, but a shiver started in her toes and kept going until everything trembled.

"You're cold." He shifted near and carefully tucked her into his arms. "There, that should keep you good and toasty until the morning. Eliza always said I was a firebox."

His heavy arm now enfolded Precious. Her stiff shoulder fit next to his chest. He wasn't moving, and soon his snores began to fill her ear.

Half-scared, half-thawed, she stole a breath and willed herself to return to full sleep. Maybe Lord Welling would come into her dreams with his rapier and murder the evil trapped in her head or drop him headlong into the abyss over the side of the boat. If only.

Something swatted at his face.

Barely opening his eyes, he caught the fingers tapping at his jaw. Fingers?

He released them as he sat up.

Wide, almost wild, brown eyes peered at him from underneath him. Somehow, he'd nearly pinned Precious beneath him. "Good morning."

"Move," her voice sounded raspier, more sultry than her normal tones. "Move."

He rolled onto his back, avoiding the temptation to pull her with him. He didn't want to frighten his mouse any more than she was. "Are you in pain?"

With a shake of her head, she shoved on his arm. "Move."

He wiggled a little and produced an inch of space and bed sheets between them. "That's all you get. Any more, I'd be on the floor. Dumped from my own bed."

The pout on her creamy face was as delightful as vexing her.

"You should be on the floor, crowding me. Don't you have a boat to steer? Someone else to tease?"

"Nope." He raked a hand through his hair, reordering the sleep-confused style. "Not for several hours."

"Then I should get up and go. You're done with me."

"Interesting, Precious. You've been injured, but your awakening under questionable circumstances with a man in bed with you. What kind of example will you set for Jonas?"

She sputtered, spittle drizzling onto her fine scarlet lips. "But it's your bed, your room. You put me here. You kissed me."

"Only 'cause you asked, actually begged, me to."

Those chestnut eyes exploded. She started thrashing about too wildly. She'd hurt herself. "Nothing happened. You're not mine, Jewell, though my men or Mrs. Narvel may think otherwise. Know that you can trust me."

One brow propped like he spoke with a forked tongue. "Like with papers? I was free and you took that away."

"Oh, you heard that. I…"

With her good arm shaking, she started to swing again but stopped. "This is why you, all men, can't be trusted. You lie when your mouths move."

The poor girl had begun to trust him. A warm feeling grew in his chest as words of explanation bubbled. "You were only free in England. People still capture blacks and take them from England to enslave them again. Now you have registered papers that will protect you in South Africa. Slavery is still legal in all of Britain's colonies."

Her frown widened. "You could've given me the chance to choose. You use that fast brain of yours to excuse your heavy hand. You didn't want me to have a true choice, just your choices. You greedy man."

He propped up on one arm and looked at the dangling braids along her long neck, the frustrated heaving of her chest. He couldn't see or think of one reason to leave the fireball in London. "London without

Welling protection would not be enticing for you. And poor Jonas, would you send him here alone? Mrs. Narvel is nice, but trying to get him to calm down after seeing you hurt took a long time. Would he do that for another Mammie?" He thumped his chest. "I doubt he'd do it for this wayward man who claims him as an heir."

Her sweet chestnut eyes narrowed. "You mean his father. Don't think I hear you say those words that often."

He pulled his fingers to his lips and wanted to smash them in for his careless phrase. Some secrets should simply die. "Yes, his father."

Her gaze sharpened, as if she could see through his shirt, straight into his fortressed heart. "I need to know everything that happened in this room, not just the bits you wish to share."

He stuck his finger on her brow and smoothed a crinkle. "Everything, Precious Jewell? I am not sure you can handle that. Besides, I think that the there's too much slave still up in that head to handle much."

"What?"

"Like clockwork, mouse, each time you do something you think has angered me, you act as if I am going to beat or attack you. That's not the thinking of a free woman. No, a woman who bears no chains, mentally or physically, will find others to assign blame. I'm surprised Eliza didn't teach you the trick."

"Then your men must be trained to enslave, for they surely thought that you should hurt me for nearly dying."

He swiped at his hair and lay back upon his pillow. "I can't excuse their horrible behavior. But, if you had listened, hadn't been so frightened of me, you'd never have been endangered. Eliza once told me of how the

115

masters treated their slaves. She never mentioned how you were specifically treated, but I can imagine."

Precious's pretty eyes went wide as she sat up and struggled to bend her feet to her. Her muscles must be stiff from lying sick so long. "You have no idea. So don't pretend you can."

He held up a hand in the air to calm her. "Then tell me."

At first, she shrank back. Then, as if she'd reached her fill of cowering, she lunged forward and slapped him with her full strength across his cheekbone.

The surprise of it made him squint at her. He couldn't decide if he should laugh or curse. "Watch it, mouse."

"Auugh." The girl kicked him in the thigh, a sharp bony thrust with the heel of her foot. She lurched as if to pop him with the arm she'd hurt. Good thing he and Mrs. Narvel had bound it tightly to her side.

"I'm no rat!"

The pacing of her kicks picked up, with the last almost punching his stomach. "And why did you kiss a rat, if that's what you think of me?"

Why had he? There could've been another way to muffle her screams. His gaze left her fiery eyes, falling upon her lips. Her very generous mouth with the plump curve of a cupid's dimple atop was so inviting with her huffing at him. "It seemed a good idea at the time. And you didn't quite object."

Her cheeks darkened. Her caramel skin reddened as if her fever had blossomed again. "You bounder baron." She started kicking again.

To stop her from hurting herself or actually connecting with one of her blows, he slipped off the bed and rolled to the floor. Laughter poured out him. "You done?"

Another long puff came out of her. "Yes, unless you come back up here. You should take two years off my sentence or I… or I'll pester you for the reason you made me stay in here with you. I know it wasn't for my benefit."

He cocked his head and almost choked on his chuckles. Only one woman understood, well, tried to understand him, and she was dead. No one but Eliza had the capacity to accept him and his ills. But it was good to see true spirit in his mouse. "Precious, there is hope for you yet."

Reaching up, he pulled down a pillow, popped it under his neck and closed his eyes. "Goodnight."

Getting comfortable on the floor, he stretched his tired limbs. He'd keep protecting Precious, and he'd get her to not be afraid of men. Like every other woman, someday she'd yearn for love, to be married. Helping her overcome her fears now felt right. Yet, could he stand to let another man take her away? Would he allow someone else to enjoy her fine eyes and spirit?

Chapter Seven: Cabin Fever

Precious sat with her back to the firm mattress of the small bed in the women's cabin. She'd never been more pleased to be anywhere than on the floor of the women's cabin, reclining on the sturdy pallet. Taking a deep breath, she rejoiced, for she was out of Lord Welling's room, away from his irritating charm, and definitely out of his bed.

He said she begged for him to kiss her. Had she done that? Deep in her heart was there something inside that wanted what Eliza had, a beautiful son, a handsome husband?

She rubbed her neck as if the shame could rub off. There was a small part of her that wanted happiness like Eliza. The day she tried on the emerald silk, she wanted to be like Eliza. But that never meant taking Eliza's place. She loved her too dearly, never wanted her hurt.

But kissing her Lord Welling? That must be wrong.

His kiss had been gentle. It wasn't sloppy or full of spittle. It was just right. And that made Precious sad.

She could never think of it again or act upon it. No more fodder could be shoveled onto that. All the crew, even her quiet cabin mate, Mrs. Narvel, had to think of her as a harlot. The captain's woman. Oh, why did she have to fall overboard?

Jonas's chubby palm lifted her chin. "Mammie sad?"

Precious gathered him up in her arms. "Not with you, sweet boy. I missed caring for you."

He surely had grown an inch on this voyage. Six weeks had passed since leaving London, but just two since her drop into the ocean.

Mrs. Narvel's voice floated down from the bed. "He's been an angel. It was my pleasure to tend to you both. Need to make myself useful before my time of confinement."

The lady crawled to the edge of the mattress and stretched, tapping Jonas's nose. The glow of the woman's tan skin had increased as her stomach grew. "Truly, I like helping. I was a governess before I married Mr. Narvel. I haven't felt so useful since. Don't mistake my words. I love being a wife. I just don't like being idle. Once the babe's born, I'm going see about helping with the missionaries. I want to help bring light to Port Elizabeth. I think that will help in Lord Welling's call for peace."

Nodding, Precious lifted another piece of biscuit to Jonas's lips. "Thank you for your kindness. I should've listened to you."

"Hoot." The little boy made another noise, blocking out Mrs. Narvel's acknowledgement or condemnation. That was all well and good. Precious couldn't hear so much over anger at herself. Well, at least she had a new nightmare of being sucked down into the abyss, instead of hungry Charleston eyes coming after her.

Mrs. Narvel leaned her head over. Her smiling gaze had become something Precious counted on seeing. Even with her own tiredness from the babe growing big in her belly, she took care of Precious when she was so weak. Precious vowed in her heart to be a comfort to Mrs. Narvel when her time of confinement came.

She took a napkin and dusted Jonas's face. "Are you and the little one done? The cabin boy will return for the plates."

At least the young fellow didn't stare at her too much, not like what the rest of the crew would do if she faced them. She wiped her fingers on her soiled bodice. "I think Jonas is done. Surely left crumbs enough."

Mrs. Narvel hummed as she curled up in her quilt. The garnet and gold sections looked quite festive and expensive. "You look like you are feeling so much better, but I think you need something different to wear. That always makes me feel better."

"I just have but two dresses. With my arm still on the mend, I didn't get a chance to clean the other."

Precious put her head in her hands. She might as well tell the nice woman the truth. "I didn't do laundry when the boat docked. I didn't want any one to see me, not even Lord Welling."

The anguish burst inside. Precious enjoyed a neat appearance. Now she was just a low ragamuffin, a lowly mouse.

Jonas's hand fisted on one of her braids. "Mammie, no cry."

Mrs. Narvel wiped a tear from Precious's cheek. "Don't be uneasy, dear. I've plenty gowns. There's bound to be something in my trunk for you."

The lady sat up and pointed to the big box in the

corner. "Check inside."

Precious ran her finger along the fine leather top. Her thumbs stopped on the brass hinges. When she opened it, the most beautiful gowns, almost as wonderful as Eliza's, were folded inside: creamy taffeta, smooth silk, airy muslin, all so beautiful. "I can't wear these. They are too nice."

"Precious, keep rooting through. There should be something simpler, if that is better for you."

Encouraged, she let her hands sweep through the fabric. That one time of playing dress-up with Eliza stirred in Precious's head. Before she could stop, she'd picked up a floral print and held it to her chin. "What do I owe you?"

"Just let me read to you. I see your caged spirit, Precious Jewell. Let me read you something to help you with your peace. You don't have much."

Another one of those Bible-toters, the ones who went to church on Sunday and kept enslaved people, sun up to sun down. "All you want to do is to read to me and I can borrow this dress?"

Mrs. Narvel nodded. "That's all. Jonas might like to hear, too."

Precious studied the weave of the gown, the embroidery of the flowers on the cuff. It looked so nice, too nice.

Again, her roommate's cheery voice sounded like the tinkling of Christmas bells. "Go ahead. I think that will look really well on you."

Precious laid the gown on the bed like she used to do for Eliza, smoothing the hem, checking the underskirt. This was a dress for a somebody, not a woman who shamed herself. "It's too much. Maybe later."

The woman started to frown. "You can wear it and I won't read aloud. I just want to be helpful."

Mrs. Narvel sounded so small, like Precious had pushed all the air out of her. Even her puffy cheeks had diminished. "Except for my husband, I don't know anyone in Port Elizabeth. I would like to have a friend. I know I am going to need one when the baby comes."

The woman was trying to be helpful and she'd just rejected her. This place, Port Elizabeth, was new. Shouldn't Precious try to be new, too? What would it hurt to trust Mrs. Narvel? Would it be so awful if Precious gained a friend?

And the woman had been so kind, taking care of her and Jonas. Being filled with so much distrust, was Precious worthy to be a friend to anyone? Oh, how she hoped there was something other than bitterness inside her chest.

Taking a slow breath, she straightened and put her gown back in the trunk. "I might try it on later. But right now, why don't you read some of that book? I reckon that Jonas and I are a little restless being in this room for so long."

The widest smile Precious had ever seen bloomed on Mrs. Narvel lips. "Thank you. I'll read you just a little of the 23rd Psalm."

Precious dressed very carefully, buttoning one silk button at a time. Her shoulder felt better now, much of the tenderness gone. She could pick Jonas up without wincing. And today she would get some air.

Mrs. Narvel had made the past two weeks in the cabin pleasurable with funny stories. Her voice had become almost melodic when she read the Bible. The woman even explained a few things and didn't try sound like a saint or a preacher. Her peace seemed true. It was something to consider.

Her traveling companion was nice. The woman didn't think her a savage. She offered kindness and friendship. Precious was a free woman and free people could choose friends. Though enslaved by the Marsdale family, Precious knew in her heart that she and Eliza had loved one another. But love was an enigma. The strength of it could break through roles and stations in life. She'd seen it.

Precious looked back at Mrs. Narvel. The lady napped, just like Jonas. Both had a quiet looks on their pink, sleep-warmed faces.

But she didn't want sleep. She wanted air. Today, she felt strong enough to get it. With one more button pinched closed on the flowery dress that her roommate had let her wear, she strengthened her limbs. Heart filling with gratitude, she tiptoed out of the room and closed the door with a soft push.

Shaking hesitancy from her limbs, she plodded to the ladder leading to the deck. The reward above of sweet ocean breezes awaited her. *Come on, Precious.* Encouragement in her head sounding like Grandmama 's wispy voice made Precious want to grab the first rung of the pine ladder, but uneasiness held her back. Instead, she took a fingernail and traced the grains of the rounded wood.

Come on, Precious. She rolled her fingers about the rung and witnessed the curling of the muscles in her forearm. The cap sleeves of the flowered dress fit near her elbows and puffed with the exertion.

With its simple skirt, the floral muslin was far from the

dresses in Eliza's closet, but Precious felt just as elegant in it as she did the day Eliza let her try on the emerald taffeta.

Sighing, with eyes widening, she again glanced at the ladder. It looked taller and more rickety than she remembered, but hadn't it taken Lord Welling's and her weight at the same time? It couldn't be that feeble.

Come on, Precious. Smoothing a braid behind her ear, she chided herself. Her nerves were stealing her peace. She'd let the faith that Eliza had in her, that even Mrs. Narvel and Lord Welling believed her to possess, begin to show. No member of the snickering crew would keep her from feeling a small bit of wind on her face.

Rung by rung, she climbed again, pushing Lord Welling's laughter, his knowing remarks, out of her head. It took more effort to reach the top, but the growing warmth from the bright sun on her temples felt so good.

Smoothing her dress of wrinkles, she tiptoed to the rail, very near the spot she'd fallen. The ocean below swirled and sparkled. Blues and greens cut through the waves, but the foam peeked out like a white petticoat. The tang of salt washed over her. She didn't hate the water. Never did, but she now understood its strength. She'd never take for granted that its beauty hid power.

Ripples came and went as the sea rolled past, dancing to some slow jig. The water amazed her. The more she stood in the strong sunlight the more she marveled at the colors, the size and lengths of the rushes. It wasn't the least bit scary now. How could she have been so frightened of it just because of the dark?

And why had she been so frightened of Lord Welling? Yes, he annoyed her. And, yes, his wit stung. But he never hurt her, never even tried to give her much of a scare. A memory of his touch, the ginger way he undid her nightgown to fix her shoulder and the firmness of his encompassing kiss settled onto her.

She shuddered.

He was someone to fear, for he knew how to set her at ease.

Shaking off the mixture of helplessness and some tortured sense of wonder about him, she turned. Looking for the baron, her gaze stuck on a burly man heading her direction.

This one she hadn't seen before. He hustled from the back of the boat. Boots clomping on the deck, he ambled near. "Mornin', ma'am."

He kept moving and soon he and his pitchy tune disappeared.

The sailor didn't stare, ogle, or threaten her. No, he acted as if the black woman in the nice dress on The Margeaux's deck was normal, nothing unusual. Precious had to wipe the disbelief from her face, giving each cheek a good pat. Maybe there was some good for being thought of as the Captain's woman.

He'd been right in allowing the charade. Boy, did it burn her insides to admit him being right about anything. Even now, she could see that impish grin on his face, laughing, smiling at her.

Cupping her hand to her face, she scoured the boat, her eyes trailing planks and the handful of men pulling ropes to adjust the billowing sails. Finally, she spied Lord Welling at the wheel. With her fingers, she measured his height. From this distance, the baron measured only a few inches.

He wasn't so scary sitting betwixt her fingers. She smashed her index into her thumb, as if that action would lop off his stupid hat or smear his grin, the one she could picture with her eyes closed.

His whole body was focused straight ahead. Even at a distance, he seemed rigid, set apart. But this was a lie. He'd masked warmth and caring that sprung free in hidden moments. Before her accident, he'd come a few evenings and played with Jonas, telling tales of the colony and how his friend, Lieutenant Narvel, was a man of honor and valor.

No, the baron wasn't so scary.

Her heart did a stupid dance. No doubt from realizing that he was just a man, one who, so far, didn't mean her harm.

With a shake of her head, she abandoned nice thoughts of the man who called her a varmint, and headed for the ladder leading to her cabin. She'd risked enough for this mouth of air.

"What's Wowski doing today?" The screechy voice assaulted her ears. The worm of a man sent by London had climbed up from the ladder behind her. He came near, fingering the buttonholes of his onyx jacket. "Looking for your prince?"

Brow raised, she gaped at him.

The squint-eyed man trudged a few more steps. "I asked you a question."

She folded her arms about her. "No, you didn't."

"Yes, I did. I called to Wowski. Or maybe I should say it plain, harlot."

This was the attitude she'd expected of all men, but it still hurt. It still crushed her growing feelings of worth on the inside. Breath burning in her lungs, she made her voice strong. "The name is Precious Jewell. Learn it if you wish to speak to me."

He rubbed his chin and the nasty shadow cleaving to his jaw. "That's not a name. And why would someone call a servant such?"

"Because it's my name. Maybe one too honorable for the likes of your tongue."

She turned her back to him. She didn't need to talk to him or pay him any attention. She wasn't enslaved and needn't pay deference to anyone, except, well, maybe her employer. But that was it.

"Well, aren't you something? I'll still call you Wowski. But I'd bet the prince's trollop had better manners than you." He came close and almost elbowed her. "By the way, you may have caught Welling's eye and think you can get away with mischief, but passions fade and you may need another friend soon. I could be such."

What was the troll angling for? Did he think her weak enough that she'd want someone who called her a harlot to be her friend? She swallowed gall and tried to answer like the baron would. "Can't be a friend to someone who doesn't like my name."

"I won't sweet-talk you, but I can be of more help than Welling. And our relationship would be transactional, information-based. His days of being in charge will end."

Didn't that beat all? The nasty man wanted her to choose him over the baron. On what side of stupid was he birthed? "I didn't think the likes of you would think I knew anything."

He tapped the rail with his stubby fingers. "You're smart. More than I'd given you credit. And since Welling is sweet on you, he'll be careless. You'll be privy to his plans."

So the skunk wanted her to be a gossip. She pivoted

and started walking toward the baron's perch. "Well, I should go see what evil he's about."

"I'm not joking." He grabbed her arm as she attempted to move past him. "And my offer is not forever."

Anger whipped through her, she shook free and then lifted her chin. The worm wouldn't frighten or hurt her. She wasn't giving him that right. "Get your hands off me, before I slap you into tomorrow."

He swung his hands behind his back. "Just remember what I said and keep this to yourself."

So the fool was frightened of Welling. Good. "You remember to mind your manners."

She didn't wait for him to reply and headed to Lord Welling's perch. Mr. Grossling was a desperate troll and that type was the exact kind of fool that could cause trouble. But what harm would he cause? And what would happen to Precious or Jonas if Lord Welling lost his power?

Through his pocket scope, Gareth spied Precious coming his way. Her hips swayed, but her lips were pressed into a frown. Putting the lens into his jacket pocket, he could feel a hint of a smile growing on his face. The two-month-long voyage was nearly over and she'd all but disappeared when he returned her to the women's cabin. Teasing her would provide a needed distraction.

Hopefully her spirits had bloomed again. He had to know he could count on her reasoning. A level head was a must, for Port Elizabeth had its own troubles.

His fingers tensed along the wheel. He'd navigated the ship past all the dangerous reefs, but the biggest danger still lay ahead: docking and unloading. That would be the most vulnerable time. The Xhosa could attack when all the men were busy carrying supplies.

With Precious, Jonas, and the pregnant Mrs. Narvel on board, the stakes were higher. Yes, they'd wait for night before embarking upon the last miles.

"Lord Welling," her voice held no notes of shyness or deference, "when do we arrive? Is this Port Elizabeth a real place?"

"Oh, it's very real, Miss Jewell." He swiveled his head from his view of the ocean to her. His breath caught for a moment. He'd never seen her in anything but her uniform. Well, that and her nightgown.

But this? A floral muslin that tucked about her bosom, alluding to her rounded hips and the small waist he knew existed. Something crossed through him, a mix of awareness of her striking appeal and a jab of raw masculine protection. "The dress...it's."

She folded her arms. "It's Mrs. Narvel's. She let me borrow it. It shows my ankles a little. Suppose I'm a little taller."

Of course, he felt compelled to dip his head and study her neat legs. With a sigh, he turned back to the ocean. "You look very nice, Precious. Well, you've had your air. Now go back to your cabin. Your wanderlust has been sated. Go prepare. We dock tonight."

Precious pushed forward and gripped the rail of his deck. Her face lit. "Is that it? There're groves of green and mounds. No buildings."

He moved to her and handed her his scope. "That green you see is a wild jade canopy of trees from a forest and the brown are dunes. The land is almost split in two with wonderful trees to serve as building materials and sandy beaches."

"What are they for?"

The breathless quality of her words made him want to scoop her up and show her everything. Instead, he took a couple steps away and gripped the wheel with both hands. "It's land for building or a barrier to separate those who can't get along."

She nodded and put the scope to one of her pretty eyes. "And what of the people?"

"They are just like in London or Eliza's Charleston."

She turned to him. Her face fell, the joy stripping away, leaving a frown. "Oh."

Catching her gaze, he felt her sorrow, the disappointments she must bear. Well, he must surely have been one for her, too. "Did I treat you poorly in London?"

"No. You didn't pay me much mind. I was glad of that. It's never good when masters...or employers take notice."

Oh, his head was in a fog in London to not notice Precious's fire. Too consumed with trying to please his own masters, his uncle and Eliza, he'd missed her blooming into a fine young lady. "I'm glad I'm not one of the memories you are running from."

She put a balled hand to her hip. "Are you sure? You haven't told me what happened that night I fell. What happened after you fixed my shoulder and kissed me? You said nothing, but I'm not sure."

"You mean, after you begged me?"

The crease between her brows deepened. "Don't make me hate you, too. Tell me."

He wanted nothing of the sort. He needed her to like him, to trust him. "Nothing happened, Precious. My doctoring was limited to your shoulder. I took no other liberties."

Her posture relaxed.

She seemed a little too happy and that stung his pride. "Did you want something to happen, Precious? Did you want more than a kiss?"

Her caramel skin glowed about her cheeks. The woman blushed and looked even more beguiling. "Nothing."

She rotated back to the sea and looked again out the scope, but it was too late. She'd confirmed that his attraction to her was returned.

That would be dangerous knowledge to any other man who had been a faithful widower, but not Gareth. His discipline and the fact that she worked for him had to be enough to withstand the draw. Still, the hope of her looking at him, chestnut eyes sparkling with desire, warred in his breast.

He pushed air out his nostrils. The one woman who could understand his shortcomings was dead. There was no replacing Eliza.

"What of the men in the trees? Do they want you to build?"

"What?" He marched over to Precious. "Let me see."

Her long fingers touched his as she handed him the lenses and energy passed through him. "Over in that thickest grove."

Putting the eyepiece to his face, he saw nothing but leaves. "Are you sure? I don't see anything."

"He was there. I saw him and the glint of something shiny, like a mirror. That's what got my attention."

The concern in her eyes with her long lashes batting made him believe her about what she'd seen and so much more. His head bent. He kissed the air near her lips. He didn't dare move closer.

At first she didn't move either, but dipped her chin and hid her expression, looking down at the planks.

"Still unsure of me?" With a shake of his head, he pivoted and searched the land again. "Well, your tree dweller is gone. We'll take more precautions. Now, below with you."

"I thought the captain's woman could be anywhere she chooses. I'd love to watch The Margeaux pull into port."

He stuffed the scope in his pocket. "Well, you're not. Are you, Precious?"

She turned and started pacing. "Everyone thinks so. That hateful war department man is calling me Wowski. Is that another British term for prostitute?"

"Wowski? No that's the name the London presses used to describe the affair the Prince of Wales, our King George's own brother, had with an island woman. She was a black, or a mulatto, of mixed race." That urge to protect Precious rose up in his bones. "Why was he talking to you?"

She started to pace. The floral gown swayed and silhouetted her lovely form. "I'd slap the little troll if he weren't set on harming you. He is out to get you."

He stopped her and took her hand in his. "You care that much of me...my reputation?

She lifted her head and caught his gaze. "Yes. But why is his or any other man's opinion so important to you? You are so much finer than they."

A joke wouldn't do for Precious. Nothing but the truth for her eyes beginning to shine with trust. For a moment, he kissed her palm along the cross of its lifelines. "If every physical need a man may have was met, he'll still want two intangible things: The want of affection from a desirable woman and an ego. Both need stroking upon occasion."

"Captain." The cabin boy stood on his deck. "I made the checks that you asked. The men are getting rested for tonight."

"Miss Jewell." He gently released her hand. "Return to your cabin. At nightfall, I am going to guide The Margeaux into port. That way, if anyone is in the trees, they won't be able to see our movements."

She nodded at him with wondrous eyes, ones full of questions.

"Boy, help Miss Jewell back to her cabin. I wouldn't want the Captain's lady distressed."

"Yes, the Captain's lady." She came close leaned up and kissed his cheek. "Good evening, Captain."

She curtsied and left with the young man.

Gareth touched his warmed jaw. Was Precious going along with the ruse? Or was there more to this open sign of affection? If everything went smoothly tonight with docking and unloading The Margeaux, he might find the time for an answer.

Chapter Eight: Docking at Port Elizabeth

Silence finally crept in and covered the boat. Precious had the door cracked so she could overhear what was going to happen, but nothing; no creaking from below, very little movement above. Everything was still and quiet but for the unease in her spirit.

Mrs. Narvel put down her embroidery. Her face didn't seem happy. It had lines, as if she had something to dread.

"What's wrong, Mrs. Narvel? Are you feeling well? It's not time for the baby."

She seemed to smile, but her lips kind of pinched and then faltered. "Call me Clara. And, no, my body feels well."

Precious looked at the door, but then drew her attention to her friend. Whatever was going on out there would keep. "But not your spirit, Miss Clara?"

She nodded. "I don't know what's the matter with me. I'm about to see the man I love. I am going to tell him of our baby. He's going to be so happy."

Precious tucked a blanket about a snoring Jonas. He

134

loved sleeping with her on the pallet. "Then, why are you fretting?"

Clara dabbed at her eyes. Her ruddy cheeks looked ashen. "I don't know. Maybe he'll think I changed. Maybe he'll think I'm too fat."

With a shake of her head, Precious came and sat on the edge of the mattress. "I don't think you have to worry. If he's the man you've been describing, he won't care about weight, 'specially since it's his doing."

"It's not that."

The weepy sound of the woman's voice filled Precious with angst. She held Clara's hand. "Then what is it?"

"I just have fear. His last letter described the violence of this place. What if something has happened to him before I could see him? What if he never gets to behold his son? What if--"

Precious squeezed Clara in her arms and held her till the lady's tears stopped. "Don't do this. The what-ifs will do you in. No more of it. Lord Welling will keep everyone safe." She picked up the lady's heavy Bible and set it on the blanket. "You calm yourself, Miss Clara, just like you did me so many nights. Read it and believe those words like you told me to do."

"Did you believe them, Precious?"

She didn't know what to say. Nothing had wiped away her nightmares, but she had more peace now than she had in Charleston or London. She patted Clara's arm. "I know you believe them. You don't lie with your faith to coerce. You're honest in it. That's what I believe. Now start in that book of Psalms. That David sounds like he's hurting, too."

Clara brought Precious's hand to her cheek. "You're right, Precious. I'm working myself up over a bad dream.

All will be well."

Precious framed a smile on her face and waited for Clara's before she got into a comfortable spot next to Jonas. Nothing could go well with her friend in a panic or with Precious joining her in letting fear run wild.

But Precious did believe in dreams. They were warnings sometimes, but she'd keep this sentiment to herself, along with her shaking limbs under the blanket. The movement she saw in the trees was a figment of her mind. Or if it was real, let it at least be a friendly person to Lord Welling and his party.

After a couple of chapters, Clara's fidgeting stilled. The woman took slower breaths. "Precious, thank you. I've been getting weak in my faith these days, fretting over the baby or my husband's safety. But none of anything that happens is in my control. I have to have peace with that."

Nodding, Precious shifted her eyes to the crack in the door, to the drifting sound of men's boots marching all about. The docking must be starting. "Yes, there's not much to do but wait and hope for the best."

Clara released a yawn. "I have to trust that, even in the bad, there will be good. God says that He wants our best. Suppose I have to believe that He will be true to His word."

Precious didn't respond. She kept her doubts tucked in her belly. Bad things always came, but hopefully it would stay away at least today and tomorrow.

When Clara's head dipped fully onto the blankets and her whistling snore sounded, Precious got up and slipped on her shoes. The movement of the boat seemed halted, almost still. She opened her door wider and saw the shadow of the ladder was the same as it had been an hour ago. Their position from the moon hadn't changed. They must be docked. They'd made it to Port Elizabeth.

Skin tingling with excitement, she pushed into the hall. Anticipation mixed with her doubts and started a rumbling in her tummy. *Shhh.* She held her middle and wondered what she would see if she took a peek.

Lord Welling warned her to stay in the cabin, but that had to be if something went wrong. Surely, it would cause no harm to crawl up and take a gander at what was happening. She'd only do it for a few minutes.

Yes, that's what she'd do.

Holding her breath, she plodded to the ladder and climbed to the top. It took seconds for her eyes to adjust to low, almost nonexistent light. Her scan of land saw endless patches of trees and mounds of beach. The curves blended into the ebony night. This place was very different from London.

She craned her neck to make out figures marching down the plank. Her pulse raced when she found the tall figure wearing the moon-shaped hat. The glow of the torch in his hand exposed him fully. Lord Welling was glorious, his jacket billowing in the breeze. He lifted his arms and he and his men started down the plank.

"Wowski? Don't you know the women should be below?"

The worm who wanted her to be a spy had come from nowhere and now stood behind her whispering, "That includes the black woman, too."

The hair on her neck rose as the scent of liquor and sweat from his sorry hide invaded her nostrils. "Hadn't you heard I'm more caramel?"

He chuckled, his tone sounding harsh with each fake

note. "Funny, Wowski."

She turned back to watch Lord Welling, but her head filled with questions. "What's going on? Why must this be done at night? And why aren't you with him?"

He moved to stand next to her. "What, your friend, the Captain, didn't tell you? The savages could be out attacking us as we unload the cargo. Once everything is stowed, someone, probably your prince, will come for you."

Now wasn't the time for his bluster. Between Clara's unease and the sense that what she saw moving in those trees was real, Precious had lost patience with his joke. "Isn't Wowski a mocking of your king? Isn't it treason to speak ill of his brother?"

The man sputtered as if caught in the snap of a bear trap. "Go on below with you. Leave this for the men."

He stepped around her and kept going.

Good riddance. But Precious wasn't moving, not until she knew all was well. The wariness in her stomach didn't quit. There was something odd in this.

Her gaze left the landing party and moved to the trees. The close ones didn't look right. A limb or two bent opposite the wind. Either her imagination had become crazed or something was out there.

She counted to ten and nothing happened. Swiveling, she again focused on Lord Welling's lantern. His light and those of his men cut through the ebony night.

This was just like the woods on the Marsdale Plantation, except the water there smelled of fish and stinky fishermen. This place had a scent of newness and some raw, unexplainable danger.

Precious wasn't scared. The bumps pimpling her skin weren't mostly from fear, but a restless anticipation. This place would be her home and she was going to set foot on it, not in chains and not enslaved.

She craned her neck to hear. Was that the sound of drums filling the wind or just her nerves? Everything within her screamed something was out there.

A party of five or six lanterns marched from the dunes to the gangplank. They must be causing the noises. But what if they weren't?

Pacing to the lieutenant, she thought of how to alert him and not give him more fodder. It was one thing to be thought of as a harlot, but a nutty one, too? That had to be avoided.

A cry pierced the air. It was man's death yell. The lead man of the party on the shore fell.

Lord Welling charged forward. "Take cover, men!"

Another man dropped to his right, but Lord Welling kept moving until he stopped at the end of the gangplank. He seized a stick and pulled it from the first man's back. Even from this distance, from the look of it, no one could survive. But her baron didn't leave him. He stayed.

She grabbed Mr. Grossling's arm. "Lieutenant, you have to go to the baron and help him."

Coward, he shook his head. "I will not. The paper-pusher's not for suicide."

Precious pivoted and saw Lord Welling's lantern go dark. Her heart nearly exploded. Suddenly, she was running to him. Just like she was a rabbit in Charleston, she bounced down the gangplank with no care for losing her balance or falling into the treacherous ocean below. She had to get to him. She had to warn him of what she sensed awaiting in the trees.

He couldn't die. He was too good a man for that.

A spear flew past her side, but she ducked and tripped flat on her stomach, the air leached out of her.

Guns belched. The air filled with the perfume of killing powder.

Lifting her head, she could see a man on horse bearing down on the baron. He was in a leathered robe. Nothing the English wore. And he was as black as ebony. His thick forearm glistened in the moonbeams. What manner of enemy was this?

Why didn't the baron move? What distracted him from the danger closing in?

She leapt to her feet and ran at full force. She saw a spear launch and jumped, arms flailing as she pushed through the air toward the baron's neck.

Wham! She hit him hard, sending him backward, but he'd grabbed her, taking her with him. As they hit the beach, sand flew everywhere. The wind of the spear sailed over her and lodged in the plank with a thud. He or she would have been sliced through if either stayed on the gangplank.

Lord Welling drew her fully into his arms, tucking her deep within his jacket. The scent of gunpowder and his musk swallowed her as he rolled with her until they were partially hidden underneath the plank.

Gunshots sounded, a bullet hitting close to their spot.

He drew her tighter in his arms. His low accent licked her ear. "What do you think you're doing? You could've been killed!"

She held him tighter, counting the hitching of his gasps. "Savin' your life. You're welcome."

"Thank you. Now we'll both be killed." He tugged her underneath him, as if to shelter her from their enemy, but his weight made it difficult to breathe.

Feet pounded overhead. More guns roared.

Fury overtook her. She kicked with her legs, beat on his chest. "I wouldn't have had to if you'd have moved. Why didn't you? I told you I saw people in the hills."

"I couldn't move. The spear hit my lieutenant. I had to tell him of his wife and the child soon to come. Narvel had to know before he died."

Precious stilled as his words crept past her anger and struck her heart. "No, not Clara's husband. Not Mr. Narvel. " Her poor friend. Precious's throat clogged, a sob filling the spaces between words. "I have to tell her."

He rolled to his side, but his heavy body blocked the way they'd come and water was on the other side of the plank. She was trapped with Lord Welling under the gangplank until some side won. "I have to help her."

He leaned over and kissed her forehead. "Not until my men sound an all clear. Then we can tend to our friends."

Port Elizabeth was to be a place of joy. With her palm, she beat the sandy floor beneath her. "Where have you brought me and Jonas?" She hit it again but he captured her hand and pulled her to him. The weight of his embrace pressing her against his chest stilled her motion.

She felt helpless and weak underneath him and the burden of her grief for her friend. "Why?"

Pistols popped, flintlocks moaned and shouts drowned out everything but the rapid beating of his heart. The light of the moon slipping through the haze of bullets and smoke showed the anguish in his eyes. "It wasn't like this before I left. I'd never..." He lifted her chin, his strong gaze searing her flesh. "I'm greedy. I wanted you and the boy here with me. I needed you here."

She shouldn't have let him kiss her, but she didn't have

the desire not to taste his strength. How could she not give in to the feel of his rough hands caressing her face, his finger tips stroking her neck, drawing her closer, wrapping her in his power?

A horn blew. He stopped the siege of lips, her very willpower. With strong arms, he nudged her behind him. "Please, stay here until I know all is well." He stroked her chin. "And, Precious, you're not a mouse. No, you're a full lion."

He scooted out of their hiding position and disappeared in the gloom.

She'd stay put, not because he asked, because she had to get all of her tears out of her, so she could tell her friend the worst. And that this crime was done by someone who Clara had come to be a missionary for, someone who very well could be a cousin to Precious. How was that news to be shared?

Extras

Sneak Peak The Bargain III

* * *

VANESSA RILEY

EPISODE III

THE BARGAIN

A PORT ELIZABETH REGENCY TALE

Episode III of The Bargain
Length: 11 Chapters (30,000 words)
Summary: Secrets Revealed

Excerpt: The Aftermath of a Kiss and the Xhosa

"Captain," Ralston cleared his throat. "She fixed me up and a number of others."

The baron's lips pursed as he nodded. "Miss Jewell is full of surprises."

His hair was wild and loose. He smelled of beach sand and perspiration. Still frowning, he raised Ralston's arm a few inches from the boat's deck. "Looks like you will live."

"Don't know how much good that'll do me here, Captain. We left here with peace. Why? What happened? And Mr. Narvel?"

"I don't know, but I'm going to find the answers." Using Mr. Ralston's good arm, the captain pulled him to stand. "Get yourself below and sleep. I've got men on watch. Our guns are ready this time for any other surprises."

The sailor shrugged as he tested his shoulder, pushing at the wrapped muscles. "Yes, Sir."

Lord Welling leaned down and took Precious's hand. "You've helped enough, Miss Jewell. I want you to go down below."

She shook her head. "There's more I can do up here."

The baron snatched her up by the elbow. "I insist."

Precious shook free and grabbed up the doctoring supplies. "We're probably going to need these again."

Ralston closed his eyes and grunted almost in unison with Lord Welling before trudging past the other men laying out on the deck, the one's whose injured legs prevented them from going below. With no rain, they'd be alright under the night sky.

Precious looked up into the night sky that looked like black velvet with twinkling diamonds. Such innocence shrouds this place. So opposite the truth.

"Come along, Miss Jewell. Now." The baron's voice sounded of distant thunder, quiet and potent. His patience, his anger, at so many lost this night must be stirring. He again put his hands around her shoulders and swept her forward.

She didn't like to be turned so abruptly, but stopping in her tracks didn't seem right either. So she slowed her steps, dragging her slippers against the planks of the Margeaux. "What are you doing?"

He stopped and swung her around so that she faced him. "I need your help telling Mrs. Narvel. It's not going to be easy telling a pregnant woman that—"

"Her husband has died at the Xhosa's hands." Precious's heart drummed loudly, like a death gait. Staying busy helping the injured delayed the building grief she had for her friend. Oh, how was Clara to take it?

Lord Welling's lips thinned and pressed into a line. "It's never easy telling a woman a difficult truth or waiting for her to admit it."

She caught his gaze. It felt as if the fire within it scorched her. Suddenly, the smell of him, the closeness of his stance made her pulse race. He wasn't talking about Clara, but Precious wasn't ready to admit anything.

And what would he think if she told him that at that moment with Xhosa bearing down upon them that nothing seemed more right than to dive headlong to save him. No, Lord Welling didn't need that bug in his ear.

But soon, he'd press. He wasn't the kind of man who waited for anything.

He gripped her hand and led her into the darkness where those stars twinkled in his eyes. "Precious, I need to ask you something."

Chin lifting, she pushed past him and headed for the hole and the ladder below. "We need to get to Mrs. Narvel."

She took her time climbing down, making sure of her footing on each rung, then she waited at the bottom for her employer, the man who in the middle of chaos kissed her more soundly than any one ever had.

His boots made a gentle thud as he jumped the last rungs. When he pivoted, he crowded her in the dark corner, towering over her. "You're reckless, Precious."

She backed up until she pressed against the compartment's planked wall. "I'm not the only one. Taking Jonas to a land of killing, that's reckless."

He clutched the wall above each of her shoulders, but

he might as well had gripped them with his big hands. There was no escape from the truth he was waiting on.

Leaning within an inch of her, his voice reached a loud scolding tone. "You're reckless. Wanton for danger."

Her face grew warm and she bit down on her traitorous lips, ones that wanted a taste of him again.

His breathing seemed noisier. His hands moved to within inches of her arms, but they didn't sneak about her. No, those fingers stayed flat against the wood, tempting, teasing of comfort. "You could've been killed. Will you ever listen?"

The harshness of his tone riled up her spirit. "Won't do me no good to listen if you're dead. The least you can say is thank you."

He straightened and towed one hand to his neck. Out of habit, she squinted as if he'd strike her, but she knew in her bones that wasn't to happen. The fear of him hurting her was long gone. Only the fright of him acting again on that kiss between them remained. "What am I to do with you?"

Get the next Episode. Look for all the episodes. Join my newsletter to stay informed.

Dear Friend,

I enjoyed writing The Bargain because I dream of Port Elizabeth, a burgeoning colony where all men and women had the opportunity to make their claim and determine their own fates. These stories will showcase a world of intrigue and romance, somewhere everyone can hopefully find a character to identify with as the colonists and Xhosa battle for their ideas and the love, which renews and gives life.

Stay in touch. Sign up at www.vanessariley.com for my newsletter. You'll be the first to know about upcoming releases, and maybe even win a sneak peek.

Thank so much for giving this book a read.

Vanessa Riley

Here are my notes:

Slavery in England

The emancipation of slaves in England preceded America by thirty years and freedom was won by legal court cases not bullets.

Somerset v Stewart (1772) is a famous case, which established the precedence for the rights of slaves in England. The English Court of King's Bench, led by

Lord Mansfield, decided that slavery was unsupported by the common law of England and Wales. His ruling:

"The state of slavery is of such a nature that it is incapable of being introduced on any reasons, moral or political, but only by positive law, which preserves its force long after the reasons, occasions, and time itself from whence it was created, is erased from memory. It is so odious, that nothing can be suffered to support it, but positive law. Whatever inconveniences, therefore, may follow from the decision, I cannot say this case is allowed or approved by the law of England; and therefore the black must be discharged."

E. Neville William, The Eighteenth-Century Constitution: 1688-1815, pp: 387-388.

The Slavery Abolition Act 1833 was an act of Parliament, which abolished slavery throughout the British Empire. A fund of $20 Million Pound Sterling was set up to compensate slave owners. Many of the highest society families were compensated for losing their slaves.

This act did exempt the territories in the possession of the East India Company, the Island of Ceylon, and the Island of Saint Helena. In 1843, the exceptions were eliminated.

Wowski
Wowski was a mocking name given to a young black or mulatto girl that Prince William, brother to Prince George (the future Regent of England) brought back

with him in 1788 while on Naval tour with Admiral Nelson. She was kept out of sight of British society. A Gilroy cartoon, depicting the couple embracing lovingly in a hammock, ran in the society newspaper *The World*. The name Wowski is derived from the name of a black servant in the play *Inkle and Yarico*, in which Inkle falls in love with an Indian maiden who saves his life but then sells her into slavery for profit.

Join My Newsletter

If you like this story and want more, please offer a review on Amazon or Goodreads.

Also, sign up for my newsletter and get the latest news on this series or even a free book. I appreciate your support.

* * *

VR

Episode IIII
* * *

***

The vastness of the cresting ocean isn't enough to drown Precious Jewell's high spirits or her dreams of doing for herself, but a false move and an old nightmare have placed her in more jeopardy, Lord Welling's bedchamber.

Captaining his schooner to Port Elizabeth was his only refuge, until his ship was invaded by land lovers, his son and his challenging caregiver. Perhaps, Miss Jewell's vivacity and audacity are just what he needs to quell rebellion amongst his crew and his heart.

The Bargain is the first Port Elizabeth Regency Tale.

Chapter Nine: Port Elizabeth, June 3, 1819

Smoke mixed with the breeze lifting from the bay. The sweet smell of the fresh water added a blanket of perfume that Precious Jewell tried to fit into every inch of her lungs. For it covered the scent of loss and despair and death. She shook herself. For fear and despair couldn't grip her. There was too much work to do; too many people wounded that needed patching. Then she'd have to tell her friend the worst about her husband. Poor Clara didn't get a chance to say goodbye.

She mopped her brow, but continued wrapping a linen bandage about Mr. Ralston's arm. The big arrow like sword that Lord Welling called an assegai had pierced the skin close to the bone. The man had bled a great deal. His lips were ashen, but when she put a thumb to his wrist, the beat felt strong. "This is gonna cause you a mighty ache for the next few days, maybe weeks, but you'll be fine."

His brown eyes shifted, but he said nothing. His tongue was probably glued in place by the pain. Finally, he licked his dry mouth and mumbled a bit before his voice became clear. "Better hurt than dead."

His words didn't shock Precious. So many sailors had been cut down tonight. It was as bad as when the plantation owners sought to squelch rebellion amongst the slaves. Precious was very young, but still remembered the torches whipping in the night sky, and the howling of the dogs and the men. Those screams filled that heavy foggy air, just like the baron's men's screams filled this Port Elizabeth night.

Tonight, two sides battle, the Xhosa and Lord Welling's men, but this time the losers didn't look like Precious. The superior force was black and bold.

And as far as she knew, the colony people here weren't guilty of enslaving folks like her. Why then should they be slaughtered? Could this place survive with Africans bent on killing?

With a heavy blink to her eyes, she steadied the shakes beginning to set in her hands. She felt some kind of way about all the violence, but would keep that to herself. "There. You're done."

"Thank you, ma'am." His voice sounded small and low. "I didn't think you'd be the one to patch me up."

She reared back on her knees, her fisted hand swinging to her hip. "Why? Cause I look like them, those Xhosa?"

When his head rocked from side to side, she stilled and unclenched her fingers. "I didn't think you would since I ain't been decent to you. Sorry for that."

She caught his gaze with his wounded mud brown eyes. "An apology? Good to hear it."

"Good to hear what?" Lord Welling stooped beside her. "What have you agreed too, Miss Jewel?"

Her spine bristled at the possessive notes in his voice. Maybe it was imagined but his clear blue eyes bore into her skull as if merely staring would unlock her secrets. He should know that wouldn't work. It'd take a lot more than his brooding to get at those. "Been helping out up here as best as I could."

"Captain," Ralston cleared his throat. "She fixed me up and a number of others."

The baron's lips pursed as he nodded. "Miss Jewell is full of surprises."

His hair was wild and loose. He smelled of beach sand and perspiration. Still frowning, he raised Ralston's arm a few inches from the boat's deck. "Looks like you will live."

"Don't know how much good that'll do me here, Captain. We left here with peace. Why? What happened? And Mr. Narvel?"

"I don't know, but I'm going to find the answers." Using Mr. Ralston's good arm, the captain pulled him to stand. "Get yourself below and sleep. I've got men on watch. Our guns are ready this time for any other surprises."

The sailor shrugged as he tested his shoulder, pushing at the wrapped muscles. "Yes, Sir."

Lord Welling leaned down and took Precious's hand. "You've helped enough, Miss Jewell. I want you to go down below."

She shook her head. "There's more I can do up here."

The baron snatched her up by the elbow. "I insist."

Precious shook free and grabbed up the doctoring supplies. "We're probably going to need these again."

Ralston closed his eyes and grunted almost in unison with Lord Welling before trudging past the other men laying out on the deck, the one's whose injured legs prevented them from going below. With no rain, they'd be alright under the night sky.

Precious looked up into the night sky that looked like black velvet with twinkling diamonds. Such innocence shrouds this place. So opposite the truth.

"Come along, Miss Jewel. Now." The baron's voice sounded of distant thunder, quiet and potent. His patience, his anger, at so many lost this night must be stirring. He again put his hands around her shoulders and swept her forward.

She didn't like to be turned so abruptly, but stopping in her tracks didn't seem right either. So she slowed her steps, dragging her slippers against the planks of the Margeaux. "What are you doing?"

He stopped and swung her around so that she faced him. "I need your help telling Mrs. Narvel. It's not going to be easy telling a pregnant woman that—"

"Her husband has died at the Xhosa's hands." Precious's heart drummed loudly, like a death gait. Staying busy helping the injured delayed the building grief she had for her friend. Oh, how was Clara to take it?

Lord Welling's lips thinned and pressed into a line. "It's never easy telling a woman a difficult truth or waiting for her to admit it."

She caught his gaze. It felt as if the fire within it scorched her. Suddenly, the smell of him, the closeness of his stance made her pulse race. He wasn't talking about Clara, but Precious wasn't ready to admit anything.

And what would he think if she told him that at that moment with Xhosa bearing down upon them that nothing seemed more right than to dive headlong to save him. No, Lord Welling didn't need that bug in his ear.

But soon, he'd press. He wasn't the kind of man who waited for anything.

He gripped her hand and led her into the darkness where those stars twinkled in his eyes. "Precious, I need to ask you something."

Chin lifting, she pushed past him and headed for the hole and the ladder below. "We need to get to Mrs. Narvel."

She took her time climbing down, making sure of her footing on each rung, then she waited at the bottom for her employer, the man who in the middle of chaos kissed her more soundly than any one ever had.

His boots made a gentle thud as he jumped the last rungs. When he pivoted, he crowded her in the dark corner, towering over her. "You're reckless, Precious."

She backed up until she pressed against the compartment's planked wall. "I'm not the only one. Taking Jonas to a land of killing, that's reckless."

He clutched the wall above each of her shoulders, but he might as well had gripped them with his big hands. There was no escape from the truth he was waiting on.

Leaning within an inch of her, his voice reached a loud scolding tone. "You're reckless. Wanton for danger."

Her face grew warm and she bit down on her traitorous lips, ones that wanted a taste of him again.

His breathing seemed noisier. His hands moved to within inches of her arms, but they didn't sneak about her. No, those fingers stayed flat against the wood, tempting, teasing of comfort. "You could've been killed. Will you ever listen?"

The harshness of his tone riled up her spirit. "Won't

do me no good to listen if you're dead. The least you can say is thank you."

He straightened and towed one hand to his neck. Out of habit, she squinted as if he'd strike her, but she knew in her bones that wasn't to happen. The fear of him hurting her was long gone. Only the fright of him acting again on that kiss between them remained. "What am I to do with you?"

His palm scooted along her jaw and curled into braids escaping her mobcap. "There's beach sand in your hair. What do these locks look like freed?"

"Thick." Why was it so hard to breathe with his rough palm skirting her neck? "Lots of tight curls."

"Tell me why you saved me, Precious?"

"Tell me why you want to know?" She jerked away. He wasn't going to push her into anything. "Nothin'.... Nothing matters but breaking the news gently to Mrs. Narvel."

With a sigh, he pulled away from the wall. "You're distracting me, Jewell. I need to know you are safe caring for Jonas. I can't do what needs to be done wondering about you, and his protection."

"There's one thing that needs to be done now." She pointed to her cabin door. "You have to tell Mrs. Narvel. She needs to hear from you that her husband has died."

He wrenched backward almost flinging himself against the wall.

Was he stalling? And all that sweet talk of distraction was that just another way to avoid breaking Clara's heart? Everything in Precious went cold. "As his captain, his employer, you must tell her what has happened."

"Such a good man. What has gone wrong here? Things were peaceful six months ago. I'd negotiated with the Xhosa and the Dutch settlers. We'd found reasons not to kill each other. And now this?"

"You negot.. negoti... you talked with the Africans? You forged an agreement? They're not savages like Palmers said they were?"

His brow lifted. "Misguided man. How much do you know of this continent or the history of slave trading?"

She put a hand on her hip. "Only first hand experience."

"Don't put stock in what old mean-spirited men say or naïve captains for that matter." He pressed at his neck again. "Some of the Xhosa speak no English and will kill any white or different looking face they encounter. Others have been taken to London or Spain and educated. Mzwamadoda, my counterpart, can speak five languages including English and Xhosa. If I get to him, he'll make sense of this."

Was it respect or fear trembling Lord Welling's voice?

Whatever she heard, it caused her skin to pimple at the thought of the baron not knowing what to do. She tucked her braids under the edge of her lawn cap. "No one can make sense of killing. Or hate. It just is."

His eyes settled upon her. Against her will, Precious felt a rush of blood pumping through her hot veins. "Yes, some things just are." He pushed closer. This time one arm snaked around her shoulders. "Why did you save me? What was—?"

"No time for this foolishness." She pressed on his chest and squirmed from him. "We have to tell Mrs. Narvel."

She turned and walked to the brass doorknob. "Maybe Mrs. Narvel's book will help her make sense of why her babe's daddy is dead."

"We will talk of distractions later, Precious. Sometimes

a man just has to know how things are." Lord Welling brushed past her. His arm touched her sending more shivers to the ones hidden inside her stomach. "Let's tell the poor lady now."

He opened the door.

Clara had Jonas in her arms as she paced from side to side.

The boy's wide eyes must've met his father's for he stretched his chubby arms toward the baron.

But Lord Welling stayed fixed in place. He pulled his arms behind his back and drew himself up straight and tall. "Mrs. Narvel, I've some news to tell you. Some very bad news."

Clara stopped moving. Her hold on Jonas seemed to slacken.

Precious moved past Lord Welling and gathered the boy from her arms. "Mrs. Narvel, you need to sit down."

The woman had frozen in place. Her normally pink cheeks turned to gray.

"Mr. Narvel was the finest of men. He died with honor."

A shriek left Clara's trembling lips. One eye started to leak then the other. "My dream. It is true. He'll never know about our babe."

Rocking a squirming Jonas, Precious bit back her tears. "He told 'em, Clara. Lord Welling told him 'fore he died."

The baron coughed as if his throat had closed in on him. "Yes, he left this world knowing you loved him and was giving him a child. I saw the pride in his eyes at knowing your love had created something that will be his namesake."

The cries from Clara's mouth increased. She sank to

the floor. Her pale dress ballooned, then flopped as the air went out of it. "Go. Everyone. Please leave me."

No, Precious couldn't let her friend be alone. She spun and handed Jonas to his father. "I'll stay with Mrs. Narvel. I'll help her through this."

The pinched up look on Lord Welling's face as if she'd just handed him a soiled rag was as hurtful as it was laughable. "I've got—"

"No, you take your son to your quarters and get him to sleep. Then you can go do what you need."

Clara started wailing and shaking her fists, beating them on the floor.

Jonas joined in and cried like Precious had taken away his favorite toy blocks.

Precious's eyes were getting pretty heavy with water too. "Please, Lord Welling. Take him now."

Slow and stiff, he nodded and left with the boy.

Precious closed the door, and then pivoted to her friend. "It's just us, Clara."

She sat down and pulled the grieving woman into her arms. "Go ahead, let it all out." Precious heard sobbing in her own voice as her heart crushed in upon itself. "No one here to pretend to be brave for."

Clara started heaving. Water like a flood of hurt poured out of her.

Precious gripped her tighter. "You were strong for me when I was filled with such shame. Let me be strong for you."

She wrapped the poor widow in all her strength and hoped the love she was capable of was enough to help.

Clara needed her now. It was something terrible to realize that the God you served rained on the just, the unjust, the free and the enslaved with the same awful vengeance. No one was protected from His wrath. How would any survive when this place seemed more evil, more readied for wrath than anywhere else?

Chapter Ten: Putting Things Away

Precious looked out the bay window at the high walls of Fort Fredrick. Lord Welling's cottage was a stone's throw from the masonry built to protect the colonists of Port Elizabeth. A big blur stood sentry next to the high cannon sitting at the top. It was probably Mr. Ralston, the baron's man. Two weeks had restored him to health, almost as if nothing had happened.

Everyone was silent on the matter, but it was there with the dark bands some wore on their sleeve or in the permanent frowns. Fifteen colonists were dead and buried. One, of course, was her friend's husband and his cousin. If Clara doesn't have a boy, the Narvel line will perish.

She shook her head. This was some kind of hurt that had been dropped onto this place.

Clop, click, clop. Boots. Lord Welling's boots. He must be leaving for his search.

Clip. Then silence.

Oh, no. There should have been four more rhythmic

footfalls. Two full weeks of avoiding him done. Precious sucked in a quick breath and turned her head toward the door.

Lord Welling stood there with his arms folded. Nary a crease existed on his crisp white shirt. He looked quite put together for a man going to hunt for trouble.

"Precious, has Mrs. Narvel come out of her room?"

She pivoted back to the window hoping something outside would be far more interesting than his handsome face. "No, she keeps to herself, barely ate a crumb today. That can't be good."

"Ralston's almost fully recovered. I'm thinking of sending her and a few of the injured back to London. I'm thinking of sending you and Jonas too."

The thought of deserting this place and Lord Welling hadn't crossed her mind. Avoiding him was one thing. But abandoning him, that was something else. "Unless you're coming too, Mrs. Narvel and her baby won't make it."

"What?" The groan coming from him could've rocked the small house. "But she isn't that far along is she?"

"Men don't ask enough specifics when it comes to havin' a baby, but if we can get her eating again, she'll do better. That babe and Mrs. Narvel will live, not like Miss Eliza."

He chuckled, a laugh full of life and maybe a touch of scorn. "Well, that is the first time you or I have said my late baroness's name since arriving. I'd hoped our words in private could be more about that question you haven't answered."

Guilt boiled within her stomach as she released the curtain. "There's no private time with so much to do. In fact, Miss Eliza would've liked for you to spend more than a minute with Jonas. But you've been too busy traipsing off to who knows where."

"So, is that what this quiet treatment of me is all about? You're the busy one with the boy or our guest. You're hiding, and this icy manner is a ruse to punish me for not detailing my whereabouts. Eliza taught you well."

She wrinkled her nose at his foolish talk. "Do you know how much there has been to put away? Or would you like to spend the day here caring for your son or tempting a broken woman with soup?"

He dropped his head and seemed to be studying his boot. "Then you haven't been ignoring me?"

"Haven't had much time to wonder about you, or where you are going or doing, or if you will return." She bit her lip. That truth shouldn't have slipped out. "Oh, just go do your job."

His head lifted. He braced against the door as if he awaited an attack. "Then why don't you ask? Or better yet, why don't you tell me what's going on in that head of yours?"

If she could figure things out, she probably would tell, but she hadn't. Smoothing her apron, she looked at the pile of crates she still had to finish before counting this room as done. "There's much to do. So, bye."

"What do you want, Precious? Surely, it's not just to tidy up the place."

"Nothing. Now shoo. Go on out of here. I've things to put away to make this home function. I've much better tasks to run in my mind than not wondering about you." She covered her mouth before something else foolish came out.

That missing grin of his stolen from mourning his men returned. "Making a home and concern for my safety? You have an odd way of showing your regard. This is the most you've said to me since we left the Margeaux." He stretched his long arms and briefly touched the top of the framing. "We should discuss *it*."

It? "What it?"

Dimples and the grin now filled his proud face. "Your leaping to kiss me. That *it*, Precious?"

The memory of that moment had made her toss in her bed every night until exhaustion claimed her eyes. It made her nearly awaken Jonas with her pacing, until she heard the baron's footfalls cross the threshold. Bristling, she moved back to the crate of linens she'd been sorting through. "I said bye. Go chase your warriors. Let busy people alone."

He tapped his lips and then took a step into the room, the hope of him leaving that kiss topic alone all but fading. "You're angry with me. I think I can tell now. Your forehead wrinkles, probably from holding in your emotions. So very different from the way Eliza showed anger."

She wasn't Eliza, and Precious sure didn't have the right to think of her man like she'd been doing. Pressing at her temples, she even pushed at the lines he'd been studying. "How am I supposed to act? Should I be happy seeing you go off into the woods to chase a people who slaughtered so many? Or maybe you want me to kiss you good-bye like a good little mistress?"

His face sobered and his big eyes bore down upon her. "Do you want to be my mistress?"

"Bye."

He crossed fully into the room and pulled off his deep blue tailcoat, sending it flying to the simple jade colored sofa. The rapier sashed to his waist gleamed, streaming reflections onto his oak colored breeches. "Miss Jewell, I asked a simple question. Do you want to be my mistress? I think I deserve a direct answer."

She bunched up the bib collar of her gown. "No. That captain's woman stuff was your lie, a crooked bargain for my safety and to check your crew. There was no truth to it."

"I'm not talking about the past. Things like desires change. You've kissed me now, twice."

She slammed her fingers into the box, jangling silverware caught within the folds of the cloth. "You just want to rile me up." She took a breath, seeking to reclaim her composure. With everything within her, she forced her tone to be low and even. "You know what happened out there. It's best to forget about it."

He pounded closer, the edge of his shadow falling upon her. The scent of sweet starch from his shirt teased her nose. Lord Welling was near enough to grab and shake some sense into him, but what could she say to keep him from chasing danger?

His foot tapped, then stilled. "Why, Precious? You were to stay in safety aboard the Margeaux. Then you risked your life to save mine. Why?"

"Don't you have something to do?" Frustrated, she shook the tablecloth hard and a dozen forks flew out the box. "I'm not your wife. I owe you no explanations as you owe me none. Come to think of it. You never offered any to her either."

"I wasn't a good husband. I accept that and the consequences of my neglect, but until I find a way to restore peace in Port Elizabeth, this could be my final time leaving this house. It might be nice to think someone in here cares if I live or die."

Before she could stop herself, she thrust her fists hard in to the crate. The silver crashed together in a horrible jingle.

"Precious?"

"Don't you think I know you might be killed? Saying anything aloud will not change that." She started stacking the scattered forks. "Nothing I say will keep you here anyway. So go."

He knelt beside her. "What if it did? What if I gave you that power?"

Shaking her head, she tried to keep her voice from straining. "Go on. Out of here. Do what you have to do. Maybe pick some rue from those woods you are heading too. It would make good tea for Mrs. Narvel when her time comes."

"What's rue?"

"We grew it in the hothouse on the plantation. But it should be natural to a warm, place like this. It's pale green all year round with three lobed leaves. The yellow waxy flowers have a musky scent."

"That will help Mrs. Narvel?"

"Yes, it will ease her childbirth. We boil it down and that will do it."

"A decoction. How do you know this?"

Heart starting to race from saying too much, she shrugged. "Pick some for me if you see it. I'll do what I have to do here to settle this house. That's all I can do. That's all I want to do."

He tossed a fork from her palm, and then claimed her hand. "No. You can do more." He rose taking her with him. "You can send a soldier away with a memory that will make him want to return. Give me something, Precious, that will make me race back here. Something that will remind me of the reward of being careful."

Pressing her against the expanse of his chest, he flung off her mobcap and put his fingers into her chignon, his thumbs tangling within her twisted locks.

Instead of getting mad at her hair not being sleek, he used the tension to crane her neck backward "Well, it seems this lovely hair has more and more advantages."

A small throaty chuckle escaped him, as his mouth went to her forehead. "Give me a hope that will make me do everything in my power to return safely."

She shook her head, fighting the temptation to be brazen and enjoy the feel of his lips upon hers again. "Your safety is not in my power. Mrs. Narvel used to talk of that Jesus helping. Must not be in His power either, not after the massacre."

His brow twitched and lifted, but her church questions didn't seem to hold his attention. Instead he dipped closer and blew onto her lips. "It is in your power to kiss me. Maybe one, freely given. Yes, that will do."

No. Not with the crated portrait of Eliza only a couple feet away. Guilt tearing at her heart, Precious ducked her face into his shoulder.

"Shy again? Oh, Precious Jewell. I thought we'd moved beyond you being afraid of me."

She didn't fear him, just that hurt that came from wanting something you couldn't have. Listening to the timbre in his voice, she forgot about guilt and allowed her arms to wrap about his waist, the rounded pommel top of his rapier pressed into her wrist. He'd be using that sword to fight the Xhosa when he left today.

The smell of his white shirt, a blend of starch, sandalwood, and musk filled her lungs. It made her take deeper breaths of him. She needed to remember this moment if he were no more. Eyes getting wet, she hugged him more tightly. Saying with it everything she felt being near him, safety, admiration, and courage. "Be careful, stupid man."

"That's not quite the sentiment I want, but it's a good first start." His lips brushed her crown kissing down the bridge of her nose. He stopped his treacherous lips above the cupid's bow of hers. "Perhaps words aren't for us."

No, no, no. No more of that and the confusion it placed upon her heart. She dropped her hold and stepped away. "It will have to be enough. Now go on before your men start gossiping about why you are late."

With a sigh, he retreated and scooped up his jacket. "This is not done, Precious. It's just beginning. With more practice, I think you'll do fine sending me off."

"No." The low breathy tone of her voice turned her traitorous stomach. "I don't want more. I'm no mistress to Eliza's husband. No more teasing the help."

He trudged away, but stopped at the entry. "It's not done, Precious. I have a horrid habit of not letting anything go."

With a slam to the front door, he was out of the house.

She plodded over to the crate with Eliza's portrait. Prying at the boards, she finally freed one end of the top and then the other, opening the box. With great care she eased out the linen shrouded frame. Yanking at the cloth, she unwrapped the layers bandaging the beautiful portrait. She'd freed Eliza. The good woman could now cast her presence here as she did back in London.

This portrait would be enough to remind Lord Welling and herself of their places, the honorable widower and the faithful servant to Eliza Marsdale. The sooner Precious made this place to look like Firelynn, the baron's home for his baroness, the sooner things would be made right.

Precious nodded and dusted the frame with her apron. "Forgive me, Eliza. I'd never hurt your memory not after all you've done for me."

Things would be restored, and this attraction would disappear. Precious wasn't going to be a mistress. No one could make her be that. No lies, or Lord Welling's charm could push her into that.

Yet, how could she resist the urge, the craving to return to his arms?

Chapter Eleven: A Reason for Evil

Unbelievable woman. Gareth pounded out of his quarters and onto the street. Frustration shook his hands so much he struggled to button his jacket. Before popping a brass button off his favorite coat, he let the fabric go and trudged forward. He needed to get his horse from the blacksmith and put his emotions in check. This day like yesterday would be filled with complaints about the Xhosa "savages" and the horrid "killers" from his men and the frightened colonists. Everyone, from the baker to the mercantile owner had complaints and fears of being murdered in their beds.

Such talk was more dangerous than the Xhosa. It made men sloppy and rash. Yes, crazed colonists pushing him to make mistakes that chilled the marrow in his bones. His score of only being wrong three times would surely go up and this time it would be deadly, ending with his own demise.

Finding Mzwamadoda had to be the answer. He could help Gareth make things right again. The scholar warrior must know what had caused the breaking of the peace.

"Lord Welling!"

A huff left Gareth as he heard Grossling's sneaky voice. He pivoted toward the oily fellow. "Yes."

The thin man ran up to him. "Was this how you left things, Welling? Intrigue and murder?"

Gareth shook his head and forestalled his temper focusing on the wind bringing swaths of fresh bay air. "Look at the mile of new road. The colony had only started cutting it in when I left for London. See the new cottages dotting the way? Port Elizabeth could thrive if given the chance. I will work a miracle setting things in order before the next supply ship arrives."

"Have you made any sense of what went wrong?"

"No. No one can tell me what went wrong." Then it hit Gareth like a thunderbolt, stirring a new sense of loss and anger. Those who knew were dead. His friend, many of the leaders he left in place in Port Elizabeth had been killed in front of him. No more words could be had from them, but did the truth have to die to?

He blinked a few times keeping his remorse hidden in his gut. No one, especially a worm like the lieutenant, could see him mourn, see him as less than. His spirit rose inside heating the breaths he sucked in as he sped up his pace. No one breathing would ever see him like that again.

Grossling worked his short legs and kept up with Gareth. "What went wrong? They are savages. You lost good men. Where do your loyalties lie?"

A huff left Gareth. He tried to stop his blood from boiling over. "I'm furious. My friend, Narvel, was cut down leaving a wife and child-to-be unprotected. Fifteen men, in total, I had to bury. I won't even count the ones like Ralston who've been injured. I don't have the luxury to be rash or caught up in emotions. I have to focus on the mission. A steady head is the only way to prevent more bloodshed."

"Let's just get on the Margeaux and go back to England."

One. Two. Three. His uncle was a balanced man. Pity Gareth never learned those lessons of patience until it was too late to matter. He drummed his hands on the fence and forestalled saying anything to cause this man to become a bigger thorn in his side. "It's staying put for now. If you will excuse me."

Grossling shook his crooked nose at him and stormed off. Good riddance. The man was doomed to cause trouble. It was only a matter of time.

Gareth stood at the halfway point between his house and the blacksmith. Lifting his face to the tropical sun, he let his cheeks warm. This wasn't cold wet London. Port Elizabeth possessed a natural beauty that should be fought for. Between the thick forests, endless hills, and bountiful thickets graced with herbs, this colony had been blessed. It would be so again, once he reestablished the peace.

Maybe if there was more time, he'd go looking for Precious's rue. When the danger passed, perhaps he could show her the restful beauty that made this great land, the ability to walk and see the soil change from white beech to sun baked tan to the rich umber of the forest, or just to catch the waves kissing the rocks scattered along the shore. She'd like that, wouldn't she?

He curled his fingers tight against his palm. No notion of anything that she liked or wanted came to him. What was going on in that head of hers?

Stuffing his hands into his coat pockets, he started plodding again toward the blacksmith and not back to Precious. Later he'd figure out if he had misread things and why she didn't feel the attraction that flared when she stood near.

A horrible notion struck, sending a pain between his eyes. What if she had suffered his attention? What if she didn't like him at all?

He pumped his arms and paced ahead, forcing his natural vanity to rise. Precious would decide that she wanted him. He'd simply have to be patient and wait. If that stubborn girl determined she'd rather be aloof, he could live with that. Caring for someone who just tolerated your existence wasn't to be borne. He'd just have to learn how to ignore her tragic form slipping from room to room, arms saddled with bundles or the babe. Nothing for Gareth.

A dray with a few men lumbered past. "Captain!"

They looked sloppy and drunk, flopping on the back of the long platform. Probably returning from the bordello two miles away. It was midday. Those fellows should be working. What happened to the discipline of the colonists?

Gareth looked down at his own uneven buttons. Where was his discipline? Would he not still be in his house plying Precious for sentiment if she hadn't sent him on his way?

Why did it matter so much to him? They were safely in Port Elizabeth. The ruse of being the captain's woman was no longer needed. She could act as Jonas's governess or even do housekeeping as she did now without anyone bothering her. As an employee of the man sent to run the colony, none of the inhabitants would be mean to her, well that was as long as he remained alive.

Yet, what would happen if he died?

She'd have to take the boy back to London. Though Jonas was heir to his barony, why would he want it after Port Elizabeth? No, Precious might be forced to send the child to his relatives in Charleston. Funny, Old Mr. Marsdale and his nephews seemed to itch for invitations to come to London. Probably wouldn't take the boy to Port Elizabeth ever again.

He jerked at the doorknob of the blacksmith and almost wrenched his arm. What was he thinking? Precious would never separate from the boy. She'd go back to America and be vulnerable to enslavement just to care for Jonas. There were far too many traders who didn't care a whit about legal paperwork. Hadn't she'd already suffered a great deal on the Marsdale Plantation? He sensed it, but wasn't sure. Now that she was of age, and her beauty undeniable, she'd suffer more.

Huffing fire, he plodded into the blacksmith's home. The hiss of the man's flame filled the small one room place like the anger or helplessness cresting in Gareth's bones. If only he could figure out what happened to Port Elizabeth, then maybe the odds of him or anyone else dying would diminish. "Mr. Dennis, is my horse ready?"

The old blacksmith stood close to the fire pit. As always, his wintry hair was pulled back into a knotted braid and tied with a crimson ribbon. Some things never changed, like the stained leather vest the burly man wore. The tongs in his large hands twirled a glowing red horseshoe in the flames. "Just this last one to finish, Captain. I mean Lord Welling. It's going to take awhile to get used to calling you by your uncle's name. My cousin's son, Percival Theol, he couldn't ever get those things right and his father was an earl. He'll be down in a month."

"Good. Port Elizabeth needs more people. Don't worry about the formality, Dennis. I've a lot to do fill in his shoes."

The swish and spit of the horseshoe sounded as the blacksmith dipped the hot iron into a bucket of water. The noise grew loud and then quieted in the cooling liquid, kind of the way Precious bubbled about him, and then froze showing no warmth until pressed.

Yet, that last embrace she offered him felt true. In spite of all the things those pert lips might've said, she did seem to care for him and that mattered to Gareth. With his condition, he knew the draw to her wasn't physical, well not purely physical. What he wanted was below the surface, trapped with her deep cinnamon skin. How could he grab hold of her raw unbridled emotion that when released shook everything loose within his jaded soul?

"I'll have you ready for tracking in a couple more minutes. Maybe you'll restore the peace again. You and your uncle reasoned with them. It has to be done again."

Dennis, a very close advocate of Gareth's uncle, had always been a bellwether for how things fared. A good Christian man who doubled as the colony's vicar, he wasn't given to embellishment.

Yet, he didn't equate the Xhosa to savage killers. That difference made Gareth scratch his head. "I appreciate your work, Dennis." He sat on the bench next to the man's tools and the readily open bible. Gareth fingered a few pages before turning his attention back to the blacksmith. "You have any idea why the Xhosa have become violent again?"

Clutching his hammer, Dennis swung and hit the horseshoe. The gong reverberated. "Vengeance is a strange thing."

Gareth's heart raced. "You mean retribution for something? Did the colonists do something first?"

"Yes." Dennis hit the shoe a final time. "Mr. Narvel, he didn't do a good job of keeping some of our men in check."

Groaning inwardly, Gareth swiped at his brow. "What happened?"

"The old Xhosa chief. They hurt him, embarrassed him something awful."

He didn't know what to react to first so he folded his arms to hide his confusion. "The old chief is now the former chief? What happened to Chief Zifihlephi?"

"One of soldiers didn't like the chief's manners, didn't like being interrupted, so he got drunk one night and attacked the chief slicing off his ears. His ears! When Narvel didn't turn over the man to the Xhosa, the old chief was deposed by his brother for being weak. And that one has been attacking and killing colonist indiscriminately until we turn over the trader."

The Xhosa weren't dumb bushmen. They were intelligent, skillful warriors. For them, revenge could easily become war. "Dennis, we have our own laws. We can deal with the traitor. We can show the Xhosa how the English administer justice."

"They don't understand that. And our justice wasn't administered. To Mr. Narvel and others, a black life didn't matter. Narvel did nothing."

The sentiments of his old butler rang in Gareth's head. His stomach churned with venom. The years his uncle and himself had spent building trust with Xhosa was gone. "Who did it, Dennis?"

"Mr. Narvel's cousin."

That's why Narvel did nothing. He endangered the colony to protect his worthless cousin. "Let me go round him up."

Dennis shook his head as he pounded the shoe then dunked it into the bucket. "Doesn't matter. He was one of those killed two weeks ago upon your arrival."

The cousin was one of those bodies, one of those deaths Gareth tried to keep faceless. The torture of Narvel dying in his arms had been enough. A tired, bitter huff slipped from his lips. "So the lieutenant didn't punish his cousin and now all the colony suffers. When is everyone going to understand that one man's sacrifice is enough?"

"They barely accepted one man's sacrifice in Galilee on an old rugged cross. How could they ever weigh the good that can come from realizing no person was more important than the rest?"

Gareth stood up, brushed off his beach colored breeches. "I don't know how to fix this."

"Maybe you're too worried about your hands trying to work things. Maybe you need to remember the Lord. Let those carpenter's hands guide you through this. Your uncle was a man of faith. He drew his strength, his wisdom from something bigger than himself." Dennis scooped up the shoe from the water and barreled over to Gareth handing him the lump of refined iron. "I've watched you tear up these hills looking for something. There's only so much you can do before it all breaks or wears like this shoe. Go to Him to find answers."

Gripping the iron in his hand, he pivoted and slunk to

the door. "Thank you, Dennis. I'll think on it."

"Do that. You'll get your answers and this colony will survive. That will make your uncle proud."

Nodding, Gareth pushed open the door and returned to the bright sunlight. Waiting for an answer was up there with waiting for anything. It just didn't sit well in his system, but how much was he willing to personally sacrifice to make all well again?

Chapter Twelve: The Price of Caring

A noise sounded outside and a shiver crept up Precious's spine. Would this be the day the guns from the fort rage again? She stomped her foot then gripped her arms tightly. In a voice as close in tone and vigor as her grandmamma, she repeated, "Stop this, Precious. Don't go hunting for trouble or expecting the worst."

Well, too many of the worst happened when she didn't look for it. And Lord Welling surely was seeking woe.

It was bad enough lying awake until late in the night to hear his footfalls cross the threshold. Then just before she could settle into bed, the creek of the door from him leaving started her pacing all over. He must be crazy working himself so hard tracking an invisible enemy.

She must be crazy too.

Fretting about him wouldn't do. Definitely didn't change nothing either. Not liking the helpless, restless feeling pulsing down her spine, Precious turned and focused on the last crate, another one of linens.

She pivoted and glanced at the hanging portrait of

Eliza. Big sad brown eyes looked back at her. Eliza wouldn't take comfort in the nearly finished house or Precious's handiwork getting Jonas settled. No, she'd be filled with betrayal.

Guilt wrapped about Precious's heart and squeezed so tightly that she felt light headed. How could she have allowed herself to come to care so much for Lord Welling?

She concentrated upon the swirls of oil paint, the gilded frame with a nick in the corner, a mark caused from the long journey. Precious had been marked by the Margeaux too, for now she couldn't shake thinking about the baron. "Sorry, Eliza."

The words left her lips and more shame poured in. "This has to be Lord Welling's fault."

A noise vibrated the window glass. Pivoting like a spinning top, she wobbled toward the bay's large panes and cupped her palm to her face. What was going on out there? Was it time to scoop up Jonas and run to the blockhouse of the fort?

A few of the men, who hadn't gone off with Lord Welling, converged onto the main street. Some with guns or hatchets. A few others ran toward Frederick's gates.

She looked away with a heart pounding like it'd bounce from her chest. Could she get Jonas from his nap and scoot to safety in enough time?

No, that'd be stupid. Running those hundred paces out in the open with a baby in her arms, well that had to be suicide. And what about Clara? Precious couldn't leave her friend. The poor woman hadn't yet come out of the guest bedchamber.

Grief had taken its toll on her friend leaving droopy cheeks and a pallid complexion. Soon it would harm the baby Narvel nurtured inside. If the woman didn't start living again, she'd never survive childbirth. She'd end up like Eliza.

Oh, Eliza. Precious peered at the portrait. That old painting, with her downcast eyes, burrowed into Precious's skull. "I said I am sorry."

Why didn't saying the words mean forgiveness? She definitely didn't feel excused. This miserable way of being was nothing like Clara described in her Bible reading. But the peace the woman described, the one that was supposed to pass all understanding did nothing for the new widow either. A tear slipped and splashed onto Precious's palm. If that book with the fancy gilded pages held no power. Then what would?

Listless with feet so mired in condemnation they seemed weighed to the floor, Precious stopped trying to move away, so she rotated and parted the curtains and stared ahead.

Another sigh pumped out when she finally saw the men nodding, lowering weapons. The street quieted when they disappeared. A false warning. She strained her eyesight, scanning the hills, the wild South African landscape but saw nothing leaving the emerald trees or brownish green thickets. No Xhosa, No Lord Welling.

All was well, right now on this clear sunless day.

She could almost imagine the easier breaths steaming out of the soldiers. Must be different for them, not knowing when terror was coming. Well, in Port Elizabeth there was equality in fearing death. Everyone possessed a little of it, not just the blacks.

Finally, those legs of hers became unglued. She pushed away from the leaden glass and plodded to fireplace. No good came from being jumpy or thinking about the worst. Lord Welling was a smart man. He'd stay safe and return here again.

So why did she continue to fret? Guilt? All he wanted was for her to admit to liking him, and she'd called him stupid.

Forget what can't be undone, Precious. Grandmamma's wisdom never failed.

Eliza of all people could understand a mistake. And Clara Narvel would mend and Precious would help with another babe. A smile lifted her lips, the joy of caring for a newborn dancing in her heart. The sweet cooing that a growing Jonas no longer offered would soon come again. She tapped her heart and wiped at a misty eye. Imagine, for someone not able to bare a child to end up helping to rear two. That was something.

As she bent to get started on the last crate, a stumbling knock came from the hall. She whipped her head toward it. Her pulse drummed matching the thump of the dragging footsteps. *Please, let Lord Welling be fine.*

Yet, the noise didn't sound like his boots. A stranger had come into the house.

Heart racing, she glanced at the heavy shears on the desk. They were too far, so she grabbed a poker. "Show yourself!"

Almost crawling, the war department man dragged to the entrance. Mr. Grossling held his left hand bandaged up in rags. "Where's Welling?"

Staring at the crimson drops collecting and brightening the cloth, the smears on his jacket, her mouth dropped open. "You've been fussin' with those Xhosa?"

He slumped at the threshold. "No! An accident." He whipped his chin violently and grabbed the doorframe.

"Where's Welling? Haven't seen a doctor about and the captain's the only one with any medical knowledge. I need his help."

Dropping the poker with a thud, Precious trudged over to the worm. Wounded, this man couldn't hurt her. "Need help. That's a lot out of your mouth. You must be pretty bad off."

He made it five steps inside before slipping to the floor. "You do what you have to, to survive. I think you know that."

Yes, did she ever. But she wouldn't let him know that. Instead, she tugged at her emerald sleeve. "You want my help or you want to wait?"

His dull blues seemed to sweep across her and maybe her black hands. "Yes. Help me please."

Other than a little name calling, Mr. Grossling hadn't been mean. And letting him die on the baron's floor couldn't be good. Shaking off her reluctance, she plodded closer and poked at the rags. Old Dr. Marsdale would stop the bleeding first. "I know what to do."

She popped up, ran and grabbed one of the sheets from the crate, then shot to the desk for the sharp scissors. The decanter of unopened brandy caught her gaze. She scooped it up too and then moved back to the man who seemed to have grown paler.

His dull eyes widened as she knelt. Fear looked so different on a man. Unnatural. "What are you going to do?"

"Hold still, you big baby." She put a fist to her hip. "Again, if you'd rather wait for Lord Welling to patch you up, I've got linens to put away."

He closed his eyes for a moment then pushed his injured arm toward her.

She undid the damp rag. A cut, thin and precise, ran along the juncture of his wrist. That didn't look like an accident, but something intentional. A drop of compassion eked out of her thawing veins. Fear just didn't look right on a man. Maybe it made them do stupid things, like staying out to all hours of the night hunting villains.

Sacrificing the fine lawn cloth, she sliced a strip and tied a tight knot about his forearm. "That will keep you from bleeding out whilst I flush the wound."

The tension in his face eased. "I was sharpening my knife, and it slipped. None of your friends did this to me, Wowski."

Friends? Her gut fumed. Precious knew it wouldn't be long before someone said something like that, tie her to the blacks that caused the massacre. She spread his palm in a jerking manner, causing a howl to fall out of his condescending lips. "Maybe I should call 'em to come get you and finish you off."

Popping the cork of the decanter, she poured the brandy onto his wound and smiled wider and wider as he pressed his lips to stop from howling. "Good, I've patched you up enough for someone else, someone with lighter hands to finish the rest. Lord Welling will be back in a few more hours."

"No!" His voice rose high almost like Clara's. "Please, I was joking."

"I don't much care for it. You can think one black is like all blacks, and all are chattel. Or you can think different. If you don't want to be left to see if someone else will help, you'll address me with respect from now on. You hear me."

Nodding, he said, "Yes, ma'am."

Ripping more of the cloth into ribbons, mimicking how Dr. Marsdale, Eliza's uncle, had showed her, Precious made bandages. One more time she lifted the decanter to pour more brandy on the cut. The candied bonbon smell of the amber liquid had tamped down the horrid iron smell of his wound. "You ready for the final sting? Hate to patch you up to have to have Lord Welling cut off the gangrene hand in a week or so."

"Just do it. I don't like the small talk."

Again, she poured the fire liquid liberally, until a clear pinkish brown puddle gathered below his open palm on the mahogany floor.

The man whimpered and closed his eyes tight.

Pushing at the cut, she overlapped the hurt skin. Then began binding it tightly with linen. Almost weaving the strips of linen betwixt his fingers, she bound his hand securely all the way to his curling his palm. Wrapping it with a final wide strip made the bandaged hand almost resemble Lord Welling's the night he cut his palm on the broken glass. That was the start of it all, the teasing, the kissing.

That was when the baron first noticed her, first rescued her, first pulled her into his arms.

The image of him waving his rapier, protecting her from the horrible lecher, it was almost as powerful of a memory as him scooping her out of the ocean, or awakening within his embrace when he fixed his shoulder.

Mr. Grossling rotated his arm, and then clasped her hand with his uninjured one. "I'm grateful, Miss Jewel."

"Miss Jewel?"

A shiver rippled up her spine at the deep masculine voice that sounded behind her.

Lord Welling's footfalls stopped behind her, his shadow engulfing her. "What happened here?"

"The war department man had an accident. He needed patching up."

Mr. Grossling's nodded. "Yes, Wo-Miss Jewel has been most helpful. You're not thinking she did this to me?"

A grunt, or was it a curse, left the baron. "She's the last person I'd suspect of treachery." He stooped down and pushed at her knots. Then dipped his finger into the spilt brandy. "You had to use the good stuff, Miss Jewell?"

"Was all I could find. The man didn't give much notice."

"Well, her knots are very nice." Lord Welling undid the cloth wrap she'd used to slow the pumping of blood in the man's limb. "Looks like you will live."

The baron pulled him to his feet. "You're lucky to have stumbled upon *my* Miss Jewel. Let me take you to your cottage."

Her heart sunk. The respect she thought she'd earned from Mr. Grossling would be stripped away with the baron's possessive address. She pushed up her mobcap and started sopping up the ruined brandy with the remaining pieces of linen.

The injured fellow put his good hand on the frame, stopping them from leaving. "Miss Jewel, thank you for your kindness, ma'am."

She caught his gaze and smiled. Watching them leave twisted her inners. A snake now respected her and the man who made her pulse race didn't. How would she ever not be chattel, a lowly possession, to Lord Welling?

Chapter Thirteen: The Lies We Feed Upon

Gareth held Grossling up with one hand and pushed into his cottage, five doors down the road. He took his obligation of protecting the colonists seriously, even the ones he didn't like. "How did you injure yourself?"

"It was an accident, sharpening a blade."

They lumbered inside and Gareth dropped the man onto a chair. Unlike his residence, Grossling's was a small two-room closet of a house with barely enough room to change one's mind. "I'll check on these bandages over the next few days."

"I suppose with this injury. I'll be no use in this place. Maybe you should rethink sending your ship back to England. That pregnant woman, Mrs. Narvel, and the other wounded should be sent back too."

"The wounded include Mr. Ralston so there is no one I trust to navigate the Margeaux. All have to recover here. And it seems Mrs. Narvel is further along than I thought. She'll have to stay and have the baby here."

"You can call it quits. No one would fault you. Many

192

thought your uncle was daft to try to colonize Port Elizabeth in the first place."

"I've told you. Port Elizabeth is a Welling calling. Others don't have the stomach for it. I will find a way to fix what has gone wrong. Apparently, we, one of our king's men, one man's drunken stupidity caused this. So one man can fix it."

"Good luck with that." Grossling leaned back against the woven bands of the back of the chair. "Well, I know you're not ready to go back with two women in your household, one a mistress, the other, wife potential. You must be very good at negotiations. Maybe this additional practice can add to your legendary peace making skills." A sharp laugh sprayed from his mouth. "If you can deal with so many women, dealing with the Xhosa should be easy."

"Mrs. Narvel is a grieving widow. And definitely not going to marry the man who virtually sentenced her husband to death by his duty here." Gareth folded his arms. "She's in no mood for marriage."

"A woman unprotected with a mouth to feed. She'll need to wed. Kind of fitting, two widowers, but what will that do for the interesting Miss Jewell."

So the man was after Precious. Gareth felt his fingers tighten and drew his arms behind his back. "I thought she was not worthy of your concern?"

"Any woman, who'll jump in front of a spear or bandage up a man who's been injurious…that's one to be concerned with no matter how dark she is. I can see why you jumped into the ocean after her."

"Leave her and Mrs. Narvel alone."

He trudged to the door, but pivoted and lifted his forearm. "And the next time you want out of here, aim your play knife about an inch higher right on that vein. Then you won't make it to my door to bother anyone."

The man chuckled. "Wouldn't think of leaving now. I think I found something to hold my interest."

Gareth trudged outside and slammed the door. Well his suspensions about Grossling were confirmed. The coward was trying to leave Port Elizabeth, but to risk bloodletting? The man was a fool or conniving coward. Either case meant keeping an eye out for the troubles he'd bring.

Yet, the man now sniffed at Precious. She wasn't the sort of woman to be easily taken in, but that heart of hers seemed awfully soft. How else could she love Jonas so well or even risk her life to save Gareth?

As he approached his door, he swiped at his hair returning some order to it. He was still mostly male; the war hadn't taken it all. He couldn't stand men hovering about Eliza and he definitely didn't want any one around Precious.

He stepped into the house and spied her on her knees scrubbing the floor. She was neat, her uniform freshly pressed with a crisp apron. How could she be the picture of order in this world of chaos? For a moment, he allowed the longing in his soul to win and imagined her in his arm, desiring his attention.

Mopping at his skull, he let his will return. She was a governess to Jonas and perhaps a confidant, nothing more. If he could keep reciting this lie to himself, maybe the heat in his blood when he saw Precious would diminish. Staying away from her these past two days had done nothing to cool it.

Feeling foolish, he pounded into the study. She rang out her rag and stretched to wipe a final spot. Her bewitching backside was toward him, and all he could do was fold his arms about himself to restrain from scooping her into his arms. Oh foolish lies.

He leaned against the door, and took in how well Precious had made the place look. Organized books, dusted shelves. A few vases on the mantle under Eliza's picture. Eliza? "When did you hang the portrait?"

Precious didn't look at him. Perhaps the notches in the oak floor were more interesting. "It was time to put things in order. Everything is now back to the way it was in London, sir."

The poorly masked hint of anger in her voice made him squint. What was bothering her? He stepped inside. "Everything back to the ways of London? Then why did you waste the good brandy?"

She looked up at him with those wonderful brown eyes, ones that held bits of fire and flecks of gold. The same, but different than Eliza's. "Well, you hadn't started drinking again. I suppose we have to make a full change to make things right. "

"I amended my no drinking rules to extend beyond God's sea to dry land when he set down a plague upon us."

She nodded, her frown growing. "So the X… Xhosa is a plague?"

The icy sadness in her voice stung. What had happened? He hadn't teased her about the kiss or her liking him, yet. He plodded to the sofa and sat. "No. They are a proud people. To be sure they don't want us here. But one of the colonists did something and drove them to do this. I need to find a way to restore the peace."

"Don't you want justice? For Mr. Narvel and the

others. You may act indifferent but I watched you caring for the wounded, praying for those you couldn't heal. You're not always about duty."

He closed his eyes and let her simple statement sink into his skull. No, he wasn't all about duty. The nightmare of the ambush haunted the little sleep he allowed himself.

For in those moments, he remembered the gleam of the assegai's knife blade catching his eye before striking Narvel through his back, clean through to his chest. The thud of dying men crashing to the ground betwixt the rhythm of pounding horses' hooves.

Gareth tensed as the strangled whispers of his friend's last breath reverberated in his mind. Why hadn't he figured out it was an ambush? Why didn't he take seriously Precious's siting in the trees? Could he have done something more to save his friend, his lost sailors? "I'm angry. My spirit is grumbling. I'd love nothing more than to stake the hearts of the men who killed my friend, my innocent crew."

His fisted palm became enveloped in warmth. Precious had covered it with her long thin fingers. Calloused in some places, smooth and silky in others, her hand, like the rest of her wasn't genteel but honest and strong, strong in ways that let him know that showing a moment of weakness would not dampen her admiration.

"This has to be my fault. Maybe Narvel awaited my arrival before setting judgment on his cousin, the man who offended the Xhosa. Or maybe he thought Xhosa would forget. Whatever the case, Narvel and the rest did not deserve to die in the dark, not seeing his enemy, with no offered chance at defense."

Anger rising at the senseless loss, Gareth blinked and

stared into Precious's warm eyes. "I don't like losing. I hate losing those in my charge. Yet, a leader can't dwell on his own gut. The greater good means you have to stomach the unimaginable. I know you understand, Precious. Firelynn's no prison. You could've run away just like you did that stormy night in London when you asked for your freedom. You stayed and suffered under Palmers' hatred to be near Jonas, your greater good."

As if it dawned on her that she held his hand, she released the boldness of her touch, grabbed at her rag and began scrubbing again. "So what did Mr. Narvel's cousin do?"

"He got drunk and desecrated the Chief of the Xhosa tribe with a knife."

Precious's eyes grew large like saucers. "What did he do with the knife?"

"I'm told he thought the man wouldn't listen and sliced off his ears."

Her lip quivered, before she lowered her gaze to the floor. "No wonder they want us dead."

"The Xhosa out number *us* by tens. If they wanted, they could've wiped the colony. These killings are a retribution, but this will lead to all out war."

Precious's head lifted, her mouth drawn into a questioning circle. "You mean more killing?"

He rubbed at his skull. "Not if we can get back to peace. That's the only way for the colony to survive."

"So there's an explanation." She nodded as if his words had started to penetrate that mobcap. "You don't think them savages?"

There was more to her question than just the Xhosa. It had to be that question of race and equality, the one he hadn't quite decided upon whilst in London. Seeing

197

the Xhosa be as cruel and cunning as his soldiers and witnessing Precious's mercy and care to all around her, Gareth knew the answer. He shuffled his boots while staring at her kneeling. She should see his face as spoke his truth. "Precious?"

She pivoted a little with those magnificent eyes set on him.

"They are not English to be sure. But different isn't savage. It's just different."

She turned back to her bucket of sudsy water. Her posture was stiff. "Your butler, he wouldn't think that. He thinks we are all savages."

His words hadn't been good enough. He needed to confess more for her and himself. "I don't think that, Precious. You should know that by now. Forget about Palmers. He's not here to torment you."

She nodded and sunk her hands into the water. "He was part of London. He and Miss Eliza, they were all part of how things were."

But Gareth wasn't trying to think of how things were. Things weren't good at Firelynn. He stood, trudged closer and then knelt beside her.

Perhaps taking a servant's posture would show her. He took her hands out of the bucket and dried them with his handkerchief. He worked at the moisture taking his time, massaging and tracing the lines of her palm. "Good work on patching up Grossling. I could not have done better. Where did you learn what to do?"

She withdrew her palm and wiped her apron as if his touch along her palm was offensive. No, the fire in her eyes told the whole story. In spite of her cool exterior, he affected her.

"Precious, it's been two days since we last talked."

She popped to her feet. "I learned a little caring for the sick in Charleston. I used to go with Dr. Marsdale on his doctoring rounds. He let me help with bandages."

That wasn't what he wanted to discuss, but the stunned look on her face like she'd given away a secret was too great to be ignored. "I didn't know Eliza's father knew medicine?"

"Not that Mr. Marsdale. His brother."

"Brother?" Gareth swept her up by the elbows and hauled her below Eliza's portrait. With both hands he framed her caramel face. There were similarities of their features, but the strength of her gaze, the fire in her eyes, all different. "You're Eliza's cousin, not her sister. That is true isn't it?"

She pushed free and snatched up the bib of her smock. "We're never to talk of it. Never."

"We ought to talk of it. In England, you'd be considered my sister if you were Eliza's sister. But a cousin is another matter. Flirtation with a cousin is lawful."

"What nonsense." She shifted and moved from the fireplace. "You are my employer. I work for you. There's nothing else."

"You know I say that very thing to myself until I come within a foot of you. Then I chuckle at the lies I tell. There is something between us just like on our Margeaux."

"People do stupid things on boats."

"And risk all when there is an attack. You saved my life, Precious. Then I kissed you. And you kissed me back and we've said nothing. "

She eyed the door as if she thought about making a run for it. "So the fact that I'm Eliza's cousin, the product of an enslaved liaison and a master, that's loosened your tongue?"

He paced ahead of her to block her path if she headed for the door. They both needed to finish this conversation. "When you came to England, you were her skinny maid, but it was obvious you were Eliza's confidant. So I gave the word to indulge you as it made Eliza happy. That is why she let you wear colorful uniforms not boring dove gray. Had I known you were family, I might have seen to your comfort."

"What would you have done? You barely had time for Eliza."

"Family is important."

"Don't start with that now. You didn't have time for Eliza. You have no time for your son, but I am to believe you would have been my champion in London. No, you always had something to do. With your drunken mourning, no one can compare to your love for Eliza. No one." She covered her mouth for a moment. Then she rubbed her eyes. "You know it's true."

He itched at his neck, trying to think of a better way to explain, but all he had was the awful truth. "I mourn heavily when I go to London. I couldn't make Eliza happy. My talk of duty, of Port Elizabeth, made her ill and I accept that my absence made her stray. I don't blame her, but it is much easier to forgive her adultery steeped in brandy. So yes, I mourn heavily my failings."

Precious squinted at him. Her generous lips flattened to a line. Was she shocked that he knew of the adultery or that Gareth had forgiven it?

The poor girl looked frozen. She truly must not have known. The lass would faint if she knew of how his inadequacy drove Eliza to sin. How could he not forgive

Eliza's need to be loved when he failed so miserably at it?

Hurrah. He'd been given a final retribution of the cannon fire that left him impotent. Now Gareth was honor bound to raise another man's son as his own.

The dear boy, innocent of his parent's horrid dealings, began to cry. His moans vibrated the rafter beams above.

Precious's gaze lifted from the floor and sped toward the ceiling. Her pert mouth remained shut as she dragged toward the door. "We can't talk of anything now. I need to get to him. He's had nothing but bad dreams since coming to Port Elizabeth."

"We are not done, Precious. We need an understanding."

"My duty is to him and poor Mrs. Narvel. They come first." She turned her back and swiveled to leave. "You understand duty, don't you, Baron?"

With her parting shot fired, Precious left.

Gareth was left to the parlor with a half empty box of linens, Eliza's sad portrait, and a nearly empty brandy decanter. He plodded over, picked up the bottle and wet his tongue. "To you, Eliza. I wasn't able to make you happy, but maybe I've learned a bit more to keep *your* son and cousin entertained."

He turned to bottle up to catch a final drop. When would the lies he fed himself ever taste this sweet?

Chapter Fourteen: Broken Homes

Precious did her best not to run from the room. Scooting up the stairs, she popped into Jonas's now quiet bedchamber. The boy had fallen back to sleep. She listened to the lull of his sweet shorts breaths and let her tears flow. Sliding down the door, she balled into the corner. No one was ever supposed to know that Marsdale blood coursed inside her skin. No one.

When Lord Welling named her as Eliza's cousin, her ears went numb. The memories of being in that shed returned. The knife, the cutting, the torment returned. And he'd said that men here in Port Elizabeth also cut people's flesh 'cause they wouldn't listen.

The air got stuck in her lungs. She hit at her chest to push air inside. She couldn't breathe fast enough. Faint, she lay there waiting for the world to stop spinning.

Having Marsdale blood had been the reason she'd been attacked. The reason the evil fiend dragged her into those woods, locked her in a shed, and hurt so bad she wished for death.

Shaking, she stared at the light filtering beneath the door. The darkness of the nursery, the sparkles of light, it all reminded her of before, the nightmare she'd been running from. Before her eyes, she was tied in that shed again, waiting for the evil to come at her. Lying on the cool autumn mud she'd counted the holes in which light sneaked through the roof. She kept waiting for things to end watching day fade into night.

He said he'd hurt her again if she told, but she had to tell someone she was bleeding so bad. Only Eliza could help. Only Eliza did.

"I didn't tell anybody else." The whisper fell from her trembling lips as forgotten tears returned. How could she ever think she could outrun the evil?

Anger rose up in her. She'd been free of the memories for almost two years. "Evil, I didn't tell."

Precious swiped at her eyes as she hushed the moans of her weeping. The last thing that she wanted was for Lord Welling to hear and ask more questions. Why did he have to be so smart?

She wiped her face on her sleeve and took a deep breath. The man in Charleston was responsible, not the one downstairs.

And what happened to her was many yesterdays past. He was too far away to hurt her again. And she was older and stronger. She had to be better able to protect herself, and maybe those Xhosa would get rid of all those men who humbled people with knifes.

All those years ago, Precious lived because of Eliza. Eliza protected her from anyone touching her again. Eliza saved her by taking her to England.

Precious stood up and eased her way to the tiny crib. "I won't dishonor your mother, no matter what I think of your father, Jonas." No matter how much she needed him to hold her and keep her fear of the past at bay.

Precious avoided the parlor and Lord Welling for the rest of the evening. He must've agreed to this silent bargain too for he took his meal of roast guinea fowl in the parlor with the door closed.

She leaned against it, rubbing a panel and trim beneath her fingers. Wasn't too much noise coming from inside. Had he left again? Was he hunting the Xhosa?

The man had slept very little in the past few days. He looked tired on that sofa.

A sigh left Precious. He needed to rest and focus his smarts on everything outside this house.

She started to moved but couldn't. Was he back to his drinking? That would mean things were truly back to normal. Why didn't that make her feel better?

Her fingers curled and she almost knocked on the door, but Precious let her hand fall. There was nothing to say to make things better. Nothing.

Returning to the cook room, she put Jonas's bowl in the tub of water. The manservant who attended Lord Welling would be here soon to clean. Maybe she could get Clara to eat and gather her dishes here too before the lad's arrival. Wiping her hands on her apron, she slipped past the parlor and dashed up to the second floor.

She passed Jonas's room. Silent, the boy could hardly keep his eyes open at end of his meal. A few more steps to the right took her to Clara's chamber.

Knocking on the widow's door produced no response.

Precious felt some kind of way about all these closed doors and quiet occupants, but unlike Lord Welling, Clara and Jonas needed her. Her brokenness didn't matter to either of them.

With a sad sigh, Precious pressed inside. Clara lay prostrate on the bed, her Bible closed beside her. Her barely touched bowl of stew sat nearby on the threadbare rug on the floor.

"Mrs. Narvel, Clara, you need to eat."

The woman shook her head. "I'm just not hungry, Precious. I'm fine."

"If this is what fine looked like, I'm fit enough to run from the top of the grassy mountain or down to the thickets and get some rue and be back, 'fore I'm missed. I'm not that fast, Clara. Tell me how to help you."

The woman sat up, the biggest frown sucked in her lips. "Can you turn back time?"

"What?"

She tugged on a drooping lock of red hair. Most of her curls had fallen away. "I want to go back in time, to when I first learned I was with child. I should've wrote him. My husband should've known."

"You wanted to surprise him. I'm sure he'd a liked it better that way. Some men are useless during your time." Lord Welling was useless to Eliza.

"Have you ever given birth?"

Precious shrank back. The horror of birthing her attacker's babe would'a killed her, and surely he had fixed it so that no one else's babe could grow. "Never." The word came out harsh and bitter. She softened her tone. "I just meant from watching others, that's all."

"Oh. My husband wasn't useless. He'd always been so kind and gentle. It would have given him such pleasure to know."

"Well, the men folk, they either hover and think you'll explode or pretend that nothing has changed, like that swelling in your fingers or feet deserves no special attention. That made Miss Eliza feel some kind away about her husband." Precious drew a hand to her mouth. She probably shouldn't say so much about Eliza's stormy feelings about the baron, but how else could she encourage Clara?

"I don't know what he'd have been like but I think a few months of planning for a future, that has to better than a few seconds. If I'd written to him at least he might have written back suggesting a name. I don't know his heart on the matter."

Precious swiveled in the small room with walls painted a peaceful dull tint the color of old bones. "When, I lost my grandmamma, I was alone. I made a rush decision to depend upon someone whom I thought liked and cared for me. I've never been so hurt or disappointed."

Clara rubbed her large tummy. "I am sorry. You don't deserve—"

"I'm not asking for sympathy. I want to show you, you are not alone. You have friends to support you. And we'll help this baby know of the love you had for his father."

Tears leaked from Clara's eyes, sliding down her pale skin. "But that doesn't change anything. He's gone."

"It doesn't change the past. The past is written in your heart, sometimes pierced into the skin. Nothing changes that. But that doesn't mean tomorrow is doomed. A big boat came and took me from my misery. After the baby comes, Lord Welling can send you on a big boat away from here."

Her friend's head shook wildly. "No. He's here. I have to stay. Nothing in England is for me. There's no balm for my soul, nothing that wipes away the loss."

She reached for Clara and wiped the tears streaming

down her cheeks. "Bare the loss. That Jesus you read to me healed by the stripes to his body. Your baby can't survive if you give in to the stripes, those wounds 'pon your heart. You're stuck with them stripes. You can't wish them away. So let them make you stronger."

Clara shrugged and pulled her shawl around her as if she were cold in the warm room. "Strong for how long? 'Till I think of him?"

"Strength won't light like a candle and just burn. It comes and goes. Yours will be back."

The lady slouched. Her head flopping onto her pillow. "I don't know what to do. Maybe you were right to question. How could the God I loved allow my baby to grow up without a father?"

No. No. No. Somebody had to believe in something more, something bigger than themselves. Precious put her hand to her mouth to keep it from falling open and saying the wrong thing.

Clara must've seen her horrified face. The woman hit at the mattress. "Just forget what I said. I surely must not know what I'm talking about."

A pain so sharp and deep pierced Precious's heart. Her friend was at the edge of a cliff looking at a valley of sadness. The woman was ready to jump.

If only Precious had that rue, a few sips of the herb's tea could ease some of it. Yet, Precious knew in her soul, she should say more. "That kind of emptiness once gripped me and had me think all kind of bad thoughts. But Miss Eliza, she saw me hurting. She got to me. She took me away from the bad places."

Clara looked up. "You think I should go back to England?"

She decided to show Clara some light, like Eliza had

207

done for Precious. "No. I might've left Charleston and those that hurt me, but I brought the bad memories with me."

She came forward, knelt close to the bed, took up Clara's hand and put them on her temples. "You see I keep them with me in here. Every cuss, every backhand, every...." Precious swallowed. "The memories will be with you, here or England."

"Then, where do I go to not feel this low? I can't stop the ache."

"You don't stop it and you don't give into it. You can't let the evil take away the joy I've seen in you. The joy that you will share with that babe of yours."

Her friend slid a handkerchief out of the folds of the bed sheets and mopped at her face.

"Clara, don't give up your light for nothing."

Precious picked up the dog eared Bible and flipped to the section that had pressed upon her every time her friend read it. Some words Precious could read, others like b-e-g-e-t-t-i-n-g, well that was anyone's guess. This page was so worn. It had to be it.

As if that God, which Precious had discounted and truthfully still burned in anger at, seemed to have decided to help. He let her fingers fall onto the creased page with the spot she wanted. "Be careful for nothing; but in every thing by prayer." She skipped some harder words and came to the refrain that now felt more true and needed to be shouted in every room of the house. "And the peace of God, which passeth all under... standing shall keep your hearts and minds through Jesus."

Clara's woe filled eyes locked onto Precious. "Peace of God?"

"I don't quite know what that means either, but I think it's that stuff both of us need to find."

A smile crept slowly onto Clara's face, maybe the first one since that last day on the Margeaux. "You remind me of peace." She put Precious's hand on her belly. "I'm going to need that to bring this one in the world and to tell him about his father."

"That baby is going to like that. Now let's tidy you up a bit."

Clara sat up allowing Precious to sit and put her head into Precious's lap.

Precious reached for a silver brush from the small table. Parting and smoothing, she worked it through Clara's hair. They all were going to need to focus on peace living in Port Elizabeth, when the next day wasn't promised.

Precious took another deep sigh. Tomorrow, she'd gather up all she could and then figure out a way to tell Lord Welling nothing more can be between them. That sacrifice would restore her peace. Surely that would make everything right again.

Tracking by foot was horrid but the best way for Gareth and his scouts to find the Xhosa encampment. They were smart, blending into trees. Probably watching them.

Scanning branches of Rooiranksaliehout, the red climbing sage, he thought he caught sight of a person hiding among the bell shaped leaves, but nothing was there. In another month, the sage would bloom with creamy orange throated flowers. That sweetish, sickly smell would make his fogged head worse. Drinking dregs always gave the worst headache and oh how his temples throbbed.

"Captain." Ralston cleared his throat. "Do we need to be out here today?"

Oh, he must look horrid for his first mate to say that. Gareth blinked and focused on a Pambatieboom, an evergreen tree with grey bark that shed its wood in fine strips. If he had a cravat, he'd have shed that in the warming air. "We need to find Mzwamadoda."

Ralston looked down at the ground and kicked a rock. "I know that, but I was thinking that after so many days, maybe we could take a rest."

Squinting, Gareth sized up Ralston. He wasn't given to laziness and his blue eyes looked clear, unlike Gareth's. "Are you feeling poorly? You look healthy. That arm hurting again?"

He shook his head. His thin trim mustache curled against his frown. "It just seems a waste of a lot of time for nothing. And I hate leaving the colony vulnerable. I don't see Mr. Grossling doing too much to protect it while we're gone."

Gareth pushed at his hair and thought of a kind way to correct the notion, but there wasn't one. Grossling would sell out the world for his own hide. Turning to the three other brave men who'd join Ralston in the hunt, Gareth cleared his throat. "Gentlemen, look for tracks, subtle signs of life. We need a trail to lead us to their encampment. You see anything, don't engage. Come back and get me. Oh and watch out for snakes. The Rinkals are spitting snakes. Those brown creatures with cream banding can get you dead in the face from two meters. If you get hit, we'll have to get you back to camp before the venom takes hold. So be careful."

His company nodded and started easing into the

brush as if they wore dancing leathers. Well, it was better to have them scared and careful than careless.

Gareth clasped Ralston's arm pulling him over to the side. "Ralston, the Xhosa are playing with us and hoping we are lulled into a placid state. Then they'll show up and cut down the rest of us. But if I find our man and prove that the guilty person, the one who attacked their chief is dead, then peace will have a chance."

The puzzled look on Ralston's face drooped into a frown. "I was just thinking about leaving camp so much."

Adjusting his rapier to hide his own frustration of the situation, Gareth softened his tone. "I know you. You're not afraid to be out here. What don't I know?"

"How is Narvel's widow?"

Odd question from Ralston. "Enduring as best as one can." Gareth felt his forehead wrinkle. "Why do you ask?"

"I heard her crying the night you told her. And that Miss Jewell, she comforted her. They've been on my mind."

"They?" Gareth loosened his hold on the handle of his rapier. "Explain."

"With Mrs. Narvel's time near, she might need help. Only you know medicine. Well, the Blackamoor does a little too, but that might not be enough."

"Her name is Jewell, Ralston."

"I didn't mean no disrespect. They just been on my mind. You remember Widow Scotts? Well, she came under more hard times when we left. She's working at that brothel. Done moved herself and her child to that wild place two miles away."

The news shocked Gareth to the core. If he was given to nausea, this would do it. A respectable widow wasn't taken care of and forced to take up a lifestyle that made a person become used up and discarded. Under Gareth's watch, via Narvel's poor leadership this had occurred. "I hadn't known."

Ralston tugged on his sloppy shirt. "I won't let that happen to Mrs. Narvel."

Gareth almost laughed but he'd never seen the fellow so serious. "What are you going to do about it? Marry her?"

"I was thinking you might."

Now that stomach Gareth questioned constricted. He whirled around as if he heard something in bushes. "Let's get back to work and put away these foolish notions."

His first mate paddled past him, cutting at vines that where too low to pass under. "Captain, a widow with a baby on the way. She's going to need protecting. And the Blackamoor, she'll need protecting too."

"What? How so?" Gareth stopped and swallowed, he might have even counted to five to forestall his temper. "I thought you said Miss Jewell wasn't pretty to you."

"No. I said she'd get prettier the longer the voyage. And with that soft spot I've seen her show to even fools like me, she done become a whole lot prettier."

Gareth's lip wanted to tug into a smile, but his discipline won out. Instead, he launched in front of Ralston. "Let them both alone. This isn't the time or place." He started to pivot to resume searching, but Ralston dropped a hand onto his shoulder.

"With all do respect, Captain, the way you keep going after the Xhosa, I or any other won't need permission from the dead."

"I don't intend to be dead. And I've been encouraged

to return in one piece." Well, that was only partially true. After figuring out Precious was Eliza's cousin, the intrepid governess had virtually disappeared from him.

Ralston pointed the blade to his ground. "But, don't you see? If you marry Mrs. Narvel everything will work out well."

"Even if I were inclined, the woman is grieving."

"It's not for you. I'm assuming your Miss Jewel is still taking care of you, but Mrs. Narvel is alone and about to have a babe. She needs to be protected since this mission got her husband killed."

Perhaps he should tell Ralston that Narvel's neglectful leadership, the same oversight that made a poor woman feel as if she had no choice but to sell her body, had led to the Xhosa aggression. No. He'd share no guilt with the dead. "Mrs. Narvel will have the widows' pension. I will see to that."

Ralston leaned on the handle of his blade. The man could fall forward and be dumped on the rich dark soil. "Look that's not enough to settle things. And what will happen if you go the ways of Narvel?"

"What, you think it's a death wish to try to reason with the Africans?"

"Yes, but you know I'll back you till the end." He lifted his knife in a swift motion and lunged it over Gareth's head.

The swooshing sound of the rotating blade deafened. The thud of it hitting a limb behind them also made the world silent and still. "Got 'em."

Gareth pivoted to see a viper chopped in two on the olive soil.

His man moved ahead and forked the ebony and yellowish body. "This wasn't one of your Rinkals, just a good old fashion Cape Cobra. It don't spit. It bites and stops your breathing."

Gareth stuffed his vibrating hand into the pocket of his coat. "Thanks, Ralston."

"Sure, Captain, but if you can't get back, there will be two unprotected women. Your Blackamoor will not do well without your presence, and I've seen how Miss Jewell and Mrs. Narvel get along. Your wife would have the influence and the respect to keep your Jewell safe in your house. And that boy of yours will have a family."

"You've been thinking about this a lot."

"Yes. If I die, I'm gone. Nothing but a headstone if I'm lucky. You got a boy and from what I count two good women that need you."

"So Jewel is good to you now?"

Ralston wiped his forehead on his sleeve, then readied his knife again as they started plodding in a new direction. "She saved your life. Yes, she's good to me. Just think about it. Think harder as we keep in these woods tracking things that can kill us."

He would think about it, because that feeling that death was laughing at him, waiting for a misstep had started again. Yes, it was too near, falling heavier upon him all the time. And if it won, two good women could be lost as well.

Chapter Fifteen: A Long Walk

Precious tied the sash for the slung she had Jonas in with a final knot. The mile or two stretch to the mercantile would do her and the little boy some good. The house really wasn't in need of anything. However, being out of this quiet place and walking far from it would settle her nerves.

A week had passed and Lord Welling was still traipsing after the Xhosa. Clara had begun eating again, but stayed in her room. With Eliza's picture consuming the parlor, the house was as quiet as a tomb.

Precious tugged on a straw bonnet and headed for the door. Before she could open it, the thing swung wide and in plodded Lord Welling.

His arms seemed to wrap about her and hold her tighter than Jonas's cloth sling. With a squeeze to her waist, he released her. "Where are you going in such a hurry?"

"To the mercantile."

"That's a long walk. Wait an hour or so and I'll

accompany you."

She backed up from him before the fragrance of fresh pine and sandalwood that was emanating from his presence made her feel lonely or vulnerable to his touch. "Won't be necessary, sir."

"Sir, is it now?" He huffed long and hard. "What am I to do with you?"

"Nothing. Just let me work my remaining three years on our contract."

He leaned against the door. "Do you think I want three more years of icy calm, when I've seen your fire?"

No talk of fire. She'd already been singed by wanting him. She shook her head and gathered up the strength to pass him. "I won't be long."

He folded his arms. He didn't seem like he'd budge. "So you wish to pretend that there is nothing between us? All of this is gone because you put up a picture and I guessed about your Marsdale blood?"

"You want a loyal crew, don't you?"

"Yes."

He gazed upon her heart. Precious looked down at the polished pine floor. "I'm on Eliza's crew. She cared for me. I owe a debt. That obligation has nothing to do with you."

"So I have to keep coming up with bargains to keep you near? Here's a new one. What if I marry Mrs. Narvel? Does that thought make a difference to you?"

Precious stepped back and swallowed the tears gathering in her throat. "If Mrs. Narvel has garnered your favor, then good for her. She'll need the help when the baby comes. That…will be good."

A frown pinched at his lips. "So you don't care? You'll let me do what ever I want and you have no feelings at all about this?"

"When does the help's opinion matter?"

He stepped closer and stroked her jaw. "It does if you've stopped pretending that I don't notice you or you me. Don't lie like Eliza. Forsake that part of the Marsdale's blood."

She scooted from his reach, just as Jonas wiggled.

The boy stuck his little hand out and waved. "Papa."

Lord Welling didn't move his gaze from her, not a dot or a moment for his son. The heated words he said about Eliza came into remembrance. All the coldness he showed for Jonas, it was because he thought Eliza was an adulterer. And this wonderful boy wasn't his.

She drew up her confidence and stood tall. "Eliza was many things, but she wasn't no adulterer. She never strayed, never broke her vows to you."

He folded his hands behind his back but his face was unmoved. "That can't be. She confessed to it."

"I was her confidant. I dressed her and helped her bathe. Don't you think I'd know the stench of another man? She may have lied to make you mad to see if you remembered her existence, but she was always faithful."

"Eliza told me differently. She laughed about it."

"Your late baroness, my mistress, was faithful. She felt alone and probably lied to you to get your attention, but she didn't undo her fancy clothes for no one but you."

As if her words had just chiseled into that thick wrong thinking head of his, Lord Welling pushed away and leaned against the yellow painted wall. "Jonas is my son. I didn't think I could..."

"Is there something?" Her words sounded airy, but she licked her full lips. She didn't need to fall into the trap of trying to figure things out. "Did you want something from the mercantile, sir?"

He reached out his hand to Jonas.

The boy gripped it with a strength that made Precious dip forward.

"Don't go. I need to think on this."

"No, you go on into the parlor and beg Eliza's forgiveness. That's what you need to do. I know I have."

"Precious, don't leave."

She put a hand on her hip and stared straight into his big blue eyes. "Is that an order?"

"I came back early to talk. Before you hid in your duties."

"Why, Lord Welling? You want to set up a time for me to visit your quarters. Some special orders for the help? I'm not doing that."

"I give orders. I'm a ship's captain and leader of this colony. And surprise, you work for me. You care for my heir, my son." He wrenched at his neck, his voice choking. "My son! But when we are alone, we can speak freely."

"As equals?" She started to laugh. "Yes, Lord Welling, whatever you say, Lord Welling."

He grabbed her arm, surely intending to haul her close, or force his skillful lips upon hers.

Not again. She wiggled free and breathed in huff as if he kissed her.

"Call me Gareth when it's just the two of us."

"It's not the two of us. It's never going to be the two of us. Your son is here. Right here. Eliza is everywhere." She shifted the bundle of Jonas onto her back.

And the boy clapped. "Mammie. Horsey."

"Yes, sweetie. We will be going, now."

"Well, leave the boy. You will be faster without him."

She barreled past him. "Jonas is all I have."

Hoping he didn't follow, she walked hard and fast. She must have traipsed a full mile before she looked back to see that he wasn't behind her.

He wasn't. And that was good right? Precious dragged forward as if she was one of the Margeaux's sails that had rolled up so it caught no wind. Lord Welling was going to marry again. "Jonas, it sounds like you're going to be getting a new mama. Clara's a good woman. She'll be kind to you. And I will only have to suffer through watching her and your papa for another three years."

Her insides hurt at the thought of the baron holding Clara. The last time she cared that much for a man, he showed himself to be evil, and he took away everything from her.

Lord Welling, Gareth, wasn't evil or even a brute. His honorable sacrifice for Clara took her breath and all the rest of that heart which she thought was gone. Three years was a lifetime. How would she survive?

Gareth paced inside the parlor. He kept looking out the window hoping Precious would cut short her walk. They needed to talk about these feelings between them. She had to tell him one more time that Jonas was truly his son.

He pivoted toward Eliza's painting. "You did this. Why did you make me think you and Jonas Hunt, Lord Jerrings, had been intimate? Did you like watching me die inside? Every time I looked at the boy, instead of seeing love, I saw you laughing at me or crying about being alone.

"Why would you take away this miracle? My fathering Jonas is a miracle." He started pacing. "I stayed away more because I couldn't be enough for you. And every time you flirted with someone else, it cut deep. The next woman I marry will know my challenges. That way they have a true choice, unlike you."

He walked to the painting and touched the frame. "I'm sorry Eliza, but thank you for my son."

"Captain?"

He pivoted to see a wobbly Mrs. Narvel standing in the threshold. "Good afternoon."

She tugged at her shawl and entered the room.

He plodded over and helped the woman ease onto the sofa. "It is good to see you about. Pre… Miss Jewell had mentioned that you haven't stirred. You need to be moving around a bit as your confinement comes near."

"I came down hoping to catch Miss Jewell before she left. She's determined to get me tea, something she called a rue. It's suppose to lift my spirits. I came to show her she didn't need to go to the trouble."

Precious wasn't going to find rue in the Mercantile. He should go after her and bring her back now. "Miss Jewell has already left."

Mrs. Narvel smiled and adjusted the heavy onyx skirts of her full mourning garb about her rounding belly. "That's a good caring woman."

Yes, she was that and so much more. Why couldn't Precious admit to wanting more?

"Is that the late Eliza Marsdale?" Mrs. Narvel's high pitched voice interrupted his woolgathering. "Is she your late baroness?"

He pivoted again and stared at the empty brown eyes of the painting. "Yes, that was she. An American from Charleston, like Miss Jewell."

"Did being so far from home… did it make things

difficult for her?"

"I never really thought of it." Well, he never really thought of much except tending to his uncle's business. "My wife seemed resilient, but I know now that some of that stubbornness just masked hurt." He tugged at his sleeve and turned toward the window. Maybe he could catch sight of Precious returning. "Are you pining for England? You are too close to your time to be sent back."

"No, not at all. I don't want to go back. I don't have any true family there. And I, if I leave, I leave Narvel too. I'm not ready for that."

He nodded and trudged to the window, flipping back the gauzy curtain. "I understand. It's difficult to move forward."

"Your late wife was lovely. Miss Jewell favors her."

He spun to see if he could detect where the woman was leading. Maybe the innocent Mrs. Narvel was a sly one.

"I can see why you are drawn to Precious, but she's not your baroness. I suspect they are two very different people. One is not a replacement for the other. And Precious deserves better than to be treated as a copy for the original."

"Why are speaking of this?"

"It took me a while to understand that you two were pretending on the Margeaux. It was hard because I see the looks you give her and the way her eyes brighten knowing you are safe and well."

Wrenching at his neck, he didn't like her conclusions. "My affairs are not your business, ma'am. That's like me telling you to marry to give your babe a father."

"This babe has a father, and he died a hero at a place he loved. I may never marry. I'll find a way to provide for the both of us, but Precious is my friend. And she's too good of a person to be made into a trollop. I don't want to see my friend used especially..."

His temper at the woman's impertinence allayed. She knew something and Gareth had grown tired of figuring things out late. "You've started down the road of intruding, madam. You might as well finish your statement."

"She cries at night sometime, when she thinks no one is listening. Your wife saved her from something terrible. Precious is indebted to her and is still trying to find a way to pay."

Gareth started pacing again. "Do you have any idea? What could've...?" Then he remembered how Precious would jerk in his arms and quiver when he came near even as her pert lips said something bold. He clasped his arms almost straining to keep them from going to his rapier and hunting some faraway villain.

When he glanced at Mrs. Narvel, the woman held the biggest smile. "You are in love with Precious, aren't you? I knew it."

"I didn't..." He wasn't ready to examine his heart that closely, not when something had injured his Precious. "Why does she cry at night?"

"I was hurt once. Deflowered by a peer." Mrs. Narvel swallowed, but her voice stayed strong. "The man gave my father some coins to make amends, but I never received justice. I kept anger and hurt in my heart for years as my shamed family shipped me off to be a governess. In my solitude, I found my worth again. God heard my cries and helped me see that I was still worthy to be loved. That though my body had been used, my soul could still be made new. Then and only then was I able to love, as a whole person, not a shadow of one, not less than one. Mr. Narvel was patient and loved me beyond my flaws, and I beyond his."

He didn't have the heart to tell Mrs. Narvel of some of her husband's flaws, that all of this nightmare with the Xhosa had been caused by his neglect. But those wrongs were now buried in the ground. He wouldn't take away her good memories. "Why tell me something so personal?"

"Because if you intend to love Precious and have that love returned, you'll have to do more than hope she comes to you and you definitely can't want her because she favors your late wife."

Mrs. Narvel wobbled to a stand. "Precious needs a man to love her and only her. If you can't be that person. If you can't show the world that you want her, and not in some unseemly way as a mistress, let Precious go. She'll never get all she deserves trapped in a man's confusion." The woman stretched and waddled to the door. "Tell Precious thank you for that tea. I'll probably be napping when she returns."

He waited for the woman to leave before plodding to the window to see if Precious was on her way back. Nothing met his gaze but an empty street, tan grasslands, and a fort facing ice blue water. How did he feel about her? Had he let that stubborn, fierce woman into his heart? Could he love her?

Could she be in love with him? And could a young vibrant woman be satisfied with him, a man enslaved to duty, one who couldn't offer all the physical closeness that someone like Eliza needed? Could he put himself through that agony again of seeing his limitations in Precious's frowns?

Whatever the case, he'd settle it tonight as soon as Precious returned.

Chapter Sixteen: Taking Too Long

Precious stepped out of the door to the mercantile. The dusty road here was longer than Precious thought, but this view from the steps with the bay and the colony in the distance was breathtaking.

Thinking of the tiring walk back with no tea made a long sigh fall out of her mouth. She didn't look forward to the sun beating down upon her again as she made it home. So what harm could come from resting on the porch of the mercantile?

The store was cut of rough oak planks. Thick walls framed the building, but it looked primitive to the stone and plaster of fancy London or for that matter the bricks and mortar of the Marsdale plantation.

Rustic and primitive, the store held all the basics: flour, sorghum, yeast, bobbins, and fabric. Nothing as fine as the fabric for the dresses Eliza or even Clara wore but enough to create something out of it. That was Port Elizabeth. There was enough here to build, enough here to fashion a life.

A breeze settled in and rustled her bonnet. It was beautiful on the porch, no ugly fort or reminders of war. She took another moment just for herself and pivoted to watch the sea.

Maybe it was viewing the openness of Port Elizabeth that made her not want to move from the steps. She took her fingers and spread them wide and still couldn't span the hills. She whirled around, making Jonas shriek with joy. Again extending her thumb and index finger, she couldn't quite fit the small strip of homes into the span. This place was so different from London. And different from Charleston. She could grow to like it here. Perhaps after her time of servitude was done, she would have saved up enough money to homestead. Maybe she too could be like one of the settlers, since all kinds of folk were building. On her way to the mercantile, she'd passed two families, one black, and the other a mix of mulatto or Spanish.

They waved and she waved back. A moment of pride had passed betwixt them. Who wouldn't be boastful seeing the fruits of their labor? Yes, they all had joy in their smiles like they were someone, like they belonged.

Precious wanted some of that too. What would it feel like to truly have a place in the world that was hers?

A lady popped out of the shop and brushed past her. She was an older woman with a large chest clothed in scarlet. Her hair was dark, with little strands of gray, all pulled back in bun under a big hat with a feather.

She stopped and took a peek at Jonas. "A fine boy, Lord Welling's son." Her accent was thick and low for a woman's voice. "That would make you Precious Jewell."

"Aye. I am. How do you know me?"

"I make it my business to know everyone, particularly

pretty little negresses. Why are you about? I had heard the captain never let you much out of his sight."

That horrible lie again. How could she ever find a place of own if every one thought of her as a loose woman? That it was her fault...? She kept her anger in check and thought of what to say to make the shrew give her some respect. Suddenly, she remembered Grandmama praying for everyone she met. "What is your name ma'am?"

"The name is Cornelia Branddochter, but most call me Madame Neeltje. I run a bordello a little ways off. "

Precious blinked, not sure of what she had just heard. "A what?"

Her small gloved hands took hold of Precious's. "A bordello, a house of prostitution, or as I like to say, a place of fun. You have a look in your eye. Restless. Things not working out with Welling?"

"My eyes are fine. I was just coming to get some rue tea."

She made a tsk sound with her red lips. Her heavily rouged cheeks thinned. "You're not with child are you? The rue can be very dangerous to a woman early in her pregnancy."

"No, I'm not. It's to ease childbirth."

"Oh, the Narvel woman. Well, if you're brave enough, go into the woods. You'll come upon some soon. They grow quite tall in the forest or even low in the thickets. But if you scared, I have new Xhosa women in my care. The Xhosa aren't afraid of anything. They could get you some."

Precious tapped her lip, like she was stupid enough to be taken in by such cunning. "Course, I'd only do that for a friend. When you want some, come find me. All the men know where."

The way she said *all* burned. Maybe Lord Welling was a patron, maybe not, but she wouldn't show Madame Neeltje she was curious. Instead she'd differ to twist in Grandmama's common saying. "With all those men knowing you, I'll pray for you, child."

The woman's brow popped. Then she flipped her head back and climbed down the stairs into her one horse harnessed gig. "Thank you, I think. But when you need a favor, come for me." She slapped at the reigns and forced her animal to move.

Whatever that was about, Precious wasn't going to figure it out. She needed all her strength to prepare for the walk back to the house and to face Lord Welling. "Come on, Jonas."

Somewhere between searching the last aisle of the mercantile and talking with Madame Neeltje, the boy had nodded off again.

Paddling down the steps, she started moving but a certain amount of tiredness came over her. Perhaps it was knowing Lord Welling would be waiting for her that made her slow down.

Why did he affect her so? And why must he torture her over marrying Clara? What did he want her to do? Pitch a fit for him? Admit to have feelings that she better not have?

She pivoted back to the bay and watched the Margeaux bob up and down in the foaming waves. Stupid boat. If she hadn't fallen overboard, he wouldn't have had to rescue her. He would not have started a rumor about her so that every one including brothel owners thought she was low like that.

And somehow that might speed the boat to Port

Elizabeth. Maybe they'd arrived a day earlier. Mr. Narvel would be alive and Clara wouldn't be available for Lord Welling to marry.

And most of all, Precious wouldn't have to know what it was like to kiss Lord Welling. She'd never have to remember the feel and smell of him. Or that throaty noise he made when passion overcame him.

Gareth had the power to do as he pleased, but his hold upon her had always been gentle, measured in his strength. He never made her feel obligated. No, he put those kisses squarely under her control, her power.

What if she were wanton? What if she didn't have to think about tomorrow? What if for one moment, she could claim all of him as hers? Oh Lord, this was too much thinking. Dangerous thinking. She shook her head. No more of him. No more dishonor to Eliza.

She stomped forward to the fork in the road as Jonas's snorts carried in the wind. Getting to that point of decision, she studied the path leading to Gareth's cottage and the other leading to the woman in scarlet.

She rested on the post. Gareth would be waiting for her. The memory of his lips tasting and teasing hers wouldn't be there when she closed her eyes. And then it would be replaced with images of Clara seeking Gareth's embraces. It made sense, two widowers, two respectable people. She could be a better asset of helping him to grow the colony. Precious had nothing to offer him to help with his dream. Her feet felt trapped in mud. She couldn't go back yet. "Not until I have my wits. Aye, Jonas?"

She pivoted ninety degrees away from Gareth's house, the mercantile, even the brothel and headed straight to the emerald trees. If the Xhosa women and the soldiers could go and come in those woods everyday, so could she. With Jonas asleep and bundled tightly in her sash, she could dash into forest find the rue and head back. The day's light should still be good.

Before she could think of all the bad that could come, she pressed forward. She used to be so at home in the woods. The bad memories had taken enough from her. No more. She trudged forward.

Gareth peaked out the parlor window for the twelfth time. The sun had begun to set and Precious and Jonas hadn't returned. Where was that woman?

And his son?

His son. Jonas was *his son*.

Those words tumbled in his mind, torturing him with each moment he stayed away from Firelynn. He'd become sick at the notion of how his inadequacies drove Eliza, the woman he loved, who said she loved him to adultery. What he should have been sick of were her lies.

Had they created some terrible circle? He'd pull away, isolating her from his affections because she flaunted the names of men who'd flirted with her or sent outrageous gifts. He turned to her portrait and let his anger pierce those soulless eyes. "Why did you make me think Jonas wasn't mine?"

Did she grow to hate Gareth because he wasn't able to dote upon her or care for her as she needed? Did she loathe him enough to take away the miracle of his son?"

And now he had done the same thing of merely being present but remote with the boy, punishing him for his mother's alleged sins. "You knew how much joy it would have meant to know I was even capable of still fathering a child, but you denied that to me. Did I enable such revulsion in you that you died with me thinking a lie?"

He stared at the portrait as if the oil paint and canvas would make that demure mouth of Eliza's move and tell him why. The one thing he knew in his gut was that Precious wasn't lying to hide Eliza's sins. He'd come to know Precious and how she thought about things. Though loyal to Eliza, Precious wouldn't state falsehoods to his face.

Oh, Precious, where are you? She'd been hurt a great deal, but the woman still gave her all to everyone. She patched up Ralston and Grossling, her kindness to Mrs. Narvel and to him all proved what kind of heart she possessed.

Do I love her?

He closed his eyes and she was there in his head calling him stupid and surrendering to his embrace.

Could she love me?

Precious was young and vibrant. Was he enough of a man for her? Would she still want him once she realized how much of a miracle Jonas was?

He pivoted and stormed back to the window. They needed to talk. Where was she? He'd let her have another fifteen minutes to appear on the street or he'd saddle up a horse and go after her. The ache in the pit of his stomach grew. What could he say that would make her want him, make her want to be with him?

The thickness of the forest loomed over Precious's head. She fought her way through some vines with thorns and made it with no scratches to her or Jonas to this patch of jade and emerald. Once she entered the looming mass of vines and moss-green branches, everything closed in upon her. She was hopelessly lost and night would fall soon.

Jonas started to stir.

She rocked the sling hoping to buy more time. The boy would be hungry in another thirty minutes. What was she going to do? How was she going to get back to the road when every way looked the same?

She threw up her hands and swatted at some low hanging vines.

She took a deep breath and let a sweet floral smell guide her. Didn't she pass this way before? Was this near the entrance or was this the fourth time she'd trekked past this stump?

Oh, Precious, this was stupid. How could she have thought this would be just like the Carolina woods, a place she knew well? Every slope of the hills, the way the sun reflected on the pond, she could picture it all. How else was she able to drag her beaten and bloodied self back to the Marsdale plantation?

She blinked her eyes and held up her fingers, but within the span she couldn't find anything distinct. Nothing to guide her back to the road, to the home she'd set up for Gareth. Oh, where was he now when she and Jonas needed him?

Gripping her arms, she took a deep breath. If she slowed her thoughts maybe she would be able to see the way out. With heavy blinking, she forced her thoughts to be happy ones, focusing on plants, broken leaves, anything that could indicate home.

Home, what a concept. The last home Precious had was Grandmama's shack. After that, it was just places to lay her head. Maybe that's why she relished fixing up the shelves, putting away the silver. She was setting up a home, one for Jonas and Clara and the baron. Their lives were intertwined. No matter what changes happened next, they were linked.

Suddenly, she didn't fear it. There was always a way out of no way. And that God that she learned about from Grandmama, had discussed with Clara, and just teased the bordello woman about was real and giving breath and renewal to everything.

She better stop teasing God on folks. For who else would get her out of this fix.

She spun again and right in the path of the setting sun was the rue tree, with bell shaped leaves and long cream colored flowers. The leaves and stems, even some bark was what she needed for the tea. Well, if she had to be lost at least it wasn't for nothing. Plodding over to it, she pushed back the brush and high grasses, the kind that snakes like to hide in.

The thought of seeing one of those varmints scared her. She hated returning with empty hands. Snakes were horrible things with a slither. And those with a rattle, oh those were from the pit of the underworld. Meant to capture folk and pull them down.

For a second, she drew back. High grasses were a hiding place for evil. Of all the things she had to be concerned about, the last thing should be an imaginary snake crawling through her mind.

There were far worse things to fear in the woods. Like those Xhosa. Oh boy, she hadn't thought of them. This tea better be the best tea ever. She'd need to gather a lot of it to make all her foolish fears worth it.

Crackle, snap.

She pivoted in the direction of the noise, but nothing became visible.

She let her pulse settle then turned back to the tree. She curled her fingers about a long runner with the flowers and leaves and tugged. Bits broke off. She gathered it in her skirt.

Crackle, pop.

This time she flinched and turned.

Nothing moved in the distance. It must have been the wind. With a deep breath she turned back to work on the rue.

That's when she felt something cold wriggle upon her outstretched wrist. Screaming, she stumbled backwards. The brown black viper with cream banding sat on her.

Before she could fling it, the snake squirted at her. The venom hit her face. It burned in her eye.

Her vision grew dim and she sank to the ground. With an unsteady hand, Precious switched Jonas around so that the sling would have him to her stomach. "Oh, God, Clara's God. Save this boy, Jonas. Don't let him come to harm."

Jonas cried but she could barely hear him as her flesh felt hot and cold at the same time.

Before her eyes shut, she caught sight of what she'd hoped was Gareth's boots, but he didn't wear sandals. And these feet appeared dark like ebony.

Chapter Seventeen: The Vengeance of Venom

Gareth had his mount circle the mercantile again. The shop keeper confirmed that Precious and Jonas had made it here, but what happened to them? How could they just disappear?

Could she have gone back to the Margeaux?

From the porch, one could see it clearly. Perhaps, the bewitching girl needed the solace of the ship. It was big and full of quiet places.

That time when it was just the two of them in his cabin was special to Gareth. It made him laugh, and think of himself as a hero again, not less than. Perhaps, she waited there now.

He reared the horse and made it soar as if it had wings. With a thud, they kicked up dirt. Sprays of brown changed to plumes of white as they hit beach sand. What if someone saw her and didn't know she was his? A lecher could've tried to abduct her.

He pulled his gelding to a halt with hands that shook

upon the leather strap. He'd just called Precious his. And he didn't mean enslavement. He couldn't quite get his mind around that L word, but it would only be a matter of time. He was hooked like a fish. He could feel the metal pierce his nose dragging him into her net. Who else had the fire to light his weary bones? Who else stood up to him and challenged him? No one but the lovely woman.

He slowed his mount and jumped off and tossed the reigns to one of his mates. "Have you seen my son's governess, Miss Jewell?"

Shrugs greeted him. "No sir."

He fought the urge to run down to the cabins or to check the hold, but there was a resounding truth in their looks and their voice. Precious wasn't there. Where could she be?

Head hanging low he turned from his beloved ship to his horse. Time ticked down and he was out of ideas. Night was about to kiss the land, leaving his son and Precious to face who knows what.

As the lad handed him back the reigns, he stopped Gareth. "I think I saw her talking to that bordello woman a couple of hours ago. Maybe Madame Neeltje would know where your governess is."

The bordello? Oh that, Madame Neeltje. She was always getting more women. Would Precious turn to her? Would she do anything to be away from him?

He clicked his horse and headed to the brothel. If Gareth knew anything, it was that Precious would never willingly sell her flesh, nor would she ever take his son to a place like that. If that woman had stolen Precious and Jonas, the witch wouldn't live until morning.

The longest two miles he'd ever trod was this dusk ride

to Madame Neeltje's bordello. He leapt down and tied his horse to the rail. The house was made of rough pine boards slathered with mortar to make it smooth. He pressed upon the door and entered into a parlor painted in red with chaise seats, each filled with scantily dressed women and bunches of drunken men.

A petite thing with emerald eyes wandered over to him. "Your lordship, fancy meeting you hear, love.

Crossing his arms, he glared at her. "Woman, go get your mistress."

She pouted, then turned and went down a hall.

Some of the men, members of his crew, denizens of Port Elizabeth, Grossling?

"Well, well, wowski isn't enough." Alcohol poured from his veins. He pulled into Gareth's face. "You done with her or she done with you?"

His fisted hand connected with the war department man's jaw sending him flying.

Grossling rubbed his jaw. "Have you lost your mind?"

"Yes, and if you make another joke about Jewell, I'll beat you to your last breath."

"Stop it. Stop it." Madame Neeltje waddled out from a side room. She pulled at her tucker to cover her jiggling bosom. "I run a decent business. If you want to act like fools, take it outside."

He pivoted from Grossling. "You spoke with Precious Jewel tonight. Where is she?"

The woman straightened a few locks of strangely colored hair, part henna brown, other strands were jet black and grey. "Sorry, Captain, I don't know. Keeping pretty girls is my trade. If you are interested in selling her, I'm very willing to take her off your hands."

"Precious Jewell is a free woman. She works for me."

"Well, it's nice work if you can get it, so I hear. My girls don't get complaints either."

"Woman, is she here? I can make your life horrible. You know I can." He plodded forward down the hall. "I'm just going to check all the rooms."

"Wait a minute. There is no need for that. I might be remembering something." She put her hands to her temples. "Let me think."

He eased his stance, though the feeling that Madame Neeltje didn't want him searching her place rocked his gut. Something was hidden here, but not Precious and Jonas. "Just tell me what you know."

"Oh my, you really care about this girl. Well, last time I saw her was near the mercantile."

Frustration boiling over, Gareth let a sigh steam out. "I know that. Do you know where she and my son could have gone from there?"

She took her perfumed hand and tapped her painted cheek. "No, but maybe I could remember something."

He took a gold piece from his pocket and held it high. "Talk."

"I think she went to get some rue for tea. She traipsed into the woods from where the road forks." She reached up and grabbed the coin. "Nice doing business with you. If you don't find them, come back. I'm sure we can help you spend your time and your money."

Cold sweat damping his palms, Gareth pivoted and headed to the door. He couldn't afford antics with Precious and little Jonas lost in the woods.

He got onto his horse and headed to get torches. God, it wasn't fair to let him know what he wanted only to snatch it away. Gareth had allowed the doubts in his mind about their differences take up too much room, but could they conjure up enough similarities to be happy?

Maybe?

Perhaps?

Yes.

It was better to dwell on Precious being his and wanting him. If only he could find her before she or Jonas became hurt.

The world outside her eyelids seemed to brighten. Someone forced one open and dumped cold water onto her pupil. The cold liquid froze the burning. With a few more blinks she could see out of it.

She struggled to move but her body ached. Her arm felt like it had been broken into pieces. But within the circle of her embrace was emptiness. No child snuggled against her bosom. "Jonas!"

She tried to sit up. Where was he? Was he with his father? "Jonas!"

Jonas was tucked in the dark biceps of a man. A large man of ebony skin held him. "Siya namkela nonke. Unjani?"

Struggling with all her might, she craned her neck and reached with her good arm. Her tongue was too thick and tired. She couldn't scream anymore.

" Welkom. Hoe gaat het met je?"

The words he spoke were so distant, but no one would keep her from Jonas. She swatted and hit at his leg.

"Bienvenue. Comment allez-vous?"

Too shocked to faint, too much a mother bear missing her cub, she pushed the words, "Put him down."

His barrel sized arms tightened about Jonas. "Oh, English it is."

She licked her dry lips. "I said put him down."

"You don't speak isiXhosa and don't sound quite English, mate." His tongue sounded crisp and clear, something she never would have thought would come from a bare chested man in buckskins. "Where are you from?"

With hair cut short and a band circling his head, he tickled Jonas's middle.

The little boy laughed and then grabbed hold of the leather strap crossing the man's wide chest.

He covered Jonas hand, with his dark, dark palm. "Oh, sorry mate. You can't touch my weapon."

Weapon? He turned a little to give Jonas a whirl. Precious could see more of those blades called assegai and the butt of a flintlock.

"He's doing well. The little fellow has been amused watching the fire glow. No harm has come to my enemy's son."

"Jonas is no enemy. He's an innocent little boy. Hand him to me."

"Yes, mate. I'm a little tired of the nanny thing. I need to check that eye and the arm again any way."

She squinted at him as his big finger stroked her cheek then pried at an eye. "Don't tense so much. I don't kill woman. Looks good. I got the snake venom out."

The smoothness of his speech sounded almost like Lord Welling's just deeper and not as proper.

He lowered Jonas to her arms and then snatched him away, causing Jonas to squeal with pleasure.

"Or I could just slit the nice little fellow's throat now. Why let him grow up to slit my people's necks? "

Like a momma bear deprived of her cub, she kicked at him. "Please, just release him. Then I wont have to hurt you."

The man bent over and started to laugh, harder and louder than he did before. "I like you, mate. Full of foolhardiness."

If he was laughing at her, then maybe he wouldn't harm them. "How did you learn to talk so fancy."

"I'm a good study. That's why I say let's do away with this one now." He made eyes at Jonas causing the boy to chuckle. "Yes, I think that's a good plan."

Panic started its dance within her heart, but her brain started working too. The man was too gentle with Jonas to do him harm. He was doing better than the child's own father. "You're going to put him in my arms now. If you meant to do harm, M-wam. M-wombat-ding-dong, you would have done so by now. And you would not've saved my sight or my life from the viper."

He bent low flexing all the muscles in his thunderous thighs. "Like I said, you're a brave one. The name is Mzwamadoda, Mm-wam-ado-da. But how did you know who I am?"

She tightened her arms about Jonas hugging his warm happy body, so much so that her arm began to throb again. "Cause I know a man looking for you, the Xhosa who speaks five languages. Let me take you to Lord Welling."

He stood up tall and brush dust from the hide draped on his hip. "You're in no condition for anything. And why were you playing in the woods with your fancy slave uniform."

"I'm a governess. No slave."

"Well the profile of nose and those full talkative lips. You're a descendant of West Africans, probably taken from Senegambia. But you are of mixed blood. How foul to have those European heels in your lineage. The only ones I know of such are slaves coming from the Americas."

This one was smart and learned. No wonder Gareth put such stock in finding him to stop the violence. She tested her arm, pumping it open and closed. "Where I am from has nothing to do with anything. You need to see Lord Welling so the killing can stop. Follow me to the settlement."

Sorry mate, but Mzwamadoda doesn't follow a woman anywhere. Secondly, that was Rinkal venom I forced out of you. You won't make it three feet without falling over. But I'll take you to the edge of the forest. Welling will find you there.

Before she could say anything his arms were about her slamming her high into his rock hard chest. She couldn't breathe with the iron bands of shirtless muscles surrounding her. She'd just gotten use to Lord Welling being this close to her. "Please, let me try to walk."

"A bit of hellcat aren't you, mate?"

A polite well muscled man jokingly threatening to kill Jonas didn't bring any comfort, even if he had saved her life and kept Jonas from harm. She tried to still the fear creeping up her spine. "Put me down. I can walk."

"No, you'll slow me down. I'm not trying to be caught by Port Elizabeth's dogs. I could hand you over to my tribe. They'll not treat you like a lady though, but as a spy or a traitor. Then they'll deal with this son of evil."

She beat on his chest, tore at the fur cloth, but nothing budged. "Let me go. He's innocent."

"Not when they grow up and try to take land that's not theirs. No, I'm thinking I really should just be done with all my troubles. That would include you if you don't settle."

If her arm didn't hurt so bad, she'd smack him in the face. But then she still wouldn't know where the edge of the forest was. So she held onto Jonas tighter and kept her trembles at bay as much as she could.

He worked his way through the trees. "What were you and the boy doing out here. Did they cast you out?

"No. I wanted some rue. I have a friend. She'll need it when her baby comes."

"So they sent a defenseless woman and a future killer to find rue."

"Stop saying that. And how can you talk such nonsense? The night I arrived you, Xhosa, killed fifteen."

He stopped in his tracks and juggled her around until he was inches from her face. "The English and Dutch have come and slaughtered thousands. We fight for our way of life, our very survival. When at great pains, we negotiate a peace and the traitors violate it. I'm not sorry if one or fifteen of them are dead."

He was cold, so matter of fact about the killing. Yes, Precious hated those who had been mean to her, but she'd never be so matter of fact about anyone suffering. Well, only one person's suffering wouldn't give her any concern, but Mzwamadoda probably wouldn't travel to Charleston to do the deed.

Yet, would the monster's death make Precious whole? Would it take away her fear of the dark? Her fear of trusting someone who in the end would only deceive and hurt her?

No, that kind of healing didn't come from a killing. What did?

"Good, mate. You've settled down. Just a note, if a man is going to get snake venom from you, he's not given to killing you or those you're caring for. Would be bad form."

Sick from having a stranger see her weak and scared, she stopped squirming and just closed her eyes. Hopefully she and Jonas would be back to the colony soon.

"Princess. We've made it. You can see…"

A horse galloping in the distance silenced him and made her heart race.

Mzwamadoda stilled and put a hand to her lips. "You're not a screamer so don't start now."

The sound of hooves came nearer.

He whispered in her ear. "We've company. Don't make me regret saving your life and keeping this one alive."

She held onto Jonas and nodded.

He put her down and took a flintlock from a sheath he had on his back.

She tugged on his fur cape. "Don't shoot anyone."

He powered his gun. "I don't make promises that I might break."

The horses leaping gait slowed, doing the opposite to her heart. Then she heard his voice. "Precious! Can you hear me?"

"That's you, mate. And you have the man himself looking for you. I knew you were special." Mzwamadoda raised his pistol. "Captain Conroy, the newest Lord Welling, governor to traitors, I think I've got someone you're looking for."

Gareth came into the clearing. Her heart beat all funny. There was an edge of shadow on his face. Had he been searching for her all night?

With his rapier extended forward, he came closer. "Mzwamadoda, is that you?"

"Sure, mate. I have your Precious and I take it the

little killer is your son."

There was fury in Gareth's stance. "Let her go. Your fight's not with her or my son."

Mzwamadoda winked at her. "She fell into a little trouble, but I was able to help her out. So far they're innocent, but you and your Narvel character that's another story."

Gareth stormed closer and whipped his rapier out from his sash. "Give me back my son and Precious, and we'll talk about how to restore the peace."

"You put down your weapon, Welling. Don't think that thin blade is going to stand up very well to a bullet pellet."

Gareth came forward as if his deep blue jacket was impervious to wounds. "Probably not, but I'll stab you as it hits. You know that I will."

The Xhosa warrior started chuckling and lowered his weapon. "That's what I like about you, mate. You're as strident to dying as much as I. Your son and your Precious are not harmed. You're lucky that it was I who found her."

"Precious, are you well?"

"A snake spit at me when I was going for rue. I don't remember much after that."

Her rescuer chuckled. "Oh, love, you forgot my whispers of sweet nothings as I searched your arm for a bite. I was prepared to drink the venom out of your veins."

The smile Gareth seemed to save for her disappeared. "Then I owe you Mzwamadoda for taking care of her and my boy." He leapt forward. His hand cradled her jaw for a second, then he stopped and scooped Jonas into his arms. "Can you stand, Precious? I need to get you both home."

"I can try, but isn't this the man you've been searching for to try to restore the peace. Talk with him."

"Oh, Precious." Mzwamadoda shook his head and smiled wide. "He knows there is no talking. Not until the man who desecrated the old chief is made to die."

Gareth bent down, put Jonas in her arms and then scooped her up. He carried her, like she were paper and put her on the back of his horse. "You've already done that. He was one of the men killed the night of the attack."

"That's an easy thing to say, a little harder to prove, mate."

He pivoted and faced the warrior. "I've got nothing else to give you, but there has to be a way to make things right."

"Well, Welling, do you have something Precious to give me?"

"No." The tone of Gareth's voice sounded hard, leaving no room for doubt of his possession of her. "You let her alone, Mzwamadoda. This is between you and me."

"No mate, it's not. I just come back from Spain to find madness. My cousin, Bezile, has been made chief overthrowing my godfather, Chief Zifihlephi. Zifihlephi and his daughter are missing. My cousin is persuading the council that you have them."

Gareth shook his head and adjusted the reins for tugging the horse. "We don't have them. I wouldn't lie to you. You know that."

Mzwamadoda popped the black packet out of the gun, stashed it in his pocket and positioned the gun to sling on his back. "The old chief is sick and the daughter, a mixed breed, like your Precious is vulnerable. Once I know that the two are well, I will go to Bezile and convince him and the council, that the culprit is dead."

Rubbing his forehead, Gareth nodded. "You have to give me time, but be assured, the guilty man and Lieutenant Narvel, both are dead. You don't have to kill any more for vengeance."

Finding a missing man might be as hard as finding rue. Precious had to help. "Please, give Lord Welling time. He can do it with enough time."

"You have seven days. Meet me here in a week with answers or the next wave of vengeance will come to pass. There will be nothing I can do."

"I'll do what I can. He jumped on the horse behind her and gathered his arms about her.

Waving at him to stop, Mzwamadoda came up beside the horse. "Oh, does she stay in your household?"

She felt Gareth's arms tighten about her.

"Why do you ask?"

"When you fail Welling, and my brethren come, I'll have them bypass your house. I like this mouthy one. Till next time, Miss Precious."

Gareth motioned his horse and started them moving.

The ride was silent. She had walked pretty far trying to find rue. How stupid? "Sorry for causing you to worry."

He released a tired breath. It cascaded down her neck to scars shrouding her spine. "Let me get you to safety. We'll talk about how much you've caused me to fret later. I'm just glad you and Jonas are safe."

Precious closed her eyes and leaned into him. If the next wave of wrath would strike in seven days. she'd savor them in Gareth's company. Nothing mattered right now, not within his tight embrace. Her heart settled down and enjoyed the feel of him, for he was taking her home.

Chapter Eighteen: The House is Too Quiet

Tired wasn't the word for what Gareth felt. Riding all night looking for Precious and Jonas had drained him, disturbing him beyond belief. He sat listless on the sofa.

As Clara attended Precious, he'd put his son to bed. He couldn't get enough of hugging and looking at this miracle. Yet, there was shame. Though he knew the child was innocent, he'd always remembered the way Eliza had laughed in his face and flaunted faux lovers. He'd been too angry to think she was lying, that she said those cruel things to take her hurt out on him. Oh how would he make it up to the boy? Would Gareth even live to do so?

Ramming his head back on the sofa's edge, he had to admit that everyone of his intellectual arguments about forgiving Eliza had been a lie. He hadn't. He'd tolerated her and slowly starved her of his time and attention. How could things have been different if his heart had known true repentance then?

He wasn't going to think of this now. There were too

many other things consuming that heart of his. When he saw Precious and Jonas; that they were alive, and being carried into the clearing by Mzwamadoda, he'd never known such joy. He had thanked God for another chance to hold his son, another chance to figure out what was between Precious and he.

Was it love as Mrs. Narvel had said?

But then he saw how Precious's caramel skin, how her face looked against Mzwamadoda dark shoulder and how out of place Jonas looked bundled in their arms. If not for the little boy, how many wouldn't have batted an eye thinking it was a Xhosa couple? How many would have shot first, then asked questions, all because the color of their skin?

Was there a rightness in how natural her flesh looked against Mzwamadoda? Did she look as natural in Gareth's arms? Did she flinch when Mzwamadoda held her as she first did with Gareth?

A light set of footfalls made him lift his head and crane his neck to the door. Precious stood there. She was beautiful with the sunlight from the hall settling on her shoulders.

"Mrs. Narvel said that you wished to speak with me?"

"Yes, come in and close the door."

The small smile on her face slipped away, but the stubborn girl complied. She pulled the door shut and traipsed near the sofa. "I must apologize Lord Welling. I put Jonas in danger just to get some rue."

With his index finger, he waved her forward. She had to come to him. That would tell him more about Precious's state of mind. Had she endured more harm before Mzwamadoda found her? Did being saved by the enigmatic warrior replace being rescued by the drunken captain? Did a joking Xhosa need to come up with all kinds of bargains just to keep her near? "Sit next to me."

She neared. Her face held strain. The last time she seemed this concerned, she thought he'd punish her and she'd turned her bewitching backside to him. He chided himself, not sure what he'd do if such an offer was made today, but it would definitely involve tossing her into his arms and holding her close.

Her jaw trembled. "I had no right to be so reckless. If Mzwamadoda hadn't found me, Jonas could have wandered off and been hurt."

Her saying another man's name with gratitude didn't sit well, but that was a problem for another day. "Precious, sit next to me."

Her eyes narrowed to slits. "Is that an order?"

"Does it need to be one?"

She blinked a couple of times as if weighing her options. Then she took the final steps and sat down.

He took her arm in her hand and rolled up the sleeve to the purple dress. Mrs. Narvel must've lent it to her. It hung well on Precious's slim form. "The venom may make this arm tingle. Mzwamadoda knew what to do as well as I would have. You are lucky my dear."

He clasped her hand and massaged a soft spot betwixt her fingers. Their skin was different, dark and light. Just like coffee and cream. But the blend made magic, a delight on the palate. And in this moment he again wanted to sample those soft lips, to taste the creamy offering of her affection. "Luck or blessings, they sit well on you."

"You're not going to yell at me. When you were mad at Eliza, you yelled." She pivoted her head toward the portrait. "She yelled too."

He reached out and stroked her cheek until she turned to look at him. "Eliza and me, our love, our whole life was stormy. When people care about one another, that's not how things have to be."

She bit her lip for a moment. "I've never seen anything but dark clouds and rain."

Had she ever known tenderness? Was her fear of men more than just some past hurt? "Precious, have you ever known love?"

She pulled away and set her shoulders back.

The comfort he'd evoked slipped away. He wanted to kick himself. "I meant to say that emotions don't have to run so high. Eliza and I, we knew some good times."

"But you never chose her? Your work, your very important work came first. It's hard to think of being a priority when there is so many other things to do."

If Precious had known how he tortured himself for not taking her and Jonas to the mercantile, she'd know he meant to fix his priorities. He rubbed at his neck. "I wasn't a good husband to Eliza. That fateful night of Jonas's birth when word came of my uncle dying, we argued. When I explained tradition of what happens with the passing of titles in my family, she didn't understand. She needled me and said 'perhaps the babe's true father would come and support her'. I wasn't smart enough to see that she was acting out of hurt."

Precious got up and walked over to the bay window. "She was mad. Your choosing your uncle must have made her say awful things."

He stood up and plodded over to Precious. With a light touch, he put his hands on her shoulders. Below the flowing fabric he could trace her slim limbs and the taut muscles. The woman was a delightful blend of delicate and bold. "I told myself that I forgave her, that it was my fault she strayed, but I hadn't."

She nodded.

"I gladly chose my duty, whenever it came to her needs. If true forgiveness was in my heart, maybe I would have made another choice. You will never know the guilt I've felt every time I am at Firelynn. My mind retraces every moment of our last argument. I think if I'd stayed, I might have been able to save her or least she and I could have parted as friends."

He spun Precious around gently. "Then you would not have had to shelter the burden of raising Jonas alone these past two years. Until you stood up to me, I would still be missing so much and begrudging him attention, just like Eliza. You saved me."

Her sweet brown eyes sparkled. "I might not do everything right, but I will do everything with my heart."

"I'm counting on that." If he bent his head and kissed her, would she put her all into it? He forestalled his need to claim those lips. Patience needed to win. When Precious chose, it would be worth it. "What made you go into the woods?"

"That Madame Neeltje woman. She said she had Xhosa girls working for her and they weren't afraid of going there. I guess she goaded me into being stupid. Probably wasn't that hard of a task."

"Madame Neeltje said she had Xhosa girls. Maybe they will know where the old chief is."

She squinted at him, but then her smile returned. "Well, don't tell her I was spit at for my troubles. I went in to the woods to get rue and didn't even get it."

He reached into his pocket and pulled out a balled up handkerchief. "You mean this?"

She took the handkerchief in her hands and poked inside the lawn cloth exposing the leaves and flowers of the rue plant. She clutched the small parcel and held it as if he had given her a gold locket or diamond. "You got this for me?"

"I found some when I was tracking you. I figured if you were, what is your pet word for things like this, *stupid*? If you were going to be foolhardy enough to go out there to chase rue, I'd better get you some to keep you from going back. I can't lose you, Precious."

Fat sloppy tears leaked from her eyes and Gareth felt as if he had given her diamonds. Forgetting his commitment to not rush her, he pulled her into his arms. She fit without any signs of hesitation, and when his mouth claimed hers, she kissed him back.

Like a first sweep of passion, she let him explore her generous mouth, taste her peppermint breath. Her breath sounded ragged, moaning her words. She might've whispered his given name. Encouraged and heady, he pressed her closer. The fit of her generous curves to him felt so good, so right.

When she pushed against his chest, he relented and dragged himself from her an inch or two. "Why not, Precious? Why can't I kiss you more?"

She tugged at her hair, catching a flailing braid. "I can't dishonor Eliza. She saved my life. I owe her."

"What do you owe yourself, Precious Jewell? You deserve to be happy."

"I don't know what I deserve, but it can't be this, Gareth." Before he could fold her into his arms again, she dashed from his side. Sprinting, she fled the room, leaving him hot and bothered. Annoyed really. What hold did Eliza have on Precious?

He pivoted to Eliza's portrait. "How did you save her life?"

The painting didn't answer, so it was something else he'd have to figure out. He put a finger to his lips. He was for certain about one thing, Precious desired him. If he could continue to build her trust, then maybe she would lend him her heart.

She called him Gareth. That must mean, even for a brief moment, she saw them as equals, not as employer and servant. With equality, there was respect, and the ability to care. He and Eliza had that once, then things changed. Even if he were willing to admit how much of his heart Precious now claimed, what would keep things from changing for the worse?

Things had to erode. He wasn't whole. How would such a young vibrant woman deal with his condition?

Whatever the answer, it wouldn't come from staring at Eliza's portrait. He lifted the painting from its nail and set the painting on the floor. Tomorrow, he'd have the cabin boy mount it in the hall or another room. This parlor of corn silk yellow walls that Precious worked so hard on to make beautiful and orderly had to be a place where two wounded souls could say anything and feel everything without the weight of guilt.

He hefted the portrait against his shoulder and put it in the hall. If only everything was as easy as removing the painting. Well, at least he had seven more days to figure out things before Xhosa waged a final attack.

The house was quiet as night invaded all the rooms. Precious couldn't sleep and hated tossing in her bed. Jonas could awaken. She'd already put the boy through too much. If Mzwamadoda hadn't found her, the boy she loved like her own would've perished in those treacherous woods. How could she have been so thoughtless? Precious was disgusted with herself.

And then kissing Gareth underneath Eliza's picture, that was so brazen. What was she to do with an attraction that made her fingertips burn to touch him? For the first time in a long time, Precious didn't know what to do. She only knew that her fidgeting would awaken Jonas so she picked up her candle and crept out of the room.

Where would she go? This wasn't Firelynn. There weren't mazes of rooms to hide inside. No. One could be found very easily in a small home like this. Maybe she'd go sit in the bay window in the parlor. That room had to be quiet with everyone in bed.

As she started down the hall, she saw light coming from Mrs. Narvel's room. Clara shouldn't be up. She needed to be resting. Her time could happen at any moment.

She pushed open the bedchamber door. Clara was up reading in her worn Bible. She lifted her gaze. "I'm surprised you are up after the evening you had, lost in the woods, bitten by a viper."

"Did Lord Welling mention that I was rescued by a Xhosa?"

"No."

Precious folded her arms determined to get to that peace in her own head. "Does that matter to you, that someone who have may have been a party to your husband's death saved mine?"

"Would I want to see you or Jonas hurt because of my pain?" She rubbed her stomach, then patted the mattress. "Precious, come here."

She complied and sat on the edge, near enough to endure the woman's backhand. For didn't she deserve it for causing trouble?

"Precious, I know or I have accepted that God reigns mercies on good and bad alike. I know it seems that bad people get away with things while others struggle. And I know now that he allowed evil to touch those who love and trust him. But I also know he will work the bad for my good."

"What's that supposed to mean?"

Smiling, Clara lifted Precious's palm and pulled it to her abdomen. "It means that I and this baby are still going to find happiness."

Their linked palms wobbled with a baby's kick. He was still pretty high in her stomach and would have to turn soon.

"Precious, I am happy that a Xhosa found my friend and saved her life and let no harm come to Jonas."

Clara pulled her into her arms. "The world may have told you shouldn't be happy because of your skin or enslavement, and I know that a man somewhere, harmed you and made you think you didn't have a right to joy. Let me show you one man who died for all to be free in him. He's that Jesus you question."

"After all your pain, Clara, you can still be so sure?"

"I had started doubting. Then He sent my friend Precious to remind me that all would be well."

She leaned in and kissed her forehead. I came here to be a missionary. I might as well start in this house."

This time Precious would listen a little better. For that God who did save her in the woods and kept Jonas safe was still pretty good at taking things away. Maybe He'd be merciful and remove these feelings she had for

Gareth, Eliza's husband.

Chapter Nineteen: A Choice

Sleepy, Precious left Clara when the lady started to yawn. The brave woman still needed to rest. The movement of the little one in her stomach was strong, but she would need all of her strength to bring the babe into the world. Even more to raise him.

Precious plodded down the hall lighter, but still not light enough to sleep. That bay window seat in the parlor had been comforting. Maybe if she sat in it, she could watch the torches lighting up the perimeter of the fort. That sounded soothing to see it quiet without guns flaring. If the old chief and his daughter couldn't be found, the peace would be gone again.

Maybe even a few turns around the parlor would make things better. She slipped past Lord Welling's chambers. It was dark, but the man was a light sleeper. Perhaps his searching for her had made him tired enough to rest undisturbed. Yet, thinking of him, his arms embracing her tightly as they rode home…well, she was still plenty disturbed.

Down the wooden steps, she held out her candle and navigated the hall to the parlor. She stepped inside and closed the door. Her small waxy flame exposed Gareth asleep at his desk.

Her heart did that crazed beat again when his eyes opened. He didn't say anything as he stood. He came near her and took the candle from her fingers and shoved it onto the desk.

He kept a steady grip on her palm and tugged her toward him. His hands, maybe a thousand of them claimed her, crashing her into him. Her robe dropped to her ankles, as did her mobcap. In just her skivvies, she stood before him. Though not naked, she felt it. All her scars, the ones on her back and along her legs, and in her heart could surely be seen. She gripped her arms about her. The shame of yesterday had to be covered.

The man she shouldn't think about seized her by the hair and bit her lip. "There's no escape." The dark laugh, the cruel smirk, it wasn't Gareth at all, but the monster from Charleston. Her half-brother. How did he get here!

Or wasn't he always there, stuck in her head waiting for when she was weak to humble her again.

Breathing hard, Precious sat up. She blinked her eyes twice and tried to focus.

Bone colored walls. A threadbare beach colored carpet. No dirt.

Her pulse slowed. She'd fallen asleep in Clara's room. Nothing had occurred but a dream. A bad dream.

How could she have made Gareth into the monster? He had never treated her poorly. His touch had never been cruel. Why was she still trapped by the past?

Well, she wasn't going to solve anything counting roof beams. She lifted from her tiny portion of the mattress and eased out of the room.

It probably would have been better to go back to Jonas's room and to sleep with that sweet smell of roses filling the air from the soap she'd washed his things in. She couldn't. She had to go see the parlor. Then she'd know that everything was well.

She slipped inside the dark room and held her breath while lighting the sconce with her candle. A gasp left her lips. Just as in her dream, Gareth was asleep at the desk.

Before she could pivot and flee, his wet, sleep voice met her ear. "Precious, is all well? Has something happened?"

"No."

"Then why aren't you sleeping? After the time you had, the venom in your system, please go back to bed and rest."

The venom. Maybe it caused her nightmare. Staring at Gareth stretching his long arms, she steadied her nerves and lifted her gaze. "I could ask you the same."

A grin, that missing one, came out on his face. "Why do that when there's more company for me here?"

"There's no company just...me." Oh, he was flirting with her. "I'll take up your advice and go back to bed."

"Don't go. If you are waiting for your new friend, we can wait together."

"New friend?"

"Mzwamadoda, the man who literally said that he's coming for you."

The Xhosa man wasn't whom she feared coming for her. She looped the ribbons of her robe about her wrist. "He wouldn't risk such, coming through town with everyone so jittery."

"Well, my friend, your new friend, seemed taken with

you. He pulled his wrists behind his head. His white shirt still held some stiffness of starch as it silhouetted the width of his chest. "Some might say he would be a good match for you. Smart, strong… black."

What was he hinting at? She squinted at him and that silly grin of his that had started whittling away her resolve to ignore his charm. "Never mattered to me what others think. It's what they do, that's what concerns me."

He stood up, pounded over to her and clasped her hand. He held the union and rolled it back and forth in the light. "What do you say about how we contrast?"

His eyes, blue and clear, tempted like a fast moving creek. What was he fishing at?

Her skin heated as he kissed the back of her hand. "Do you think about how different we are, sea captain and his woman, the governess?"

He wasn't grinning anymore and the touch of his hand made it hard to think. "The governess should listen and go back to her charge."

His lips lifted. His voice sounded amused and not amused. "Oh, now Precious Jewell listens."

"Guess I should start some time. I figured I should do so if we only have seven days before the next attack."

"That business will wait. For now, we should discuss you liking me and I you."

She took a step back and then a few more until she stood near her bay window. "Gareth, don't talk like that. Nothing good can come from it."

He strolled to her, boots pounding. Clop, click, clop. "If something could come from it, what would that be?"

No answers could be had, not for the impossible.

Clip.

His boots rested. His eyes pierced hers.

Stretching, he put his fingers to her temples, with his index fingers rolling lightly over her skin. And before she could refocus, he'd taken off her mobcap. With both hands, he framed her face and sunk them deep into her tumbling braids. "Oh, yes I remember how useful this wonderful hair is."

He was nothing like the man in her dream, but wasn't he as determined? One hand left her cheek and smoothed its way to her waist. His actions were deliberate and slow. Her pulse soared as if he'd been the opposite. "Well, Precious, what do you want?"

There were inches between them. She breathed heavy and long as if he'd kissed her. She tried to move to him, to taste his mouth if only for just a moment but he kept her at a distance.

Maybe that was best, who knows what stupid thing she'd say or do if he did kiss her like he had on that beach with the world going crazy all about them.

"I'm waiting, Precious. I need to hear what you want."

"Nothing."

"Truly." He moved her a little closer in his arms.

It was torture to be so near, smelling the scent of him, almost feeling his heart beat. "You can't give me what I want."

He stilled and released her. He plodded away from the window. "Perhaps, but it doesn't stop me from trying."

There was hurt in his voice. She didn't mean to do that. She rushed to him and put her hand on his shoulder. "I don't want to be a mistress. I don't want Jonas or Mrs. Narvel's child growing up in a house that everyone thinks is sin riddled like that Neeltje woman's brothel. It's my home. It should be an honest one."

He turned. His eyes looked larger. His chin nodded to

some sort of silent agreement. "Then you shouldn't be a mistress. Marry me, Precious."

She folded up her arms. "You have lost your mind."

"Why? Then this thing between us will be respectable."

She bunched up her collar and backed from him. "I can't marry Eliza's husband."

His steady gaze pierced her heart. "You want to dishonor her? Marriage is an honorable institution."

This couldn't be true. He must be sotted. "You've been drinking. Where's the brandy? It—"

"Taste me. You will see I'm spirit free."

Head spinning, looking for what his game was, she stomped her foot. "So this must be some twisted bargain. How can you be so cruel?"

"Woman. This isn't a bargain, but if you need one make it up."

She turned to look at Eliza, but the portrait had been moved. She was alone with a man who made her feel treasured, frustrated, and confused, all at the same time. "I don't know what to do. Why do you want to marry me?"

"Maybe I want to make sure you are protected with rights and privileges, if I can't stop the Xhosa's attacks. Perhaps, I am afraid of losing you or just maybe I need a reason for you to be legally obligated to awaken next to me without squirming away." He lowered his voice as he pushed at his dark hair. "I'm just trying to give you a choice, but it seems a hopeless business. Perhaps, I'm using too many words."

She stiffened as he reached for her. He let his hand drop away.

"Back to that I see. When you decide what you want,

let me know. Maybe I'll still be alive to enjoy it."

He left the room, slamming the door.

The vibrations cut through as Precious sank onto the sofa. What did she want? What could she reach for and not be cut to pieces? And by the time she figured things out would Gareth be alive and still want her?

Look for the final episode of the season coming soon. Sign up for my newsletter and be the first to buy upcoming episodes and other books.

Episode IV
* * *

Episode IV of The Bargain

Length: 10 Chapters (25,000 words)

Summary: Saving The Colony And A Soul

Status: Available

In Episode IV:

Time is running out for Port Elizabeth. A missing chief and his daughter, tensions among frightened colonists, and the trembling of a difficult labor threaten to break the fragile bonds of its survival.

Precious Jewell will do what is right to protect those she cares for, even for the man she won't admit to needing.

For Gareth Conroy, death doesn't matter anymore.

He purposes that his spilt blood will bring the salvation of the colony, but will he realize too late that no single man of flesh and blood can bring redemption?

Will the burgeoning hope of two stubborn, wounded souls fray or smolder in this exciting conclusion of The Bargain, Season I?

Don't miss the exciting conclusion.

Chapter Twenty: London, July 1, 1819

Precious pushed on the door to Jonas's bedchamber to peek at the sleeping fellow.

The little boy had rolled up in his bed sheets with his blonde head poking out. His sweet little snore sounded like birds chirping.

No one would guess that his stupid governess or maid or whatever Precious was had put him in such danger. If not for finding the noble Xhosa, Jonas, well both of them could've been so hurt. Why had she been so foolish? What would she have done if the boy, this lovely little person who depended upon her had been injured?

Would Gareth have proposed to her if Jonas had hurt himself?

She put her hands to her thick hardheaded skull and pressed her thumbs into her temples. "No more being careless. Grandmama didn't raise a fool."

Or did she?

A lazy chirp croaked. Wide blue eyes, blinked open, then offered a smile. Oh he was his father's son with that smile. "Mama, fine?"

"It's…Yes, I'm fine." She crossed the room to tuck in the wiggling boy. He reached up and slapped a big juicy kiss on her cheek.

She let a smile grow on her face. "Now go on back to the land of fairy's that Mrs. Narvel read us about."

He yawned. "No, Esther. Nice lady saved people."

Her heavy heart warmed. Clara was good to read to both of them from her Bible. It wasn't strange anymore. And more often than not, it had begun to bring comfort. "Yes, Esther was brave."

He nodded and shut his eyes. "Yes, brave."

Before she could blink, his snores sounded again.

With a shake of her head, she crossed to the window and cracked it open. The sweet air slipped in freezing her tear-stained cheek. She wiped her face and inhaled the hint of flowers stirring in the breeze. Looking down, she saw something that looked like an aloe plant with bunches of yellow blooms. That had to be the source of the fragrance. The freshness, that scent of hope, would help Jonas claim all the naps he'd missed yesterday.

She tiptoed back to the door, took a final sniff and let her gaze fall again on the child. That boy had her heart. She'd never allow her foolishness to harm him again. Having a careless stepmother was like spilled kerosene falling on a lit match. The blaze would consume everything. "I won't put you in that kind of danger again, sweet boy. Never."

"Sleep, Mammie Mama."

Mama. With a sad huff, Precious closed the door. It would be so easy to claim him, for she loved him as if she'd birthed him. But Jonas was Gareth's and dear Eliza's.

Tomorrow, Precious had to be firm with Jonas and herself. She couldn't covet the child or make it harder for him to accept someone else more proper for a stepmother.

As soon as Gareth figured his way out of this crisis with the Xhosa, he could concentrate on finding a mama for Jonas. One who read really well like Mrs. Narvel, and could hold her head high in Port Elizabeth with no scars from the past.

She swiped again at her wet cheek and weak eyes. Her body must still be feeling the effects of the snake venom for surely she wasn't given to such emotions. The lack of sleep didn't help. Rest didn't come last night. Over and over, her traitorous mind repeated Gareth's proposal and showed the light dim in his blue eyes when she said, 'no'.

Tempted to bang her forehead against the door, she stood up straight. Why would he ask a formerly enslaved servant to be his baroness? What was in it for him?

And what if for one moment, she could dream and said yes?

Would being able to his accept his kisses without feeling like they were sneaking outweigh the sneers of the town folk when they rode side by side in a wagon or again boarded the Margeaux? Would it cover the shame of her scars, the reminder she saw etched in her flesh every time she washed?

Nonsense. This thinking of marrying. No one could accept or forgive her humiliation. And how could she be thinking about becoming attached to Eliza's husband. That just wasn't right. Eliza had saved her. Though gone for two years, didn't she owe her more loyalty than to make eyes at her husband? Shameful.

Shrugging in hopelessness, Precious swiveled and

pivoted into Gareth. Colliding into his big chest, she smashed a cheek on the buttons of his jacket. She forgot herself and clung to him. But those big strong arms of his didn't move to embrace her back.

"Precious, is all well?"

Frozen, she continued to lean into him, smelling every inch of his starched shirt, with its hints of the pine soap he used. The beat of his heart danced like it had last night. Still, he didn't move, didn't put one of those well-muscled arms about her.

"Has something happened, Precious? Tell me."

Sinking deeper into the want filling his perfect blue gaze, she stood still. What could she say to him? She'd turned down his proposal. How could she ask him to hold her and make the world seem right?

Her throat clogged with a sob. She couldn't even grunt past the lump of shame filling her mouth. She wanted Eliza's husband, needed to be kissed by grown up lips. Ones that knew all kinds of words, big ones, small ones, ones that made her heart burn within her bosom.

He stroked her cheek. His thumb lightly brushed its fullness, and then lifted her jaw. "Precious?"

Her eyes closed as she surrendered to his touch. Suddenly, she blinked away the darkness, remembered herself and pulled back.

His hand moved. Cool air swept around her as he stepped away. "You still don't know what you want, Precious. But I do. I have a colony to save."

Save? That meant he would put himself in danger. She pulled at her shawl and spun around catching sight of his straight spine as he descended the stairs. "Wait."

He unbolted the door, and tapped at the brass as if he counted the reasons why he should wait and listen versus leaving. Finally, opening the door, he lifted his foot to go outside.

"Gareth, please don't go."

He dipped his head and pushed the door closed. He pivoted. "I'm listening."

"Mrs. Narvel. The baby hasn't turned."

The blank veneer of his face slipped. His clear blue eyes hardened. "That's it?"

She nodded.

"If that's your only caution, dismiss it. There's still plenty of time. The babe will find the right way."

Precious chewed her bottom lip. She was a guilty coward for making him feel unwanted and not telling him how she felt. She tugged on her collar and straightened. "No one listened to me when I said Miss Eliza was in trouble. I'm telling you that baby should've turned by now."

A harsh sigh blasted from his flared nostrils. He looked to the ceiling and whipped a hand through his thick hair. "I've checked on her. The babe and Mrs. Narvel will keep until I get back in a few days."

He was going away, and not for just a couple of hours. Did rejection push him out of his wits? Did he want to make a wife out of Precious that much?

Gareth stared at the most frustrating woman of his acquaintance and counted the shallow breaths filling her bosom. Goodness, why did she have to be so stubborn and beautiful with that flared nose of hers? Those full lips tucked into a dot. She needn't make herself ill over Mrs. Narvel when there were other things like the Xhosa tribe pushing everyone into the bay cutting the life out of Port Elizabeth. Those were things to fear.

He sighed, spread his legs apart and held to attention, as if he addressed an admiral. "I have to leave. I will return in three days."

"Three days." Her eyes grew big like saucers. They showed fear, an emotion he didn't think the brave girl possessed.

What was going on in her head? Gareth had never understood Eliza or any other female. He shrugged and rotated to the door.

She sped her steps behind him. Her fingers clasped onto his rapier slowing his exit. "No, don't go. I…We need you here."

He half pivoted as he slid her palms from the fennel of his blade. "What are you doing?"

She shook her head hysterically, but that wasn't Precious. "You are not listening."

Tapping away her fingers, he almost smiled. Maybe he wasn't listening. It was hard to do as he watched the same lips that had turned him away. "You don't touch a man's greatest weapon, unless you're prepared to use it."

Those eyes, lovely and dark, swirled and popped wider. She pulled her hands back and tucked them beneath her grey shawl. "Babies don't follow a schedule."

"Then you will know what to do. You've told me again and again you don't need me, Precious Jewell. Why start now?"

Her voice sounded strangled. "So now you are leaving me just like you did with Eliza?"

Oh, the girl knew how to throw a dagger to the heart. Maybe he should just give her his rapier too and let her finish him. He pushed at his hair and tried to come up with a softer way to reply. This could be their last meeting. Anything could happen in the wild. He opened his mouth, but the pout hanging on her frowning lips stripped away his caution. "Woman, this isn't the same. I've a colony to save. And why would Port Elizabeth matter to you? Eliza only cared because she was my wife. What is your reason?"

Her gaze lowered. "Because I do, and I want to help you. But stay. Let's keep Mrs. Narvel safe then—"

"No. Not good enough. I'll see you in three days."

She sprang forward again and clasped his arm creasing the sleeve of his blue jacket. "Where are you going? At least tell me that."

"To the blacksmith now and then off to the inland settlements. The chief's daughter is part Dutch. They may be hiding there."

She nodded, grasped him by the coat lapel. Face to face, gaze to gaze, he saw fury and hurt and something else in those magical irises of hers. Breathing heavy and long as if he'd stolen the air from her lungs, she crossed the inches that separated them and kissed his cheek. Turning, she fled and almost tripped as she ran up the stairs.

With a shake of the head, he trudged out of the house and stood on the short portico, if one could call it that. He rested his hand on the thin beam that held up the smallish roof. Gareth needed to calm his thoughts. His notion to pretend he wasn't affected by her refusal of his proposal hadn't gone so well. Yes, he burned inside from her rejection as he had last night.

Any one other than that stubborn American would understand the honor he bestowed upon her. Any one else would be appreciative, and respond in kind.

But not Precious. She didn't give a whit, and that was one of the reasons he cared so much for her. That's why he…

Gareth sucked in a breath, but the air must've sputtered out of his pierced chest. The gaping hole to his vanity held nothing inside. Good thing he was as stubborn as Precious. Yes, far too stubborn to admit painstakingly obvious things.

He shook his head, clearing it of Precious and the fearful look in her eyes. Time to be about the mission, something he had a better chance to control. He pounded off the portico and started down the road to Dennis's shop and the accompanying stables.

Funny, if she'd said yes last night or even now to marrying, he'd be hauling her down to Dennis's with the family ring. They'd be married in minutes just as if they'd eloped to Gretna Green in England.

He sighed. It wasn't to be. The woman who just kissed his cheek, who clutched his arm and his rapier like it was a rope keeping her from drifting away, didn't need him.

Stubborn girl. If she'd said yes, at least he'd know she'd be protected if he died during this hunt for the missing Xhosa chief. No, she had to take that notion from him, too.

He almost looked back at the solid door of his whitewashed house as thoughts of the stubborn, foolhardy, lovely woman continued to press. "Well, I better return in one piece."

Footsteps pattered behind. He spun around hoping to see Precious there, hoping she'd come to her senses.

She hadn't. It was just Mr. Grossling, the war department officer.

A thousand pounds of disappointment crushed his innards, but Gareth strengthened his voice. "Grossling, are you looking for me?"

The man pulled a pistol from his pocket.

Before he could aim it, Gareth drew his rapier and forced the tip at the fool's neck. "What are you doing?"

Grossling's Adam's apple vibrated, shaking the rapier, causing it to nick his weak flesh leaving red marks. The laggard cursed then said, "Easy captain. Let's lower our weapons."

Gareth didn't budge. In fact, he wished for the chance to cut something into shreds, just to feel fully in control. Yet, how would it look for the leader of Port Elizabeth to kill a denizen on its first street? He eased the pressure back on the sharpened iron but didn't withdraw his rapier. "Why don't you go first, and then I'll follow."

Grossling kept his gaze level, but lowered the gun and shoved the muzzle into his coat pocket. "I'm not trying to kill you, but I'll be ready when it's time to kill those Xhosa. You can count on me to help murder the heathens."

Putting his rapier back into his sash, he shook his head. "No. You will return to filling out your forms. The last thing I need is a trigger happy warrior. And when I say so, you will protect the colonists. That is your mission before you think about harming anyone."

Pushing at the small cut on his neck, Grossling worked his jaw. "Use that hot head of yours to kill the Xhosa."

"I'll use my temper to neutralize threats, all threats."

"Wouldn't that make you a threat to be neutralized?" Grossling followed up his words with a laugh full of bluster, as if the levity would take away his careless words. "Good day, Captain."

Something in Gareth's gut said watch that one, but he shrugged and set his focus on the impending problems with the Xhosa tribe. Fury still roiled in his innards as he headed again toward the blacksmith.

Boots crunching on pebbles and dried leaves, he stumbled forward.

The low breeze kicked up dust along the road. Specks of cinnamon and umber danced in the wind then settled back down on the road, Port Elizabeth's first road. He couldn't let it be the last.

With each footstep, he tried to discern his growing anger. Was it possible to vanish all the hard work and sacrifices to make a go of this place? That couldn't happen. Why couldn't Precious see Port Elizabeth as the reason he had to leave her?

Maybe Eliza told her of his inadequacies. With virile charismatic men like Mzwamadoda around, why should she want Gareth? Was it Gareth in Precious's mind when she kissed him or her brazen rescuer?

Gareth's fingers clenched as he shoved a fist into his pocket. The thought of Precious and Mzwamadoda burned a hole in his gut.

She should be grateful to Gareth. He always respected her regardless of the trouble her deep passions drove her to.

She should admire the enormity of the task at hand and support him without complaint.

She should ask him to spend time with her for her sake, not another woman.

She should want his kisses as much as he enjoyed offering them.

She should love him!

Love?

He stopped short and nearly tripped again. Did that word just flash before his eyes? Was Mrs. Narvel right?

Gareth swallowed hard at the implications. He tried to blink away the notion. The fury of jealousy over Mzwamadoda dripped away as his palms dampened. Could his unconscious mind have settled into loving her?

Now wasn't the time to figure it out, particularly since she didn't want him. She'd refused his offer and blamed it on Eliza. Long since gone, how could Eliza's hold be stronger than any thing the feisty governess felt for him?

Unwilling to measure the depths of his feelings or admit defeat, he stomped the rest of the way to the blacksmith, kicking an occasional rock that dared lie in his path.

Dennis leaned against the doorframe with his arms folded across his dark leather vest. "Whoa there, Welling. What has you chewing dirt?"

Gareth didn't need homespun wisdom or some assertion about God solving all his problems from the colony's makeshift pastor. He looked at the ground. "Nothing of consequence."

"I saw you tearing up that road for at least a half of a mile back. Something's eating at you."

"I need sturdy shoes on my horse. I've some hard riding to do to locate some of the Dutch settlements."

The old man didn't move. He forced Gareth to look in his face. "I can't dawdle."

"Seems an odd time to take off. That will take you three days round trip. With Narvel's widows about to pop, and the Xhosa problem, I'd reckon you should stay."

"This expedition might just stop the hostilities. As for the former, she will keep and my boy's governess will take care of things until I return."

Dennis shook his head, still not moving from his

position. "You trying to convince me or yourself? Nothing ever quite follows man's timing. At some point, a fellow needs to think beyond his own notions."

"I'm sacrificing for Port Elizabeth. It's bigger than Narvel's widow or a feisty governess."

"Speaking of her." Dennis pivoted and went into his shop.

Gareth should've headed straight for the stable around back, but curiosity over what the man was going to say about Precious made him follow.

Dennis swung his blackened tongs from a hook and plunged it into the water. "This shoe is about done."

The thick char on the tool showed its age, the passing down of the implement through the generations. Oh, how Gareth wanted this place and his leadership to be something Jonas and Precious could hold onto with pride.

"You've been sweet on the negress. I hear talk of her being more than just the help."

Unprepared for the interrogation, Gareth folded his arms. "What does my household arrangements have to do with anything?"

"Proximity can make things seem right. Close quarters have led to all types of hasty decisions, unchristian behavior. Miss Jewell's from the Carolina's right? The slave trade is very big there." Dennis popped out the shoe and felt the edges. "Yes, this will do. "

Gall flooded Gareth. "I'm not one of those men. I don't order employees to my bedchamber. My late wife's family enslaved her. But she's not as the American's say, a fancy. She is free. She has her own mind and does as she pleases."

Taking a big file with ridges, Dennis rubbed at a short

corner. "We have too many women who lose their means and end up selling their bodies to survive. I'd hate to see the colony's leader make the same mistakes."

He wasn't going to admit to the man Precious had refused to marry him or that he'd ended her indentured service with the paperwork on his desk. It had to be to done prior to asking her to consent to wed. He couldn't risk telling Precious and have her walk out his door and his life. No, he couldn't share his lack of trust, so he just stared at the shine forming upon the shoe as Dennis polished it.

"Perhaps you are correct, Welling. A self-focused mind makes our wants and desires both seem like the true path. But desires can just be selfishness in disguise."

He wanted to say he wasn't selfish, but Gareth knew that he was. Deep down, he wanted Precious to love him without him ever having to utter those words again. Eliza had married him for the prestige of his name. Why couldn't that be enough for Precious? Or why couldn't she succumb to the desire arcing between them like sweet lightning and wed for that alone? He snorted a quick breath, attempting to cool the heat coursing in his veins. "Yes, but sometimes desire is right."

"Is it now?" Dennis scrubbed at his chin and started toward the rear of the building, exiting to the stables. "I don't think it works like that."

Gareth followed close. He wanted with each step to be on his horse riding as far and as fast as he could. "Things just need to keep for a little while longer. I'll be back before trouble."

The man opened up the door to the hut like structure where Gareth's grey horse stood with its bushy silver mane. "If you hadn't noticed, there's already trouble.

Folks are short on tempers. The small service we had last Sunday ended in a brawl."

"Open in the road? Your parishioners fighting?"

Just out front of the shop. If we make it, this place should have a fine chapel built.

Gareth swung his leg over the gelding's strong back. "Well, with a bit of luck, we'll be able to break ground on it next year."

Dennis handed him the reins. "Some things take more than luck. And it's fine to admit the truth too. You don't have all the answers, but God does, Lord Welling. You're trying to do this all on your own. Don't you think others want to help? Don't you think if you asked, help would come?"

Gareth rolled the leather strap of the horse's harness betwixt his fingers. Asking didn't suit him. The possibility of no was too great. Telling others what to do felt comfortable. Hadn't he asked Precious to marry him, only for her to say no? Yes, asking wasn't for him. "I'll be back as soon as I can. Keep everyone in order. Ralston is prepared to evacuate the colonists if…"

"If you don't return?"

No, he'd be back. Regardless of Precious's refusal, she still needed protecting. His son and Mrs. Narvel all needed protecting. "I'll see you in three days."

Dennis blocked his path. He reached into his vest and pulled out a folded up parchment. "This was something your uncle wrote to me. He gave it to me the last time he was here before setting off to London. I think you might need it more."

Taking the paper, he traced the edge of the worn foolscap. It was his uncle's private stationery and from the depth of the creases, something Dennis must've studied from time to and time.

"Read it, Lord Welling. It may bring you peace."

Gareth started his mount but then slowed him at the door. "You haven't struggled with my title today.

"Haven't needed to. This colony is yours to lead. I'm praying that like your uncle, you find the way to do right."

Thinking of his beloved mentor and how close Gareth was to losing Port Elizabeth hit deep and hard. But he made his face like stone, unmoved from the weight of the angst growing inside. He urged the horse forward. "I'll be back in three days with news of the missing chief. I'll stop the Xhosa aggression."

A mile or two on the open trail, Gareth let his veneer slip. His confidence in his own abilities waned. What did one do when one realized for the hundredth time they weren't enough? His will and desires weren't enough for Precious or Port Elizabeth. He turned his face up to the low clouds. A soft mumble fell from his lips. He cleared his throat and said in a loud commanding voice. "I understand. I can't do any of this alone. Make things right anytime You're ready."

Chapter Twenty-One: No to the Dress

The cabin boy dragged the last big pot of water into the hall for Precious to inspect. "Ma'am, that's the last one. If you don't need anything else, I'll be on my way."

She handed him a glass of cooled tea. "Thank you. Your captain would be proud."

A small smile popped onto his face as he swatted his brow of sweat. The fifteen or sixteen year-old guzzled the liquid. Hopefully it was a good reward for hauling eight jars of freshwater from the bay to the house.

He yawned and rubbed his reddish blonde mop. "I'll sleep good tonight at the fort."

"You've done good. Go on and get your supper. I've packed you up some stew in the kitchen."

The lad's face brightened as he bounced down the hall toward the back kitchen. Mid stride, he stopped, rotated, and sprinted out the front door.

What in the world could he be doing? So far, everyone loved her cooking. Even Ralston, Gareth's first mate came off his post twice yesterday for another dip of her fresh bread and fish. The first time, he probably nosed around on Gareth's behalf. But the second time had been pure gluttony.

Maybe when Gareth restored the peace, he could let her open the house for a Sunday meal, sort of like the field hands coming to Grandmama's. It was one of the memories of Charleston she liked. The only one.

She rubbed at her temples, chastising her mind for stumbling back to Gareth. She tried not to fret about him, but failed every minute. He should be here, not out there facing who knows what all alone.

Oh, she really needed to push harder on her skull to keep from seeing his sea blue eyes everywhere. She missed him too much.

Scraping noises made her look up from the barrels.

The lad dragged a wide flat crate inside. She hoped he hadn't scratched up the floorboards. "This was on the ship. The last in the hold. It had your name on it." He set it down, nodded his head and almost tripped over himself as he lunged toward the kitchen.

A smile wanted to force its way onto her lips but the curiosity of something having her name on it kept them tight. How many times had she seen her name written out? Three, maybe four. She plodded over and pulled it past her jugs to the light at the bottom of the steps.

She ran her fingers over the stamped letters. P-R-E-C-I-O-U-S—J-E-W-E-L-L. What could it be? She'd brought all her possessions in her bag from the Margeaux herself.

The need to know made her pulse race. She pulled at the boards and pried at a corner until she got the slat of wood moving. With a final tug, the lid flipped free. The scent of lavender hit her. Her heart almost stopped as she pushed the folds of tissue paper aside. With the last piece of paper out of the way, her breath caught.

The emerald dress.

Eliza's emerald striped gown with the low bodice, that clung to her curves. The silk that was to be given away.

Why was it here?

And why did it have Precious's name?

Swallowing, she lifted her gaze to her late mistress's portrait. Her mind filled with the sounds of Eliza's laughter and memories of that one day she let Precious try on this dress. Slipping the silk over her palm, she remembered Eliza saying she looked well in it. She said no one could see her scars. For a moment, Precious believed her.

Then time passed. The butler and others took every opportunity to remind her that the scars, the stains would never go away. Maybe their words like the scars, where right. For what other than a wh-- she couldn't bring herself to even think the word. What kind of person would want their friend's husband?

Guilt wrapped about Precious. It strangled her in the shadow of the portrait. It was bad enough Eliza's son clung to Precious's bosom as if he was her own. Now she'd drawn in Gareth. She was no better than those words. Her scars ran too deep.

Sweating, she tossed the dress to the floor and backed up to the largest urn of the eight she had the boy fill. She stuck her hands in the cold water and drew up some to drink. The water refreshed her, taking the stiffness from her body. It was just a dress. A nice gesture. Something that if not saved would've been given away.

That last week in Firelynn, Gareth offered it to her while staring at Eliza's picture. Precious's forehead crinkled with new suspicions. Was this a ploy, another trick to sway her? He'd teased her about being a tentative rodent playing with a fast thinking Tomcat.

She shuffled her hands against her apron. There would be no way Gareth would know that they, that she would come to care for him. Could he? Had all the tenderness been some build up to confuse her? Had he been planning a new bargain of some sort? Was it is his mind to give that fancy silk gown to his fancy, his new bed chamber mistress?

She closed her eyes and relived every kiss. She recalled the tone of his deep voice has he asked her to marry him. He didn't want a fancy. He wanted a wife. Heat ran up her limbs. Her heart pounded as if he stood before her. No, Gareth wasn't playing games anymore. He'd caught his mouse.

"What are you doing down here?" Clara's voice floated from behind.

Precious jerked as if she'd been caught doing something naughty. She swallowed and tugged at her collar, making sure the scars on her neck didn't show. "Now, Miss Clara." She slowed her tone and steadied her voice. "You shouldn't be out of bed. And you shouldn't be walking down these steps. What if you fell?"

"Precious," The woman tugged at her woolen robe and cupped her swollen abdomen.

She leaned against the rail of the steps. "I can't lay about, not when I hear doors slamming and other noises. I had to see what was happening. Maybe I can help."

Precious understood not wanting to be idle, but the woman shouldn't be risking her health. She wiped her palms on her apron. "Lord Welling's cabin boy, he helped me fetch water. You must've heard the front and back doors opening and closing."

Clara lifted her index finger and pointed, moving her mouth as she counted. "Seven. Eight. Eight jugs of water. Precious, are you expecting a drought?"

Precious wiped her hands on her apron. "I am getting ready for you to birth little Narvel. Clean water is necessary."

"And did the cabin boy bring that dress, too? Is that dress for you? Oh, it will look lovely on you. Go—"

"Stop." Precious wrung her hands. Her voice sounded too loud. Clara was delicate and didn't need scolding. "Sorry, Clara."

"Precious, your name is on the crate. It's yours. I don't understand."

"The box has my name, but it was Miss Eliza's dress. It can't be mine."

Clara seemed to squint and then looked toward the oil painting of the late Mrs. Conroy, Gareth's Eliza. "Well, she can't use it now. I don't see any harm in you having it. Your chestnut eyes will glow in it."

"Miss Eliza's eyes did. We have the same eyes. But I have to stop wanting things that were hers. It's not right."

Clara folded her arms as her smile faded. "I see. She pivoted fully to the painting. I'm surprised that you haven't moved this back to the mantle in the parlor, the main room in the house."

"Ga...Lord Welling placed it here."

"Well, why don't you put candles about it and pay your respects daily." Clara's tone wasn't sweet. It bore an edge Precious didn't think the lady possessed.

"Come on, Precious. Let's get them now. Then you can teach Jonas and me how to be stuck in the past."

Precious pushed at her brow. "You're a widow. You've

months before you can go on about your life."

"When I'm able, I may go out in black crepe as proper for a widow, but I won't blanket it about my heart or cut myself off from feeling."

"You don't understand."

"I understand plenty. So does Lord Welling. We've loved and lost, but I believe I can love again. I know he's found love again."

Precious put her hands to her ears. Fire crept up her neck. The scar hurt as if it burned. She stuck her hands in the water again and patted her throat. "He can't love me. He just can't. He doesn't realize what I am."

"I think he does. I think he sees you and your beautiful spirit. Surely, you're not thinking of race? Black and white didn't matter much when he jumped into the ocean after you or when you dove headlong after him to save him from the Xhosa."

Precious wasn't thinking about their difference in skin. Something far worse was branded in her skin. Scars that wouldn't go away.

Clara came down the last step. Before Precious realized it, the woman grasped her hand. "I don't know why you can't let yourself be happy, but you should be happy. No one as loving or as caring as you should keep herself away from love. No memory or claims from the grave can begrudge you."

She kissed Precious's knuckles. A wince crossed her face as she did.

The baby. Enough of her own foolishness. Her friend needed help. Precious put her arms about her and guided her to the stairs. "I told you, you need to be laying down."

She put her weight on Precious and slowly took the

stairs. At the top, she pressed Precious's palm against her big belly. "He's mighty active in there. Hopefully, Lord Welling will be back soon. I hate that he will miss this one's arrival."

The kick felt like a foot. That baby was still pointed the wrong way. "He rode off to a Dutch settlement." Precious's voice croaked on the word settlement. "But he'll be back tomorrow."

"Now you sound nervous. You don't think he'll be back?"

How could she tell her friend? Maybe if she just blurted it out, the knots in her stomach that kept showing up and twisting would finally leave. "He's going to try and stop the Xhosa, but I don't think his head is on straight. He's gonna be reckless."

Clara shook her head and waddled to her door. "You mean he might try to run out in the middle of a snake forest to get rue for me?"

Precious wanted to pull her mobcap over her eyes. Instead, she drew back her shoulders. "Yes, I've been reckless. But I had good cause. He needed savin' and you needed rue. Wouldn't you have done so for your husband?"

Smoothing the front of her robe, Clara nodded. "For a friend, I'd like to think so. For my husband. For the man I love, I'd survive just about anything. Is that how you feel?"

Pressured to admit things that she couldn't possess, Precious backed away. "You need to be going and resting. You'll need your strength when that little one starts pushing to come."

"Why is it so hard for you to admit how you feel? Why won't you let him love you?"

Desperate, she bunched her collar and came up with the first excuse she could. "A servant can't love her employer. It's not done."

"It's been done. And I know several governesses who've married their employer or his son and changed their stations. So social class can't be a hindrance. What is the real reason?"

"Woman, open your eyes. I am not like your governess friends. I was enslaved by his wife and by her marriage, enslaved to him. How can I covet his love?"

Leaning on the threshold, Clara lifted her chin. Her eyes closed. She was praying again. Something she did more often and more visibly since that time in her room when Precious broke through her sadness. "You are not enslaved now. I've seen the respect and admiration he holds in his eyes for you. He doesn't see you as less than. And I think he loves you too."

"I didn't do anything to cause it. I didn't lure him to me. I haven't been wanton."

"Precious, calm down. If you weren't so far away, I'd hug you and make you see the truth. You've done nothing wrong. Even when you pretended to be the captain's woman on the Margeaux, neither of you took advantage of the other. Nothing but respect and regard for one another is what I've seen. But this isn't about being property is it? I'm beginning to think that it's not about Miss Eliza. What is the real reason you are terrified of loving the captain?"

Precious bit her lip. Uttering anything about not wanting Eliza's man or dishonoring her friend wouldn't be accept by this wise woman. The truth was far worse.

Clara opened her bedchamber door. "No one could love Jonas more. The debt you feel to Eliza Conroy has been paid. If Lord Welling is in love with you, he's ready to move away from the past. No one can take a heart that's unavailable."

She turned, then paused again. "One day I hope to be as lucky as Lord Welling to find love again. To find someone who can treasure me and this child. I think my Mr. Narvel wouldn't want me to be alone. I don't think any true friend would."

Precious watched the door close. Tomorrow, she'd have the cabin boy gather up as much wood as possible to get the water warmed and linens washed. That baby would be coming soon. Hopefully, he would turn and make his debut without a fuss.

Taking a few steps, Precious' slippers slowed. She started thinking again on Jonas's birth and how it drained the life from Eliza. She couldn't let that happen to Clara. But how?

Head aching, filled with doubts, she sank and stared at her reflection in the wall mirror. Quivering lips and wet eyes met her gaze. Pitiful.

If she'd seen a thief or husband stealer in the mirror, then maybe the turmoil in her gut might just calm, but the reflection of a girl with scars on her neck poorly hidden by braids reminded her of what she was. These were the visible marks, nothing to the ones hidden about her. Eliza put balm on them, and took her to England to save her from more pain. Loving Jonas, maybe that debt was paid. But Precious's innards still felt bankrupt.

She put her face into her hands, and wept. Hot tears dumped against her palms as she tried to muffle her whimpers with her roughed skin. She was still those hidden scars. Gareth's proposal hadn't changed that. Nothing ever would.

Chapter Twenty-Two: By the Waters

Pressing closer to the Dutch settlement, Gareth slowed his horse. He'd spent too much time in Bethelsdorp. The little mission village with the rows of whitewashed almshouses seemed like the perfect place to hide the chief. Conversing with the locals, he heard more Irish and Spanish tongues than he had in a long time. The small plaque on the last row of pews in the Van Der Kemps Kloof Church was etched with the name Joseph Conroy, The Baron Welling. It reminded Gareth of his uncle's influence and how hard he'd worked at bringing different sides together for the good of this land. What would his uncle say now, with the peace threatened, and everything about to be lost?

The gong of a bell, probably the brass one hanging in the middle of the village filled the quiet. What did it announce? Prayer, a worship service, maybe a babe's birth? He'd never figure it out, but his mind was still there, listening and watching the missionaries.

Gareth knew the reasons he risked all, the need to

make his uncle's work live on, the legacy of blood that pushed his uncle, now sat squarely on him, squeezing at his chest. But what drove these missionaries?

Converting the Xhosa to faith, as well as being a place for all the foreigners to stop along the coast and renew before journeying further inland touched him, more deeply than it should. Failing held dire consequences. He knew in his bones, the Xhosa wouldn't stop at punishing Port Elizabeth. Their new leader, Bezile, wanted all foreigners dumped into Angola Bay. He would turn his wrath to these people. Gareth had Fort Frederick and cannons to protect the colonists for a few hours against an onslaught. What did Bethelsdorp have? Almshouses and prayer? A brass plaque to a man long gone?

He sunk in his saddle and waited for the last toll to fade. An hour or two later, his concentration hadn't returned. With the sun lowering more and more, he might as well break for camp. He pulled at the reigns, made his mount stop and then jumped down. Leading the gelding to a grassy patch and tying him to a tree overlooking a river, he saw the midden pile and allowed himself to smile. Some person, either Xhosa or Strandloper had bedded in this spot and used the midden to dump shells, making an outdoor kitchen for abalone and crayfish. This was as good a place as any to get a few hours of sleep and start again fresh in pursuit of the missing Xhosa.

He spread out his bedroll and kicked a pink shell out of the way. Precious wouldn't like this outdoor kitchen with untidy shells. The orderly miss always had things in its place.

He rubbed at his face, released a frustrating grunt for thinking about the stubborn woman then started a fire.

He cocked his head, and turned toward his gelding. "Hey boy, do you still think about mares? Maybe that one stubborn one, boy."

The horse ignored him, munching on the wild brown grasses.

As the fire blazed, he settled on to his bundle. Tugging on a blade of tall grass, he stared at the night sky. It was beautiful. Diamonds lit the dark strands of deep blue and purple. Oh, how his uncle loved this place. The man saw hope in the faces of the colonists and the tribes he negotiated.

His sturdy horse nibbled dry brown brush and edged closer to the water. Gareth couldn't blame him. The swirling noise of the river sounded peaceful. His own eyes grew heavier. Yet, if he closed them what would he see?

Precious's quivering lips trying not to show fear.

Or worse. Eliza. Would she approve of Precious taking her place, having the title she so craved but never claimed? A bitter chuckle sputtered from deep inside. No, that woman wouldn't want to give anyone anything that she felt was hers. Yet, she entrusted Jonas to Precious. What was the bond? Was it really Marsdale blood that threaded them together in this mashed up tapestry? Or was it something worse, something that transcended station, slave and slave mistress?

And how could he break it? What would he have to do or say to help the blasted jewel of a lady experience true freedom?

He was one to talk.

What could Gareth say of true freedom, when fear of acceptance kept him from being vulnerable to those he should trust? His mistrust had led him to alienate his own son. A debt he didn't know how he would ever repay.

Folding his arms behind his head, he pulled at his jacket. The letter from his uncle tumbled out. Luckily, it didn't fall into the flames. He tugged at it, quickly wrenching it back to his chest. Thumbing the well-worn creases, he unfolded it. His uncle's sturdy script filled the parchment. There was a section of pleasantries, the usual compliments over a sermon Dennis had preached, but then one solemn sentence.

Blessed is the man that endureth temptation: for when he is tried, he shall receive the crown of life, which the Lord hath promised to them that love him.

Dennis was the colony's reverend. Temptation wasn't a problem for him, or was it? Maybe all men struggled with it in some form or another.

He shook his head as he pondered the matter. Until now, Gareth's own struggles with his war injuries made it easy to forego physical temptations. When his men would go ashore at the various ports or even to Madame Neeltje's, he never had the inclination to be a whoremonger. Even after Eliza's death, when such pleasures wouldn't be adultery, womanizing wasn't at the forefront of his thoughts. No, Port Elizabeth and seeing her survive was his only focus.

Until now.

Now his mind lay divided between his leadership of the colony and his household, bonding with his son and dealing with the delectably unpredictable Precious Jewell.

He hefted the paper again to his face. The firelight glowed behind it, outlining the words the Lord had promised to them that love Him.

Gareth closed his eyes. He was back on his naval vessel. He could see his men lighting the fuse of the cannon, the one that exploded injuring him and killing three others. He smelled the salt in the air, the flint, and the char of the fuse. His heart pounded. The small voice in his head grew loud. Why hadn't he listened? Why didn't he stand back? No, he trusted his own gut, the hunger for victory. The need to witness the enemy vanquished led to his own defeat. Laid up for the rest of the war. His proud command given to another. Then a bride arranged by his uncle betrothed to man, a wounded man sight unseen. Eliza's disappointment was understandable, hard to bear, and utterly humbling.

Pulse exploding, Gareth lurched forward. He thrust open his eyes and glanced about him. The night enveloped him, thick and black. Even the fire had grown cold and died. As he gulped the fresh clean air, the bitter taste in his mouth receded. The past was no more. He'd healed enough to relearn to walk, even sire a son.

Gareth's temptation wasn't about womanizing. It was about loving God enough to trust Him. It was about loving Precious enough to trust that she could love him back. Maybe he could trust that God would help him save Port Elizabeth.

He folded up the paper and avoided the urge to toss it into the flames. Stuffing it deep into his pocket, he stared at the sky. Was Gareth a big enough man to trust anyone's judgment other than his own?

He rolled onto his side and listened to the river and the latent whinnying of his horse. If he couldn't find the chief, he supposed he'd have to come to terms with God quickly. He was ready to die for Port Elizabeth, for Precious and Jonas. It would be good to firm up his salvation to be assured of his final destination when the end came.

Precious shifted her hands against her apron and peered out the window again. Two days and no Gareth. The stubborn man hadn't returned. Was he staying on the Margeaux, just to make her fret?

The nerve of him. She fumed and paced some more. He should have been back by now, safe in the house, not finding ways to vex her. She clicked her short heels against the floorboard. He should've never went in the first place. Clara was ready to burst and the baby hadn't turned.

What did Old Doctor Marsdale say to do? Every pot in the house had fresh water. The fireplace in the parlor and in the kitchen had some warming. Surely, that would be enough to keep things cleaned, just like the old man would do.

Oh, what would he say to get that baby pointed right? Grandmama said that Precious's own mammie just stopped in the fields, squatted and had Precious. Eliza wasn't built for that rugged life and from the looks of it, neither was Clara.

She started pacing again. Oh, what would Old Doc... her pa say to do? The more she thought about him and Charleston, the sadder her heart got. She would always feel some kind of way about never being able to acknowledge her pa. She had so many questions for him.

Her ma was a field hand at first. So she wasn't bred to be her master's fancy, but things can change. Was she forced...abused? Was she a mistress, if there could be such a thing when his family owned hers?

All Precious knew was that Old Doctor Marsdale had

been a widower for many years when he took up with Ma. He made her a house slave until she died. Ma ain't had no choice of the field or the big house. So what could a captive do with the advances of a captor?

These questions couldn't be answered with both Ma and Old Doctor Marsdale dead in the ground. One thing for sure, Old Dr. Marsdale wasn't nothing like his son. He didn't trick Ma into the woods, abuse her, cut her brutally, and then lie on her saying she was a runway, insuring a whipping that scarred Precious on the outside too.

With shaky hands, she set about dusting. Not being idle would force the evil from her mind. Gareth's desk lay full of papers. That was as good a place to start.

Taking a cloth from her apron, she started polishing the mahogany top. She took care not to disturb his papers. But the mishmash of parchment and foolscap wouldn't do. A little stacking wouldn't hurt and would make his work surface very fine. Careful not to get things out of order or separated, she made a neat pile, but stopped on something that looked like her indentured papers. She examined the lines of bold print. It proved to be them. Running a finger along his tidy script and her mark, she saw the date of service had been scratched through. A new date had been written in and initialed, June 3, 1819. That date marked the night they landed at Port Elizabeth. The night she saved his life. The night they kissed beneath the Xhosa battle. She'd been freed from service. He'd ended her indentured term, but why didn't he tell her?

She forced her breathing to slow. Precious Jewell was free, not property or a forced servant. If she wanted, she could walk at the door. Truthfully, she could've without these papers. Since they'd left London, he'd given her the ability and opportunity to do as she pleased.

When she'd refused his proposals, he didn't make any bargains or threats to persuade her. He didn't like her answer, for sure. But, he respected it. She felt that in her bones. Gareth was a good man. But could he truly be her man? Her heart was willing, but the terror in her head said no.

She heard a noise from upstairs. Precious trembled until silence again swept over the house. Why was she always so fearful?

She'd refused the master of the house, her employer. Surely, she'd hurt his pride. However, unlike all the other men who had power over her, Palmers the butler, the Marsdale men, retaliation never entered her mind with Gareth. Yet, dread still found a home in her brain. She lifted her shivering palms in the air. Maybe being enslaved so long had ingrained fear into her nature. Maybe her mind hadn't embraced freedom. When would she ever gain the strength to listen to her heart and not the darkness in her head? She shook her fists with fury. "God, Clara's God, Grandmama's God, take care of Gareth. And show some mercy on me."

The rain had started again. She looked out the window. Clouds blocked the view of everything, yet Precious was sure she'd be able to see Gareth's outline, the sway of him as he trudged to the door.

But he wasn't there.

Maybe God didn't answer little black girls playing wife in the big house. It was like she'd always known. God didn't care. He didn't care when her half-brother brutalized her in the woods. He didn't give a jot when he branded her flesh. God just didn't care.

She struck at the window. The chill of the windowpane met her palm. Moisture beaded on her skin, but she couldn't tell if it was from the window or the tears that leaked from her eyes.

The only man that did care was gone. He was out there in trouble with no one to help him.

A sigh built inside then spilled out. What if he were in trouble? What if he needed help?

What if he needed her?

She wrapped her arms about her mobcap as if that would smother her thoughts. It didn't. Nor did it push from her skull the look on his face when she refused him.

Like the rain outside on the glass, water now streaked her face. It wasn't God that didn't care. It was Precious. She let Gareth go without telling him how much she cared for him. How nothing would seem right if he didn't come back. She didn't tell him that the weeks here in Port Elizabeth, making this house into a home for him and Jonas were the happiest she'd ever spent.

"God, forgive my stubborn heart. Please take care of him."

Thunder clapped. Precious jumped. She wasn't given to fright of the weather, but there was this thudding in her chest. Time was running out. The Xhosa would attack in three more days. Gareth's dreams of Port Elizabeth would be gone.

Jonas squealed. Must be the booms of the storm.

With slow steps, she pounded from the parlor and headed upstairs.

Before she could grasp the knurled post at the end of the pine treads, a weak sound filtered between the boy's wails.

That heart of hers that had started to slow ticked up

again.

"Precious." Clara's voice trailed to her. It was so small, absent of any cheer.

Precious swallowed and pattered down the hall. "Yes, Clara?"

"P—. It's time."

Precious wiped her face dry on her dark jade sleeve, and stole up the stairs. Her feet barely hit the treads. She swiveled for moment, unsure of whom to attend first - her Jonas or her friend.

"Precious!" This time the shriek was louder than the babe's. She pivoted and went into Clara's chamber.

The lady was on the bed. The sheets about her legs looked soaked.

"I'm leaking."

The baby's done kicked through. He's coming. Precious put her hand to Clara's stomach. The positioning was still all wrong. That little Narvel hadn't turned. Both the baby's and her friend's life was in danger. She tried to sound hopeful. "You just need to sit back. Keep calm and keep your feet up. We need to wait a little longer. The contractions haven't started. Lord Welling will be back soon."

Clara flopped her back onto her pillows. "I don't know, Precious. I just don't know. Doesn't the baby need this water to survive?"

Precious ran and gripped her friend's hand, "It's not blood. You're still giving that baby everything he needs. Give him your hope too."

"I'm in trouble. I feel it. My baby. I can't lose him, too." Big fat sobs flopped down Clara's red cheeks.

The air in the room drained away. It was all happening again. Just like Eliza except for no blood with the baby water. There was still time to make things right. Here in Port Elizabeth, there was no butler or doctor man to argue with about how to care for Clara. So Precious could do everything to help.

Well, there should be one man to argue with. Goodness how she missed Gareth's deep funny accent.

Clara reached up and touched Precious's lips. "That smile of yours gives me hope."

Nodding, Precious clasped her friend's hand to her heart, close to the imprisoning bib collar she always wore. "Well, nothing good can come from us both crying. You are going to be fine. Your baby's going to be fine."

"How do you know?"

"I will help you, Clara. And that God of yours... our God, He's going to guide me."

Admitting aloud that she was ready to trust in the Lord, felt right. Her spirit felt light in her bosom. At least for this moment, Precious chose to believe everything would be well.

Clara took in a deep breath and eased back onto the pillows. A smile crept over her strained features. "I believe too. We just need to convince this little Narvel."

Jonas wailed again. Precious whipped her head to door.

"Go check on him. I am going to be fine. The shock of the water frightened me so."

Precious swiveled to the closet and took out fresh sheets, the ones she'd cleaned to prepare for this moment. "I will go, but let me get you fixed up.

From her pile of clean linens, she pulled and tucked new sheets about Clara. While she worked, everything seemed to quiet. The ruckus Jonas made stopped. Her pulse raced. Perhaps his daddy had come home and held the little boy. She backed from the room, biting back a big grin. "You rest, Clara. The pains to push that baby out will start soon. You'll need every bit of your strength."

Clara nodded and closed her eyes. Her fingers sank into the Bible by her side.

"Once I see to him, I'll bring you some rue tea. Lots of fresh warm water downstairs to brew it fast."

"You don't have too rush. We'll be fine."

Precious nodded but she could've been agreeing to anything. She needed to go see Gareth. Almost breaking into a full run, she leapt to the boy's room and threw open the door. "You're…"

"No." She lit a candle and spun. Her mouth dropped open. Her feet felt cold and numb. Someone had picked up the fussing boy, but it was not his father.

"What are you doing?" Precious hated the sound of her voice. It sounded weak, full of shock and disappointment. "Mzwamadoda, why are you here?"

The African, tall and black, bounced the boy in his arms. The boy's white pinafore contrasted like night and day in the warrior's grasp. "Decided to come for a visit, to see the Precious one and meter the progress of my friend, the captain. Has he found my chief?"

She unglued her feet, and charged forward with arms outstretched. "Gareth's not here. Give me my boy."

Thick chuckles fell from the man making eyes at Jonas. He was perfectly dark, almost hidden by the night sky that shone in the window. The small candle didn't do justice to the strength of his outline, but the distant lightning strikes silhouetting him did. He was powerful. A man others would fear.

Yet, Precious wasn't frightened by him like she was of

most. Though, maybe she should be. This man had saved her life and taken care of Jonas until her wits returned. Gareth thought of him as a friend, a man of reason. Deep in her bones, she knew this man, though different, had principles just like the baron. She waved her hands again. "Please, give Jonas to me."

A laugh bellowed out of him. He spun a bit, causing Jonas to giggle. His chubby little arms flopped and swayed with the quick movements. "You like that, little mate. Aye?"

The warrior stopped twirling, but still lifted and lowered Jonas. The boy spread his arms like a big old eagle. "Tell the Conroy to come up."

She put a palm on the man's arm, her fingers sinking into his soaked cloak. The smell of wet fur mixed with the scent of fresh rain, filled her nostrils. It made her nose wriggle. "You are getting water on him. Just give him to me."

"My pretty Precious, the lad and I are old friends, and you must be busy since you let the future killer scream his head off."

She fisted her hand and drew it to her hip. "I told you not to call him that." Mother bear growling within, she wrapped her arms about Jonas and stole him from the brash man. "Go down to the parlor and dry your cloak in front of the fire so you'll stop dripping on the floor."

"What, no care for me? If I catch illness, will you smash me against your bosom, too? An ample one such as I can tell."

"Look you." She yanked off the babe's wet pinafore, and tossed it at Mzwamadoda. Precious put Jonas back into his crib, and bundled him tightly in the blankets. "How did you get in here?"

The man hit at his chest. "I've seen better days and my kaross, or cloak as you call it, is designed for rain. I am not soft like the ones from England or from the Americas."

Undoing the folds, he let the fur drop. Only eight rows of a beaded necklace and a pair of buckskin breeches kept him from being naked. This time, the dim light of the small room showed everything. She didn't need the lightning to see the muscles and leanness of the man. "See, I am not worse for the wear. If you care, Precious one."

Like Gareth, he didn't allow idleness to make him soft and weak. And he definitely didn't need the threat of knifes to get his way. "How did you get in here or is there a path of water from here to the front door?"

"The English don't lock the windows. Maybe none of them can climb. I am gifted with agility."

With a few more rubs to Jonas's forehead, the boy drifted to sleep with the biggest grin plastered on his sweet face. Mzwamadoda must have frightened him or thrilled him, coming in through the window. She spun back to the warrior. "Come with me. I can get you a towel."

The warrior sighed long and hard. "I will give exception to being ordered around by a woman because you are foreign, from the American soil. But these heated words can grow painful quickly."

She bit her dry lips and leveled her shoulders. She wasn't going to let him intimidate her. "Then take this final order, get out of my house. I've a woman about to give birth and she is in trouble. I don't need no foolishness."

Mzwamadoda straightened. The fun in his lean cheeks

disappeared. "She is troubled in her birth?"

"Yes." Hope stirred inside. Maybe he knew something to help since he was good with children. She came closer to him, trying hard not to wring her hands. "The baby hasn't turned. Do you know how the Xhosa women fix such problems?"

"No, nothing about birthin' babes. But my people don't do it like the English. The women stand, not lay out." He folded his arms about him. His voice grew lower. "But Conroy knows medicine. He can help. He can save them before the shadows take them."

The sadness in his voice, the distant look in his eyes said he'd lost someone dear.

Pregnancy was so dangerous for women. She shook her head. "That's what I been trying to say. He's not here. He's gone off to the Dutch settlement to find your king."

"Not a king, a chief."

"Well, Gareth has left to go find him, to save this colony. You must go. Go find Gareth. Get him and hurry him back here. I will keep Mrs. Narvel calm and try to slow the pain with tea from the rue. But if you can go get him that will solve everything."

Mzwamadoda looked her up and down. "I came to tell Conroy that my cousin, Bezile will attack the colony in two days. He's moved up the schedule. He wants a surprise attack to catch your cannons off guard."

Her palms shook picking up the wet hide, the kaross. "No, no, no. We need more time. Gareth has to come back. You must go get him."

One brow of his popped up. He eyed Precious. His head moved up and down. "I could go, but what's in this business for Mzwamadoda?"

She handed the tanned hide back to him. "What do you mean?"

"You know exactly what I mean, woman. Helping one of the English bring another little warrior into this world to threaten and kill my people is not something I wish to help with, nor is taking orders from the Precious woman. But I could be persuaded. What do you have to give me?"

Though his tone wasn't sinister, she still bunched up her collar. "I've nothing for you."

"Easy woman. I said give. Not take. I want a kiss from the Precious lady. That will be a token to pay Mzwamadoda to go and retrieve the Conroy."

Precious looked to the floorboard as if it had answers. Mzwamadoda was not ugly. In fact, he was dark polished ebony like fine furniture, and his quick smile made him handsome. He even had that fast wit like Gareth, but he wasn't Gareth.

"Tick tock, time is wasting. Do you want me to go get Conroy?"

"Precious!"

Clara's groan sent a shiver up Precious' spine. She'd put up with advances from worst looking men even ones that never bothered to ask. They just took. Fingering her apron tied above scars that told her she was foolish to think her resistance or pride meant something, she lifted her chin. "If one kiss is what it takes for you to bring Lord Welling back here…done."

"Yes. One lovely, precious kiss, and I will bring back the man with two names. I will even hurry."

She nodded and came toward him.

Inches from him, she felt her breath stop. The fear of being this close to any male always made her insides stew. She would be stoned for this. It'd be over, and then Mzwamadoda would bring back Gareth.

Grinning, the warrior bent his tall frame toward her. He smelled of wild pine and wet hair. His full lips touched hers. Before she could step back, he swept her up in a full embrace.

His lips pressed to hers and made them open. He'd locked her palm against his as he scooped her from the floor. All she could do was cling to the tall African to keep from falling onto the rug. The floor was the last place she needed to be with any man, especially one built for quickness. His hands became more urgent. He molded her against him. When he began searching her corset, her wits returns. Precious managed to free a hand and slugged at his back. Moving more, she might've even kneed him in the stomach.

He dropped her. "Wild cat!"

She rolled and tried to absorb the sting of her backside against the floorboards.

He bent again and offered a hand. "Now why did you have to ruin the moment?"

Anger pumped through her veins. She took his arm but only as leverage. With all of her might she swung at him and tried as best she could to slap him into tomorrow.

Her palm connected. The sound of his head snapping shook the room.

He moved back a few feet and rubbed his jaw. He scooped up his fur cape from the ground. "What kind of woman are you?"

She looked to the left and the right and then it dawned on her. "I'm the captain's woman. I'm Gareth's woman. Now go get him and bring him home."

He tied his cloak back on. "Well, I had to know what it was like, but I am a man of my word. I will bring back the Conroy."

"Hurry."

Mzwamadoda turned and went to the window. He stuck a leg out the frame. "I will try, but nothing but the chief will stop the Xhosa from killing every one of the colonists."

"You just bring back Gareth. Everything will be well. He'll solve everything."

Mzwamadoda nodded then went out on the ledge. Between flashes of lightning, he disappeared.

Precious closed the window and locked it this time. She felt some kind of way about having to rely on the warrior. Though he might be a rogue when it came to kisses, Precious knew he'd keep his word and bring Gareth back. But would it be in time? "Lord, it's me again. Clara and I both are standin' in the need of prayer. God, let this be one of those times you show."

Chapter Twenty-Three: Saving Her Loves

The sun rose over his shoulders, but it didn't enliven Gareth's spirits. The storm of the previous night made him seek shelter in the settlement of Grahamtown. The town was rife with squabbles over cattle disputes with Xhosa. He kept his identity as the leader of Port Elizabeth a secret and broke up his brogue to sound more Irish than English. The Dutch didn't take too kindly to English incursions on land they wanted to claim.

Yet, the search, the questions led to nothing. No Xhosa was hiding in this town and none was being held hostage. If the chief and his daughter came here, it wasn't willingly and they most certainly weren't around now, at least not living. Hatred of the Xhosa was very high.

Gareth shook his head and kicked his gelding into a faster pace. There was another settlement a couple hours away, but what was the likelihood that the two were there?

For three days, he'd checked places up the coast and by the main rivers. It led to nothing. Avoiding the warring Xhosa and the belligerent Dutch had consumed most of his time, time he didn't have to spare. All he had to show for his efforts was a sore back and wounded pride. Precious hadn't wanted him to go. Maybe she was right.

Perhaps he should turn back now and head to Port Elizabeth. He needed to plan the resistance to the onslaught or even an evacuation. No help would be had from the folks in Grahamtown. It was time to give up.

Failure.

Lost cause.

Words that should never be uttered out of a Welling now pressed on his mind. As Port Elizabeth's leader, wasn't it better to give everyone a chance to live than be slaughtered over his foolishness? Boy, did he sound like Precious. How were the stubborn girl and his son? Narvel's widow? Maybe he'd head back after checking this last outpost. Then he'd take his time riding back plotting how to tell everyone of his failure.

He stopped at the top of a ridge. From here, he could see the bay in the distance. It looked like part of the sky, endless and blue. For a moment, he closed his eyes. He allowed his heart to admit how vast and empty he felt. He needed God to fill him back up, pour some of that rain water that dotted the trail with puddles and filled the limitless bay into him as well.

"I understand, Lord. I'm done. If evacuating and giving up on Port Elizabeth is what You want of me, then that is what will be done. Is that what You've been waiting for me to do? To trust You more than my own strength?"

No amount of drink or stubbornness ever changed things. He still awoke each day with the same feeling of hopelessness. "I submit. Do you hear me, Lord? This isn't the Damascus road. I'm not Saul. I have people to save."

Rubbing at his mouth, he slumped in his saddle. His poor horse refused to move another step. Blast it.

Gareth soon heard what his gelding must have. The sound of hooves pounded toward him. He jerked the reigns and forced his horse to turn. Bracing for confrontation, he looked toward the brush.

The blurs came into view. Dark and tall. Warriors on bareback. The Xhosa. The fuzzy plumes above their head meant these were the most skilled of their clan.

He unhitched his rapier and prepared. He wasn't going to die on this dirt road alone. His heart thudded. *Lord, forgive me. My stubbornness, my doubts, my lack of forgiveness, my lack of trust are all sins to You.*

He raised his sword and spurred his horse forward. *Take care of those I love, of those I have led.*

The wind moved past him. Dust from the oncoming men reached him. It was raw, blending with the musk of his lathering horse. Fitting, his last smell would be pure, the pureness of South Africa. He ducked down and drove harder.

When he reached within five hundred paces of the three riders, he saw a fourth coming full bore at his left. This was an ambush. The Xhosa liked hiding in the brush then springing into attack. He must've stirred up too much noise looking for the old chief. Now Bezile's men were coming to finish him.

It wasn't the time to die with so many things undone, unspoken. And Precious, not enough time to love her. A sense of peace lifted him as he raised his rapier. He wasn't going to be murdered here. God would give him the chance to make amends. He'd trust in this renewed peace.

"Yima! Yima!"

The shout became louder, clearer as did the warriors coming toward him.

"Y-I-M-A!"

Wasn't yima, the Xhosa command for stop? Trickery. This had to be how the Xhosa had become so skilled in their warfare techniques.

Gareth sped his horse more intent to engage and win.

The fourth man shouted anew. "Yima!"

This time the line of warriors slowed. They lowered their assegai. One by one with their sharp hunting spears by their side, they turned from Gareth's path and sped back into the tree line.

Gareth lowered his rapier. He wasn't to kill today. Or to die. His lungs filled with the dust of the retreating horses. Maybe some of things unsaid to Precious could be relayed after all.

More commands came forth from behind. He turned his gelding toward the voice that had stopped the assault.

"Mzwamadoda?"

The black man on the silver and ebony Arabian pounded closer. "You aren't a hard man to find, mate. Countless numbers have witnessed the white man seeking the old Xhosa chief. I've been on your trail the past five hours. Seems like I found you just in time. Wonder what the Precious one will do for me?"

Gareth hadn't been discreet, not with so much at stake. He wiped the perspiration off his brow with his jacket. "Precious?" Gareth felt every muscle tense at the cheeky look on his friend's face. To avoid turning his rapier on the man who had just stopped a fight, he eased back in his saddle. "She sent you? Is that why you are here?"

"Well, it wasn't to save your life. Though I suppose I'm glad I did. I promised the Precious one to retrieve you. She should know I'm a man of my word. I don't suppose that meant dragging a dead Welling back to Port Elizabeth."

Gareth should say thank you to the man who'd just stopped unnecessary bloodshed, but hearing Precious's name leaving Mzwamadoda's mouth made him burn. "You saw Precious?"

A grin grew on Mzwamadoda's face as he rubbed his jaw. Mirth clouded his dark eyes. "Yes, I saw her."

He pulled his horse alongside Gareth's. "I came looking for you. Seems I was right too. Bezile is a little anxious for revenge. He's not going to wait the full seven days. They are gathering to attack as soon as tomorrow."

No. No. No. Gareth swiped at his skull. "I haven't had enough time. The chief has vanished."

"That's not good. But time has run out for Port Elizabeth and that sweet lipped Jewell of yours. She's the reason I've come for you."

Sweet lipped? Gareth balled his fist. He took a breath and relaxed his muscles. He wasn't going to take the man's bate. Blasted. Maybe he should encourage Mzwamadoda to pursue her if the warrior could handle someone as aggravating and loving as Precious. But Gareth wasn't that big of a man. He was selfish. Precious was his, even if he still had to convince her of that fact.

He pointed his mount back to Port Elizabeth and

urged him forward. "Then I better see what she wants."

Mzwamadoda caught up to him, squinting at him. "So you are not going to ask anything? Nothing of our kiss?"

As long as he'd known Mzwamadoda, the man never lied. He just embellished the truth. It must be so. Gareth's heart sank. He should've told Precious how he felt, not fallen into false pride. Swallowing contempt, he shook his head. "She'll tell me."

A frown covered the man's face. "Then it must be as she said. You are a lucky man."

Gareth tucked hope back into his heart and clicked his foot into his horse's side.

Mzwamadoda's Arabian matched Gareth's gelding stride for stride. I'll ride with you to the town's edge. It will be too light for a Xhosa to venture into Port Elizabeth. The English are trigger happy. I'll let them save their bullets for the battle ahead."

Riding a little faster, Gareth waved him forward. "You're under my protection. No one would dare harm you."

"You might think that. I don't believe the colonists think that." He thumbed his chest. "My dark life doesn't matter to them. They'd rather we were enslaved or dead."

It did matter. Just as Mzwamadoda saved Gareth's life minutes earlier, his was worth saving as well. Xhosa lives mattered. "Anyone helping to save or build Port Elizabeth matters. Go back to Bezile. See if there is another way. A ransom payment. A public flogging. There must be a way to avoid an attack."

"We'll see, Welling. Once you are back to Port Elizabeth, I will go find my cousin and hope he can see reason. But for now, I will make you ride faster. Perhaps, you could still wheedle out of me the details of my visit to your Precious Jewell."

Smirking on the inside, Gareth turned his gaze solely to the dirt trail. Though he wanted to know more than anything what had transpired betwixt the two, he wouldn't give his friend the advantage. Five more hours of hard riding, Gareth would know all. Then maybe, he would say all.

The rue started working a few hours after Mzwamadoda left. Precious watched her friend sleep and the occasional movement of her tummy. It gave her a moment of peace. She took a deep breath, maybe the first filling one of the day. The night Eliza died felt too close. So much so, Precious dared not shut her eyes.

For like that day, everything had been overcast. And Gareth wasn't there. Not that he could've saved Eliza but surely he could've made peace with her. Then Jonas wouldn't have been nearly abandoned for two years. Maybe the guilt Precious had for liking Gareth wouldn't be so strong.

Why did she like that man? Why did he go away when she needed him? Well maybe if she had told him, things could've been different. She folded her hands and almost started to pout. She and Eliza had a lot more in common than Marsdale blood.

"Precious." The rue made Clara's voice sound distant, as if she talked in a dream. "Get some sleep. I am fine."

"I'm not leaving you. I've nowhere else to be. Jonas has been fed and went down easily to sleep." Being awakened by the storm and a late night visitor seemed to have tuckered him out all day.

"I've made it through the night and most of the day

without another large contraction." She wiggled a little on the pillow Precious had put under hips to get the baby moving in the right direction. "Where did you learn these things?"

Precious sat up straight and stared into Clara's cheery eyes. A comfort gripped her. For once, saying the truth aloud didn't make her fear. No, there were much bigger things than ghosts of the past filling her head right now. "My pa. He did doctoring in South Carolina. He used to take me with him on his rounds sometimes."

Clara smiled and shut her lids. "That's nice. It's the first nice memory you shared of growing up."

Precious drew her shawl up tight about her. A chill set in her bones but she didn't crumble. As good as it was to say the truth, it still didn't change things. There would always be a hole on the inside for not being able to call Old Doctor Marsdale, Pa or Eliza, cousin. A sigh leaked out. "There weren't too many good ones."

"Please, dear friend. Beautiful precious friend, get some rest. In a couple of hours, you will hear me yelling for you."

In her heart, Precious knew this was true and she feared it. Clara was so nice and caring. And she'd lost so much. She and the baby had to survive. *Sunday God.* Well, it wasn't Sunday, but Thursday. *Sometimes God, please save these two.* "Lord, tell me what I need to do."

A tear sprinkled from Clara's lashes. "I said go get some sleep."

Precious put a hand over her mouth and popped up. "I...I think you are right."

She leaned over and batted a red curl back from Clara's brow. "You rest. Then you and I will fight for this baby."

Clara lifted her palm from the bed sheets and clasped Precious's. "You promise to put this baby first. If things go wrong, my husband's legacy must survive. And you will love him just like Jonas."

Another deathbed promise. Her heart ripped as she nodded. "But don't talk like that. Just focus on this baby coming out the right way."

Clara's fingers became light and slipped back to the mattress. Precious bent and kissed her forehead. Leaving the room, she gently closed the door. Thirty more minutes and it would be fifteen hours since her water broke. By dark, the labor should start again and this time that baby would come out or Precious would lose another dear friend and the babe. "Oh, Sometimes God, could this be one of those times you showed up."

She slipped down the stairs into the parlor. The sofa, the dusted mantle, Gareth's orderly desk, everything looked in place. A portrait of him sitting in his chair, going over correspondences, would've made the room complete and as fine as anything in Charleston or London. Well, maybe not as fancy, but it was good, solely good. No bad memories here. This place had to survive. But how?

Flopping onto the sofa, she tried to close her eyes, but every creak of the wind made her lids open wide. She could lose Clara and the baby tonight. If Mzwamadoda didn't find Gareth, he could be lost too. She'd never have the chance to tell him how much she cared for him or how angry she was at him for leaving, even if it was to save everyone. Stupid, heroic, lovely man.

Turning again and again for comfort, she fell off the cushions onto the floor. Sleep wasn't to be hers. She stood, dusted off her skirts and went to the window.

Maybe sitting there, watching the sun set on Port Elizabeth would restore her calm.

Parting the curtains, she saw a familiar blur. The blur took form, a decidedly masculine form. Before she could stop herself, she fled the parlor, slid through the hall and unbolted the front door. She started running.

"Precious!" he called out to her. She ran straight to Gareth.

She hugged him, enjoying the strength of his arms, the earthy musk of his neck, but the pent up fear for his safety, the angst of him walking away, merged with her easy temper.

She beat on his chest. "I told you trouble was to come. You didn't listen."

Instead of saying anything, he wrapped his arms about her tighter. She wanted so much to just melt into him and feel that strong heart of his. But how could she get past her hurt? "I told you things would be bad, but you didn't listen."

His man Ralston came from behind laughing. "Captain, glad you're back. But I see you still can't handle your woman."

"Ralston, I know exactly how to handle my woman." He flipped Precious over his shoulder; just like he did the night on the Margeaux when he saved her from drowning.

Breathless, she hung to his back. Blood drained from her face. "Put me down."

"Nothing doing, woman." He pivoted to his first mate, making her head bobble. "Ralston, head back to the fort. Make sure the men are on alert. No one shoots unless we are shot at first. They may send a lone emissary. He is to arrive and leave in safety. Is that clear?"

Upside down, her vision blurred. She couldn't see Ralston but heard the respect in his voice. "Yes, sir."

Precious watched Ralston's boots trudged back toward the fort.

"Now it's time to deal with you, Miss Jewell." His steps quickened as he marched back to their residence. He kicked open the door and pounded into the parlor. "You just don't know how to do a homecoming do you?"

Still dangling down his back, next to his smelly grass stained rucksack, she didn't have a chance to respond. All she could do was push against his thick legs to keep from smashing into him with each of his movements.

With a flip and a light swat to her fanny, he tossed her onto the sofa. "Woman, I'm home."

He dropped his sack, came round and plopped onto the floor in front of the sofa. He folded his arms and leaned his head back against the cushions.

They both sat there in silence with the sun fading. Soon the rays would stop pouring through the lead glass. Only the candle's light would remain. Who would speak first?

Finally, he sighed long and hard. "Precious." His voice sounded tight, as if he struggled to sound calm and reasoned. "Tell me what that was about. Mzwamadoda told me you actually wanted my return. I've ridden like a crazy person to be here."

"You should've never left."

"If he'd said I was to be made a fool of on Main Street, I might have taken more time. Maybe even gotten a nap. We will be the talk of the colonists. The captain and his argumentative governess."

He was right. She'd shamed him, but none of that mattered now. He was back. He could save her friend.

"Miss Clara needs you. The baby is in trouble. Her water has come out."

He swiped at his brow. Is the babe still quickening?"

"Yes. He's still active, though I've slowed her contractions with the rue."

He stood up and peeled off his jacket and sank on to the sofa. The man was sweaty and tired. The most wonderful man she'd ever seen. "Well, its seems I'm back in time for her. Is she the only one who needs me, Precious?"

She couldn't say it, could she? Pushing up on the cushions, she got on her knees and reached up to his dusty mop to order his hair. "No, she isn't the only one who needs you."

He clasped her hand and pressed a kiss into it. "Maybe you should tell me who else needs me. Is it Jonas?"

The moan in her throat evaporated all her reason.

Gareth splayed apart the fingers she used for measuring. He kissed the soft spot at the crevice. "Maybe you did miss me."

She couldn't be wanton right now. Her friend needed him more than she. "Wash your hands really good. There's hot water in the kitchen. I've been keeping it warmed to prepare. Then come upstairs, and save my friend."

He didn't let her stand. Instead he pulled her back. His powerful arm swept her into a full embrace. She didn't resist and rested against him. The counts of his heartbeat were musical. She could stay like this forever.

His lips graced her forehead and nibbled an ear. "The next time I come home, I expect a much warmer greeting. Is that understood?"

Who could think with him teasing her? She pushed at his chest. "Go wash up and put on a fresh shirt. You've a baby to deliver."

He nodded and left the parlor.

Precious smoothed the collar of her smock and tried to push away the feeling of warmth and love bubbling inside. Or the craving to fully submit to the emotions running through her crazed veins. But she shouldn't think of herself right now, only Clara.

Chapter Twenty-Four: Addition & Subtraction

At Precious's insistence, Gareth put on a fresh shirt and breaches. He didn't quite see the purpose since birthing was a process that left things soiled. And difficult ones meant a great amount of soiling. He left his chambers at the darkened end of the hall and went back down to the kitchen.

After scrubbing his hands for the third time, he plodded back into the parlor. Surely he would pass inspection now. He swallowed. Turmoil built inside. This was again one of those time where good intentions and best efforts didn't lead to success. *I get it, Lord. Let Your hands drive mine.* There had to be joy in this house for a few more hours, if even if war drove it away tomorrow.

Letting his hands air dry, he trotted up the stairs. With a breath and another quick prayer for guidance and mercy, he crossed Mrs. Narvel's threshold.

"Captain." The woman's eyes shone brightly though her voice was weak. "So glad you are safe."

He nodded and approached the bed. "May I?"

Her head whipped up and down as she bit down on a whimper. "No need for shyness now, Captain. Seems we are going to be very familiar soon."

"About that familiarity. For the record, I know some about births. My ship rescued a slave ship during the war. It had women from Jamaica on board. I had to deliver a child or two, but that's it."

The poor woman nodded as she gritted her teeth. "That will have to be enough, Lord Welling. Precious knows some things. She's helped me to last until your return."

He looked over to Precious as she mopped Mrs. Narvel's brow. She looked threadbare, about to fall over with concern. The lovely girl had a big heart. He couldn't let it break with the loss of Mrs. Narvel. Pivoting back to the panting woman, he nodded. "I suppose together, we'll make a good team."

"We're gonna have to be."

He leaned down and started to poke at the blanket covering the lady's legs. Then stopped himself.

Precious crept closer to his shoulder. The whisper of her soft breath fell upon his neck again pushing his thoughts far from this bedchamber to his own.

"Go on, Gareth. We can't delay."

He stood back and folded his arms. "It's not that simple, Precious. This may not be England, but I'm an English gentleman about to compromise a widow woman to view her privacy. "

The feisty governess latched onto his shoulder. "Clara just told you she didn't care."

"Captain." Clara's strained voice came between them. "You're going to marry Precious. She's the captain's woman. I heard her tell that to someone yesterday. Nothing changes that. Isn't that right, Precious?"

He tried to hide a smirk, but failed miserably. "So that is what you told Mzwamadoda? Well, you made your own bargain this time or did your dear friend hear wrong?"

Precious thinned her lips as if she tried to think of an excuse. She spread her shoulders back. In a voice that sounded almost prideful, she said. "Yes. That's exactly what I told the bounder. Now, help me bring this baby in the world."

He wasn't going to hold her to something said in duress, but she didn't have to know that now. Smiling, he moved back to the sheets. "I'll do my best, my intended."

The glint of humor in Mrs. Narvel's eyes faded as another contraction hit. "You have my permission to do what ever is needed to save this baby. And if you have to do a caesarean do it. My dearest husband's baby must live.

Precious whipped her head from side to side. "But that will mean you'll bleed to death." Her voice became a strangled tumult. "Gareth, no. Don't let that happen."

He took her hand and squeezed it hard. "I'm not going to let any more bad happen to those you love. You've heard my words."

The frown lines on her temples cleared. "Yes."

He took a peak at the bed-ridden woman. She was quite ready for life to spring forth, but he didn't see the crown. He observed what looked very well like the top of a shoulder. "Precious, go get a clean sharp knife and more towels."

Eyes wide as saucers, Precious paled. "You're going to take a knife to her. No, no cutting on her like she has no value."

Not sure of what the woman spoke, all he could do was make her believe all would be well. "I need you strong, Precious. Trust me. Now hurry."

She was back before he could blink. Her ashen, shaking hands held a shiny knife.

He took it from her before she dropped it. "Good, now go hold on to your friend. Mrs. Narvel, I'm going to cut a little of the membrane, to make his path easier. Then I'll see if I can pull the babe out. "

Mrs. Narvel closed her eyes, and nodded.

Putting on the bravest most confident expression he could muster, Gareth started. All the while, he prayed for this baby, Mrs. Narvel, and Precious who looked as if she would fall dead if things didn't go well.

Incisions made, blood pooled about his fingers. He wiped them on a towel, one taken from the pile that had been gathered in the corner next to a huge jug of water. Then he went to the head of the bed. "Precious, we are going to lift Mrs. Narvel up. We'll hold her upright and hope that gravity guides the baby out."

Precious's chestnut eyes expanded. "He could drop to the floor. Strangle with the cord."

He put a clean thumb to her lips. "Trust me. It's how the Xhosa women give birth."

She nodded. "That's how the enslaved in Charleston do it too."

He nodded. "Then it should work. Ready, Mrs. Narvel?"

The widow waved her hands. "No choice. Get this baby out of me."

He scooped her up, set her on her feet and positioned her to lean against Precious. He lifted Mrs. Narvel's arms and draped them about Precious's shoulder.

He dropped back into position to catch the babe. This all had to be well. These ladies were too entwined. Precious's giving heart would ache so if things went wrong. He lowered his head and prayed anew, trusting this was the right thing to do.

Precious held Clara tight, gripping her underarms.

Her friend shook. The tremors of birthing took more and more of her strength.

"Push, Mrs. Narvel." Gareth's voice sounded low and strong. "Help that baby come to me."

Clara's hold weakened. Precious bolstered her. "I'm with you, Clara. We've come too far, from London to Port Elizabeth."

Dull sherry eyes locked onto hers. "I can only do what...auggh... I can."

"The head is coming. A bit more."

Precious rubbed Clara's back, and bore her weight. It was all she could do. Well, there was one more thing. She swallowed and held Clara tighter. *Sometimes God, please save my friend and this baby.*

Gareth poked his head around. "Stop."

His face disappeared behind Clara's nightgown.

Precious could see his arms moving, though he said nothing. There were no baby noises. Her heart beat loudly. A dozen sentiments of things to say to Clara came to mind, but she kept quiet and hoped God was just a little late this time. That everything would still be well.

A sharp wail filled the silence of the room. A baby's strong cry finally started.

Hearing the baby scream at the top of its lungs was

like church bells to Precious. Eliza had taken Precious to a yuletide service their first year in England. She had to sit on the last pew with the other servants, but the majesty of the hymns and the ringing of those brass chimes reached all the way to the back of the church.

For that hour, the beauty of the stain glass, the sound of the organ, it made her forget all - her station, her past. Those were the sounds of God. She even spread her fingers wide to measure the distance from the preacher man to herself. God didn't seem far away that day.

With the wide toothy grin on Clara's face, He didn't seem far away right now. Sometimes God showed up for her friend.

Gareth stood. He wrapped the tiniest little thing in one of her fresh towels. "The cord is cut, Mrs. Narvel. You have a beautiful daughter."

He put the babe in Precious's arms as he carried the new mother back to the mattress.

Precious wiped the infant's nose and mouth then settled the sweet girl in her mother's arms. "Hold on to this bundle, Clara, while I clean you up."

Her friend's face was a sea of tears, yet her smile so bright. "Thank you, Precious. Captain, thank you."

Gareth stood in the corner with his arms folded. His eyes closed.

In no time at all, Precious had the room and everything in it spotless as if this birth had been easy.

She turned to Clara and listened to the baby settle down, no longer screaming.

Clara touched the little one's nose. "You sure did make a fuss for one so little."

Gareth came closer. He batted up sheets, tucking them about Clara. It was funny to watch him play healer, still trying not to look. His hands were soiled, as was his shirt. A smear even sat on his forehead. All stained, he never looked more handsome.

"Mrs. Narvel, you tore a little but you should heal with no problem. As a precaution, remain as still as you can."

"Can't stay still. I have to nurse this one. She'll need to eat a lot to catch up in weight."

She fumbled with her robe. "I want to be alone. Go clean the captain up. And Precious, you need to sleep. She hasn't slept in two days."

"Yes. You should go to bed, Precious." He swiveled and looked out the window. "We've a few hours before dawn."

Gareth pivoted and headed to the door. "Come along, Precious."

She scooped up a clean towel dipped it into the jug of water and followed after him.

With the door closed, he leaned against the wall. His proud shoulders sagged. His shirttail hung over his buff breaches. In the small light of the tallow candle affixed by his head, he looked so tired. His handsome face puffy about the eyes. "Go on to bed, Precious. I can't have you getting sick. Jonas and Mrs. Narvel and her daughter, they'll need you strong and healthy."

"What about you?"

He lowered his gaze and picked at the towel. "I'll manage some sleep." He pivoted and walked away heading to his room.

She felt a frown swallow her lips. But in the partially lit hall, the darkness shrouding them gave her courage. "Wait, Gareth. I was talking about the needin' part."

He stopped in the shadows, then turned back to her. "Precious."

"Yes."

Silent for at least thirty heartbeats, he swiped at his forehead and must've figured out he'd gotten a stain there for he examined his fingers.

"See, you need me to clean you up. She moved closer and raised the wet towel. He caught her palm and lowered her arm. "In Nigeria, they have a strange custom for people to marry. A goat is killed. Its blood is spread on the roof of the bride's home. She's asked if she's pleased with the groom. If she is, the couple is considered married. Since you and I are stubborn like goats." He wiped his finger along her brow.

Her forehead felt sticky.

His voice was low. The tiny bit of light shed on his face showed large eyes full of purpose. "We are now marked with blood. We'd be married if you were pleased with me."

"Gareth, I--"

He wiped his hands and face clean on the towel, then hers too, and dropped the cloth away. "Well, neither you or I are Nigerian. Maybe, I should go about this more directly."

Her skin vibrated when he held her palms within his.

"I need you, Precious. You must know that I am in love with you."

Her heart stopped. He couldn't be. "Don't say that."

He let her go. "Don't say what? Things that are true. Well, we know who is more stubborn." He turned and headed deeper into the shadows plodding into his bedchamber. "Goodnight, Precious."

Hadn't she vowed not to make him feel unwanted? "Wait."

The whine of his door met her ears. If she didn't tell

him now, she'd never tell him.

No more being a coward. She ran straight to him and lunged into his chest knocking him backwards. Though his arms went about her, they crashed to the floor. Surely, he took the brunt of the fall since he kept her aloft from the floorboards. Gareth winced, but kept her close. He hugged her deeply about the waist.

It was good and dark in his room. That gave her courage. With timid hands, she traced his jaw, his cheek. When she found his lips, she took them, and kissed him with all she had and then some. Gareth would know tonight how much she cared for him.

He rubbed her back. His fingers massaged her tired muscles making her fidgeting relax against him. His touch didn't frighten her. The fear came from wanting this man to soothe all her aches.

He lifted her chin and took a deep, long breath. "When you decide something, there's no holding back."

"Been doing that since we landed in Port Elizabeth. Only so much I can hold in."

Confidence building, she drew her thumb to his open collar and smoothed the top of the exposed scar on his chest. "What happened to you?"

He stilled her palm against him. "War and stupidity. They don't mix."

Though he'd tried to make a joke, she knew him now. Humor or brandy hid his pain, just as much as the dark covered hers. She wasn't going to add to his burdens anymore.

He took a sharp intake of air. The moonlight drifted in from his window. It made the edges of his hair wild with parts going every which way. Surely it was too dark to see her, but maybe the light of the hall could expose her.

With her foot, she closed the door. No light needed. In the dark, she could be beautiful, and escape everything as long as Gareth held her.

Quieting all the voices in her head, the ones of caution she rarely listened to and the ones calling her wanton, she snuck her hands beneath his shirt. Precious grasped him tighter. The lifeline of her palm wed fully against his scar, then to the right, over his beating heart.

Nothing shiftless or flabby on him. Gareth was a handsome man and he said he loved her. Maybe that meant all of her.

The thudding, the feeling of his skin pulsed beneath her fingertips. It wasn't enough. For the first time in a long time, it wasn't enough just being at his side.

Wanton. Who…

She pulled away. All her words about not being a mistress gathered in her throat and mixed with a sob. Even if she put words to what she felt, how could she voice it. What if he could still see her with his captain's eyes? Would he agree with her scars?

"Precious, what's wrong? Did you hurt yourself when we fell?"

"No." Her voice sounded so weak. But, was she weak? Hiding in the darkness, she hoped Gareth didn't see the water streaming down her face. Could his love be enough to make her whole?

"Precious?"

No sounds could be uttered without starting a full crying jig. Any words would just show how mixed up her insides were, how confused every bone in her body had become by touching him. Desire and need, weren't they right in the dark?

Gareth sat up and pulled her against him. His arm folded around her. He weaved his fingers through hers. A nip at her ear, set with a whisper melted her into him. "We're going to go to Mr. Dennis tomorrow. He'll marry us, properly. No goat required."

Unlike hers, his tone sounded strong, no doubts or questions clouded it.

"Then I am putting you and Jonas, Mrs. Narvel and her babe, and all the rest of the colonists who aren't so pigheaded onto the Margeaux."

She spun to him. She almost wished for light to see if his face held a joke, but she knew in her heart, he was serious. "Leave Port Elizabeth? No."

"The Xhosa are going to attack. No more deaths over this land."

"Gareth, you worked so hard. All that can't be for naught."

"I went to every Dutch settlement, betwixt here and Grahamtown. No chief. No daughter. And with it our hopes of Port Elizabeth surviving."

"Dutch? Like the brothel owner?"

"Yes, like Mrs. Branddochter. The Madame Neeltje as they call her, but she won't leave."

She released a frustrated grunt. "More people with two names?"

He chuckled. Then his tone sobered again. "I'll try to make sure the Xhosa leave her alone, but all may be lost."

His words of sending and not coming cut through her fog. "You're staying? That's crazy."

"The captain goes down with the ship or in this case the Welling goes down with the dream."

"No, Gareth, no." She put her wet cheek to his face.

"No."

But now his mouth was on hers, changing everything to yes.

With this longer kiss, she moaned into him and again snuck her arms about his neck. Nothing could be wrong with him close to her and darkness covering all. Maybe allowing him to love her would erase all the self-hate inside.

Buttons were undone. Ribbons loosened. He lifted her up from the floor. It was quite like flying, but the crash, the fall back to earth would soon come. She didn't care anymore.

She'd been branded as wanton, as a harlot. Maybe Gareth's touch, the love he claimed to have would make all the bad go away.

He placed her on his mattress, his hands raked over her bodice, the edges of her corset. She waited for him to touch the scars, to brand her with love. Maybe she'd finally forget the hate that had abused her so long ago.

His hands stilled.

Then nothing.

He'd moved away. Taking a pillow, he left her shaking, and raw. "You'll not be a mistress to me, but a wife, Precious Jewell."

This wasn't the time for her foolish excuses to come back to her. Had he felt the scars through her blouse and guessed the words carved on her skin? Or did he guess what she really was and wanted her no more?

She bunched up her collar. "I don't understand."

He sat on the edge of the mattress. "I was injured in the Peninsula War, very badly hurt. I suffer from bouts of impotence. And being up for the last day and a half, I haven't the strength."

The bed rocked as he lifted then settled down on the floor.

She moved to the edge to watch him. To make sure she understood. "Don't you want me?"

"More than I can say. I want to appear noble and take you as my bride like you deserve, not a mistress. But that wouldn't be true. I simply can't. This is my struggle."

A sigh hissed from him. "Let's both get some sleep. We'll see Dennis in the morning. Then I can send my baroness and my boy to safety."

"Gareth--"

"Please, don't. As a man, I need to know you and Jonas are safe. Don't take that from me, too."

What could she say to restore his pride? Most of the men she'd known boasted about their exploits and even hurt women to prove their fortitude. The night Gareth had plucked her from the ocean, he took such a teasing by his own men. What could the captain's woman utter to be salve to his wounds?

Nothing.

But Precious wasn't big with words anyway. No, she was more about action. She'd wait for Gareth to start snoring, and then she'd sneak to that one Dutch woman who'd teased about Xhosa women being brave. Mrs. Branddochter's taunts had made Precious go into those snake woods. Where else could the chief and his daughter be hidden so well?

She laid back and waited. The captain's woman would save Port Elizabeth for him. If there was any hope for Precious to be happy, it had to be here with Gareth in Port Elizabeth and not on some boat away from him.

Chapter Twenty-Five: Time to Get Married

Light touched his lids. Gareth had seen better days.

And better nights. He groaned inside and let his eyes adjust to the daylight spilling into his bedchamber. He stretched his arms trying hard to ease the ache of his back. Between his days of horseback riding to falling on the floor with Precious, it really hadn't stood a chance. But it was morning. His energy always restored then.

With a yawn, he turned to peak at the rumpled bed sheets. Oh, Precious. In a few hours, he'd make an honest woman of and perhaps be able to make up for last night's disaster. His pride as a man, his love for that woman demanded he make amends. Thoughts of her melting in his arms filled him.

Last night. Sad wasn't the adjective that sprung to his mind. He remembered the days on the Margeaux taking care of her, snuggling near. Would those images eclipse the memory of her shimmering eyes filling with rejection?

He sighed with frustration. The woman had decided

she wanted him and there wasn't a blasted thing he could do about it. She hadn't been jittery to his touch. Perhaps he'd finally bridged over the hurt some scoundrel had inflicted upon her. If Mzwamadoda bought at least one more day of delay, he'd take the opportunity to focus solely on her, on loving her, of giving her everything within him before setting her and his son on the Margeaux.

She hadn't stirred from the lump of bed sheets. In the light of day, he'd be able to tell if her tears where the vestiges of frustration or something else. Maybe she didn't regret how things had changed between them. Could Precious love him too?

He had to know. Gareth slogged to his feet.

But the bed lay empty.

A twinge of sadness touched him, but Precious wasn't the kind to lay about.

He'd make himself presentable and then march her down to the blacksmith. Under the protections of marriage, she could be assured of his commitment. Her rights and her ability to care for Jonas would be strengthened, if he weren't able to survive the Xhosa attack.

Rubbing at the growth of shadow on his chin, he angled to his dresser with his razor. A good shave would set him straight. He thought about Precious again, of how close they'd become, of how close she'd wanted to be. Maybe, there would be a moment, where they could find a haven, a final lasting memory as husband and wife. The notion made him hurry his toiletries.

Dressed in his best blue coat, Gareth left his chambers and wandered past Mrs. Narvel's open door. Sitting up, she adjusted the blankets about her little one and sang. He half-expected to see Precious fussing about her, but didn't. A bit of disappointment filled him. He brushed it away. "How are you today? How's the baby?"

"We are both doing well. You don't know how grateful I am. God knows how to give the best blessings, even if we have to wait a little while for them. "

Gareth folded his arms, and pushed away the notion that somehow this was in reference to his and Precious's situation last night. "Have you seen my fiancée this morning? We are supposed to wed today."

"Earlier." A smile blossomed on Mrs. Narvel's face. She tucked her little girl against her flowery pink robe. "Oh! I am so happy for you. No wonder she was dressed so fancy. That emerald striped dress will be a wedding dress."

Emerald stripes? Eliza's gown, the one he'd brought with them from Firelynn? The one Precious had refused. Something in his gut started to twist, but that must be wedding jitters or angst over Precious in his first wife's clothes. A bad feeling settled in his gut. Did Precious know he sought to marry her, not a copy of Eliza?

Jonas's strong giggle came from down the hall.

Gareth turned his head in the direction of the noise. "Well, let me go greet my son. I suspect that is where my bride will be."

He bowed, then took a few steps toward the boy's bedchamber. Maybe they should take Jonas with him since she would become his stepmother as his Mammie. Mrs. Narvel might not be up to watching the little fellow and her new girl. Yes, that would be a good idea. Jonas must be having a marvelous time.

Maybe she was explaining about marrying Gareth.

Heart pounding, he turned the knob. He wiped his eyes in surprise.

Mzwamadoda sat on the floor playing with Jonas, rolling blocks between his thick tree-trunk legs.

Gareth wiped at his brow again and just stared. "What are you doing here?"

"I came before daybreak to tell you that Xhosa will be attacking at noon. I could not get Bezile to agree to new talks."

Gareth went to the window and looked out at his desperate colony. "That's only a couple of hours from now. How am I going to get all the colonists on the ship? Why didn't you tell me as soon as you got here?"

"Your woman asked me to watch the small one and let you sleep."

He spun and looked at the warrior. He wanted to sneer at him as if he'd become crazed. "Why would she need you to do that?"

"Because she left. She says she knows where the chief is."

He raked a hand through his hair. He couldn't believe his ears, but then he thought about the most rash, crazy, loving woman in the world and knew it was all true. "Why didn't you stop her?"

"They don't let Xhosa men in the white man's brothels. And she thinks if too much fuss occurs, they'll hide him. I have to say I agree."

Madame Neeltje's? "You both are crazed. Come with me."

"She has my horse. And remember, your people are ready to kill anyone that looks as handsome as me."

Gareth bent and hugged Jonas good morning. For a second, he held his boy tight.

"Papa." Soft and sweet were those words. Love filled him almost as much as the fear he felt for Precious's safety.

"I'm going to need you to be good for Mrs. Narvel. Your new friend must come with me."

Mzwamadoda sat back against the wall, folded his kaross over his arms. "Oh no, Welling. It is safer in here with the little one and the blocks."

"You are with me. You are protected. And you need to see the chief to verify for Bezile and the Xhosa that he's not a prisoner."

The man shrugged and stood. "Perhaps. But I must say, I want one of these women of America. These seem determined to give their all for their men."

Yes, that was exactly what that blasted woman would do, even if it got her killed.

Chapter Twenty-Six: One Reckless Act

Precious followed Mrs. Branddochter down the pink painted hallway in the Neeltje brothel. She tried to pretend wearing the low cut gown felt normal. Eliza's dress was pretty, with the emerald stripes, but it showed too much skin. Precious was embarrassed. She balled her fingers in her shawl. "This is a long house."

The buxom Dutch woman nodded and continued to lead her through the corridor. "It will do."

With the woman's back to her, Precious tried to hold her shoulder level, tried to appear ready to sell her body. Yet, what did that mean?

The man before took her virtue, no asking. Last night she was so weak for Gareth, she was willing to give it away on a promise in the dark. Promises in the dark didn't last. Maybe she was the words cut into her flesh.

Did Gareth truly love her? Or was it just his way of manipulating her to agree to marrying him? He liked to win and he liked to get his way. If he were going to send her and Jonas away, why did it matter?

If Precious had any hope of finding out, she needed to discover the Xhosa chief. So many doors lined the hall. Which one could hide the king? She twisted her fingers again in the fringes of her shawl. This had to work, and not just be another reckless thing. Mzwamadoda said the attack would happen today without a miracle.

Precious bumped into the woman's back, for the madame had stopped short. "Sorry."

Mrs. Branddochter turned, her face ladened with a heavy frown. "Your head seems somewhere else. I was very surprised that you showed up. You're not thinking of going back to Lord Welling are you?"

"I…ah. No."

She grabbed Precious's arm as if to shake some sense in her. "You weren't happy with the captain? When I heard the brute put you over his shoulder yesterday, I knew it was only a matter of time before you came to me. I don't let the men get physical. If they hit you or do anything you don't like, they never come back. My girls are clean. I take care of them."

Precious's heart was flooded with thoughts of last night with Gareth's hands on her. Blood rushed to her face. She wondered if the woman could see her warming cheeks. "No. He's not. Just when…I."

"Child, you don't have to say. Though I dearly want to hear." She released her and exposed a grin like an alligator. "Oh, I so want to hear about the bad captain."

The lady's brow lifted. Her round face moved from side to side. "You don't look bruised up. Maybe you are use to being his fancy."

That horrible word, the sorry fate that fell upon some of the other women enslaved in Charleston, possibly her own mother. A shudder rippled over her exposed bosom.

She drew her shawl down about her. The cut of the dress wasn't indecent but much more than Precious would ever feel comfortable with out of her home. "He was a man to me."

She meant a good one, a decent one who treated her like a lady even if it didn't serve his purposes. She couldn't admit that now and ruin her plans to find the chief and his daughter. And wasn't it safer to believe, he didn't love her? You can't hurt from losing something you never possessed.

Mrs. Branddochter cackled, her teeth looked extra pointy. "Well most men are a little rough. But I protect my girls and this place." She put her large hands on Precious again and made her spin. "Except for that scar on your neck, you are pretty."

She tugged at Precious braids, but the coils sprung back into place. "I guess It will do. I'll save you up for the best penny. Men like different. And you are very pretty even if you are dark. Now go on in and meet the other girls. I'll come for you when the customers arrive."

Precious sucked in a breath. She planned on being gone before the selling commenced. "They don't just come at night?"

The woman laughed. "Men are men all the time. Once their drinking has worn off, they come to pay for loving. Now go on."

Panic fluttered her heart. What if the chief wasn't here? Or worse, what if she couldn't get out of the brothel before customers arrived? No rethinking her plans now. She shrugged inwardly and entered into a room.

The chamber was sparse save a couple of beds. Three women looked at her as she entered. They weren't disheveled or chained about as slaves. Except for one, they looked healthy, like regular women.

Mrs. Branddochter pushed her forward. "Ladies, this is Precious Jewell. She's come to me, so I'd like you to be neighborly to her."

Two of the three said in unison, "Yes, Madame Neeltje."

Precious turned back to the brothel owner with a brow popped.

"That's what my girls call me." She marched past Precious to the lump in the closest bed, the unresponsive woman. "Mrs. Scott, you have to work tonight. Your boy's been gone long enough. I can't keep this bed for you if you don't work. I'll find you someone nice."

Precious's hand flew to her mouth. The lump was a grieving mother.

The poor woman lifted up. "He ain't dead. He's been stolen, I say."

Shaking her head, the Madame turned. "Can't satisfy my clients if you've lost your mind. I'll give you another week. Then you have to get to work."

A girl with dark black hair got up and patted the bed. "I'll work extra good for her. And you've got a new one here to make up the lost income. Please give her time."

Mrs. Branddochter folded her arms and shook her head. "We will see." She plodded to the door. "I'll see you in a few hours, Miss Jewell. Stay in here. You're new, and I don't need trouble."

With a slam, the matron left.

Precious felt out of place here, until she saw the hurt in Mrs. Scott's voice. She knew what to do with other folk's pain. Moving near, Precious bent and rubbed the woman's palm. "Tell me about him."

Mrs. Scott's hazel eyes were vacant. "He's not dead. He's just gone."

The dark haired girl who'd stood up for Mrs. Scott came near and sat on the small grey blanket that covered the bed. "Millie's lost a lot this year. A husband, now her boy. But welcome for what that's worth."

This one was pretty, with long dark hair and eyes that slimmed like slits. She held her head up with dignity. But how could that be, when she sold her body nightly? Maybe you gave so much of yourself away, it didn't matter anymore.

"What is your name?" Precious ask the composed woman.

"I'm Cai De. I ran away from a settlement when my mother wanted to marry me off. Maybe I shoulda done it. Couldn't be any worse than this."

A runaway? That happened outside of Charleston, too.

Still clasping her hand, Precious lifted Mrs. Scott's cheek. "Was your husband in the colony's military? Did he serve for Lord Welling?"

The woman nodded then crumpled back on the bed.

There had to be something that could be done for this widow. Precious looked at all these women. There had to be something that could be done for all of them.

The last girl, one with brown hair, came near and circled Precious. With a thick crisp accent, she asked, "You've a name?"

"Precious. Precious Jewell."

She sauntered back to her bed. "Precious Jewell sounds hoity. You'll probably be like the other darkie, thinking you're better than the rest. So Captain Welling has come to his senses and threw you out. Now we get another Xhosa to contend with."

"Sahara, the other one, isn't working yet." Cai De put her feet up on the mattress. Her slippers were worn. "And this one seems nice."

The other Xhosa? The answer Precious had come for. "Where's the other one like me?" She put a hand on her hip and hoped the action made her sound worldly, not scared. "And why isn't she working for her keep? I don't like those who can't hold up their end of a bargain."

Sahara started to smile. "Well, if you do your part around here, maybe you won't be so bad."

Precious moved away toward the empty bed. Another woman black like her. Oh, Lord let it be the Xhosa daughter. "Why is the Xhosa not with us?"

Cai De put her hands above her head as if she wore an imaginary crown. "She's a princess."

Sahara forced her hand down like she wanted to slap Cai De. "I'm going to tell Mrs. Branddochter. I'll let her know the new girl's snooping."

The horrible girl stomped out of the room.

Precious was desperate. Time was running out. "Where is the Xhosa girl? Is she with an old man?"

Fear clouded Cai De's eyes. "How did you know? That's suppose to be a secret."

Precious' pulse raced as she came closer to the woman. "Tell me where. It's very important I find her."

Millie lifted her head. "I'll tell you if you help find my boy."

"Tell me, Millie. I will help you. I promise, I will help. I will help all of you."

Nodding, as if she understood, Millie sat up and pointed. "Down the hall. Take the stairs to the root cellar. She's there with her father. My boy, he's got red hair. Small for his age."

"Thank you, Mille. I will get help for you." She slipped from the room into the hall. She'd keep her promise. One of the widow's of Gareth's men shouldn't spend her days here.

Precious spied the stairwell and made a dash for it.

Heavy footsteps sounded. It had to be Mrs. Branddochter.

Before they came into view, Precious bounded down the stairs like a rabbit. It wouldn't take long for the madame to find her missing. *Sometimes God, let this be the answer.*

She strengthened her courage and searched the dark corridor. Not seeing the way she felt the damp rock walls, and moved until she saw a hint of light. She followed the light until she came upon a door.

Precious held her breath and prayed again that she hadn't risked everything for foolishness. She made her way inside.

Warm candlelight surrounded an old man in a bed. His eyes were closed on his black face, his skull wrapped in bandages. A slim lady with tawny brown skin and long straight hair sat by his side.

The girl, maybe Precious's age, maybe younger, lifted her face. "What do you want? Mrs. Branddochter knows my father needs his rest."

Emboldened, Precious decided to use some of Gareth's wit. Well, the sharpness he taught her. "I've come on behalf of Lord Welling. Your people must know the chief is alive."

"My people?" Her mouth slimmed. "The same who have taken my father's throne? Go away."

Hallelujah, Praise the Lord, Precious had found them.

She pranced over and knelt. She was in front of a king after all. "You don't understand. A war is about to take place. The colonists will all die because the Xhosa thinks you and your father are prisoners."

The girl's face changed as her lips pressed into a line, no longer serene but marred with hatred. "Let all the sons of men burn. They led to my father's disgrace. They made him weak. They are the cause of his lost of the nation."

Precious tugged on her shawl. It was cold down here, too cold for a sick man. "I don't care a wit about all that happened before, but I do care about innocent people dying."

The old man's eyes opened. A horrid cough left his throat. "Thembeka, are you here?"

"Yes, Father."

"The land of the shadows are calling."

Tears fell from the girl's eyes. For all her anger, Thembeka was nothing more than a scared girl about to lose her father.

"Don't answer. Stay with me, Father. Together, we will get back all you have lost." Thembeka put her face in her hands. "Please leave us."

Precious backed away. She'd give the Xhosa privacy, and go tell Gareth. The war would not happen now.

Heart beating, she made her way back up the stairs and headed for the door. A hand clasped her arm, stopping her.

Mrs. Branddochter tightened her fingers around Precious's elbow. "Where are you going?"

"I wanted some air."

"You can have that later. Your first client is here. Go into this room."

Precious panicked. Her pulse raced. "I don't want to do this. I've changed my mind."

She shoved Precious from behind, and almost tossed her into the room. "You just need to get this over with. Then, as one of my girls, we'll see if you can go back to the captain."

The door closed.

The click of a lock sounded.

Precious beat on the door and twisted the knob. "You let me out of here."

Laughter poured through the door. "Your customer has a key. See what you have to do for him to release you."

Precious pounded on the door until her knuckles stung. So close to saving Port Elizabeth and now she was locked away. The world was going to end here and she couldn't even be with Gareth and Jonas or Clara.

She pounded again. This wasn't that shack in Charleston, but fear still coursed through her. Her heart doubled in speed when humming hit her ears.

The notes made her turn. She forgot that she wasn't alone.

"Why don't you come over he...here?" The man hiccupped again. The madame had locked her in the dim room with a drunk.

She pivoted hoping to reason with him.

A customer sat with his shoes off, waiting for her on the bed.

She took a step forward. When she was closer, the candlelight exposed him. Mr. Grossling shook a key at her.

She almost let out a sigh of relief, until she saw him unbutton his coat. "I couldn't believe Welling would break with you. Now I get to sample the captain's woman."

Fear and anger twisted in her gut, wrestling to allow the right words out of her mouth. "You've lost your mind. I came here to find the missing Xhosa to stop the attack. So go on and give me the key."

She stuck out her hand.

Mr. Grossling whipped a gun from the nightstand. He put a bullet in it and peppered it. "It's not that simple, Miss Jewell. If we die from the Xhosa attack, I'll die with a smile on my face. Now come away from that door."

A battle inside erupted again. Those same words were uttered to her in the shack in the woods in Charleston. She didn't listen then and it had made her punishment worse. He'd taken a knife and branded her forever.

She folded her trembling arms. "I have to get to Gareth. You're not an evil man. And you're not going to take me against my will."

"You've been a mistress to Welling. Why not be my whore, too? Come give me my due. I've paid for you. You're not leaving here unless you make me happy."

He pulled out his watch. "Time is running out. I could've had you and been done by now, if you were willing. Then you can run and tell Welling whatever it is you think will stop the Xhosa." He blew her a kiss. "Tick tock."

Maybe if she gave him his due, he'd let her go to Gareth and stop the war. She was in a house where women gave they their bodies for a few pence, a little food and water. This giving would save the colony. Wasn't that enough to endure this final shame?

It had to be. She dropped her shawl and watched his eyes get bigger as he seemed to ogle the low cut of her bodice. Marked as such so many years ago, playing dress up in Eliza clothes, even gaining Gareth's love, none of it changed what she was. Now she'd be wanton to save Port Elizabeth.

Chapter Twenty-Seven: Saving His Loves

Gareth muttered every thing he could under his breath. That darn woman was going to be the death of him. It took forever to get his household stable. Rousing the cabin boy to come attend Mrs. Narvel, her babe, and Jonas took needed time. Precious was in Mrs. Branddochter's house of flesh. The girl had been horribly abused in Charleston. Those men wouldn't take no for their dalliances. It wasn't safe for any woman, especially not Precious. Someone might look at her and miss the passion in her eyes, the intelligence that worked when she wasn't doing something stupid.

Mzwamadoda rode up next to him. "My people are gathering on the ridge. The attack is imminent. You should turn back and get your people to safety."

"My people is in a brothel, doing something she thinks will stop the coming slaughter. I've got to get her out of there."

"She means that much to you?"

He looked at Mzwamadoda. If he could use his rapier

to end this futile chatter, he might have cut his friend down.

"So Xhosa lives matter to you, Welling." Mzwamadoda smiled. "Then let's go retrieve the Precious."

The sound of horns started small then grew. They must know that this would make the colonists fearful. Ralston said he'd be steadfast. The English wouldn't draw first blood. Well not Xhosa blood. If some fool laid a hand on Precious, blood was going to be shed.

They arrived at Madame Branddochter's. Gareth jumped down and pounded to the front.

The Dutch woman blocked him at the door. She had a gun barrel in her hand. "Lord Welling, what do you want here?"

"I've come for Precious Jewell."

"She's my Precious now. And she's busy. I'll tell her you stopped by."

He hefted his spear, knocking at the gun butt. "Neeltje Woman, get out of my way or I'll tear this place to pieces."

Mzwamadoda was on his heels. "Dutchy, he will." He took his spear from his side. "Can't shoot us both."

"Gareth?" It was Precious's voice. She sounded hurt.

He flew down the hall past the woman. Again Mzwamadoda was right behind him.

Precious stood at the door of a chamber. She bunched her shawl about her shoulders. "Gareth?"

As he started toward her to scoop up the scared girl into his arms, Grossling popped out of the chamber behind her. "Xhosa!"

The world moved in slow motion. The flint exploded, the bullet sailed through the crook of Precious's arm.

Gareth pushed Mzwamadoda out of the way and took the metal's sting. His side felt on fire as he fell to his knees. He placed his hands to the gaping wound. His hands last night were covered in Mrs. Narvel's blood. His own now stained his fingers. Now wasn't the time to die. Nothing was done.

Precious screamed and ran to him. She took her shawl and bunched it into his leaking side. "No, Gareth. This wasn't supposed to happen."

Mzwamadoda jumped over them, knocked the gun from Grossling and pinned him to the wall. "I told you they were killers, Precious. Now they kill each other too."

His hands were on Grossling's windpipe.

Turning purple, the war department man squealed. "I was protecting myself. I meant to kill him not you, Welling."

Precious pulled Gareth's face into her bosom. She kissed his brow. "You have to be well. I found the chief and his daughter. Your Port Elizabeth can be saved. You can't die."

Pressing her hands to his side, he sat up. "Where are they, Precious? Maybe there is still time to stop Bezile. Tell us."

Mzwamadoda punched Grossling so hard he fell down in a silent lump. "The Precious one, where are they?"

She fussed over Gareth, touched him, and kissed him. He felt the depth of her care, but so many things were undone between them.

Her voice held tears. "Mzwamadoda, down the stairs."

The warrior flew down the hall. His feet barely touched the ground.

Mrs. Branddochter rounded the corner. The woman

paled. "Blood! Oh, dear lord, what is going on?"

Precious leapt up. "This is your fault, you horrible shrew. You locked me in that room with that fool. And he just shot my Gareth."

Her Gareth. What a fine time to claim him. "Precious, don't waste your breath. The Xhosa will burn this place down first. She'll lose her livelihood. It's the only thing she cares about."

Precious nodded and came back down to Gareth's brow. "I'm not going to let you die in here, you hear me." She took his hand in hers and pointed his rapier at the Madame. "She's been keeping the chief hostage."

Mrs. Branddochter looked unnerved, almost frightened. Precious with his weapon in hand was a little scary.

"Lord Welling, the girl is nuts. She said you manhandled her."

Precious lifted his sword and looked like she might actually use it. "I said nothing of the sort. I let this snake go on with her foolishness to find the Xhosa. I had to save Port Elizabeth for you. I needed to do something for the finest man I know."

His heart warmed, but he leaned over and grasped her about her ankles. "No need to slice anyone up."

Feeling faint, he fell over. "Precious, get some cloth or bandages."

She spun. Indecision crossed her features. "Cai De, I need some bandages!"

Gareth tried to press the shawl into the bullet hole, but he couldn't feel anything.

When he refocused, Precious had cloth from two women. They held it in place while she tore at his shirt.

"It went straight through, but we have to stop the

357

bleeding. We must clean good to keep the fever away." There was hope in Precious's voice as she spilled brandy on his wound. "I'm going to make you better."

He couldn't hold in the wince. "Such a waste of liquor. How 'bout a sip?"

She bent down and kissed his lips. "I'm going to take care of you." She ripped the cloth and wrapped it about him."

The sounds of the horns made the house rumble. Xhosa horns. He tried to sit up, but didn't have the strength. "It's too late."

Mrs. Branddochter leaned over him. "I didn't want trouble."

Mzwamadoda plodded back up the stairs. "A war is going to happen because my people believe the chief and his daughter are captive. The Madame woman will be the death of your people, Welling."

Once more, he tried to sit up. "There has to be a way to get to Bezile."

Tears streamed down Precious's face. "Don't move, Gareth."

"It's not about me anymore, Precious." He tried to mouth, all that was in his heart. "Love you, crazy woman."

Precious took her fingers sticky with Gareth's blood. She wiped it against her brow. "Your crazy woman. I'm not letting your legacy die."

The horns blared again. Precious shook her head and rose up from Gareth. If he was going to die, he'd know that his life work would be saved. "Mzwamadoda, can you go tell him that their chief is here? The daughter is here."

"Bezile is set to kill. At this point, only the chief himself could stop him. And he's in too bad of form to move."

Gareth coughed. His face looked ashen. "Maybe there is someone else." His hand raised and pointed. "Thembeka, go stop the war."

The princess had come up the stairs. Her pretty face held the deepest frown. Maybe Gareth's bloodshed would change her care-for-nothing attitude about the war.

Precious rushed to her. "The Xhosa are about to attack. They have to know you've been held captive here not Port Elizabeth."

Mrs. Branddochter came to them. "Girl, you need you stop this. I don't want no trouble."

Thembeka folded her arms about her, creasing her silvery moss colored dress. "Mrs. Branddochter is not holding us hostage. She is my aunt. She has given us respite in spite of what you English have done to my father."

The madame's snide veneer collapsed. Fear trembled her lips. "Are they going to attack, girl?"

"Maybe."

"They will kill me too. Did you think about that, girl?" Mrs. Branddochter took Cai De's hand and ran to the room where she kept all the girls. "Ladies, we need to get out. Thembeka has killed us all."

In a low voice, Thembeka said, "Maybe they should destroy this brothel too for what my aunt has done to women."

The princess turned as if she was going to head back down the stairs. Precious panicked. The princess couldn't leave. Something had to be done.

Precious came to this house of sin to save Port Elizabeth. She didn't matter. Her flesh didn't. She'd go out to meet the Xhosa herself and die trying to help. "Wait, Thembeka."

Gareth looked at her. There was love in his eyes as he gazed at her but his strength was leaving.

She lifted his rapier. "Thembeka, you will go set this all straight. You have to tell the truth. They will listen to her, won't they Mzwamadoda?"

"I am going to sit with my father."

Precious took her arm. "I said, you are going to set this right. Gareth can't die without his Port Elizabeth living."

Thembeka shook free. "I don't care. And take your hands from a Xhosa's chief's daughter."

Think Precious. What would Gareth say to her if he was able? She looked around and then it came to her as shiny as the sword in her hands. It was all about worth. "Go to him. Let him see the coward you are before he dies."

Mzwamadoda stepped in front of Precious. "Please don't talk to my cousin like that. She's young and woman. What can she do?"

Thembeka spun and poked him in the arm. "You take that back, both of you."

Precious came forward held out her hands that were stained with Gareth's blood. "I know the hate you have inside. I have it too. All these men, even a relative has stolen your dignity. You hate them and you hate yourself."

The princess balled her fists. She nodded.

"You are bigger than your pain. There is evil out there, in here." She pointed to her chest. "But you are bigger than the pain. Come with me. Let's show them."

"The Precious one is right. You know your father wouldn't want the innocents to die, mate."

"If you call me mate one more time, I will take this one's rapier to you."

The sound of the horns grew louder. The Xhosa had to be close.

Gareth pushed up for a moment then fell back. His head banged on the floor. Precious felt every ounce of his pain. "Careful with my rapier. All lives matter, even the ones who've wronged you. Go stop this war, brave daughter of Zifihlephi, Chief of the Xhosa."

Precious looked at the unconscious Grossling. She had to suck in a breath to keep from wretching.

Almost panting, she took Thembeka's hand. "Set aside the pain, the hurt. Come with me and save Port Elizabeth. My friend, she reads to me about a queen. Esther went against fear to save life. Come on, princess."

Precious turned to Mzwamadoda. Help Gareth to live until I get back. Her eyes locked with Gareth's. Maybe he knew how she felt for him, always would feel for him.

Rapier raised, Precious and Thembeka ran out of the brothel. They charged up the path from the brothel, waving their arms and shouting.

The horn blowing stopped. A few of the lead horses charged down the hill.

Thembeka took hold of the rapier. "How do you deal with the hate, Precious one?"

The wind whipped up the dust. It flew about them. Precious thought about her half-brother, her enslavement in Charleston, Palmers the hateful butler, nasty Grossling. Then fresh images of Gareth, and Jonas and Clara. The love of that Sometimes God who felt as if he was near today. "I'm still learning, Thembeka. But I know it begins with believing that there is something better for me. That I'm not my scars."

The lead horseman came closer. "Great Thembeka, have you escaped the English dogs that held you captive? Where is your father?"

The princess lifted her chin to the man, big like Mzwamadoda, but with large grey eyes. "Bezile, if you care so much for my father, give him back his reign."

The warrior laughed with a bitter chuckle. The two plume of feathers from the band on his head shook. "I ask again, where is your father?"

Precious stepped in front of the bronze man and kept him from Thembeka. "Her father is sick. He is dying. Let him be in peace."

"Is it true, Thembeka?"

"Yes." The princess made her voice loud. "We are not prisoners. Call off the attack." Her voice gained strength. It became louder, ringing as if she had cupped her hands to her mouth. The words, the sounds were so strange and foreign but held power. The lines of warriors on the hill put their spears back into the sheath on their backs.

Thembeka yelled again. Her voice sounded like a song.

In response to whatever she said, the line of warriors backed away. Soon the hills became bare. The threat for now had gone away.

Thembeka held her head high, every inch a queen. But the nasty Bezile and two of his henchmen stayed. "Where is your father? He can come back and be at peace with the Xhosa. You will join with me and rule Xhosa at my side.

She reached for the rapier, but Precious held it firm.

She wasn't going to let the girl do something reckless.

Letting go of the weapon, Thembeka drew her arms to her side. "I will not justify your rule. Go enjoy what you have stolen."

"No, you shall return." He reached to grab the girl and take her with him.

Without any hesitation, Precious stepped in front of her and lifted the rapier so the sharp point would stab the Xhosa man if he tried to come at them again. "She told you good bye."

He drew himself up, escaping the point of the blade and made his horse circle them. "Woman, who are you to stop me?"

Dirt kicked up, choking and blinding Precious. She waved Gareth's prized weapon and stood up tall. She'd defend Thembeka as if she were protecting her love's colony or his son. This young woman didn't let pain win today, and neither would Precious. "I'm the captain's—"

"Wife!" The voice said strong and clear.

She turned to see Gareth supported by Mzwamadoda coming toward them. Though he leaned to the side and held his ribs, her love propelled toward her, handsome and in control. Was it an act?

Gareth took the last few paces unassisted. "Go back to your people, Bezile, and let mine be. The peace between my uncle and the greatest Xhosa chief is still in effect."

Mzwamadoda shouted a command to the henchmen. They responded in kind. The language didn't sound like music but the tones and changes in their expressions seemed to be working for the two henchmen withdrew. They moved at least fifty paces away, a full stretching of Precious's fingers if she were to measure it.

"Mate, I've seen the chief. He's not a prisoner, and he

is more shamed by your attack on the colonists than the loss of his lobes. He's forgiven his transgressor. He's made his peace. Go back to the inlands. Seeing Thembeka not in shackles might make the Xhosa think you lied. Some one else may be bucking for your throne."

Bezile turned his horse. "You are crazy, Thembeka. Maybe you do belong here with the other half-breeds and the unworthy English. You will be sorry."

As the warrior rode away, Thembeka pivoted. "You will all be sorry. I will find a way to get back the kingdom."

Her words were whispered, mixed with the fleeting hoof beats but Precious heard them clearly. The poor girl trudged back to brothel. Rage still filled her, and it would only grow worse when her father died. Precious promised herself to figure out a way to help Thembeka and all the trapped girls of Mrs. Branddochter.

Gareth hobbled to her and took back his rapier. He stabbed the ground with it and pulled her into his arms. "Woman, when I get you home…"

She tried to hug his neck, and spied the reddening spots of the makeshift bandage. She pulled at his coat, just as he fell again to his knees.

She lifted her face to Mzwamadoda. "Help me get my man home. I need to tend to his wounds."

Gareth stretched out on the ground, a smile grew from his wincing lips. "Yes, get us home, Mzwamadoda. I need my woman, my Precious, to doctor me now that Port Elizabeth is safe."

"Mate, the Xhosa are not done with Thembeka or Port Elizabeth. Bezile will try again."

Precious knelt by Gareth and applied more pressure to his wound. None of that foolishness mattered. She needed to get him home where she could tend to him, so no fever would set in. He had to live. She needed to feel pure in his love again.

Chapter Twenty-Eight: The Scars That Won't Fade

The light outside his lids seemed brighter. Gareth opened one eye then the other.

Pain shot through him. His side ached. He sniffed the foul smell and hoped that one of Precious's rues or other weed poultices hadn't been stuffed near his bullet wound. He felt well enough to know he wouldn't die, but the smell just might cause him to lose his composure.

He peaked under his blanket and saw wide white bandages wrapped about his waist.

The bullet missed his organs or anything else vital. One thing was for sure, bullets hurt just as badly as shrapnel.

What if he lost more than he knew? He wiggled one foot then the other. So far so good. He lifted the blanket again and saw that the rest of him survived as well.

The door swung open and Precious came inside. She was back to her usual mobcap and high necked collar. Nothing like Eliza's gown she'd worn to the brothel. He closed his eyes and tried to forget how fetching it looked on Precious's curves or the look of sheer horror on her face when she stepped out of that bedchamber. What had happened in that room with Grossling? Had she suffered more trying to save Port Elizabeth?

She came close and lay a palm on his head. Her wrist smelled of his pine soap. It smelled nice on her skin.

A sigh sounded. "No more fever, but he hasn't awakened. Please, Sometimes God, let him be well again."

Between his lashes, he watched her float about praying aloud. He must've given her some kind of scare. When she started wiping at her eyes, he coughed to let his voice sound strong. "Lass, you seem to be fretting over a little metal."

She pivoted and gazed at him. Her lip, that full tender work of art, quivered. "I've been so worried, Gareth."

Tears dripped down her cheeks. "Please, tell me you are well. I'll do anything to fix this."

Anything? "Then, come to me lass."

She tugged at her collar, but came near and sat at his side. His brave girl looked tentative, almost afraid to approach. This wasn't to be. He caught her hand. "You still don't follow instruction well."

With all his strength, he pulled her into his arms, folded her against his chest and embraced her. "Much better."

He held on to her until she stopped crying, taking the opportunity to caress the curves he'd admired moments before. It took a little effort, but he had her off her feet and snuggled next him, just like on the Margeaux.

"Gareth, I thought I'd lost you."

"Woman, if you ever leave this bedchamber without

telling me where you are going, you just might."

"I just knew they were there from what Branddochter had said to me before I got lost in the woods with those spitting snakes."

He tossed her mobcap and fingered a braid or two. It was time to ask. "She can be dangerous, but what of Grossling?"

Precious tried to pull away from Gareth, but he held her fast. Her tears were ragged and loud.

He kissed the scar on her neck. His suspicions had to be correct. Grossling must've forced himself upon her. Anger burned inside, more than the sting of his wound from tensing. Now wasn't the time to plan revenge. It was time to show love to this jewel of a woman. "Nothing matters. You trust me, Precious, right?"

She wiped her face. "Yes, Gareth, with everything in me."

"Do you love me?"

She spun in his arm and held his gaze. Fear and questions dotted her eyes, but was there love too?

"Can you love me, all of me, even the scarred parts?"

Before he could answer, the door opened. She tried to squirm away but he held her fast.

Mrs. Narvel poked her head inside, and then pushed fully into the room with Jonas and Dennis. "Sorry to interrupt, Lord Welling, *baroness*, but this little boy and your friend wanted to see you."

Mrs. Narvel let Jonas loose.

Like a released hot gas balloon, he ran to the headboard, squealing and holding out his hands to come up.

With Precious firmly locked in one arm, Gareth reached down and picked up his son. He lay back with two squirming bodies. The two he loved most dearly.

"Jonas has been good, helping with my little Clara. But he wanted to see his Papa and his Mammie."

The boy bounced on the mattress. "Papa's going to be fine. Mammie and I prayed."

Precious's cheeks held a full blush. Others might miss it against her warm brown skin, but to him it looked like autumn leaves appearing against the umber bark of an oak. Lovely woman.

Blushing more, she smiled. "We've all been praying, Jonas."

The little boy bounced up and down on the bed. If not for Precious's protecting his bandaged midsection, the tike's fast movements might've caused damage.

Gareth raked his fingers through his boy's blonde mop. "So what brings you to me, Dennis? I'm not quite able to dress and attend you downstairs."

"I know, but the colony's abuzz about you and your wife saving us from the Xhosa. I just came to officially perform your marriage ceremony. Regardless of the African tradition the miss tried to explain, we need to make sure that this bond can't be broken by London."

Gareth squeezed her hand. "It can't, Precious. Can it?"

Her pretty chestnut eyes locked on his. "No."

"Good." Dennis hefted a big book and took a quill and a bottle of ink from his leather vest. "Mrs. Narvel, can you get this feather pen ready for the bride and groom?"

"It is my pleasure." The woman plodded over and took great care in opening the small flask. She dunked the tip of the quill twice and then handed it to Gareth.

Dennis neared and put the book close to the bed. "Put

369

your mark in here, both of you."

Precious sat up a little and fussed with his bandages. "Wait, I need to tell you."

Gareth was done with excuses and delays. He linked his hand with hers, gripped the quill and made his mark for Gareth Conroy, the Baron Welling and then a quick P and a J. "What else, Dennis, do we need to make this marriage official for the folks back in England?"

The blacksmith rubbed his beard. "An exchange of a ring will do it."

The family ring, where was it? Oh, somewhere in his dresser or trunks. Getting up to search for it might give Precious more time for excuses. She was his and he hers, no matter what anyone thought. "I've none at the moment." He heaved a heavy sigh. "Perhaps there is a substitute condition?"

"Use this, Lord Welling." Mrs. Narvel took off her ring and gave it to him. "It can do until you give my friend something proper."

The simple gold band would more than do. "Thank you." He took it and slipped it on Precious's finger. "Done."

Dennis closed his book up. The thud was loud, definitive. "Well then, it's done."

Mrs. Narvel put her hand on her hip. "It can't be that simple. Make them say some vows."

Frowning for a minute, Dennis scratched his jaw. "Well, alright. Do you Gareth Conroy, love this woman?"

"I do."

Dennis looked down at the fidgeting bride. "Do you, Precious Jewell, love this man?"

She was silent for a moment and shut those big chestnut eyes. "Yes. With everything that is in me, yes."

Gareth didn't wait for permission. He leaned over his son and kissed her. He made it a slow one, taking time to savor her trembling lip. He lifted his head and peered at his son, who clapped his hands.

The cheery Mrs. Narvel in her widow's black crepe and Dennis joined in too, but things weren't done between Gareth and his new wife. He sat back on his pillows and coveted Precious's hand, pulling it along his bandages. "As much as I enjoy you all, the baroness and I won't be joining you for the wedding breakfast."

Dennis offered an arm to Mrs. Narvel. "Newly wedded people need privacy for theirs is an honorable marriage bed."

That wasn't quite the verse, but close enough for Gareth's purposes. He hugged his boy one more time. "Papa will play with you later, Jonas. I need to have a long talk with your Mammie. Would that be fine, son?"

Jonas smiled and nodded. He climbed down and ran to Mrs. Narvel's waiting hand.

The three left and closed the door snuggly behind them.

Straining, he tugged Precious to his side. Her chin rested on his abdomen above the pristine wrapping of bandages. "Now what is it you had to tell me, Mrs. Conroy?"

She put her hand with the glimmering band to her eyes. "That I don't deserve to be. I'm not a pure bride."

"A little late for that complaint since we've been officially married. Yet who needs perfection? I'm not that pure of a groom, but the Lord can make things new."

Gareth studied the serious pout on her face. His jests didn't bring her comfort. It was painfully obvious that her freedom wouldn't be until they talked about what happened at the brothel. He'd arrived too late to save her from harm. Insides beginning to boil, he placed his palms flat on the mattress. "Just say it, Precious." Then he could go and kill Grossling for taking advantage of her.

With tears pooling in her eyes, maybe she feared for Gareth's safety. Or worse, that kindness in her soul didn't want him to harm the villain. He blew out a breath and opened his soul. She had to see Gareth and know his love. "Precious Jewell Conroy, you have the biggest heart. Nothing you could say will ever stop mine from flowing to you."

Precious sat up, taking care to not touch his wounds. "The room is so bright."

"Precious, don't delay." His tone sounded quiet, but she knew him. The hunger to defend what was his would always define him.

"Come now, Mrs. Conroy. You can tell your husband anything."

She blinked her eyes again. The room was so light. That Sometimes God had been here. He'd made it so Gareth's fever would break and gave him a sunny day to awaken to. But the Lord left His glory shine. No secrets of the past could be hidden.

"Your lips aren't moving, Precious. What makes them so quiet?"

He took a short breath and raised her up. His gaze set upon her. His eyes scooped up the candle's shimmer making them a deeper blue than she'd ever seen. Oh, why couldn't he just tunnel into her mind and see the darkness within her?

"Precious, we aren't sneaking about. You are legally

obligated to lie next to me. There's nothing to fear, but I need you to tell me what troubles you."

His calm voice didn't do anything for her heart. It raced more and more as his lips came closer to hers.

She turned away to the window. "Let me close the curtains. Dim a candle. I want to be in the dark when you see me."

"You know a captain's vision is pretty good, day or night." He eased back on his pillow again. "Nothing escapes me much. What don't you want me to see?"

How could she tell him of the scars, the ones that said what she was? Putting herself with Mr. Grossling. "Please, just make it dark."

"How about I just hold you in my arms until your courage returns?" His hands played with the buttons on her blouse. "But while I wait, perhaps we should rid you of these confining clothes. It's not quite fair for you to be fully dressed, while I'm not."

She scooted from his heated hands and dangled her feet over the mattress's edge. "You are not being serious. How am I to tell you something awful?"

He reached over and brushed her cheek. Gareth turned her chin toward him. "Just say it. Then lie back down next to me. The best sleep I've had in years was when you were the captain's woman on the Margeaux."

"Stop making jokes. Another man has looked on me, Gareth. Mr. Grossling at the brothel."

"Did he violate you?" His voice was low and cold. "I will kill him."

She pivoted to face Gareth.

His palms fisted. His gaze burned. "Don't tell me not to."

"No, it is worse." Hands shaking, she reached for his

but couldn't make it that far.

"Precious, come to me."

She wanted to but couldn't move. Shame gripped her; hogtied her feet to the floor.

Grunting, he pulled forward. His arms snaked about her middle. He gathered her in his arms.

The scent of him, liniment and woodsy, filled her nostrils. He smelled good. His arms felt good.

"You can tell me anything, Precious. Nothing changes what's betwixt us."

As long as his hold was tight, nothing mattered. "Grossling had been drinking. He had a gun and said he'd paid for me. I had to get to you, to tell you about finding the chief. So I didn't struggle with him. I figured I'd let--"

"You'd let him get his due, that stupid concept you tossed at me back at Firelynn." He growled deep in his chest. His arms bound about her more tightly as if he thought she'd flee. That wonderful heart of his thudded against her. "So what happened?"

"He made me lie down and bunch up my skirts."

Another growl left Gareth. Air rushed of her braids; the low tone vibrated on her neck. "But you said, he didn't?"

"He was going to until he looked at my scars. Then he let me go. I was too ugly for him." She couldn't hold in her emotions anymore. Sobs came from everywhere. "I'm afraid you'll think that too. I don't want to be my scars for you. "

"Scars?" He fingered the one that peaked from her collar. "What scars?"

"When my half-brother molested me and thought he'd killed me, he took a knife to me hoping to make sure I couldn't bear children with a drop of Marsdale blood."

"Your half-brother, Eliza's cousin?"

"Yes."

She rubbed at her stomach; almost wishing the motion would take away the memories. She wished it were dark in Gareth's room so he couldn't see her or read the letters cut on her stomach and thighs.

He didn't say anything. His fingers started that dance along her back. When her overdress fell to her shoulders, the fog of his touch had worn away. His motions were purposeful. Her fingers trembled as he stripped away her blouse. Layer by layer, her outer dress dropped to the floor.

Like she was paper, he lifted her and freed her stocking. It wasn't a noise of passion, but of pain. The bullet had done him damage, but none of that seemed to be on his mind.

She started to clasp his hand, to make him stop and save his strength, but the look on his face said he wouldn't, not until nothing separated them.

Gareth was her husband now. He had a right to see her. So she put a shaky finger on the front lacings of her corset and undid it for him. Only a thin chemise now remained.

He sunk his hands into her braids and guided her lips to his. It was all a distraction for as his deep kisses took over her; he removed the stiff muslin from her.

The room was bright. He could see all of her, including the scars. Her flesh held words so horrible that even a drunken fool didn't want her.

"Trust me, Precious." Those hands of his, rough and powerful, smoothed her knotting stomach.

She was on edge, hardly able to breath. "I don't want

to be ugly to you."

Her next intake of air was sharp. Her innards knotted tighter as his hands wandered lower to the scars.

With his fingertips, he traced the W, the H, then the O. Soon, he'd traced them all, every repeated letter that evil had carved upon her skin. "You've been treated so cruelly. A woman whose heart is so filled with love never deserved this. You're beautiful, Precious Jewell Conroy, every bit of you. You are not these words."

"But the scars are still there for any one who sees me. With layers of clothing, I know they are there. I remember—"

"I'm the only man, Lord willing, who will ever see them. And I tell you, you are not these words. You are this." His pinkie wrote a new word, L, O, V, E over her wounds. "You've bandaged me up. I'm not a perfect specimen either. You know my struggles."

She reached up and grabbed him by the ear and tugged his face to hers. "If you never touch me again, you've loved me better than any man ever could."

That lopsided smile of his burst forth as he snaked her beneath the bed sheets. "We'll see."

He didn't say anymore. His mouth was too busy caressing her. Those hands of his that have brought forth life, and could wield a rapier like it pirouetted in the air, started working to draw her nearer, spinning Precious into the light of his love. So close to him, she could feel his pulse racing. He trembled against her as he sunk upon her loving her, all of her.

Epilogue: The Beach

The bright sun warmed his skin as Gareth walked to the bay. It felt so welcoming. Three weeks of bed rest under the love and care of his new wife had restored him back to health. He folded his arms and sat back against a boulder. Brown grasses surrounded this remote area of the bay. More middens piled high with shells dotted this escape. He lay back folded his arms and counted the white puffy clouds. Hints of pink outlined the sky. Oh, how he loved Port Elizabeth and his family.

Truthfully, he could've been up about his duties in a week, but there was something wonderful about staying in bed with a young wife, one who brought her zeal for life into her passion and her patience. Though he was sure he had enough drive to produce another son out of this new bargain, he still struggled with bouts of nothing. Yet, this wonderful woman made him feel loved and powerful, never weak or less than. She was the right one for him.

Precious's laughter met his ears. He sat up and

watched the barefoot sprite twirl in the sand, whirling Jonas. The two fell down, laughing.

Hard to believe the girl who'd been through so much, enslavement, a brutal attack and mutilation, now danced and smiled, seemingly with no cares. She didn't even wear one of those restrictive collars today. The sunlight fell freely upon the scar on her neck.

If this was a dream, he needed to keep guzzling brandy and never wake up. But, this was true. God hadn't forgotten him, and He'd given him much more than Gareth thought possible.

Precious waved. "Let's see if your Pa can name the seashells for us. He's smart like that."

"That sounds like a challenge, my dear. Do I win anything if I am right?" He moved toward them, dropped his rapier into the white sand and sat next to his son.

She shrugged and laughed again. "Not like we know enough to correct you."

It was so good to see her happy and carefree. But he needed to bring up something that surely might steal her smile.

His boy proceeded to plop at least four different types of shells into Gareth's lap. One abalone, the rest different size crab.

He took them up one by one and made a big show of studying them. The sound of hoof beats approached. Mzwamadoda on his silver horse galloped near.

A pout filled Precious's countenance. "Oh, here comes trouble…during the day, too."

Mzwamadoda, taking risks during broad daylight? That wasn't good. Gareth tensed but tried to keep his demeanor calm. Strain between the Xhosa and the colonists had lowered but antipathy remained. It wouldn't take much to start hostilities again. He cast a gaze to Precious. More gratefulness poured through him. Time was a precious gift, something he'd never ever take for granted.

Precious pulled Jonas into her arms, almost crushing the boy. Fear pinched at her lips, but she didn't want Gareth to think she'd lived fretful of the next moment. "I hope this doesn't mean the chief has died. This war foolishness can't start again."

Mzwamadoda slowed his mount and then popped off. His friend stood in his traditional kaross robe, save his English breeches. "This looks like a homely scene. Surely, the captain of the Margeaux with his cannons and sword hasn't become domesticated? The lion is now a kitten."

Gareth purred as he put his arm about Precious's shoulder.

Precious clasped his fingers. "The old chief? Is he dead?"

"No, but soon that day will come. He seems to linger for a reason. Something is undone."

Precious brow furrowed. She couldn't help it. There was such agony in waiting and watching the suffering. Everyone should go like Grandmama. She went to sleep after making dinner. Precious was glad it was a good meal for it was what Grandmama loved.

She swallowed and pressed down her sadness. "And Thembeka?"

"She won't leave his side. She barely touched the food you sent, but Madame Neeltje's other girls ate everything."

Her husband sighed. "I thought they didn't let Xhosa

into Mrs. Branddochter's."

Mzwamadoda grinned with his old arrogant smirk. "The Dutch are no better than the English at locking windows."

A smile couldn't help but form on Precious's lips. Though she hadn't had the courage yet to go back inside the brothel, she hadn't forgotten the women. Sending baskets for each of them by Mzwamadoda was a good start.

Gareth pulled to his feet. "Then what brings you? You usually are a nightly guest."

The Xhosa's joy disappeared from his face. "Bezile's not done in his war. He'll find another way to make trouble. I'm hearing things."

Her husband reached over and pulled his rapier from the sand and swung it about. "I figured as much. I..." He looked down at Precious. "I mean we, we will be ready."

Mzwamadoda grabbed at the shaft and lowered Gareth's weapon. "What have you done with the shooter?"

"Grossling? I've confined him to his quarters until I can send him back to England."

The sound of the fool's name made her sick. He'd seen the scars. But maybe there was something human in him, since he did let her go. Precious bounded up and brushed sand from her palms. "No more talk of war or anything else. Time to head home."

She tried to scoop up Jonas, but Gareth blocked her.

"Our day at the beach isn't done, my dear. Besides, if you go back to the house, you'll be cooking or fussing with the baby. I like it here, with just us and you at ease."

She shook her head, and tried hard not to let her eyes become glassy. He made her happy, made her feel so special. "A little longer then, but Jonas needs a nap."

Gareth raised his arms in a yawn. "A nap might be good all around."

With the lift of his brow, the wink of his eye—he wasn't thinking about a nap.

Mzwamadoda shook his head. "Domestic bliss. Well, I like playing with the future, k—leader too. Don't I get that weepy look?"

Precious put a hand on her hip. "You will be lucky if I leave you dinner tonight."

"Delicious food. I want a Precious, Welling. Where can I find one?"

Gareth pulled her fully into his arms. "There's only one and she's mine. So run along or go find you some nice Xhosa woman to settle down with and become domestic."

Mzwamadoda smiled and jumped onto his horse. He set off down the long stretch of sand. "Maybe Xhosa or someone else. Or maybe the Precious one day will grow tired of you, mate. Till next time."

Annoyance at the Xhosa warrior battled in her chest, but the irksome man had saved Gareth and her and Jonas, too. So she couldn't really complain too much. "You don't mind me serving all these people at your table, Xhosa, idiots?"

"Well, it's not Palmer's stiff meals of Firelynn. But it's more of how my uncle saw things. Everyone had a seat at the table."

Their dinners had grown over the past week with Mr. Ralston coming more and more, even the preacher man Dennis too. Maybe Clara might know love again. "You're not still fretting over Mzwamadoda. Are you, Gareth?"

His lips found her neck. She released her own purr.

"No. I love you. And I know you love me. And now that you are legally obligated to stay in bed next to me, I am quite content. There are even papers showing it. I know how fond you are of papers."

She turned her head from Jonas picking at the abalone shell to seek Gareth's eyes. "Like my indentured servant paperwork?"

He winced and fingered the sand. "I signed the release the night we arrived. Any debt was paid when you saved this sorry hide of mine."

"Why didn't you say something?"

"I'm selfish, Precious. I needed more time to show you that we should be together, especially with a flirtatious Xhosa underfoot."

"Well, I found them straightening your crowded desk and as you can see I didn't run off with him even when he kissed me."

The frown crowding Gareth's face warmed her heart. "Remind me that I owe him a bout of fist-a-cuffs."

She sank into Gareth's embrace. "Selfish silly man, I just have to learn to love you more to set your mind at ease."

The wind kicked up as a wave pushed close to their spot. They'd need to move nearer the rocks, but there was something wonderful, just being in this moment locked in loving arms with God's sunlight all about them.

Gareth sighed, tucking her head underneath his chin. "I'll have to release Mr. Grossling from arrest soon since the shooting was not intentional.

She didn't want to think of the odious fellow, but knew Gareth had to do what he must. "The leader of Port Elizabeth is to do what is right."

"There could be redemption for him you know. When I send him back to England, he will clear up the paperwork and get Mrs. Scott her widow's pension. I'd like to send her back but she won't leave. She still thinks her boy will come back. I've had Ralston go reason with her, but she's not inclined to believe otherwise."

Her heart went out to the widow. "She's trapped in the past as I would be if not for you."

"The past is no more Precious Jewell Conroy, my Baroness Welling. In fact, since you single handedly saved Port Elizabeth, perhaps we should dedicate a statue to you."

With Jonas waddling and picking up more shells, she looked out at the clear blue bay and thought of how far she'd journeyed for love. "If we build one, let's make it for Eliza. If not for her, we would never have come to be."

"Maybe so. Eliza set us on this path. But know it is you, not some slight resemblance that has my heart."

She dug deeper underneath his patched blue coat. "I know."

"My dearest, speaking of legal obligations to be in my bed. Maybe you are right about having enough bay air today."

"But you just said, you weren't ready to… You can't be tired?"

He scooped her up and swung her high in the air just as she had been turning toward Jonas. "Who said anything about being tired?"

The wicked glow in his face spoke volumes. She grasped his neck as laughter erupted. "Come on, Jonas. Time for you to play with your blocks in your room."

He set her onto the sand then scooped Jonas up and

put him into her arms. The boy barely had a chance to grab more than three of the things he'd gathered.

"Shells for Mammie, Papa?"

"Later, my son. Mammie and Papa have some obligations to work out."

She gripped Gareth's hand and settled the boy on her hip, walking in step with her husband. Yes, these obligations were something she wouldn't grow tired of. And she'd keep working to help him build Port Elizabeth, so he'd always have the time and energy to focus on these obligations in the Conroy home.

Extras

Author's Note

Dear Friend,

I enjoyed writing The Bargain because I dream of Port Elizabeth, a burgeoning colony where all men and women had the opportunity to make their claim and determine their own fates. These stories will showcase a world of intrigue and romance, somewhere everyone can hopefully find a character to identify with as the colonists and Xhosa battle for their ideas and the love which renews and gives life.

Stay in touch. Sign up at www.vanessariley.com for my newsletter. You'll be the first to know about upcoming releases, and maybe even win a sneak peek.

Thank so much for giving this book a read.

Vanessa Riley

Here are my notes:

Slavery in England

The emancipation of slaves in England preceded America by thirty years and freedom was won by legal court cases not bullets.

Somerset v Stewart (1772) is a famous case which established the precedence for the rights of slaves in England. The English Court of King's Bench, led by Lord Mansfield, decided that slavery was unsupported by the common law of England and Wales. His ruling:

"The state of slavery is of such a nature that it is incapable of being introduced on any reasons, moral or political, but only by positive law, which preserves its force long after the reasons, occasions, and time itself from whence it was created, is erased from memory. It is so odious, that nothing can be suffered to support it, but positive law. Whatever inconveniences, therefore, may follow from the decision, I cannot say this case is allowed or approved by the law of England; and therefore the black must be discharged."

E. Neville William, The Eighteenth-Century Constitution: 1688-1815, pp: 387-388.

The Slavery Abolition Act 1833 was an act of Parliament which abolished slavery throughout the British Empire. A fund of $20 Million Pound Sterling was set up to compensate slave owners. Many of the highest society families were compensated for losing their slaves.

This act did exempt the territories in the possession of the East India Company, the Island of Ceylon, and the Island of Saint Helena. In 1843, the exceptions were eliminated.

Glossary

The Regency – The Regency is a period of history from 1811-1825 (sometimes expanded to 1795-1837) in England. It takes its name from the Prince Regent who ruled in his father's stead when the king suffered mental illness. The Regency is known for manners, architecture, and elegance. Jane Austen wrote her famous novel, *Pride and Prejudice* (1813), about characters living during the Regency.

England is a country in Europe. London is the capital city of England.

Image of England from a copper engraved map created by William Darton in 1810.

Port Elizabeth was a town founded in 1820 at the tip of South Africa. The British settlement was an attempt to strengthen England's hold on the Cape Colony and to be buffer from the Xhosa.

Xhosa - A proud warrior people driven to defend their land and cattle-herding way of life from settlers expanding the boundaries of the Cape Colony.

Image of South Africa from a copper engraved map created by John Dower in 1835.

Abigail – A lady's maid.

Soiree – An evening party.

Bacon-brained – A term meaning foolish or stupid.

Black – A description of a black person or an African.

Black Harriot – A famous prostitute stolen from Africa, then brought to England by a Jamaican planter who died, leaving her without means. She turned to harlotry to earn a living. Many members of the House of Lords became her clients. She is described as tall, genteel, and alluring, with a degree of politeness.

Blackamoor – A dark-skinned person.

Bombazine – Fabric of twilled or corded cloth made of silk and wool or cotton and wool. Usually the material was dyed black and used to create mourning clothes.

Breeched – The custom of a young boy no longer wearing pinafores and now donning breeches. This occurs about age six.

Breeches – Short, close-fitting pants for men, which fastened just below the knees and were worn with stockings.

Caning – A beating typically on the buttocks for naughty behavior.

Compromise – To compromise a reputation is to ruin or cast aspersions on someone's character by catching them with the wrong people, being alone with someone who wasn't a relative at night, or being caught doing something wrong. During the Regency, gentlemen were often forced to marry women they had compromised.

Dray – Wagon.

Footpads – Thieves or muggers in the streets of London.

* * *

Greatcoat – A big outdoor overcoat for men.

Mews – A row of stables in London for keeping horses.

Pelisse - An outdoor coat for women that is worn over a dress.

Quizzing Glass – An optical device, similar to a monocle, typically worn on a chain. The wearer might use the quizzing glass to look down upon people.

Reticule – A cloth purse made like a bag that had a drawstring closure.

Season – One of the largest social periods for high society in London. During this time, a lady attended a variety of balls and soirees to meet potential mates.

Sideboard – A low piece of furniture the height of a writing desk which housed spirits.

Ton – Pronounced *tone*, the *ton* was a high class in society during the Regency era.

Sneak Peak: Unmasked Heart
* * *

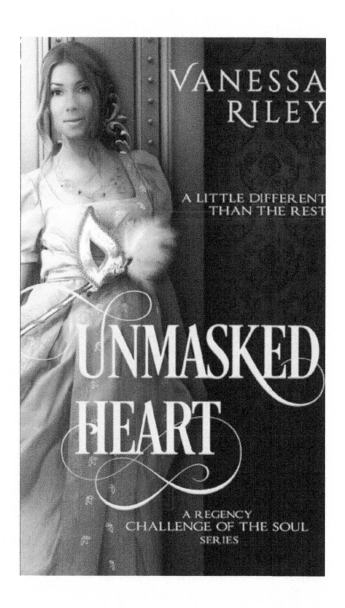

VANESSA RILEY

A LITTLE DIFFERENT
THAN THE REST

UNMASKED
HEART

A REGENCY
CHALLENGE OF THE SOUL
SERIES

Shy, nearsighted caregiver, Gaia Telfair always wondered why her father treated her a little differently than her siblings, but she never guessed she couldn't claim his love because of a family secret, her illicit birth. With everything she knows to be true evaporating before her spectacles, can the mulatto passing for white survive being exposed and shunned by the powerful duke who has taken an interest in her?

Ex-warrior, William St. Landon, the Duke of Cheshire, will do anything to protect his mute daughter from his late wife's scandals. With a blackmailer at large, hiding in a small village near the cliffs of Devonshire seems the best option, particularly since he can gain help from the talented Miss Telfair, who has the ability to help children learn to speak. If only he could do a better job at shielding his heart from the young lady, whose honest hazel eyes see through his jests as her tender lips challenge his desire to remain a single man.

The Bargain

* * *

Unmasked Heart is the first Challenge of the Soul Regency novel.

Excerpt from Unmasked Heart: The Truth

Her father sat near Sarah. Nodding his clean-shaven face, his long ash-blonde sideburns curling to his ears, he waved her forward. "Come in, Gaia."

She hadn't expected him to be in here. He usually took refuge in his study on the far side of the house; that is, if he made it out of bed. This couldn't be good.

Gaia swallowed and almost clasped the pianoforte tucked in the curved niche at the threshold. Maybe she could lean against it to regain her composure.

Sarah smiled at her before lowering her gaze. She motioned for Gaia to cross the paisley rug framing the sitting area close to the fireplace. "We need to speak with you."

"Does this mean I can't have the fabric? You can see I'm much grown." She tugged at the snug lines of her bodice.

His lips flattened to a line. "Your mother and I have decided you should be aware of all your responsibilities."

"My responsibilities?" At this, she slipped onto the couch. Why did she have the feeling her cheeks would soon color the same shade of burgundy as the sturdy seat?

Sarah tugged upon her treasured coral necklace then started working embroidery thread from the coiled jute basket near her caned chair. Her gaze seemed to be wandering as her tapping foot lifted her cream-and-rose skirt. "You know your father's estate is entailed to the males of the Telfair?"

"Yes, Timothy will inherit everything," Father coughed. His lungs raged as if he were coming down with another cold, the third this year. "You've made much progress with him. If you continue to keep him, I think he'll be prepared to manage Chevron Manor."

She stopped her fingers from twitching and then squinted at her unusually silent stepmother. Her hands shook as she passed a needle through a snowy handkerchief. Something definitely was amiss. "Sarah, Father, I don't understand."

"We, your mother and I, feel you should be his permanent companion."

"Permanent?" Gaia clutched the arm of the sofa, her nails denting the swell of the cushioning.

Sarah raised her head. Her mouth opened and closed and opened again as her voice went from non-existent to low. "You... will be mistress of Chevron, making sure that he runs things well. My Timothy will always need supervision."

Gaia bounced to her feet and headed for the fireplace. Clasping the dark poker, she stoked the low flame and allowed the heat to dry the water leaking from her eyes. "But what of my hopes?"

Father wheezed, and he pounded the arm of his chair. "You've never been inclined to anything but books. And this will make sure that your sisters and mother will be taken care of always."

"My mother is dead." Gaia spun around and pointed to her stepmother. "This is *her* work. She's only worried about herself."

"Don't talk to her like that." His feeble fingers gripped

the woman's hand. "And she's a good woman, unlike…"

"No, dear," Sarah wiped her leaky eyes. "You see she does not wish it."

Father left his chair and took the poker from Gaia's tight fingers. His clammy palms contrasted the blackness of the implement. "If my cousins press that Timothy is unfit, or they dupe his easy mind, all the family will be in jeopardy. I'm convinced your care will keep things well. You're levelheaded. You will be the guardian of this manor. That's a worthy calling for you."

With the back of her hand, Gaia swiped at her cheek. The lenses of her spectacles steamed. "Abandon my dreams? Don't you think I want to marry?"

Father guffawed, placed the poker by the fire's grate, and twisted the fob of his pocket watch. "It's not possible. You've never had any inclination."

Why wasn't it possible? She squinted at his creasing forehead. "I want to. In fact, I want to marry Mr. Elliot Whimple."

"You want your cousin's leavings?" Father chuckled. "I can tell you now, Whimple is not looking for a bluestocking. We're even too poor for your sister's pretty face to catch anything. She'll be home on Friday with no offer."

No marriage for Julia. She must be crushed. Tears for her slipped down Gaia's chin.

"Mr. Telfair, she's in love," Sarah put down her needlework and approached. Her almond eyes scanned up and down. "I suspect she's loved him for a long time."

Father moved toward the boxy pianoforte, his spindle legs drifting. "I wasn't aware, but it is of no consequence. The man doesn't look at you that way. Though he's good to his brother's household, I see him going to study in

London. That's too far to watch over Timothy."

"I need a chance to convince him. If he could like me, I'm sure he will help in my brother's care."

He leaned on the instrument. "I can't be at peace if all my children are tossed to the streets. You owe this to me, to all the Telfairs."

Owe? "What do you mean, Father?"

"Don't, Mr. Telfair. She doesn't need to know. Gaia can be reasoned with without saying anything more."

The warning sent a chill down Gaia's spine, but she had to know. "Tell me why I owe my flesh and blood."

Father took her hand and pulled it to his pale face. "Do you think it's possible that fair Telfair blood could produce this?"

Her heart stopped, slamming against her ribs. "My mother's Spanish roots have browned my skin. That's what you've always said."

He dropped her palm as his head shook. "It was a lie to cover my first wife's harlotry. You're a Telfair because I claimed you."

Gaia couldn't breathe. She crumbled to the floor. Hot tears drenched her face as she wished for a hole to break open and swallow her. "A mistake. Please, say this is a mistake."

The man whom she'd called father, whom she'd worshipped, shook his head again.

She lifted a hand to grasp his shoe but stopped, missing the black leather.

Was this why she'd always felt as if she could never grasp a hold of his love? Is this why he treated her a little differently from the rest? "Then who am I? Whose am I?"

"Some traveling bard, some African poet who

captivated *her* whilst I travelled. When you came out so close to white, with so little color, the ruse was borne; no scandal would befall my name. I'm just lucky you weren't a boy. Then, Chevron would fall to a mulatto. How would the Telfair line handle that tragedy?"

She waved her fingers, studying the light pigment coloring her skin. Mulatto. All this time she'd blamed her flesh on fate or heritage, not lust. She tugged at her elbows, feeling dirty. Glancing at him between tears, she silently begged for him to say it didn't matter, that he loved her still. "Father?"

With a grimace painting his silent mouth, he buttoned his waistcoat. "I'm going to lie down. Talk to her, Sarah; make her understand."

Desperate, Gaia's hand rose this time, but his back was to her in a blink as he plodded from the room. Her fingers felt cold and numb as they sank onto the thin rug. The breath in her lungs burned. Adultery, not a Telfair by blood – these thoughts smashed against her skull.

Sarah knelt beside her and stroked her back. "I'm so sorry. You should never have known."

Gaia shook her head and pulled away. "No more lies."

"Please, I'm not the enemy."

Rearing up, she caught the woman's beady gaze. "You want me to believe you don't want the almost-bastard to be a servant to Timothy? Would you wish one of your children be given this sentence, to become a governess to their own flesh and blood? Well, at least they can claim to be flesh and blood to Timothy."

Sarah reached again and wiped tears from Gaia's cheek then opened her arms wide. "You are his sister. You love him so. This is no failing of yours."

At first, Gaia fell into the woman's sturdy embrace,

then she stiffened and pulled away. She needed to flee, to let her brain make sense of the emotions whipping inside. Her slippers started moving. "I must go."

"Sweetheart, wait!"

Gaia shook her head and backed to the threshold. "Why? Is there something else you have to disclose to steal the rest of my dreams?"

Without a thought for a bonnet or coat, she rushed down the hall and out the front door.

Wham! She slammed into a man in fancy, sky-blue livery. The servant was tall and black. Black, like some part inside of her. Her eyes fixed on his bronze skin and wouldn't let go.

"Miss? I've come from Ontredale. Are you well, miss? You look pale enough to faint."

Not pale enough; never would be. "Sorry." She ducked her eyes and sidestepped him.

"Ma'am, I bear a note——"

"You want a Telfair. They are inside." She started running and kept going until not a cobble of Chevron Manor could be seen. Salty drops stung and blurred each step. She strode forward, deeper into the welcoming woods. A hint of spring blooms stroked her nose, but the streaks lining her wet face obscured them.

A fleeting thought to go to Seren's crossed Gaia's mind, but she couldn't let her friend see her like this. She was even more pitiful than normal. Would Seren even want to be her friend if the truth of her birth became known? "God, I have no hope."

As if her slippers bore a mind of their own, they led Gaia back to her special place. Heather grasses and lousewort danced about her mighty oak, like there were something to celebrate. Her dance card was now filled with pity. Her fortunes forever changed. Nothing good ever changed for Gaia. "God, spin back time. Let me be ignorant again - ignorant and meek and unnoticed. I won't complain this time."

Anything was better than what she was, a secret bastard. If not for the covering lies of the Telfairs, she would be a by-blow. She studied her shaking hands. If she'd been dark like the servant she'd collided with, would she have been tossed away?

Making a fist, she beat against her oak. The snickers of her *friends*, did they know, too? How many sly remarks were actually hints at her mother's infidelity? The village was small. Gossip burned like a candle's wick, bright and fast.

Did it matter with white and black, all trapped inside her limbs? Her stomach rolled. Nausea flooded her lungs. She lunged away, dropped to her knees, and let her breakfast flow out. Maybe the ugly truth could drain away too.

Wiping her mouth, she crawled back to her oak and set her wrist against a thick tree root. Her skin was light like butter, compared to the bark. The skin was almost like the Telfairs', just a little tan, a little darker. Not good enough.

She wasn't good enough.

Now she knew she could never be good enough.

Envy of her sisters' fair, pretty skin, had it not always wrestled in her bosom? The English world said the lighter the complexion, the more genteel and the more one would be held in esteem.

But she should have envied their blood instead. They knew with certitude who their father was. Julia, the twins, each had a future that could include love. What did Gaia have?

She stood and wiped her hands against her skirt. The grass stains and dusting of dirt left her palms, but the off-white color of her skin remained. She brushed her hands again and again against the fabric, but the truth wouldn't disappear.

A light wind whipped the boughs of her tree, as if calling her for an embrace. Tripping over the gnarled root, she fell against the rough bark. Arms stretched wide, she held onto the trunk. Moss cushioned her cheek while the rustle of crunching leaves sounded like a hush, as if the oak knew her pain and tried to stop her tears.

More crackling of leaves made her lift her chin, but the strong sun shining through the jade canopy of leaves blinded her. She clutched the scarred bark with trembling fingers, and hoped whoever was near didn't see her. No one should witness her shame.

A white handkerchief waved near her forehead.

Gaia surrendered to the fact that she'd been discovered. Slowly, she stood, smoothed her wrinkled bodice, and turned. Nothing mattered any more, not even the opinion of a stranger. Shame mingling with tears, she took the fine lawn cloth from the man who'd caught her Sunday, praying aloud about Elliott.

Read more about Unmasked Heart at VanessaRiley.com.

Join My Newsletter

If you like this story and want more, please offer a review or give a shout on social media: @VanessaRiley.

Also, sign up for my newsletter and get the latest news on this series or even a free book. I appreciate your support.

VR

Made in the USA
Monee, IL
05 October 2020

44029509R00239